High Moor 3: Blood Moon

HIGHMOOR III
BLOODMOON

I0690038

Graeme Reynolds

First published in 2015 by
Horrific Tales Publishing
http://www.horrifictales.co.uk
http://www.facebook.com/HighMoorNovel
Copyright © 2015 Graeme Reynolds
http://www.graemereynolds.com
The moral right of Graeme Reynolds to be
identified as the author of this work has been
asserted in accordance with the Copyright,
Designs and Patents Act, 1988.

A CIP catalogue record for this book is available from
the British Library
ISBN: 1-910283-09-6
ISBN-13: 978-1-910283-09-7

Dedicated to the memory of
Tony Smith
and
Kat Yares

Tony used to run a small flash fiction website called Flashes in the Dark and published my first short story, giving me the confidence to go on and produce the book you have in your hands (as well as the first two books in the series.) Tony was always very supportive of my work and it was a tragedy for him to die so young.

Kat was another writer that I knew from Facebook. She was always very cheerful, supportive and was always there for people, giving freely of her time, knowledge and compassion. She volunteered her name to a character in this book and, tragically died before she could learn what happened to her namesake.

Rest in Peace and know you are both missed.

Graeme Reynolds

A WORD FROM THE AUTHOR

Well, here we are. The end of the line and the final part of the High Moor trilogy. I realise that many of you wondered if this day would ever come. For that I apologise and am grateful that you stuck with me. I hope that the book you now have in your hands is worth the wait.

It's something of a bitter-sweet moment for me. I have lived with this series and these characters for over five years now, pretty much to the exclusion of anything else. They are a part of me and I am sad to bid them goodbye. On the other hand, I really cannot begin to describe how happy I am that I don't have to come up with yet another way to describe a werewolf transformation. Most of all, I am very happy that you all get to finish reading the story I've been growing in the back of my mind since I was a child.

As many of you may have guessed, High Moor 1 was a very personal book for me. The first part of book one was essentially a snapshot of my childhood (without the werewolves, admittedly). Some of those scenes were embellished (and we didn't burn the school down) but it was as close as I will ever get to writing an autobiography and so it means that much more to me that it struck a chord with so many of you – especially those of you who grew up in similar small towns in the 1980's. That the characters then took on a life of their own was, I will admit, something of a welcome surprise. It's very hard trying to tie the threads of a densely plotted trilogy like High Moor together, but I am fairly sure I've managed it and, most

4

importantly, have given the story a satisfying conclusion with no more ongoing cliffhangers.

As ever, I need to extend my thanks to the fantastic people I have working with me at Horrific Tales Publishing. Stu Smith has yet again pulled out all of the stops and created a truly exceptional piece of cover art. Kerri Patterson is one of the most talented structural editors I have ever worked with. Vix Kirkpatrick continues to be my beta reader of choice who always gets to read my work before anyone else. And special thanks to the editorial team – Simon Marshall Jones – my last line of defence and probably the person I trust more than anyone else on the planet, as well as Chris Barnes who brought the audiobooks to life in a way I never imagined possible. This book – this series in fact – has been a team effort in every way possible and I could not have done it without those listed above and countless others who helped me shape this book and the preceding two.

And most of all, thank you to those of you who read and enjoyed this series. Those of you who left reviews or contacted me on social media to tell me how much you enjoyed the book. Those of you who were there to support me when I went through some difficult times in my life over the last few years and those of you that nagged me incessantly to finish the bloody book :)

Here is High Moor 3: Blood Moon. Hope you enjoy it

Graeme Reynolds October 2015

Prologue

28th August 1995. Kozara National Park, Bosnia. 20:15

Michael burst from the trees and sprinted towards the old oak in the centre of the village. Filth and drying blood covered his naked body and, as he slowed, the last twinges of transformation began to fade from his aching limbs. He paused in front of the assembled villagers, struggling to catch his breath.

"They're... coming. Over the mountain pass from Dera. Maybe five miles away, if that."

Marie stepped forward and placed a blanket around her brother's shoulders, then passed him a cup of water. She glanced at the other pack members before casting her eyes downward, cheeks flushed scarlet with shame. Without a word, she shuffled backwards, away from Michael.

A murmur of uneasy conversation broke out among the pack members. A mixture of fear and outrage. Connie and Isaac held little Megan close to them, whispering to her that everything would be all right. The action was mirrored by the other parents as they attempted to soothe their worried children, while the more militant pack members bristled and snarled in outrage.

Markus, the pack alpha, motioned for silence, and the murmuring faded away. He turned his attention to Michael, fixing him with his clear green eyes. "How many, Mikhail? How many of them are coming?"

Michael shook his head. "I don't know. Maybe a hundred

or more. Most of them looked like they were regular army. But there were some special ops with them, and they had armour. I spotted two Gvozdika howitzers before I had to get out of there."

Markus stroked his silver-flecked beard, considering the information. "Are you certain they are coming here? For us?"

Lukas Kassik pushed his way to the front of the crowd, his face a mask of barely suppressed rage. "Of course they are coming for us." He motioned his head towards Marie. "That stupid whore left one of them alive after she went on her little excursion. They had a damn Moonstruck tear through their garrison on the last full moon. They know the legends, and they know the paths their ancestors avoided. There can be no doubt as to their intentions."

Krysztof Balazs, a huge, muscular Armenian with jet-black hair and a thick beard moved up beside Lukas. "Then we make them understand why their ancestors feared this place. We should attack them, now, while they are still preparing themselves. Make the rivers run red with the blood of these dogs and leave their corpses to rot in the forest."

Markus shook his head. "What good are teeth and claws against armour? These troops are worse than the Nazis our fathers fought. They know what we are, and their legends tell them how to deal with Vukodlak. If we slaughter these, more will simply arrive to finish the job."

Krysztof's eyes bulged. "Alpha, with respect, you cannot be suggesting that we run? This place has been our home for centuries. To leave now, at the first hint of a threat and without a fight is unthinkable."

Markus placed his arm on Krysztof's shoulder. "I understand your anger, my friend, but think for just a moment. We have spent decades keeping our existence a secret. Killing Moonstruck before they exposed us. The beast that attacked the garrison two weeks ago was unfortunate, but the superstitious fools burned the body after they killed it so there is no evidence beyond a few mangled corpses. We cannot hope to beat them in an open confrontation, but if we leave, then they have nothing but a few empty cottages in the middle of the forest. Our secret remains exactly that, and the peasants will have nothing more than some new stories to frighten their children with."

Michael looked up at the faces of his pack mates. Fear was quickly turning to anger, although those with children looked more relieved than anything. He paused for a second, unsure of how to impart the next piece of information, then pushed down his uncertainties. "There is one more thing. Their weapons are loaded with silver bullets."

Lukas snarled at him. "And how can you be sure of that? Are your senses so acute you can smell the silver in their rifles?"

Michael's mouth went dry. There was no point in trying to hide his condition any longer. He shrugged off the blanket and brought his wolf up to the surface of his mind, focusing the transformation on his right index finger, wincing as a razor sharp talon burst through his flesh. Without a word, he sliced into his abdomen, biting his tongue until he tasted blood to keep the scream of agony in check. He dug around, and after a few seconds, retrieved a flattened lump of bloodstained metal. He then handed the bullet to Markus.

The pack leader's eyes widened as he examined the round. "Mikhail. This is silver. How did you...?" He shook his head, although his expression remained troubled. "It doesn't matter. Not now anyway. How you managed to heal from this is something to discuss another day. And we will discuss it. At length." He held Michael's gaze for a moment longer, and Michael thought he saw fear in the eyes of his alpha. Then Markus turned back to the others. "This settles things. They won't attack at night, and the sun will set in less than an hour. We'll burn this place to the ground and leave under cover of darkness. Take nothing. We'll steal what we need on the way."

Another burst of angry conversation sprang up from the assembled villagers. Some had already begun to move towards their homes, intent on retrieving precious keepsakes, while others like Lukas and Krysztof protested their alpha's decision. Michael noticed a glimmer in their eyes as they exchanged veiled, conspiratorial glances. Surely, though, they wouldn't go against Markus's decision? Not even Lukas would dare to make such a move? Would he?

Markus raised his hands and silenced the arguments with a look. He opened his mouth to speak, but then paused and angled his head upwards, a look of confusion crossing his face. Michael took an involuntary step backwards, unsure as to the meaning of his alpha's actions. Then he heard the noise. A low rumble, as if an express train were bearing down on them. But there were no train lines for forty miles in any direction. His confusion mirrored that of his pack leader, until he remembered the mobile artillery units he'd seen on the road.

He reached out his hand to Markus and screamed his name. Then the world exploded in a flash of noise, hot metal and pain.

Michael lay still for a moment, his body struggling to knit torn flesh back together. The pain overwhelmed his senses. His ears rang, and the stench of blood and burning meat assaulted his nostrils. He shook his head, as if to clear it, and opened his eyes.

A smoking crater dominated the centre of the clearing, its epicentre almost exactly at the point where Markus had stood seconds before. There was no sign of his alpha, but pieces of torn flesh and blood covered everything within twenty feet. The other members of the pack stood in mute silence, unable to believe what had just happened. Several of them were wounded. Dmitri, who had brought Michael from England nine years before, was missing most of his right leg, while Kasha, his wife, struggled to push her intestines back into her rapidly healing stomach cavity. Even Lukas and Krysztof seemed unable to process what had just happened. Their faces were blank, bloodstained masks of shock, and they stood by the side of the crater, gazing at the smouldering ruins of their alpha.

Michael's ruptured ear-drums popped back into place, and he felt a warm rush of fluid stream down each cheek. Noise flooded back, as if he'd emerged from underwater. The cries of pain and fear from his pack mates filled the air. And something else. The rumble of another inbound artillery shell.

He pushed himself to his feet and ran towards the others. "Go! Get into the forest. Now!"

One of the log cabins exploded in a fireball, sending vicious shards of wooden shrapnel slicing through the flesh of the villagers. His eyes sought his sister, who cowered beneath the branches of the grand old oak tree along with Connie, Isaac, Megan and James. He ran to them and pushed them towards the trees on the northern side of the village. "We have to get out of here. Now. Head to the east, towards Grbavci, and I'll meet you at the edge of the forest."

Marie shook her head. "No, come with us. I won't leave without you."

He pushed her away. "I'll be right behind you, but I've got to get the others moving. I won't leave anyone behind."

Marie looked like she was about to argue, but her shoulders started to sag and she nodded her head in agreement. She put her arm around Connie and led her and her friends towards the edge of the village, while Michael tried to help Dmitri and Kasha to their feet.

Kasha's face was pale and streaked with sweat, but she'd managed to push her innards back inside, and her wound had already closed. Dmitri was another story. Tattered strips of flesh hung from his severed leg, and several wooden splinters the size of baseball bats protruded from his chest. Michael looked around and saw, to his relief, that the rest of the pack were stumbling after Marie. He called out to one of Markus's closest advisors, who was close to the rear of the retreating group. "Steffan, I need some help here. I can't carry him on my own."

Steffan looked back, and without hesitation, ran to Michael's side.

Dmitri was on the verge of unconsciousness, but managed to shake his head and growl at Michael. "Leave me. Get Kasha clear instead. I'll just slow you down."

Kasha struggled to her feet and yanked one of the splinters out of her husband's chest, eliciting a scream from Dmitri. "Enough of that talk, Dmitri Kosovan, or I'll twist the next one as I pull. Stop whining like a kicked puppy and get on your foot."

Another cottage erupted in a fireball, and Michael felt a warm rush from his leg as wooden shrapnel shredded his flesh. He ignored the burning sensation and the metallic aroma of his own blood, and, with Steffan's assistance, dragged Dmitri up from the ground.

They'd made it halfway across the clearing when, above the cries of pain from the wounded pack members and the crackle of flames from the burning buildings, came another sound. The rhythmic thud of an inbound chopper. Michael exchanged a worried look with Steffan, and they pushed themselves harder, but it was too late. Above the trees to the south rose the sleek, insect-like shape of a Soko Gazelle helicopter. Weapon pylons protruded from the aircraft's side, and almost immediately, the Gazelle began to rain heavy machinegun fire and rockets down on the fleeing werewolves. The trees to the north erupted in a column of flame and smoke, scattering bodies like confetti across the clearing.

Michael felt his heart lurch. Marie had been heading for those trees. He screamed her name, just as the nose of the helicopter tilted towards him. Then the world turned red.

***

20th December 2008. Underhill Military Base, Sublevel Four. 08:27

Michael's eyes snapped open. He felt a moment's disorientation at the bright fluorescent glare of the overhead light and the overpowering stench of disinfectant. Cold metal pressed against his bare skin, and when he tried to sit up, he found his arms, legs and chest restrained by thick nylon bands. He struggled to piece together his thoughts, his mind groggy with the remnants of a narcotic haze. It came back to him then. The battle at the cottage in Scotland, against pack mates he'd known for years. Fire. Blood. The military units falling upon him as he tried to heal the terrible burns he'd received. He was still in the military base they'd brought him to. This was bad.

A face peered at him. Bald, with a pair of horn-rimmed glasses and a forest of nasal hair protruding from wide, flaring nostrils. Terrible halitosis. The face smiled. "Ah, good. You're awake. I would have been rather disappointed if you weren't conscious for the experiment."

The man backed away, out of his field of vision. Michael attempted to turn his head, but found that another wide strap across his forehead prevented him from moving.

"What are you doing?" He asked, his voice thick with the lingering effects of the drugs.

The man ignored him and busied himself with some metallic implements that scraped and rattled on a tray somewhere to the right.

"Hmm, now, let's see. The date is 20th December 2008 at approximately... erm... zero eight thirty hours. The subject is a male lycanthrope, Caucasian origin, possibly from Northern England based on his accent."

The man's face appeared once more. He held a vicious looking blade with serrated edges that glinted in the harsh glare of the overhead lights. "Today, we shall attempt to ascertain the limit of the subject's regenerative capabilities and pain threshold."

Chapter 1

20th December 2008. Underhill Military Base, Sublevel Three. 11:43

Steven's eyes snapped open and he sat bolt upright in the metal-framed bed. The movement tugged at his stitches, setting his chest and shoulder alight with a sudden flare of pain. He'd been dreaming. A nightmare, really. Hardly a surprise, given the events of the last few weeks. There'd been a little girl, crying, begging him for help. Something in the shadows, stalking them both. Something with glowing red eyes that cut through the darkness like laser beams. The details of the dream danced on the edge of his consciousness, insubstantial, ethereal and fleeting, fading into nothing until all that remained was a persistent feeling of unease.

He licked his lips, grimacing at the foul taste in his mouth. A glass of water sat in a wire holder attached to the bed. He reached over with his uninjured arm and drained the tepid liquid in a single gulp, relishing the moistening of his cracked lips and swollen tongue.

First job done. Now for the hard part.

Steven swung his legs off the edge of the bed with exaggerated care, so as to minimise the howls of protest from his injuries, and detached the saline drip from its holder.

So far so good.

He steeled himself for the inevitable surge of agony and staggered across to the toilet in the corner of the room.

He honestly couldn't remember feeling worse than he did right now. Even the chemotherapy he'd undergone in a vain attempt to fight his cancer hadn't been as bad as this. The bullet wound on his shoulder throbbed, but was almost insignificant compared to the damage that Connie Hamilton had inflicted on him. She'd shattered his collarbone and done a damned good job of chewing through his rib-cage before she died. He knew he was lucky to be alive, even if he didn't feel that way. Even the smallest movement felt like someone grinding shards of broken glass into his torso.

He reached the toilet and, steadying himself against the featureless concrete wall, released a stinking stream of dark yellow urine at the porcelain. At least his gracious hosts had allowed him that dignity. The pain he had to endure to make that small journey was terrible, but it was immeasurably better than being strapped to a table, pissing into a bag through a plastic tube forced up his dick. In fact, since his conversation with that slimy tosser of a politician, his captors had been quite accommodating. Downright pleasant even, if you ignored the fact that he spent his days locked in a soundproof room in the arse-end of some military base.

As if on cue, the lock on his door clicked, then swung open on reinforced hinges. A young woman with dark hair and vivid red lipstick appeared, flanked by two muscular men with machine guns. The woman, Rose, frowned at him.

"Mr Wilkinson, you know you're not supposed to get out of bed on your own. Pull the cord if you need to go to the toilet and I'll come and help you."

Steven shook his head. He liked Rose. She was friendly, attractive and always smiled at him, even when she was telling him off. The last thing he wanted her to be doing was standing there watching while he took a piss. Even in a place like this, where his movements were monitored twenty four hours a day by CCTV, he preferred to at least retain the illusion of some privacy. He thought about saying that to her, but instead just returned her smile. "That's okay, Rose. I'll manage."

Rose sighed. "Well, don't come crying to me if you rip all your stitches out. You'll have no one to blame but yourself."

"I know, but a bloke has to keep a little self respect. Besides, if I show all the goods off now, you might lose interest."

Rose rolled her eyes in mock exasperation. "Mr Wilkinson, I don't know what I'm going to do with you."

"I could make a couple of suggestions, and please, call me Steven." He winked at her, taking small satisfaction at the flush of colour in her cheeks. "Now, as much as I enjoy your company, I somehow doubt you came in here for the pleasure of mine. What is it today? More blood samples?"

Rose stood to one side and let one of the machine gun toting meatheads push an antique wheelchair into the room. "Not today. If you're feeling up to it, there are some people who'd like to meet you."

Steven sighed, then nodded his assent. "Lead the way, Rose. It'll make a nice change to get out for a while."

He allowed Rose to help him into the chair while one of the guards held it steady. The other guard watched him like a hawk, and Steven couldn't help but notice that the safety catch of the man's MP5 was disengaged. It felt strange to be in a sitting position after spending days lying flat on his back, and the sensation was far from pleasant. His abdominal muscles pushed against his ruined ribcage, and he ground his teeth together to prevent the cry of pain from escaping his lips. Rose must have noticed his discomfort and, after she'd attached his saline drip to a holder on the back of the wheelchair, administered a liberal dose of morphine into the line. The warm glow of the opiate filled him, diminishing the pain until it was barely noticeable. A glimmering ember that would, in a few hours time, flare back up into a raging bonfire.

They pushed him through a series of plain white concrete corridors, illuminated by harsh fluorescent bulbs whose light glared from the sterile walls. Doors lined both sides of the corridor, all of which were reinforced and had magnetic card and keypad access. Some of the rooms had been set up as cells, while others were being used as offices. As he passed the windows, he could see military personnel sitting behind shabby, cramped desks, working on antique computer equipment. It looked like the place had been outfitted with whatever old junk they had in storage, and Steven realised that probably wasn't far from the truth. No doubt in a month or so, once orders were approved, the rooms would be filled with new desks and modern computer systems with flat screen monitors. For now, they were making do with whatever they could get their hands on.

They eventually arrived at a pair of double doors, which Rose opened. The guards wheeled Steven in and positioned him next to a conference table, then stepped back to the corners, weapons at the ready.

Steven recognised some of the people at the table. Phil Fletcher and Paul Patterson sat next to each other at the far end of the room. Steven was glad to see them both. He'd heard nothing about their fate since they'd been taken by the military. Both men's heads had been shaved, and their scalps were red and blotchy from the acid burns they'd received while rescuing him. Phil nodded a greeting, while Paul barely registered his presence. The firearms officer's jaw was clenched and he stared into the middle distance. Steven had to remind himself he'd only lost his family a short while before. He struggled to reconcile the fact that it was only a little over a week since he'd woken from his coma in a hospital bed. It seemed like a lifetime ago.

Steven didn't know any of the room's other occupants, but he didn't need to. They were clearly military. One of them, an older man with a moustache who stank of expensive aftershave, was obviously the commanding officer. The other five men and women held themselves with a casual alertness that only came from combat experience. Even in the safe environment of the conference room, their eyes were continually flitting around, checking for potential threats.

The officer got to his feet, a smile on his lips. He extended his hand to Steven, shaking it in a vice-like grip. "Mr Wilkinson, it's good to finally meet face-to-face. I'm Colonel Brian Richards, the CO of this base. Mr Fletcher and Mr Patterson you already know. The rest are Lieutenant Derek Foster, Sergeant Jayne Peyton, Corporal Aaron Raines, Private Roland Lewis and Private Fay Cross. We're just waiting for one more person to join us before we begin." He turned to Rose. "Doctor Fisher, would you see if Doctor Channing is going to grace us with his presence?"

Rose nodded and got to her feet. She'd almost made it to the doors when they burst open and a tall, thin man wearing horn-rimmed spectacles, a white, bloodstained surgical smock and gore-encrusted rubber gloves strode into the room. The man glared at the Colonel. "What is it now, Richards? I'm in the middle of something important."

The Colonel gave Doctor Channing a thin smile. "We'll try not to keep you long, Doctor. In fact, we might as well start with you. What have you found so far?"

Doctor Channing huffed and rolled his eyes. "The creature's blood is unlike anything I've ever seen. The cells are more animal than human, although I'm *still* waiting on the DNA analysis from those imbeciles in Wroughton. The two I've examined so far appear to have similar regenerative abilities, however, Mr Wilkinson's capacity for healing is seriously inhibited by silver. The other creature appears to be unaffected by it."

Steven raised an eyebrow. "You have one in custody? If it's healing from a silver wound then it's a member of a pack field team. I'd watch your back. They don't tend to leave their people behind."

The room went silent for a moment. Steven noticed Paul clench his fists into tight balls, while Phil looked physically sick. Given their recent experiences with pack werewolves, Steven couldn't say he blamed them.

The Colonel gave Steven a thin smile. "I can assure you, Mr Wilkinson, we have taken every precaution. Please, Doctor, continue."

Doctor Channing exhaled in irritation at the interruption. "Anyway, I've yet to determine exactly how the transformation occurs, however there appears to be some evidence of a viral vector that I'm attempting to isolate, which may explain how an individual becomes infected. Beyond that, it's almost impossible to learn more with a living subject. The damn thing heals before I can do any real exploratory surgery. If you'd only allow me to dissect him properly, then we might get somewhere."

The Colonel shook his head. "We've discussed this before, Doctor. With the exception of Mr Wilkinson here, who is our guest and is not to be harmed, I can't sanction the termination of our only living werewolf. As far as we know, he's the only one in captivity anywhere in the world."

"Then, Colonel Richards, I suggest you get me something else to work with. There are too many disparities between the two subjects we currently have, and the Hamilton woman was too badly damaged to give much insight. I need more subjects to continue my work."

Colonel Richards smiled at this. "And that, Doctor, is precisely why I've brought us all together today."

21st December 2008. Trecorras Cottage, Llangarron, Herefordshire. 15:30

"Marie, he'll be here in a minute. Can you please do the drying up? Like I asked you to do an hour ago."

Marie groaned and tried to push herself up from the sofa. The makeshift stitches across her side tugged at her tender skin, and she felt a couple pop loose. A warm trickle of blood ran down the inside of her t-shirt, staining the white fabric a deep crimson.

"Marie?"

She bristled at the sound of his voice, but bit down her irritation, almost managing to keep it out of her voice. "Alright, I'm doing it now."

"And can you pick your clothes up off the bedroom floor? And did you remember to clean the toilet?"

"Why would Daniel go into our bedroom? Just close the fucking door and he won't see the clothes."

"Marie, just do it, please." John's voice had acquired an edge that Marie didn't like, however, she decided not to push the point.

She shuffled through to the kitchen and began half-heartedly drying up the cutlery and plates, keeping one eye on the long gravel track that was the only route to or from the isolated house.

John bustled into the kitchen and began spraying down the worktops with disinfectant and scrubbing them vigorously with paper towels, even though, as far as Marie was concerned, they looked perfectly clean. The chemicals burned her nostrils, causing her to sneeze. He stopped, threw the towels in the waste bin and turned to her. "Did you pick your clothes up yet?"

"For fuck's sake, you only asked me ten seconds ago. I've been doing this, in case you hadn't noticed."

He arched an eyebrow. "Ten seconds? I asked you last night. And this morning. And half an hour ago."

"Can you give me a break? I'm supposed to be recuperating here. And I doubt Daniel is going to care about the odd dirty sock or wet cup."

John glared at her and lifted his shirt to show the blood-stained bandage beneath. "You aren't the only one with injuries. And it doesn't matter if Daniel cares or not. I care. I don't want him coming in here thinking that we live like pigs. Can you stop moaning for five bloody minutes and help me get this place looking presentable?"

"Okay, okay. Just stop firing lists of fucking instructions at me. I'll sort it out before he gets here."

John looked past her, down the snow-flecked track, to the plume of dust rising above the bare hedgerows. "Too late. That must be him now."

"Alright."

"And Marie..."

"Yes?"

"Can you change your t-shirt before he gets here? That one's got blood all over it."

Marie sighed in exasperation and trudged out of the kitchen, into the long hallway, towards the staircase.

"And put your fucking dirty t-shirt in the wash basket," John yelled from the kitchen.

Marie bit back the comment that was on the tip of her tongue and made her way up the stairs. She was not looking forward to this. Not one little bit.

***

Marie sipped her tea, feeling the hot liquid burn the inside of her mouth. If she was honest with herself, the momentary pain was a welcome distraction from the tense atmosphere in the living room. Daniel clearly wasn't comfortable with coming out here to live under the same roof as two of the most wanted people in the country. It was a necessary compromise, however, as neither John nor she could exactly pop down to the local shop when they ran out of milk, or deal with any unexpected visitors. The local vicar had made the half-mile trek to the cottage a couple of days ago, forcing John and Marie to hide upstairs until he'd gone.

Then there was John. He'd been behaving like a complete arse ever since he'd found out Daniel was coming out here. Actually, she corrected herself, he'd been behaving like an arsehole ever since their escape from Scotland. Clearly, he had no idea how to share a living space with other people. She bit back her irritation and tried to break the leaden silence.

"So... Daniel... this is John."

Daniel held out his hand, but John didn't reciprocate.

Instead, he glared at the big German and said flatly, "We've met."

"What do you mean? When did you ever meet Daniel?"

John's lip curled up. "Well, he wasn't wearing an Armani suit last time." He leaned forward in his seat, fixing Daniel with his gaze. "Fur coat, wasn't it, mate?"

The penny dropped. "Oh, fucking hell. You mean..."

John's eyes blazed. "Yes, I fucking mean. In the woods outside of High Moor. That was you trying to kill me, wasn't it, *Daniel*."

Daniel put his hands up. "It was, but that was before. Things are different now. Circumstances have changed."

"You talk about it like it's ancient history. It was a week and a fucking half ago!"

Daniel's shoulders tensed. "Yes, and I can't help but wonder if we would be in the same situation if Gregorz and I had succeeded in our mission. I..." Daniel stopped himself from finishing the sentence and exhaled, as if to rein in his anger. "No. The situation would have remained the same. Connie would still have slaughtered that police woman. Michael would still have ordered her home, and she would have gone after Wilkinson anyway. The unfortunate position we find ourselves in is not your fault," he gave Marie a sideways glance that made her cheeks flush scarlet, "not entirely. Please, accept my apologies."

Marie glared at John. "You have nothing to apologise for, Daniel. We should be apologising to you." John looked as if he were about to speak, but Marie silenced him with a look. "Like you say, everything's different. We have to deal with what's happening right now and not get caught up on the past. Right, John?"

John murmured his assent and seemed to, if not relax, at least shift his body into a less threatening posture.

Satisfied that the situation had been defused for the time being, Marie turned to face Daniel. "Have you heard anything else from Russia?"

"The situation is not good. Krysztof and Lukas are taking control and they have the support of the Moonborn pack members. They've issued a death warrant for you, alongside the one for Simpson, but have stopped short at declaring Michael a traitor. There are still a lot of members loyal to him, and they don't want to risk dividing the pack. Not yet, anyway."

"Then the sooner we break Michael out the better."

Daniel laughed. "Marie, there's not a great deal we can do just yet." He motioned to John. "Simpson's injuries won't heal until the next full moon, and then there's you..."

Marie bristled. "What the fuck is that supposed to mean?"

"Well, as I understand it, you're human now."

"So what? I'm still a trained pack operative, and if anything, that'll work to our advantage on an infiltration mission. Their IR sensors won't pick up anything out of the ordinary, and their bloody sonic countermeasures won't do a damn thing to me either."

"And if they shoot you, you'll die."

"I'm not leaving my brother locked up in that base for a second longer than he needs to be."

Daniel shook his head. "I know, but you need to be realistic. We have to do a proper reconnaissance and come up with a workable plan. We can't just go charging in there unprepared. Are you even sure that your information is correct?"

Marie's shoulders sagged. "Alright. We'll do it your way. For now. And yes, I'm certain Michael is there. We have a couple of field operatives within the UK military, and one of them tipped me off. I've already been checking the place out, and a few of the staff have Michael's scent all over them. I've got a couple of ideas of how we can get in and out without raising the alarm. With any luck, they won't even notice Michael's gone until we're far away."

Chapter 2

22nd December 2008. Parklands Close, South Molton, Devon. 14:17

Sophie Riley flopped down on the bed and glared at the back of her cousin's head. "Adam, it's my turn now. I want to play!"

Adam Kosovan ignored her and continued to blow zombies into bloody fragments. Sophie felt her annoyance grow, and she tugged on the older boy's arm just as a particularly fat zombie stumbled from an open doorway, vomiting green bile across the screen.

Adam's shoulders tensed as the screen blurred and hordes of undead attacked him from all directions. Seconds later, the screen turned red, and he swore under his breath.

"Adam! You're dead now. It's my turn."

"Yeah, but it's *your* fault that I died. I'm having another go because of that."

"But it's *my* Xbox, you ball-bag. Mum told you to let me share. Can't we play split screen or something?"

"No, I don't like split screen games. You can't see what you're doing, and you're too young to play this anyway. Can't you play on your Nintendo or something and stop bothering me? It's bad enough that I've had to come all the way over here with my bloody parents, without you buzzing around me like a fly."

"I don't want to play on my DS. It's crap. I want to have

a go on my Xbox and play *The Sims*."

Adam arched an eyebrow at her, stuck out his tongue and then hit restart on his zombie game.

Sophie jumped up from the bed and stomped to her bedroom door. "Right, I'm telling my mum. Then you'll be in trouble."

Adam's attention was back on the game. "Suit yourself. You'll be the one that gets in trouble though. They told you to stay up here and not bother them while they talk."

Sophie spun on her heels, strode to her bedroom door, then let herself out onto the landing and crept downstairs. She knew her parents had been serious when she'd been sent to her room with Adam. Her father had made it very clear that both children were to stay upstairs and not bother them because they had important things to talk about. But this was important as well. It was *her* Xbox. Just because Adam was older than she was shouldn't mean that he got his own way all the time.

She made her way down the staircase, carefully placing her feet so as to avoid the creaking floorboards. If her parents heard her coming down, she'd be sent packing without having a chance to explain herself. Besides, she quite wanted to know what was so important that her Aunt Kasha and Uncle Dmitri had come all the way from Bristol, bringing Adam-the-snot-eater with them. It didn't even look like they'd brought Christmas presents, unless they were still hidden in the car somewhere. Yes, she decided, they must be still in the car. Even so, she wanted to know what was going on. She reached the bottom step and sat down, straining her ears.

"Please. William, Sonja. We can't stay here anymore. It's too dangerous. You have to see sense. The news is filled with reports of Connie's betrayal, and another incident in Scotland." Her Uncle's voice had an edge to it that Sophie hadn't heard before. "They're talking about extra security measures at the airports being used. And Connie said she'd sent the authorities a list of families..."

"Dmitri," her father answered, "I know what you're saying, but honestly, the best thing we can do is keep our heads down and wait for this to blow over. You, Kasha and Adam are more than welcome to stay here with us if it would make you feel better."

"Bah, this won't blow over and you know it. You weren't there in '95. You and Sonja were out hunting Moonstruck when they came for us. Krysztof says that..."

Her mother's voice cut Dmitri off mid-sentence. "Krysztof says? Since when have you given a shit about what Krysztof says? The man's a fool. A dangerous fool. From what Kasha told me, he wanted to fight men with tanks and helicopters back in '95. In the open, for the world to see. Don't talk to me about Krysztof. If you do as he says, then you're as big of an idiot as he is. Krysztof can rot in hell for all I care. Are you so eager to betray Michael?"

"And if they come for you?" her Aunt Kasha replied. "What then? If they come through that door in the middle of the night with machine guns, what will you do?"

Her mother's voice dropped an octave, into a deep,

threatening and unfamiliar tone. "Then I'll tear their fucking throats out where they stand. I'll…"

The door burst open, and Sophie looked up into the enraged eyes of her mother. "Sophie, I told you to play in your room with your cousin."

"But he won't let me play. He's shooting zombies on my Xbox and I want to play something else."

"I don't care, young lady. You *will* do as you are told. Go to your room. *NOW!* And don't let me catch you down here again. This doesn't concern you."

"But, Mum, he's horrible. He farted and tried to make me smell it, and he keeps punching my teddy bear. Can I go and play at Karen's house instead?"

Her mother stood with her hands on her hips, lips pursed. Sophie worried that she'd be sent back upstairs to sit with her stinky cousin, but after a moment, her mother's posture relaxed. "Alright, but you're to be back here for dinner at five on the dot. Not a second later or there'll be hell to pay. Okay?"

Sophie's face burst into a huge smile and she gave her mother a brief, fierce hug before grabbing her jacket and heading for the front door. "Thanks, Mum. I'll be back in time for dinner. I promise." Then, before her mother could change her mind, she ran out of the front door and along the street to Karen's house.

A freezing wind whipped along the street as Sophie rapped on Karen's front door. After a few moments, Karen's mother answered the door with a smile. "Come on in, Sophie, before you catch your death of cold.

Karen's upstairs in her room. Would you like a drink of anything?"

Sophie smiled. "No thank you, Mrs Davies." Then she removed her shoes and scampered up the stairs to Karen's room. She pushed open the door to absolute carnage. Karen's room was normally spotless, with dolls and stuffed toys neatly arranged on her bed. Now the toys were in disarray. One doll's head and arm were missing, and a cuddly penguin had its stuffing pulled out through a ragged tear on its stomach. Karen sat on the floor holding a naked Barbie that seemed to have strands of Karen's hair stuck all over it with PVA glue. Puzzled, Sophie gave a polite cough. "Hey, Karen. What'cha doing?"

Karen smiled at her friend. Her fringe was a ragged mess where she'd cut into it with a pair of craft scissors. "Hiya, Sophie. Malibu Barbie turned into a werewolf, and she's on a killing spree. Wanna play?"

Sophie closed the door behind her and sat down on the bed. "Werewolves don't *all* go on killing sprees, you know. Some of them are quite nice."

Werewolf Barbie ripped another chunk of stuffing out of Mr Pingu. "Yeah, they do. That's what the man said on the news. Who made you the expert on werewolves all of a sudden, anyway?"

Sophie grinned. "I know *loads* about werewolves. More than some stupid fat bloke on the news. Sit down and I'll tell you, and later I might even show you something cool."

***

It was dark as Sophie hurried along the street to her home. Spider-fingers of frost had begun to form on the windscreens of the parked cars, and Christmas lights twinkled from every window. She couldn't wait. Only a few more days to go until Santa came, although the missing presents from Uncle Dmitri and Auntie Kasha still bothered her. Perhaps they would be under the tree when she got back. She stuffed her mitten-clad hands into her pockets and made her way along the street, careful not to slip on the newly formed patches of ice that covered the pavement.

As she got closer to her house, she saw Uncle Dmitri, Aunt Kasha and Adam coming out of her front door. Uncle Dmitri wasn't wearing his false leg, and he negotiated the slippery driveway on his crutches while Aunt Kasha bundled a complaining Adam into the rear seat of their car. That was strange. She thought they'd be staying for dinner. At least she'd get her Xbox back and wouldn't have Adam stinking her room up anymore.

Her parents stood at the doorway, grim expressions on their faces. Dmitri reached the passenger side door of the car and turned to them. "I wish you'd reconsider. It's not too late. We can go online, book your flights and you can come with us."

Her father shook his head. "We've made up our minds, Dmitri. We think its better that we stay where we are. Please be careful, and phone us when you get to Salzburg so we know you got there okay."

Dmitri nodded. Kasha hugged both her father and mother, then, spotting Sophie on the road, hurried over and held her tight. "Be safe, little one. We love you," she whispered. Then she got into the driver's seat and closed the car door.

Sophie stood next to her mother and father, watching as the car started, backed out of the driveway and drove away. They stayed until after the car had disappeared around the corner of their cul-de-sac. Her mother had tears in her eyes. Sophie gripped her mother's hand, looked up to her and said, "Did Uncle Dmitri and Auntie Kasha remember to leave my Christmas presents?"

22nd December 2008. Exeter Airport, Devon. 17:58

Dmitri gazed out of the car windscreen and sighed. Banks of freezing fog had begun to drift in from the moors, billowing beneath the glare of the security lights. Ice crystals glimmered on the other parked cars like diamond dust, and the grass verges were already white with frost. He turned to Kasha, whose beautiful face had creased into a harsh mask of worry. He forced a smile and squeezed her knee. "Don't worry, Kasha. Yes, they have security in the big airports, but you know what this country is like. They could not have gotten around to the smaller places like this in such a short time." As he said the words, Dmitri was only too aware that he was trying to convince himself as much as his wife.

Adam shifted in his seat, a sour expression on his face. "I don't want to go away. It's a week before Christmas. And I don't know why you made me leave my things behind, either. I've hardly got any clothes and I've got nothing to do. I'm bored already."

Dmitri's head snapped round. "Listen to me, Adam. The

things that have happened in the last week have put us all in danger. You've had a soft, easy life up until now. That life is over. It's time for you to become a man."

Adam rolled his eyes. "Yeah, yeah, I've heard it all before. When you were a boy you and mum lived in a log cabin, with no electricity, no phone, and no internet. You ate what you grew yourself or what you killed. Am I missing anything?"

Dmitri struck Adam across the face, leaving a red palm print on his son's cheek. Adam recoiled in shock, his mouth hanging open and his eyes welling up with tears. Dmitri felt a swell of shame for striking his son, but realised he still hadn't got the message through. He grabbed Adam by the front of his shirt and pulled him close, until they were almost nose to nose. "You listen, boy, and you listen well. We are not fleeing this country because we want to. We are leaving because once they tighten the noose, there will be nowhere to hide. On mainland Europe, we can go anywhere, cross borders undetected, live in the forests if need be. This is hard enough on us all without your selfish whining. Now, pull yourself together, hold your tongue and try to pretend we are going on a family skiing holiday."

Adam looked at his feet and nodded. "I'm sorry. I know this is serious, and I won't let you down. I'll do as you say."

Satisfied with his son's response, he turned in his seat until he faced his wife. "Are you ready?"

Kasha took a deep breath and exhaled a plume of warm vapour into the cold night air. She managed to force a wan smile. "Yes. I'm as ready as I'll ever be. Let's do this. Adam, get the cases out of the boot while I help your father."

She got out of the car and walked around to the passenger side, allowing Dmitri to steady himself against her as he tried to get his crutches in place. "I wish you'd reconsider wearing your leg."

"You know I can't. If things go badly and we need to turn, then I can't do anything with that damned false leg flapping around behind me. It will just get in the way."

"Then let us hope that everything goes to plan."

They left the car behind them. Adam carried his own luggage over his shoulders in a rucksack and pulled Dmitri's case behind him as they left the car park. The main terminal lay a few hundred yards along the road, although the fog obscured their view of the building. They made their way along the footpath towards the glowing lights, taking care not to slip on the icy pavement.

As they approached the terminal, Dmitri paused, beckoning Kasha and Adam close. "If I'm wrong and they've installed the security systems here, remember that they work on body temperature. Push your wolves down as far as you can. We can't risk setting them off. Understand?"

Kasha and Adam nodded, then turned back towards the large glass entrance to the main terminal and walked inside.

The rush of warm air was a sharp contrast to the frigid temperatures outside, and Dmitri already felt a few pinpricks of sweat break out on his forehead. He balanced himself on a single crutch while he struggled out of his heavy winter coat, while Kasha and Adam did the same. Then they joined the check-in queue behind a group of young men carrying skis and snowboards.

The line seemed to take forever, and Dmitri couldn't help but glance around the rest of the terminal building as he waited, looking for potential threats and escape routes. Old habits die hard, and even though he'd not been on a field team for almost twenty years, the training persisted. He noticed Kasha doing the same thing. Not that the threats were hard to find. Armed police officers brandishing submachine guns stood along the concourse, casting their eyes over the crowded check-in area. He counted three. No doubt there would be more by the security station and customs. The realisation that it was too late to back out struck him. It would arouse too much suspicion if they were to turn around and leave now. They were committed. No choice but to go through with the plan and hope for the best.

The check-in went smoothly, and he even managed to smile at the girl behind the desk when she asked if he'd packed his bags himself. Most of his luggage was filled with survival equipment, false passports from a number of different countries and several thousand Euros in cash. Kasha's and Adam's bags contained similar items. Clothes they could buy or steal anywhere. They'd packed what was important. Things that would help them survive the coming months. Clean clothes and Adam's portable games console were luxuries they didn't need.

Once they'd checked in their bags, they headed for the escalators to the air-side facilities. Dmitri could feel his hands sweating, slipping against the hard plastic handles of his crutches. He forced down the hard knot of fear forming in his stomach and wiped his hands against his trousers. Only one more obstacle remained. He took a deep breath, gave Kasha and Adam what he hoped was a reassuring smile, and then made his way towards the security station.

The airport was busier than he'd anticipated, filled mostly with young people on their way to skiing holidays. The group that had been ahead of them at the check-in desk were in front of them now, laughing and filming each other with their telephones. There were not many flights out of Exeter at this time of the night, and Dmitri groaned as he realised that they would probably have to share a plane with the loudmouthed youths. The stench of alcohol billowed from them like a cloud. Several of them appeared well on their way to being drunk already, and one was clearly suffering from the beginnings of a nasty case of influenza. Dmitri could smell the sickness on him beneath the stink of cheap whiskey.

The line wound its way along rows of fabric cordons, ending at a number of metal detectors and x-ray machines. Behind each gate stood another armed policeman. Dmitri wondered if those guns held silver bullets, then forced the idea away. It was too late to worry about such things, and the last thing they needed to do was look nervous as they passed through the barrier. Nothing appeared different from the last time he'd flown, so it was likely that the countermeasures had not yet been installed in this small, insignificant airport. There was nothing to worry about. Once they made it past the security check, they would be able to relax in one of the bars, have a drink and wait for their flight.

The group of young men reached the barriers and began emptying their pockets into black plastic trays that fed into the x-ray machines via conveyor belts. One of them tripped the alarm and was quickly searched by a security guard who'd been standing off to the side, while the armed police officer stood by, watching them closely. One by one they passed through. Dmitri and his family would be next, after the sick one made it through.

The sick one. The one who burned with the beginnings of a fever.

Oh no.

The boy stepped through the metal detector, and Dmitri's world turned upside down. The high pitched shriek tore through his skull, causing agony like nothing he'd ever experienced before. His crutches fell to the floor and he collapsed beside them, his hands pressed over his ears. The sick youth, and the other passengers didn't appear to be affected, although Kasha and Adam were as badly stricken as he was. The police officers raised their weapons and pushed their way through the passengers towards them. Dmitri looked at his family and saw that Adam's eyes had begun to turn yellow.

"No... Adam... Don't"

It was too late. Adam began to transform, no doubt hoping to fight off the aggressors and save his family. Once the change began, his ears became that much more sensitive to the high frequency noise. Dmitri could see blood running in bright red rivulets down the side of his son's face, his eyes filled with rage and pain as his transformation progressed.

Then the police officers raised their weapons, and the world erupted in a red maelstrom of fire, noise and pain.

Chapter 3

23rd December 2008. Trecorras Cottage, Llangarron, Herefordshire. 10:05

John took a sip of coffee and stepped back to admire his handiwork. The dusty box of Christmas decorations he'd found in the attic looked like they'd been there since the early 1970's at least. The tree was plastic with silver branches instead of the usual fake green needles, and had clearly seen better days. The trunk was badly bent and held together with ancient, yellowing sellotape, while half of the branches were bare. John had carefully positioned it so that the kink was face on to the rest of the living room, then covered the sorry-looking thing with pretty much every piece of tinsel and bauble in the box. The lights had been a particular triumph. He'd spent over an hour working his way through them, a bulb at a time, until he'd found all of the broken ones. Now the silver tree twinkled in the corner of the living room, bringing some much needed seasonal cheer to the place.

Sharing a house with others was harder than he'd expected. He'd been on his own from childhood, not daring to even make any close friends, let alone actually live with anyone. Now that he found himself co-habiting with two other people, he began to realise just how used to being on his own he'd become. Of course, there had been many times over the years where the loneliness had been crushing, and he'd wander around his house, not knowing what to do with himself. Now that he had company forced upon him, however, he couldn't help but resent it, no matter how hard he tried not to. It didn't help that Marie was such a damn slob. He loved her. Having someone there to talk to and curl up next to at night was amazing. It was a closeness he never thought he'd experience, and he cherished it. He just hadn't expected it to be so difficult to allow someone into his life and to share his personal space.

"Where the fuck did you find that?" said Marie from the doorway. She wore a pair of tracksuit bottoms and the oversized t-shirt she'd slept in. Her eyes were half-closed and her hair looked as if she'd been dragged backwards through a hedge. Marie, John had discovered, was not a morning person.

He grinned at her. "I found it in the loft, along with a box of decorations. Apparently this place used to be a children's home, and I thought it'd be nice to put them up."

Marie cast a quizzical eye at the tree. "You know that it's bent? And you might have overdone the tinsel a bit."

John's face fell. "I just wanted to try and brighten the place up. Make it feel a bit more like Christmas, you know?"

Marie walked over and kissed him on the cheek. "It's the thought that counts. Is there any coffee left?"

"Yeah, there's still some in the pot. It's been there for a couple of hours, though. I can make a fresh one, if you want?"

She shuffled out of the living room, towards the kitchen. "No, it's alright. I could do with something strong enough to stand a spoon up in this morning. One bloody glass of wine and I still get a hangover. I am officially a lightweight. Where's Daniel? I thought you'd have roped him into your little decorating project."

John stood back from the tree and tried to reposition it so the bend in the trunk was less visible. "He went shopping in Ross first thing. Said we needed a few things and he wanted to pick up a newspaper. Should be back soon. He's been gone for a couple of hours now."

Even with his enhanced hearing, John couldn't make out the details of Marie's grunted response, but he heard the clink of china and the burble of coffee being poured, and figured that any further attempts at conversation were probably better off left until she'd caffeinated herself. She trudged out of the kitchen, mug in hand, and made her way back upstairs without another word. A few moments later, the hiss of the shower drifted down the stairs, and John turned his attention back to the Christmas tree.

***

Daniel drummed his fingers against the steering wheel and sighed. The tractor ahead of him had blocked the single track road for over three miles now and showed no signs of turning off any time soon. Vehicles coming from the opposite direction had been forced to reverse back along the road, adding more delay to proceedings. He pushed the irritation down and tried to relax. No easy matter given what he'd found out that morning. Still, there were only a few more miles to go before he reached the stone bridge that marked the boundaries of the village, and then only another mile and a half before he reached the isolated cottage he'd been forced to co-habit with Marie and Simpson. If nothing else, the journey gave him time to gather his thoughts.

The situation was a difficult one. His orders were clear. Marie and Simpson were to be executed on sight and their corpses disposed of. However, Krysztof and Lukas didn't run the pack. Not yet anyway, despite the way they were behaving. While Michael lived, there was a chance that things could be turned around. If Michael had been killed by his captors though, or if the council voted to depose him as pack alpha, something that seemed increasingly likely as the days passed, he would have no choice but to carry out his instructions. His loyalties were, and would always be, to his pack. At least, if it came to that, he'd be able to make sure they were put to death quickly and painlessly. He owed Marie that much.

The tractor turned off onto a side road as they reached the outskirts of the village, and Daniel breathed a sigh of relief. In reality, the village was little more than a collection of houses and farms, centred around an old church. There had been a public house at one time, situated next to the river, however it had long since been boarded up. Other than that, there was only a post office that opened for a few hours each morning and a small garage that survived by maintaining the agricultural vehicles for the nearby farms. Most of the houses seemed to be occupied by commuters, the array of BMWs and Audis parked on the neatly maintained driveways testament to the fact that most of the village's original inhabitants had been priced out of the area. He doubted if there was much remaining by way of a community here anymore. The only focal point would be the church, where people would gather each Sunday to pay lip-service to the hymns and prayers before retreating back into the self-contained bubbles of their lives.

He passed through the village, turning off onto a long gravel track that ran for half a mile across open countryside before it reached their cottage. Pheasants burst from the hedgerows before him, squawking their alarm at the intruder in their midst. They did this every time he drove through here, and their impromptu honour guard always made him smile. Besides, they also provided a useful early warning system in the case of unexpected visitors.

The track branched off into a field where a flock of sheep huddled in the far corner, no doubt able to smell the wolves in their midst but unable to retreat any further from them. The day he'd arrived, one of them had attempted to throw itself across the cattle-grid to escape and had broken its legs as a result. He'd been tempted to take it up to the house, butcher the corpse and put it in the freezer, but decided against it. If the farmer had come up to the house, enquiring after his missing livestock, and he'd caught sight of either Marie or Simpson, then things could have become complicated. Better to let him find the creature where it lay. He had, at least, broken the animal's neck to prevent it from suffering unnecessarily.

The cottage came into view as he crossed the field. It had red sandstone walls with a grey slate roof and a partially rotted wooden conservatory that leeched the heat from the building in the evenings. Light flashed from the living room window, and another blazed from the double bedroom that Marie shared with Simpson. At least they were awake. He didn't feel like breaking his news to Marie before she'd had at least one cup of coffee. The car rumbled across the cattle-grid separating the cottage from the field beyond, and he parked by the property's rear door, retrieved two plastic bags of shopping from the passenger seat, then got out and went inside.

Marie was walking down the stairs with a towel wrapped around her wet hair as he entered the hallway. Simpson seemed to have spent the morning turning the living room into a tasteless parody of 'Santa's grotto'. Daniel shook his head, disgusted.

Marie smiled at him as she reached the bottom of the stairs. "Morning, Daniel. Everything alright?"

He put the bags on the floor and removed two newspapers, putting them on the dining room table. "No, I'm afraid it's not. We have a problem."

Simpson crossed the room and picked up the first paper, a copy of the *Daily Mail*. The headline read "Illegal Immigrant Werewolves on Benefits Stopped at Airport." He sighed. "Well, that just ticks every bloody box, doesn't it? The fucking Tories will love that, and the blue-rinse brigade will be up in arms. They seem to be more bothered by the fact that one of them claimed benefits than the fact that they were werewolves."

Marie picked up another paper and scanned the text, then looked up to Daniel with tears in her eyes. "Dmitri and Kasha? Do any of the reports say what happened to them? Are they okay?"

"I don't know. The tabloids have sensationalised their accounts so it's difficult to understand exactly what happened. What is certain is that the situation is now so much worse than it was. People in the coffee shops and supermarkets were talking about little else."

Marie retrieved her laptop from under the empty box of decorations. After a few moments, a grainy video appeared on the screen, obviously taken on a camera-phone. It showed Dmitri, Kasha and their young son, Adam, fall to the ground, writhing in agony amidst a group of panicked travellers. Then Adam began to transform. Fangs burst from the boy's mouth and hair surged from his pores. While the quality of the footage was poor, there was no question of what was happening. The image shook as the person filming was shoved out of the way by armed police who then opened fire on the three werewolves with submachine guns. Bullets tore into Adam, Dmitri and Kasha. The police clearly weren't taking any chances with them and emptied their entire clips into the trio. Then the video ended. Marie stifled a sob and closed the lid of the laptop.

"I... I knew them. Dmitri was like a father to me and Michael. They weren't hurting anyone. They just lived here, quietly for years. And Adam was only a child. How could they do that?"

Daniel put his hand on Marie's shoulder. "They only saw the monster, Marie. They didn't think of them as two parents with a child. They thought of them as wild beasts and put them down. We knew it would be like this. After what Connie did, how could they think otherwise?"

"I know, but seeing it like that, reading those fucking rags that make it sound like some kind of massive victory, it... it makes me sick." She got to her feet, jaw clenched and red-rimmed eyes blazing with fury. "I'm not leaving Michael in the hands of these fuckers. We need to accelerate our plans. God knows what they've been doing to him."

"We've been over this. It's all Simpson can do to stand up, and your injuries need more time to heal as well."

Marie glanced at Simpson, then back to Daniel. "There's a way to sort John out before the next full moon, and it's not like he'll be going into the base anyway, unless things go tits up." She walked over to Simpson and put her hand on his shoulder. "If you're up for it, we can have your injuries healed by lunchtime."

Daniel hadn't expected that. "You can't be serious? I know what you're thinking and it could kill him. Please, for the sake of a few more weeks, think about what you're suggesting."

Marie took Simpson's hands in hers. "It'll work. It won't be nice, but it'll work. And it's our only chance of getting to Michael in time."

Simpson seemed to take a moment to consider it, then nodded. "Fuck it, I've spent the last month or more held together with stitches and I'm getting sick to death of it. What do I have to do?"

"Okay, there's a reason that injuries inflicted by another werewolf don't heal until the next full moon. It's to do with the curse, or whatever you want to call it. When a wolf causes an injury, the wolf spirit is passed along and, in a normal human, it turns them on the next full moon. In your case, you're already afflicted, so your wolf fights against the new one and they cancel each other out until the moon rises and your wolf becomes powerful enough to defeat the other. You'll still heal from normal injuries, though. So, in theory, if we cut out the wounds inflicted by the other werewolves, you should then heal normally."

Daniel shook his head. "In *theory*, Marie. Gregorz said he'd done it to himself after that Moonstruck in Prague took a bite out of his leg, but he also said that he almost bled out in the process. Simpson's injuries are much more extensive than that. The damage we'd have to inflict would be dreadful. It may be too much for him to cope with."

"It's up to you, John. I can't force you to do this, and it's really not going to be pleasant. But if it works, then we can move the plan forward and get Michael out of that hell-hole."

Simpson took a deep breath. "Okay, I trust you, Marie. Let's do this. What do you need me to do?"

Daniel shook his head. "All you'll have to do is keep your wolf under control while we perform the operation. Unfortunately we don't have any tranquilisers left. If we're going to do this, then we should get on with it. Marie, can you get the plastic sheeting and rope out of the garage? I'll make sure the kitchen knives are sharp enough."

Daniel took a small amount of satisfaction in the expression on Simpson's face. He looked like he was about to throw up. Beads of sweat had broken out on his forehead, and his skin had turned pale and waxy. The stench of fear billowed from him. Daniel tried to give him a reassuring smile. "Don't worry, we'll do this as quickly as we can. You might want to get changed into something else, though. Something you don't mind bleeding on."

23rd December 2008. Underhill Military Base, Sublevel Two. 18:20

Phil balanced the tray of food on his left arm and brought his hand up to knock on the door, hesitating for a moment, unsure of what he'd say. He shook the feeling away and rapped twice on the plywood panel, then, without waiting for an answer, opened the door and stepped inside.

The room was dark, but enough light seeped in from the hallway for him to make out the outline of Paul Patterson sitting on the metal framed bed. "Paul, I've brought you some food from the mess. Nothing fancy, just bangers and mash."

Paul didn't turn around. "Just leave it on the table, thanks, Phil. I'm not that hungry, but I'll have some later on."

Phil put the tray down and turned on the lights. The fluorescent bulb flickered into life, illuminating the bare walls with a harsh, unforgiving light. Paul squinted at him through red-rimmed eyes. He hadn't shaved for a couple of days and Phil could smell him from where he stood. "I said I'm not hungry, Phil. Can you turn that fucking light off?"

Phil moved to the bed and turned on the small lamp on the bedside cabinet, then extinguished the main light. "Better? Listen, mate, I know that it's been shite, and I can't imagine what you've been through, but you need to talk to someone. Just saying that I'm here if you need me."

"And what do you think I need to talk about, Phil? The fact that I stitched up my mates and got them killed, or that my wife and daughter got torn apart on the fucking Internet?"

Phil sat down beside him. "Either. Both. Jesus, Paul, no one blames you for what happened. I probably would have done the same thing if that bitch was holding Sharon hostage. And you couldn't have known what she'd do."

"Yeah, well I should have known. I should have told you all what was going on, and then maybe Rick and Mark might still be alive. We could have set something up, ambushed the bitch and..."

Paul began sobbing. Phil had no idea what he could say that would even begin to help. Instead he put an awkward hand on the other man's shoulder and waited for the tears to subside.

"Christ, Paul, I don't know what to say, but you can't let this destroy you. Emma and Sam wouldn't have wanted that. You need to try and get past this. Grieving is one thing, but you're going to pieces here."

Paul looked up at him, his eyes glinting from the deep shadows cast by the lamp. "The Colonel wants me on their response unit, and I've said yes."

Phil's eyes widened. "Are you sure that's a good idea? I mean, fucking hell, Paul, after everything you've just been through, going back into the field's the last thing you should be doing."

"Oh, it's exactly what I need, and anyway, apart from Wilkinson and you, I'm the only person that's had combat experience against these things. They need me, and if it means I get to kill some more of those monsters, then I'm all for it. Should save Durham Constabulary a shitload of therapist's fees at the very least."

Phil could hardly disguise his shock at this. Paul Patterson was a wreck. No one in their right mind would give him a letter opener, let alone a firearm. He and Colonel Richards were going to have a fairly pointed conversation about this in the immediate future. He didn't allow Paul to see his alarm, however, and instead tried to force a reassuring smile onto his face. "Don't rush into it. That's all I'm saying. The Colonel asked me and I told him to go fuck himself. I'm an old-fashioned copper. I hunt bad guys, not monsters. If I never see another of those things again it'll be too soon. Just take some time to think it over. Please."

Paul's lips curled into a humourless smile. "Too late for that, Phil. They've got an op coming up, and I'm going to be going in there with the rest of them. Those hairy fucking bastards aren't going to know what hit them."

Chapter 4

24th December 2008. Crickhowell, Powys, Wales. 19:45

Rose Fisher swore under her breath as she pulled up outside of her rented flat and discovered that some inconsiderate bastard had parked their car in her space. Crickhowell was not a large town, and parking was difficult at the best of times. She'd hoped that at this time on Christmas Eve she might have had a chance to actually park outside her home, get inside and spend the night with a Chinese takeaway, a bottle of wine and the *Gavin and Stacey Christmas Special*. Apparently it was not to be. She'd have to park in the public car park behind the tourist information office, and then make the rest of the journey on foot. Feeling her mood rapidly deteriorate, she accelerated round the one way system, back onto the A40 and towards the town centre once more. She parked in an empty space close to the alleyway that led back to the High Street, not bothering to pay for a ticket. Not even the over-zealous local traffic wardens would be out at this time on Christmas Eve, and she had to go back to the base first thing in the morning anyway. All leave had been cancelled because of the werewolf situation. Better to work than sit around the flat on her own, getting fat on Christmas food and watching crap TV.

A fine drizzle filled the air, forming orange coronas around the street lights. The moisture soaked through her uniform within seconds of leaving the car. It had been sunny and unseasonably warm when she'd headed out this morning, and she'd forgotten to pick her coat up from the kitchen work surface, an oversight she already regretted. Despite the rain, the pubs were already busy, overflowing with drunken merrymakers in Santa Claus hats who spilled out onto the streets, singing bawdy versions of Christmas carols. After the day she'd had fending off the lecherous advances of Steven Wilkinson, dealing with Doctor Channing's emotional outbursts, and trying to come up with a mix of anti-depressants and anti-psychotics for Paul Patterson that wouldn't render him a drooling mess, the last thing she wanted to do was fight off the wandering hands of amorous Welshmen on her way home. The first one to push things too far would learn a lesson he'd not soon forget.

She hurried through the dark alleyway and, despite there being no cars on the road, walked further along the street to use the crossing in order to avoid two of the high street's busier public houses without making it look too obvious. A few wolf-whistles and lewd comments were hurled in her direction, but she quickened her pace and reached into her bag for her keys, looking forward to her food and wine away from the Neanderthal locals.

She unlocked the door and made her way upstairs, not bothering to turn the light on. The kitchen was to the right, and she planned on dumping her things, getting out of her army uniform into something a bit more comfortable, and settling down for the night. Once at the top of the stairs, she reached out for the light switch.

A hand grabbed hers from the darkness, and a shape moved from the shadows behind her and clasped a hand firmly over her mouth. Her takeaway and wine fell from her grasp. The bottle shattered on the tiled floor, while the foil takeaway cartons scattered her beef in black bean sauce across the kitchen, mingling with the shards of glass and red wine to form a dark, steaming puddle.

Her attackers held her firm. One had an iron grip on her wrist, while the other one restrained her from behind, preventing her from screaming for help. They probably thought that they had her right where they wanted her.

Their mistake.

Rose brought her heel down hard on the foot of the man behind her, feeling satisfaction at the hiss of pain that escaped from his lips. The bear-hug loosened, and she bent her knees, sliding forward while lowering her centre of gravity. The movement put her assailant off balance and he flew over her shoulder onto the shards of broken glass scattered across the kitchen floor. If these bastards had broken in here expecting to find some poor, defenceless girl, then they were about to get the shock of their lives. Plus, by now, all of the shops would be closed. She'd not be able to replace the wine or food, meaning that she'd have to spend Christmas bloody eve sober, hungry, and no doubt cleaning this mess up. Not to mention the tedious task of having to deal with the police. They were going to pay for that.

"Bastards!" she hissed.

The shape on the kitchen floor struggled to get to his feet, while the one grabbing her arm tried to shift his grip to get a better hold. Rose delivered a sharp kick to the prone figure's chin and he slumped face down into the puddle of glass and wine.

One down, one to go.

She twisted her hand, then stepped backwards and brought her other hand up to her captor's, locking the other man's wrist in a very uncomfortable position. In theory, she could hold him like this until the police arrived, but her anger and outrage at being assaulted inside her own home boiled up from within, and instead, she struck out at the joint, delivering an open-handed blow that shattered the man's wrist like porcelain. The grunt of pain was immensely satisfying, but it wasn't enough. It wasn't nearly enough. Twisting the broken joint further around, she locked out the man's elbow, and was about to deliver a vicious strike that would break the intruder's arm when the unmistakable click of a pistol being cocked came from behind her, and a woman's voice said, "I'd rather you didn't do that, Rose. Why don't you be a good girl and let my friend go."

Cold metal pressed against the back of her head. There was no way she'd be able to disarm the woman before she blew her brains all over the kitchen. Not while she still had hold of the man with a broken wrist, anyway. Her stance was all wrong. "Look, there's not a lot here. I don't have any cash, and the TV's a piece of shit. Just take what you want and go, alright?"

"Oh, Rose. You honestly didn't think we came here to steal your telly, did you?"

Before she could reply, the handgrip of the pistol came down on the back of her head, and bright bomb-bursts of pain lit up the inside of her skull. Then the darkness claimed her.

***

Rose had no idea how much time had passed. As consciousness returned, she kept her breathing steady and remained motionless as she tried to assess where she was. The back of her skull throbbed, and she'd probably have a mild concussion, but couldn't feel any more injuries, which was good. She also still had all of her clothes on, which was even better, even if the wet fabric felt uncomfortable against her skin. What was not quite so encouraging was the fact that her wrists and ankles were tightly bound with what felt like electrical cable. Her best chance to get out of this was to play dead for a while longer and see if any opportunities for escape presented themselves.

"She's awake," said a male voice with a thick German accent.

Bollocks. So much for that plan.

Rose opened her eyes and looked into the faces of her captors. The man was tall, grey-haired with a muscular build, while the woman was much smaller, her hair cut short and sporting a bad black dye-job. Both wore army uniforms, and the woman looked familiar. Rose cocked her head and narrowed her eyes, instantly regretting the sudden movement as the throbbing at the back of her skull erupted into a white-hot blaze of pain and a wave of nausea surged up from her stomach.

Yep. Definitely a concussion.

The woman smiled at her, crouching down on her haunches until they were face to face. "The reason we're here tonight is that we'd like to talk to you about the base you work at. And we'd especially like to talk about some of the people there. Michael Williams for one.

"I don't know any Michael Williams. I just work at the training camp up the road, for God's sake. Patching up TA grunts who hurt themselves on the assault course."

The German spoke again. "She's lying. You were right. She's got Michael's scent all over her. Wilkinson's too. And, Marie... I can smell blood on her. Michael's blood."

The woman's eyes widened, and she grabbed Rose's chin. "My friend had better be wrong about that, Rose. Because if you've hurt my fucking brother, you won't like what happens next."

Rose began to connect the pieces, despite her concussion. The woman was Marie Williams, the corpse which had vanished from the morgue in High Moor six weeks ago. She recognised her from the newspaper photograph now, even though her hair was different. If her brother was the werewolf that Doctor Channing was experimenting on, and the German could smell his scent on her, then that meant that she was in a hell of a lot more trouble than she'd realised. She'd seen the photos of Olivia Garner and her husband after Connie Hamilton had attacked them and she knew she didn't stand a chance unless she co-operated.

"Alright, but I've not hurt him. I'm just a doctor. He had a lot of injuries when they brought him in, and I've been taking care of him."

Marie Williams curled her top lip up into a snarl. "You'd better hope that's the truth, pet. And you'd better not bullshit me anymore. We can *smell* it when you lie. If I think you are being anything other than completely truthful with me, then I'll let my mate, John, teach you the error of your ways."

58

Another man entered the room, wearing nothing but army combat trousers. He turned to her and smiled, and Rose couldn't stop the whimper of terror escape from her lips. She recognised the man instantly. How could she not when his face had been on the front page of every newspaper for the last month? John Simpson. The *thing* responsible for all of those deaths in High Moor. She knew then that her chances of getting out of here alive had reduced to virtually zero.

Her terror must have been plain to see because Marie smiled at her. "Good girl. I can see we're going to get along like a house on fire."

24ᵗʰ December 2008. Underhill Military Base, Sublevel Two. 21:35

Phil hurried along the corridor to where Colonel Richards was talking to a junior officer. "Colonel, can I have a word please?"

Colonel Richards looked up at him and acknowledged his presence with a nod. He returned his attention to the young lieutenant, taking the clipboard from his hands and scrawling a signature onto a piece of paper. The lieutenant gave Colonel Richards a hasty salute before hurrying off through the double fire doors, leaving the two men alone. The Colonel smiled at Phil. "Mr Fletcher. What can I do for you?"

"I was hoping we could have a chat about Paul Patterson."

The Colonel made an exaggerated show of checking his

watch. "Of course, but you'll have to make it quick. I've got to attend the mission briefing in a few minutes."

"Well, I'd really rather that you didn't use Paul. Not this time around, anyway. He's been through a hell of a lot, and I don't think his head's in the right place. He should be getting psychiatric care, not being sent back into the field to face those bloody things again. It's too soon. You give him a gun and he'll probably just stick it in his mouth."

"Under normal circumstances, I'd agree with you, but unfortunately our options are limited. The only people we have access to with combat experience against these creatures are Paul Patterson, Steven Wilkinson and your good self. Clearly, Wilkinson is in no physical shape to go out into the field, and if I'm honest, I'm still not comfortable with the idea of having a werewolf out there alongside my men. Yes, Paul has been through a difficult time, but he's a trained firearms officer, and unless you are prepared to take his place, he's the only experienced asset we have that I can send into the field. Are you saying that you want to go along instead of him?"

Phil's shoulders sagged. "No, I'm not weapons trained. I'd be an even bigger liability than Paul is, and there's no way you'll get me to face down one of those things by choice. I've seen what they can do."

"Then I'm afraid we aren't left with any alternatives. As valuable as Mr Wilkinson's intelligence has been, there really is no substitute for first-hand experience. Now, if you'll excuse me, I have to brief the combat teams on their respective missions."

"There is one more thing. I was wondering when I'd be

allowed to go home."

"Ah, yes. I'm afraid that it won't be for a little while yet."

Phil had been expecting that response, but his stomach still sank with disappointment. Sharon was staying with her sister in High Moor, and while he'd been allowed to speak to her on the telephone, it just wasn't the same. There'd been times over the last couple of days where he'd locked himself away in his room, weeping silently into his pillow, wishing that his wife was there to hold him close. He'd never spent more than a few days apart from her in over twenty years, and without her he felt lost. "I realise that you still need me here, Sir, but all I'm asking for is a few days to see my wife. Maybe spend Christmas with her at her sister's?"

Colonel Richards shook his head. "I'm sorry, Phil. I really am, but it's out of the question. At the moment, you are one of the few people on the planet who has first-hand experience of these things. You're too valuable an asset to risk at this time. Other governments would quite literally kill for the knowledge you possess, and let's not forget the creatures themselves. You'd put yourself and anyone around you in terrible danger if you were to leave this facility now. If it would make you feel better, I might be able to arrange for your wife to be brought here instead?"

Phil was taken aback, and for a moment seriously considered the offer. Then he shook his head. Sharon would hate being confined to this place, even if her presence would make him feel better. He couldn't do that to her. She was better off at her sister's house. He shook his head. "No, thank you, Colonel. That won't be necessary."

"Well, if you change your mind, let me know. Now, if you don't mind, I really must get on."

Phil sighed as the Colonel turned and walked down the corridor to the briefing room. He felt useless, impotent, frustrated and more than a little bored. Steven Wilkinson was the werewolf expert, while Paul, despite his state of mind, was a highly capable firearms officer with combat experience. In contrast, Phil was little more than a bystander. There really wasn't anything he could offer that the others couldn't do better. With nothing else to do, he went back to his room and lay on the bed, wishing that Sharon was there beside him.

***

Phil looked at his watch and groaned. He'd been alone with his thoughts for almost two hours now. There was nothing on television that managed to hold his attention, and his mind was too active for sleep. The base was quiet now. There'd been a flurry of activity about an hour ago as the combat teams finished their briefing and departed on their respective missions. The corridors had been filled with the sound of boots and shouted commands, but now there was only an eerie silence. He picked up his phone and thought about calling Sharon, but at this time she'd either be in bed or at the midnight Christmas Eve mass with her sister. Better to leave it until the morning. Still, he was tired of looking at the plain beige concrete walls of his room and wanted to talk to someone. Anyone. He sat up on the bed, wincing at a twinge of pain in his lower back, slipped on his shoes and walked out into the corridor. With Paul gone, there was really only one other person he could speak to. He just hoped that Steven Wilkinson was in the mood for a visitor.

The elevator to sublevel four, which housed the medical and detention facilities, was situated at the far end of the underground complex, along a twisting maze of identical corridors. Phil still found himself becoming disoriented in this place on occasion, and as he made his way through the labyrinthine passageways, was acutely aware of the sharp echo of his own footsteps. There was no sign of anyone else. The military personnel that had not gone out into the field would be in the situation room on the next level up, monitoring the mission. He reached the elevator and punched the call button, a vague feeling of unease nagging at the back of his mind. He'd not actually been forbidden to go down to sublevel four, but it had certainly been implied quite heavily that he was not to stray beyond the accommodation level. Still, if he was discovered, he could always plead ignorance.

The doors slid open, and Phil found himself face to face with two stern looking army officers: a powerfully built man and a dark haired woman who seemed familiar, but whose name he was unable to place. His heart sank and he cast his eyes down to the floor, expecting to be challenged, but after a second, when nothing was said, he got into the elevator and pressed the button for sublevel four. All he could do at this point was to act as if he was supposed to be here and hope for the best. Still, in the cramped confines of the elevator, he had the uncomfortable feeling of eyes boring into the back of his neck. His heart began to race, and sweat beaded on his forehead. He forced himself to regulate his breathing and calm down. He'd know soon enough if they were going to prevent him from progressing any further.

The elevator lurched to a stop and, after what seemed like an eternity, the doors slid open. Phil stepped out and turned to his left, towards the medical facility, very much aware of the numbness in his legs and the hammering in his chest. He glanced back over his shoulder and saw that the two army officers were walking in the opposite direction, toward the detention area, and breathed a sigh of relief. They might mention having seen him to Colonel Richards at some point, but they clearly weren't going to place him under arrest there and then.

He reached the door to Steven's room, rapped twice on it, and let himself in, allowing the reinforced door to swing closed behind him. Steven lay on a metal hospital bed in the centre of the room with a drip running into his arm and an array of machines behind him that monitored his condition. "Hi, Steven, hope you don't mind me dropping in unannounced. Just wondered if you were up for having a visitor?"

Steven winced in pain as he sat up on the bed. "I'm glad of it, Phil. I've been going stir crazy in here on my own. It's..." Steven's eyes widened and the machines behind him let out a cacophony of warning alarms.

Phil rushed to his side. "Steven – what is it? What's wrong?"

Steven grabbed Phil's arm. "They're here. Oh, God, they've come for me."

"What do you mean? Who's come for you?"

"Who do you think? The fucking pack. I can smell them on you, Phil. You stink of the bastard that was hunting me on the last full moon. There's a pack assassination team down here with us."

Chapter 5

24th December 2008. Underhill Military Base, Sublevel Four. 23:52

Marie breathed a sigh of relief as she watched Phil Fletcher disappear around the corner. "Thank fuck for that. I thought he'd recognised me for a second."

Daniel smiled. "The human mind is adept at rationalising things. The last thing Detective Fletcher expected was to see you here. He's never actually met you in the flesh, remember. I doubt he made the connection."

Marie frowned. "Well, let's make this quick. The last thing we need is him to work it out and raise the alarm."

Daniel stopped outside of a store room and put his hand on Marie's arm. "I'm not comfortable with this approach. By rights we should be burning this place to the ground and getting rid of anyone who knows too much. Destroy any evidence. It's what we were trained to do."

Marie shook his arm away. "I know, but our priority has to be finding Michael and getting away without anyone noticing. We're in a bloody secret military base, for fuck's sake. We can't fight our way out of here."

Daniel nodded his acceptance, then paused and sniffed the air. "There's one more thing you should know. Wilkinson is here. I just caught his scent."

"Shit. That explains why they know so bloody much about us." She paused, then shook her head. "It doesn't change anything. Getting my brother away from here is all that's important right now."

Marie turned away from Daniel and strode down the corridor. Daniel caught up to her and grabbed her wrist. "We might not get another chance like this. Their werewolf expert is here. Their research is here. If we can get Michael out, destroy their work and kill Wilkinson, then we have to try. There's more at stake here than just your brother."

She snarled at Daniel and pushed him against the wall. "Michael is our priority. He's the only one that can stop the pack from tearing itself apart. Once we get him out of here, feel free to come back and tie up the loose ends. Until then, we stick to the fucking plan. Am I making myself clear?"

Daniel raised his hands in surrender. "As crystal. Let's get this over with."

They hurried along the plain corridors, passing darkened laboratories and offices until they arrived at a reinforced steel door with a numeric keypad inset into the wall beside it. Marie punched in the code they'd got from Rose, and the lock disengaged. As the door swung open, Marie's hand went to her mouth.

Michael lay naked on a metal autopsy table in the centre of the room. Thick nylon straps across his limbs, chest and forehead prevented him from moving, while an array of machines monitored his vital signs. An IV drip fed a cocktail of drugs into his system, while a metal tray beside the table contained an array of vicious, bloodstained surgical implements. Even without enhanced senses, Marie was almost overwhelmed by the stench of blood and excrement that billowed from the room like a noxious cloud.

"Fuckers!"

She raced into the room, tore the drip from her brother's arm and loosened the restraining straps. "Michael. Can you hear me? It's Marie. I've come to get you out of here."

If Michael registered her presence, he made no sign. But for the shallow rise and fall of his chest, her brother could have been dead. The drugs they had him on were clearly doing their job well. Marie turned to Daniel, who stood in the doorway, and shook her head. There was no way they'd just be able to walk out of here with Michael in this condition. It was time to take more drastic action.

She unplugged the machines that monitored her brother's condition and ripped the sensors from his body. "Michael, I'm really sorry about this, but it's the only way." She reached into the pocket of her combat jacket and removed a large syringe, then probed his torso with her fingers until she found the faint beat of his heart and stabbed the adrenaline injection into her brother's chest.

Michael's eyes snapped open and he let out a scream that echoed through the empty corridors. His body convulsed in agony while Marie and Daniel tried to hold him down. "Michael, it's Marie. I'm here with Daniel. We've come to get you out of here."

Michael, however, didn't seem to recognise her, or even acknowledge her existence. His eyes flashed a phosphorescent green and hair began to flow from his pores like a writhing tide of serpents. Bones popped and crunched, and razor sharp fangs burst through his mouth in a spray of blood-flecked foam.

Marie's heart raced. She'd known that there was a risk the adrenaline would trigger Michael's transformation, but in his drug-addled condition, there was a good chance he would lash out at anything nearby. His wolf would react on instinct, fighting off the perceived threat. It would tear apart anything it saw, and that included her and Daniel.

"Michael, please, it's me. You need to stop. You need to change back."

Bones twisted, shattered and reformed. Michael's face elongated into a snarling muzzle. The transformation would be complete in a matter of seconds. She looked at Daniel and saw her own terror mirrored on his face.

Then, just as Michael's transformation completed, an alarm began to sound, echoing through the empty corridors outside.

25th December 2008. Parklands Close, South Molton, Devon. 00:07

Sophie lay on her bed and watched the glowing digits of her alarm clock count the passing of another minute. Her parents were downstairs, arguing again. They'd been doing this for days, now. Her mother's mood swung from tearful to incandescent rage and back again more times than Sophie had been able to count. Her father had weathered the storm, accepting his wife's fury with a resigned look on his face, doing his level best not to make things worse, with varying degrees of success. Sophie had no idea what was going on. It was Christmas, and she thought that everyone was supposed to be happy at Christmas. She just hoped that in the morning, her mother's sadness would go away. Perhaps the present that Sophie had made for her would cheer her up. She'd worked very hard on it, after all.

The clock's display clicked over once more, just as her mother stomped upstairs and slammed the bedroom door closed behind her. A few moments later, her father's careful footsteps followed. He paused on the landing and opened Sophie's bedroom door to check on her. Sophie closed her eyes and pretended to be asleep. She was glad that her parents were *finally* going to bed. Santa wouldn't leave any presents with them arguing like that downstairs. He'd come down the chimney to face one of her mother's moods and wouldn't know what to do with himself. That would just be awkward for everyone. Hopefully her father remembered to put the mince pie and milk out for him before he came to bed. The last thing Sophie wanted was for Santa to think that they weren't grateful. He might not come next year if they didn't put his treats out.

The thought nagged at her. Her father always made sure that Santa's mince pie was out before she went to bed, but tonight he'd been preoccupied. There was a chance he'd forgotten, and the consequences of that were too terrible to contemplate. She'd have to make sure.

Sophie slipped out of bed and moved silently towards her open bedroom door, taking extra care to avoid the creaking floorboard beside her dressing table. She strained her ears, allowing her other self to come up a little to improve her hearing. Her parents were talking in their bedroom.

"William, it's not safe here anymore." Her mother's voice. Strained. On the verge of more tears. "If they work out that Dmitri and Kasha were here before they went to the airport..."

"Sonja, there's nothing we can do. There's no way out of the country, at least, not yet. Krysztof said that we should carry on as normal and not draw attention to ourselves."

Her mother snorted at this. "Normal? How can anything ever be normal again? My sister and her entire family are dead. *Murdered!* And you expect me to carry on as if nothing has happened? And worse, take orders from that fool, Krysztof?"

Her father's voice took on a hard edge. One that Sophie rarely heard him use, especially not to her mother. "You need to pull yourself together. For Sophie's sake, and mine, if not for your own. We'll mourn them later, once Krysztof and Lukas come up with a plan to get us to safety. In the meantime, we're going to act like nothing is wrong. Tomorrow, you and I are going to smile and give Sophie a nice Christmas day. We'll deal with everything else after that."

Sophie felt confused. Her parents were talking as if something had happened to Uncle Dmitri and Auntie Kasha, but that was just silly. She'd only seen them a few days before, and they'd gone on holiday. They must have been talking about someone else, she decided. Perhaps her mother had another sister she'd never met.

Sophie pushed the worrying thoughts aside and concentrated on the task at hand. She'd never be able to sleep until she was certain that Santa's mince pie was in its usual place on the coffee table. With exaggerated care, she crept out onto the landing and made her way downstairs, placing one foot slowly onto each step before shifting her weight to it, in order to avoid any tell-tale creaks. Her mother could hear a mouse fart halfway along the street, so getting past her unnoticed was no easy task. Fortunately, it was something that she'd spent her entire life practicing, and could be as silent as a shadow when the need arose.

She reached the bottom of the stairs and stood on the soft, pale carpet of the hallway. The door to the living room was closed. She'd not considered that. The handle on that door always gave off a distinctive little squeak that would bring her mother downstairs in a second. That meant she'd need to go through the kitchen and dining room to get to the lounge, but that presented a different challenge. A set of wind chimes hung just behind the kitchen door. The slightest breeze would set them off. She'd have to be extra careful.

Sophie pulled open the kitchen door, millimetres at a time so as not to create a draft, and slipped through the gap onto the cold slate-tiled floor. Her parents were still talking upstairs, their voices muffled, but understandable to her sharpened hearing. She ignored them. They were talking about boring, grown-up things, and she needed to concentrate on what she was doing or risk getting caught. With the mood her mother was in, that really wasn't an option. The last thing she wanted was to spend Christmas day confined to her room in disgrace.

There was just one more obstacle to overcome. The sliding door at the far end of the kitchen. From there, she'd have a clear view into the living room. Fortunately, the door was partially opened. She'd never have been able to open it without making noise, even by the small amount needed to see into the next room. She allowed herself a small smile of victory as she crept across the kitchen and peered through the doorway.

The lights on the Christmas tree twinkled, casting multi-coloured shadows that danced across the room. An empty glass, and a saucer covered in mince pie crumbs sat on the coffee table, and on her father's armchair in the corner of the room sat a large pile of presents. Her father hadn't forgotten, and best of all, Santa had already been!

The crunch of a footfall on the gravel path outside. A bright light shining through the kitchen window. Sophie's heart fluttered and she brought her hands up to her mouth, barely able to contain her excitement.

"Santa?"

She hardly had time to scream as the kitchen window exploded, and shards of glass tore her face into tattered, bloody ribbons.

25th December 2008. Underhill Military Base, Sublevel Four. 00:10

Marie threw herself away from Michael's thrashing form. Klaxons echoed along the corridors and red strobe lights flashed against the concrete walls. She could see clouds of steam billowing from Daniel as he struggled to restrain the disoriented beast that had been her brother. He was on the verge of transforming himself, his wolf as close to the surface as he could get it. Grey fur burst from Daniel's pores then retreated back into his skin. Even so, Michael would be free in another second, and in the distance she could hear the sounds of boots against the concrete, getting closer. "Daniel. You can't hold him. Move your fucking arse."

Daniel threw Michael across the room with every ounce of strength he had left and dived for the open door. The werewolf scrambled to its feet and followed close behind, snarling in rage. They tried to slam the door closed, just as Michael crashed into it. The door pushed open a fraction, but not enough to allow him to escape. They both put their weight behind it, but even their combined strength wouldn't hold against the frenzied assault for long. Marie looked up and saw four armed men in Special Forces uniforms turn the corner, weapons raised as they hurried towards them.

Marie looked at Daniel and nodded. She turned to the armed men and yelled. "It's okay. We've got it." Then they pulled the door open and let Michael out of his cell.

Gunfire echoed through the narrow confines of the corridor. Bullets peppered the reinforced steel door, leaving visible dents on the side that Marie and Daniel cowered behind, and the air was filled with the stench of gunpowder. Michael yelped in pain, then roared in rage. After a moment, the weapons stopped firing and the screaming started. Before long, that stopped as well, and the only sounds Marie could hear were the shriek of the klaxons and a wet ripping noise.

Daniel began to remove his uniform, obviously intent on transforming so that he could meet Michael on even terms. Marie put her hand on his arm and shook her head. She'd not come this far to let Daniel and Michael kill each other. She took a deep breath and stepped out from behind the door to face her brother.

The Special Forces team hadn't stood a chance. Two of them had been torn in half, their bodies ripped open and spread across the walls and floor. One of them tried to crawl towards them, blood bubbling from his mouth and one eye hanging from the shredded ruins of his face, his guts unravelling behind what remained of his torso. The last one's mouth opened and closed like a fish out of water, mouthing a silent scream as Michael buried his snout into the exposed chest cavity and chewed on the succulent organs within.

Marie put her hands out and took a step forward. Michael lifted his blood-drenched muzzle and snarled. Her legs betrayed her, and every instinct screamed to get back behind the comparative safety of the ruined steel door. She pushed the fear down and took another unsteady step forward. "Michael, it's me. Marie. Come on, big brother. Stop acting like a twat."

There was no flicker of recognition in Michael's eyes. His lips curled back to reveal rows of bloodstained fangs, and he let out a thick, guttural growl. Marie took another hesitant step towards him. "Michael. Snap the fuck out of it." A note of anger and impatience had crept into her voice. It would not be long before more armed men arrived to contain the situation. Time really was not on their side. Michael crouched down and sank his teeth into the arm of the half-dead soldier, then began dragging the corpse away from her. She recognised the signs. The body language. This was all wolf. The behaviour of a wild animal protecting its meal from an intruder. She'd woken up the beast, but not the man. She took another step, very much aware of the growl's ferocity increasing as she invaded the beast's personal space.

Her voice took on a hard tone as she pushed the fear out of her mind. "Michael. I'm not going to ask you again. Stop pissing about and let's get out of here." She stared into the huge creature's baleful yellow eyes, searching for any sign that it knew who she was. The werewolf's muscles tightened. Its posture shifted into a crouch. Marie knew what was coming next. With a snarl of pure rage, the beast leaped into the air, jaws agape and black talons slashing out.

As Michael attacked, Marie dropped to the ground, and when the monster sailed over her head, she brought her foot up sharply, kicking it in the testicles. The werewolf's snarl of rage turned into a yelp of pain before it collided with the reinforced steel door of the cell with a sickening crunch.

Marie scrambled to her feet, slipping in the blood of the dead soldiers, and breathed a sigh of relief as she saw Michael's body twist and contort back into his human form. He looked up at her with glassy eyes and tried to get to his feet.

"What? Marie I... oh, God. Did you kick me in the balls?"

Despite the circumstances, she smiled at him. "You had

it coming." She reached down and poured the remains of a dead soldier out of the bloody scraps of his uniform, then threw the dripping rags at her brother. "Put these on and let's get the hell out of here."

Michael's nose crinkled. "Haven't you got anything a bit less... blood-soaked?"

"Yes, but these are better. Stop fucking moaning and get dressed. We've got to get out of here before anyone else shows up."

Daniel helped Michael into the tattered uniform, and Marie slipped under her brother's arm to support him. He went to shake her off. "It's okay. I can manage."

She shook her head. "Seriously, you wouldn't last five bloody minutes in the field. Let us support you. Act fucked up."

Michael's eyes widened as the details of his sister's plan fell into place. Once Marie and Daniel had positioned themselves under each arm, he slumped, allowing them to support his weight. They'd not made it far along the corridor before another fire-team emerged from the stairwell.

Marie looked over her shoulder, then turned to the squad of armed men. "It's loose! Somewhere down near medical. The rest of them are... oh, God... we tried to... It ATE them!"

The squad leader nodded. "It's okay. Get upstairs and find help." He motioned to his team and they spread out into the corridor in a standard formation, weapons raised. He made a series of hand movements, and they moved away into the depths of the base.

Marie hit the call button for the elevator, and once the doors slid open, ushered Michael and Daniel inside before pressing the button for the surface level. She glanced over to Daniel, who arched his eyebrow.

"What's the matter?" she said in an innocent voice. "I told you it'd be a piece of piss."

The lift arrived at the surface level and juddered to a halt. After a moment, the doors slid open to reveal a squad of soldiers standing before them with weapons raised. A grey-haired man with a bristling moustache smiled and stepped forward. "Miss Williams, I presume? So glad you could join us. I'm Colonel Richards, commanding officer of this facility. Please, come with me."

Chapter 6

25th December 2008. Parklands Close, South Molton, Devon. 00:10

Paul Patterson tightened his grip on the submachine gun and tried to bring his racing heartbeat under control. His hands were slick with sweat, despite his fingerless cotton gloves, and the polymer handgrip felt as if it could slip from his grasp at any moment. The silhouetted outlines of the other members of his team were just visible in the darkness. They flowed through the mist-shrouded trees without making a sound, their movements slow yet fluid. Not even the crack of a breaking branch underfoot betrayed their passage through the small patch of woodland. Paul's own movements, while measured and stealthy, felt lumbering and clumsy by comparison. Not for the first time, he wondered what the hell he was doing here. The rest of the squad were elite Special Forces troops, whereas he was just a police firearms officer. To say that he felt out of his depth was an understatement.

Sergeant Peyton raised her right arm and made a fist. Corporal Raines and Private Lewis froze in place, then dropped into firing positions in a single co-ordinated and sinuous movement. Half a second later, Paul mirrored them, only too aware of the fact that he'd reacted slower than everyone else. It felt like he'd lost a game of musical statues for the tenth time in a row. The woods began to thin a little way ahead of them, and the hazy sky visible between the trees glowed orange with the reflected glare of the sodium streetlights against the drifting fog. Their target was just beyond the treeline. The realisation unleashed a surge of adrenaline that deadened his limbs and brought on a wave of nausea that he struggled to control. His mind felt fuzzy, heavy with the combined effects of the drugs he'd been given back at the base, and the first hints of panic began to bubble up from his subconscious.

I shouldn't be here. I can't face these things. Not again. Phil was right. Oh, God, I feel sick. It'll be a massacre. Those fucking werewolves will tear through us like cattle. I've got to get out of here.

He shook his head and fought against the rising tide of terror. Remembering the reason that he'd agreed to come on this mission. The faces of his wife and daughter the last time he'd seen them. Happy, smiling and looking forward to the Christmas break when they could spend some time together as a family. The look of pain and terror on their faces when they'd died. The screams of Emma as she tried to shield Sam from the savage teeth and claws of Connie Hamilton, and the high-pitched shrieks of terror from his daughter as she watched her mother being slowly torn apart, turning into hitching, pleading sobs as the monster turned its attention to her.

He grabbed hold of the fear and doubt, forced it into submission, and moulded it into something he could use. He poured in the ache of his loss and his guilt, forging it on a cold flame of rage until it became a razor-edged blade of raw emotion. His heartbeat slowed and his vision cleared. He became acutely aware of the frozen, dead woodland around him. The distant hoot of an owl as it searched the frost-covered fields for prey. The shriek of a fox behind them and the answering call from its mate. The sporadic rumble of cars on the main road. The position of his squad mates, spaced out before him in the darkness, invisible but for the plumes of their breath as it reacted with the frigid air.

Sergeant Peyton gave the signal to advance, and this time, when the squad started towards their target, Paul's movements were as graceful and silent as the rest of them.

The dark skeletons of the trees thinned, then vanished abruptly at a low, wood-panelled fence. Beyond it lay a neatly maintained garden. A frost-covered climbing frame and slide glimmered under the reflected light. A gravel path ran along the length of a small lawn, and a sand-pit sat beside a small wooden shed, its contents frozen as hard as concrete. The house at the far end of the garden was dark and silent, save for the twinkling lights of a Christmas tree, barely visible through the kitchen window.

One by one, the team vaulted the fence, clearing the gravel and landing on the lawn without making a sound. Sergeant Peyton gave a series of hand gestures, and the squad spread out in a combat formation, weapons trained on the dark openings of the kitchen window and back door. A shadow momentarily obscured the shimmering lights of the tree and Paul felt his heart lurch in his chest. Then Sergeant Peyton gave the signal to attack.

Private Lewis raised his weapon; a modified SA-80 with an under-slung grenade launcher, and fired one of the explosives directly at the kitchen window. The squad threw themselves to the ground as the 40mm grenade shattered the glass and exploded inside the house. Shrapnel peppered the wooden fence, and the rest of the glass in the window and back door blew out. The squad were on their feet before the blast had finished echoing around the neighbouring houses.

Sergeant Peyton, Corporal Raines and Private Lewis began making their way toward the smoking ruin of the back door, while Paul stayed back to provide cover. He knew that Lieutenant Foster would break through the front door with Private Cross in a matter of seconds, and they'd proceed to clear the house of hostiles. That grenade should have annihilated anything in the kitchen, but according to the intelligence reports, that still left two lycanthropes in the property. And Paul doubted they would go down without a fight.

Corporal Raines reached the doorway first. He didn't bother checking the remains of the kitchen, no doubt assuming that the grenade had done its job and killed everything within a five meter radius. Instead, he shone his tactical light through the shattered doorway that led to the front hall and stepped inside the building. Paul couldn't believe his stupidity. He'd *told* them how hard these bastards were to kill. Connie Hamilton had healed from a point-blank headshot in less than twenty seconds. He opened his mouth to warn the soldier, but before he could get the words out, the huge, muscular form of a werewolf burst through one of the upstairs windows in an explosion of glass and wood.

Private Lewis and Sergeant Peyton swung their weapons around to face the threat, but hesitated once they realised what they were facing. The beast was huge. Triangular, pointed ears lay flat against the monster's

82

head, and it's long, tapered snout was wrinkled into a snarl, revealing rows of vicious, gleaming teeth. Muscles flowed like liquid beneath layers of coarse, black fur, giving a sense of the thing's raw power. No matter how well trained they might have been, their minds struggled for that vital fraction of a second to comprehend the nightmarish creature before them. And that fraction of a second was all the werewolf needed. It tensed its muscles and leaped into the air, jumping over the hail of bullets the two soldiers unleashed with ease. It slammed into Private Lewis and clamped its jaws down around his neck, severing the man's head in a single bite. Sergeant Peyton threw herself backwards just as the monster lashed out with its claws. The movement, along with her Kevlar vest saved her life. Just. The claws ripped through the protective clothing, but from where Paul stood, it didn't look like the attack had penetrated all the way through. She scrambled backwards and brought her weapon to bear on the werewolf, just as Corporal Raines began screaming from inside the house.

The scream snapped Paul out of his stupor. He'd faced these monsters before. That was the whole point of him being here. As the massive creature stalked towards Sergeant Peyton, he raised his SA-80 and opened fire.

The attack seemed to take the werewolf by surprise, almost as if it either hadn't noticed him, or had discounted him as a threat. He stitched the creature's flank with bullet holes, sending it crashing against the side of the house, and fought to control the wave of revulsion that washed over him as he watched the werewolf's bones shatter, twist and reform as it turned back into a naked man. Paul wasn't finished yet, however. Drawing his pistol, he strode over to the creature and fired a silver bullet straight into its skull.

Sergeant Peyton's mouth hung open. "What the hell are you doing, Patterson? We're supposed to take these things alive."

Paul felt his lip curl up into a sneer. "You're fucking welcome," he said to her, then shouldered his SA-80 and strode through the back door, into the darkness of the house.

It didn't take Paul long to find what was left of Corporal Raines. His eviscerated corpse lay in several pieces along the hallway. Dark puddles of blood had stained the light carpet crimson around the stumps of his severed limbs, and his throat had been slashed. The front door hung open on shattered hinges, and the wood around the lock was splintered. He could make out a boot print just beneath the lock. The other fire team had clearly executed their part of the plan, but were conspicuous by their absence. Sergeant Peyton pointed to the closed living room door, then to the staircase. Paul nodded his understanding and crouched at the bottom of the stairs, his weapon pointed into the darkness while the Sergeant carefully turned the handle of the living room door, then pushed it open.

The twinkling of the lights on the Christmas tree glittered in his peripheral vision, but Paul kept his weapon trained on the stairwell. Sergeant Peyton stepped through the door, weapon raised, then fired two shots. A high pitched yelp came from the living room, followed by a thick, guttural snarl from the darkness at the top of the stairs. A pair of green eyes glowed in the shadows. Paul squeezed off three rounds in rapid succession as the werewolf burst from cover and launched itself into the air towards him. The rounds slammed into the creature's body and he side-stepped out of its path as the naked, bloodstained body of a woman crashed into the wall behind where he'd been standing. He drew his pistol to administer the coup de grace, but felt Sergeant Peyton's hand on his arm. She shook her head, then tapped her throat mike. "Charlie Oscar, this is Fire Team Tango. Targets neutralised. Requesting immediate evac and medical assistance." She nodded to Paul, her face a grim mask. "We got the bastards. Now let's see if anyone else is still alive."

25th December 2008. Underhill Military Base. 00:18

The soldiers led Marie, Daniel and Michael through the upper levels of the complex, keeping a respectful distance from their captives, until they reached a pair of double doors that led outside onto a flat expanse of tarmac. Marie risked a backward glance at the nervous soldiers, and took some satisfaction in the fact that they all pulled their weapons harder into their shoulders. "Where are you taking us?" she asked.

Colonel Richards said nothing at first. When she repeated the question, he gave a grim smile. "Clearly this facility has been compromised, so we'll be taking you to a new, secure location for interrogation. Now, please keep moving. I'd hate to be forced to have you shot."

A hard knot of fear clenched her stomach. The fact that

Michael's injuries had healed so quickly meant that they were probably armed with standard silver bullets, not Steven Wilkinson's silver and mercury rounds. Michael and Daniel would most likely survive a confrontation. The same could not be said for her, and she realised that her companions were only going along with this to protect her from harm. A wave of guilt and nausea washed over her. Whatever happened to them next would be her fault, and she couldn't see any way out of the situation.

They made their way across the tarmac, away from the subterranean complex, towards the dark silhouette of another building that loomed up from the swirling mist. To her left, she could just make out the orange glimmer of the streetlights on the main road. Two hundred yards across open ground to safety. Even with the darkness and inclement weather on her side, she knew that she'd have no chance of crossing the distance before a bullet found its target. Their captor's SA-80's were equipped with IR scopes which would light her up like a bloody Christmas tree. She'd be lucky to make it ten feet.

Attacking them was also out of the question. The men were well trained and maintained a set distance of about three meters behind them, spread out in a loose semicircular formation. Daniel could probably close the distance and kill one of them before the rest opened fire. Michael *might* be able to, but she had no way of knowing how badly the drugs they'd been pumping into him had affected his reactions. The adrenaline would be wearing off now, and her brother had never been on the field teams. Despite being silver immune and possessing his lycanthropic gift, Michael was nowhere near as efficient a killer as Daniel or herself. She cursed Stephen Wilkinson again. Six weeks ago, she could have taken these soldiers out without breaking a sweat. Now, in her maimed, weakened, *human*, state, she'd be lucky to beat one of them in a fair fight. Not that fighting fair was ever high on her list of priorities.

As they drew closer to the row of buildings, she began to make out the details. Heavy steel roller-doors opened up to reveal the cavernous interior. The rumble of an idling engine and the smell of diesel fumes reached her. The building was the base's motor transport section, and somehow she doubted that they'd simply be loaded aboard a standard troop carrier once they reached the garage. An armoured prisoner transport vehicle would be more likely. Once they were secured inside of that, the chances of escape reduced to pretty much nothing. She glanced at Daniel and he gave a tiny, almost imperceptible nod. He understood what was about to happen, and knew that if they were going to act, they had to do it now. Marie tensed her muscles in preparation and visualised what she was going to do next. A feigned stumble, a roll beneath the firing arc of the weapons. Get in close and kill without hesitation or mercy. Her eyes flicked to Daniel one last time. The German's nostrils flared and he slowly shook his head. His body language was clear. He'd caught a scent on the breeze. Something that had made him revise their attack strategy. Marie felt a momentary confusion as to what would make him change his mind. A second later, a long, mournful howl echoing out from the swirling fog answered her question. John.

The soldier's reaction was instantaneous. Cries of

"Stand to," rang out, and while two of them kept their weapons trained on their prisoners, the remainder of the squad brought their weapons up to their shoulders and scanned the darkness for the new threat. Colonel Richards held a 9mm Browning semi-automatic pistol in a two handed grip, a sheen of sweat visible across his forehead and a look of barely contained panic on his face. He momentarily caught Marie's eyes, and she took great pleasure in slowly curling her lips into a smile.

The Colonel grabbed her and pressed the barrel of his pistol against her temple. "How many more are out there? Tell me, or I'll blow your brains all over the road."

Marie didn't flinch and kept right on smiling. "Enough. More than enough. You and your men were dead the second you set foot outside of that building."

A dark shape darted between two trees. One of the soldiers screamed "Contact!" and opened up with his rifle, filling the empty air with 5.56mm rounds. Another one followed suit before their squad leader, an older man wearing sergeant's stripes, yelled at them to hold their fire and check their targets.

Another howl rang out, reverberating between the buildings. Even without enhanced senses, Marie could almost smell the terror emanating from the soldiers. Colonel Richards removed the pistol from her head and cast quick, nervous glances around him. Marie looked across to Daniel and Michael and saw clouds of steam begin to rise from them as they brought their wolves close to the surface of their minds. Daniel's eyes had already become flat, phosphorescent discs, and she could smell an unmistakable animal musk emanating from the two men.

The sergeant, to his credit, seemed to recognise the signs of rising panic in his men and took steps to take control of the situation. "Right, you lot. Form up and get ready to move. We are heading to the MT section as planned. Double time it. Weapons free, but for fucks sake, check your targets. Dobson, I'm talking to you. Now, move out."

The soldiers closed ranks and took on a defensive formation before moving as one towards the open roller doors. Marie, Daniel and Michael were ushered forward at gunpoint, their captors so far failing to recognise the signs of Daniel and Michael's imminent transformations. They'd made it almost halfway across the open expanse of tarmac when a scream rang out from the darkness. A body flew through the air, covering almost fifteen feet before it was cut down by a volley of automatic weapons fire and crashed to the floor in a tangle of bloody limbs. What remained of the corpse wore standard army fatigues and was still twitching as the last of its blood leaked out to form a dark mirror on the ground.

"Damn it, I told you to check your targets. Does that look like a bloody werewolf to you?"

They began to move forward again, more slowly this time, the men's fear beginning to override their training. They were focusing their attention on the unseen threat in the mist, and seemed to have forgotten, just for a moment, about how dangerous their prisoners were.

A pair of glowing green eyes shone out from the dark shadows between the MT building and the adjacent hanger. A thick, guttural snarl filled the air. The soldiers swung to face it as one and, as their weapons trained on the lurking werewolf, Daniel, Marie and Michael made their move.

The vinyl ties around Daniel's wrists snapped, and the big German stepped back, grabbing the stock of the nearest soldier's SA-80 with one hand, while slamming the other into his throat. Michael kicked out at another man, shattering his kneecap. As the soldier cried out and fell to the ground, Michael grabbed his head with both hands, twisting it clean off before hurling it at Colonel Richards. It connected with the commanding officer's skull with a sickening crack, and he collapsed, seemingly unconscious.

Panic spread through the troops. Several of them opened fire at the dark shape of John, who had burst from cover and ran directly towards the soldiers and their captives, seemingly oblivious to the bullets that buzzed through the air around him. Marie grabbed the rifle from the man Daniel had killed and swung it like a club at the head of the sergeant. The plastic stock of the weapon shattered in her hands, but the man fell forward and didn't move. She grabbed Michael's arm as he finished off another soldier. "Come on. We need to get to the truck."

Her brother looked at her for a moment, his eyes shining with joyous bloodlust, before he snapped out of it. More soldiers were running from the subterranean complex, and bullets exploded into the tarmac at his feet. He nodded his agreement and they sprinted towards the open hanger doors, with Daniel following close behind them.

More bullets slammed into the concrete walls of the garage as Marie reached the comparative safety of the building. The air was filled with screams and the sound of automatic weapons fire. Daniel passed her and reached the idling prisoner transport vehicle, yanked open the driver's door and hurled the startled soldier behind the wheel into the side of an adjacent truck. Marie pulled open the rear doors and threw herself inside just as another hail of bullets peppered the reinforced walls of the vehicle. Michael joined her less than a second later. She crouched behind the closed door and risked a glance outside. John had reached the squad that had been escorting them, and was hurling bodies away from him as if they were stuffed toys. His muscular form lashed out at anything in a uniform, but, she realised, without inflicting serious injuries. His attacks were restrained, avoiding fatal blows to the armed men, or even anything that would break the skin and transmit the curse. He was fighting like a man in a bar brawl instead of letting his animal side dictate the flow of the battle.

"John, get your fucking arse in here," she screamed at him.

John dropped another unconscious soldier and looked in her direction. Then Colonel Richards staggered to his feet, almost ten feet from where John stood, raised his pistol and emptied it into John's back.

Marie couldn't believe what she was seeing. She screamed John's name as more soldiers poured from the complex and opened fire on him. Plumes of blood burst from John's body as the troops emptied their magazines, reloaded and continued firing. His body began to twist.

Bones shattered and reformed. Hair retreated into pores, and in a matter of seconds, John's naked body lay face down on the tarmac.

"No! John!" she screamed, and tried to get out of the truck, but Michael grabbed her, holding her still.

"He's gone, Marie. There's nothing you can do for him."

She fought against her brother's grip. "No, that can't be right. He can't be dead."

Michael pulled the rear door closed as more bullets slammed into the truck, then slapped his hand against the rear wall. "Daniel, get us the fuck out of here. John's down."

The truck began reversing at speed, the plink of bullets echoing around the interior. Michael put his arm around his sister, who sat on the floor with tears running down her face. "We have to stop, Michael. We have to go back for him."

He held her close, running his hand through her hair. "Marie, I'm sorry, but there's nothing we can do. John's dead."

Chapter 7

25th December 2008. Trecorras Cottage, Llangarron, Herefordshire. 02:15

The journey back to the cottage had been tense. They'd abandoned the prisoner transport vehicle in a small patch of woodland close to the English border and finished the journey in a stolen Ford Focus that Daniel had parked there earlier. Michael sat in the front passenger seat, while Daniel drove. Marie hadn't said a word since they'd escaped the base, her grief poisoning the atmosphere in the vehicle until Michael hadn't been able to take it anymore and turned the radio on to listen for news reports of their escape. The near constant stream of old Christmas songs had made things even more uncomfortable, and after a few minutes, he turned it off again. The rest of the journey had been undertaken in an uneasy silence.

Michael struggled to understand the severity of his sister's reaction. She'd lost people before. Friends, family members, even lovers. However, he couldn't remember seeing her like this since their older brother David's death when they were children. This wasn't like her. She was stronger than this. John's death was a tragedy, but a lot more people were going to die before this ended. Michael shook his head. The way things had escalated, he struggled to even envision an ending to this. It was his worst nightmare. The thing he'd spent most of his adult life trying to prevent. They were staring extinction in the face, and the loss of one person was insignificant compared to that, even if that person had once been his best friend.

He glanced across to Daniel. The German's eyes shone green as he drove along the dark country road. They couldn't risk having headlights on. They'd heard the distant noise of a helicopter a few times now, and the risk of detection was too great. Instead, Daniel had used his enhanced senses to navigate the twisting, ice-covered road. Michael was loathed to distract him, but the oppressive silence was beginning to gnaw at his nerves. "How are things in Russia, Daniel?"

Daniel kept his eyes focused on the road. "Not good. The Russians have been raiding known organised crime gangs, armed with flamethrowers and silver. So far, they've only hit the Mafia, and the pack are staying on the move as much as they can. Still, it's only a matter of time before they get lucky. Or unlucky, as the case may be. Krysztof and Lukas are busy consolidating their power base, but Steffan and a few others are managing to moderate their actions. There's still support for you, even within the Moonborn members, but it's only a matter of time before Krysztof declares you dead and calls for a council session to proclaim a new alpha."

Michael sighed. He'd expected something like this to happen, but he'd hoped that things wouldn't escalate this quickly. "I need to get back there as soon as possible. What are our transport options?"

"Limited. The airports and major ports are out of the question. They've installed countermeasures, and by now they'll have put all of our descriptions out to the authorities. We might get lucky with a small fishing boat, assuming that they've not started blockading the waters.

Other than that... well, there's always the tunnel."

Michael's stomach lurched. "Let's leave that as a last resort. The chances of surviving a tunnel run are pretty slim at the best of times."

Daniel turned his head to face him, one eyebrow raised. "And yet, that was exactly what you ordered Connie to do. With respect, Michael, part of me is not surprised she went rogue, considering that you effectively sentenced her to death. What she did was inexcusable, but not entirely unexpected."

Anger and guilt surged within him. Daniel was right. He'd fucked up. It was his orders that Connie had been following when she'd slaughtered that policewoman, even if she'd gone way over the top. And it was his order to abandon the hunt for Wilkinson and return via the Channel Tunnel that pushed her over the edge. He was as responsible for this situation as she was. Maybe more so. "I know. And obviously, with the benefit of hindsight, I can see that I made a grave error. All I want to do now is to try and salvage something from this mess. I know that I can't fix it. Not completely. But I'm not ready to roll over and die just yet."

Daniel turned away from him and focused on driving. "We may not have a great deal to say in the matter."

After another uncomfortable silence, the car turned off the narrow country lane and onto the half-mile track leading to the cottage. Daniel pulled up on the driveway, got out of the car and opened the garage door. Michael turned to the back seat. "Marie? We're back. Listen, if you want to talk..."

Marie didn't respond at first, just carried on looking at her hands. When she looked up, her face was streaked with tears, and her voice was low, barely above a whisper. "I'm fine, Michael. I just want to get inside and sleep, if that's okay with you?"

He nodded, "Okay. Fair enough," then got out of the car and walked to the rear entrance of the cottage. Marie followed a couple of seconds later, inserted the key and pushed past him as the door swung open.

If anything, it seemed colder inside the building than it had been outside. Still, Michael couldn't fault Daniel and Marie's choice of safe house. There wasn't another property for half a mile in any direction. With luck, they should be safe for a little while at least. Hopefully long enough for them to work out a plan to escape the country. The need to get back to Moscow weighed heavily on him. Steffan had told him not to come over here, and to let the field team do its job. Of course, if he'd listened to Steffan, Marie would be dead by now. He wasn't sure what bothered him more. The fact that he'd gone against people who trusted him in order to save his sister, and had completely lost control of the situation as a result, or that he was beginning to doubt that he'd made the right decision. He needed to know what was going on back in Russia.

He shook off the self-doubt, refusing to allow it to take hold. His mind was heavy with fatigue and the lingering effects of the drugs he'd been pumped full of. Not only that, but the bloodstained clothing felt sticky and uncomfortable against his skin, while the coppery stench of the dead soldier's vital fluids inflamed his wolf side. He needed to have a shower and a good night's sleep, and take stock of the situation in the morning. He just hoped that when he closed his eyes, he wouldn't relive the torture he'd been put through over and over again. He suspected the mental scars would not heal quite as quickly as the physical ones.

Marie stood in the hallway, gazing into the living room at the flickering lights of a tastelessly decorated Christmas tree propped up in the corner of the room. She didn't turn to face him as he walked up to her. Her voice was still hushed. "Bathroom is upstairs, first door on the left. Your room is the first one on the right. You'll find some clean clothes in there."

He put his hand on her shoulder, but she flinched away from the contact, not taking her eyes off the tree. "Thanks, Marie." Then, in an attempt to lighten the mood, said, "Nice job with the tree by the way. I didn't think it was possible to get that much tinsel on one."

She turned to him, a snarl on her lips. "What's wrong with the fucking tree, Michael?"

Michael put up his hands. "Look, I'm sorry, I didn't mean anything by it, I just..."

Her eyes blazed with pain and anger, and more tears streamed down her cheeks. "No, you're right. I'll get rid of the fucking thing so that it doesn't offend you anymore."

Before Michael could stop her, she strode across the room and began tearing into the dilapidated, aluminium tree, hurling baubles and decorations across the floor. "Marie... please... you need to calm down."

"Don't you fucking tell me to calm down. I'll calm down when I feel like fucking calming down."

"Marie... please... stop for a second and look at your arms."

That got her attention. She glanced down at the layer of thick, light brown fur that covered her bare skin. Her head came up, and she looked at her brother with feral, yellow eyes. "What? ...I don't... I can't..."

Michael rushed over to her, gathering his sister in his arms as she fell to her knees. She sobbed into his blood-soaked shoulder. "Why now? If I'd known before... I could have saved him... I could have..."

There was nothing that Michael could say to that. Instead, he held her close until the tears had subsided, and the coarse, brown fur had retreated back into her skin.

25th December 2008. Nauchnnyy proyezd, Moscow. 07:37

Steffan wrapped his coat around him and suppressed a shiver. The snow that had been falling for weeks showed little sign of abating, and he'd struggled to keep control of the Zil limousine as he drove towards his destination. The traffic had been light for a Thursday morning. Despite the Russian Christmas not being until the 7th January, many workers had apparently decided to take the day as an impromptu holiday to coincide with the western tradition. While this meant that there were fewer accidents on the busy roads leading out of

Moscow than he would have expected given the conditions, the quiet roads left him feeling isolated and exposed.

He pulled into the industrial estate and drove past empty factory units. Only a few of the buildings showed any sign of life. Rusted cars were parked outside of prefabricated offices with twinkling Christmas lights in their windows, however, most of the units in the estate remained deserted and dark, with long tendrils of ice covering their doors and a thick layer of frost blanketing the windows. He pulled up to a large complex, the same one he'd visited with Mikhail less than two weeks ago, and nodded to the pack member that opened the heavy chain gate. Steffan couldn't remember the man's name, and the thought nagged at him momentarily until he dismissed it. He had bigger things to worry about, if the number of vehicles filling the parking area was any indication. There were dozens of cars. He doubted if this factory had been this busy when it was operational. It looked suspicious. And suspicion was something they could ill afford in the current climate.

He parked the limo beside a Japanese 4x4, got out and cursed as the dirty slush seeped into his shoes. He would have preferred to wear something more practical, but appearances were important, especially if the reason for this impromptu meeting was what he suspected it to be. Trying to ignore the cold wet sensation in his feet, he strode towards the rusted metal doors of the factory's administration block, pulled them open and stepped inside.

He didn't need his enhanced senses to guide him to his destination. The roar of raised voices came, not from the offices themselves, but from the main factory floor. One voice stood out above all the others, Krysztof's distinctive Armenian drawl, shouting down any who would dare talk over him. This situation would require careful handling. One wrong word or misjudged sentence could spell disaster for them all. Steffan took a deep breath, walked down to the double doors at the end of the corridor and stepped through into a wall of noise.

It seemed as if every member of the pack living in Moscow was present, plus a few that Steffan had thought were living in other countries. Families stood alongside members of the field teams, and at the front of the crowd, as he'd expected, were Krysztof Balazs and Lukas Kassik. Krysztof was a hulking brute of a man, muscular and bearded, with flecks of grey peppering his once jet-black hair, while Lukas was a much smaller, older man with piercing blue eyes and sharp, aquiline features. While Krysztof was the muscle and mouth, Steffan knew that Lukas was the one that supplied the words. The brains behind the would-be pretender to the throne.

Krysztof raised his hand to silence the assembled pack members. "Ah, I see that Mikhail's lapdog has decided to join us. Thank you, Steffan, for honouring us with your presence. Now, perhaps, we can deal with the matter at hand?"

Steffan nodded to Krysztof and made his way to the front of the crowd. He would only speak if he needed to, but if it became necessary, he didn't want to have to shout over everyone else to make his point.

Krysztof puffed up his chest. "Brothers and Sisters, the

atrocities that occurred last night have shocked us all."

Steffan's mouth fell open. Atrocities? He'd heard nothing. He glanced around the room, and from the looks on the faces of the other pack members, it seemed that he was in the minority. That could not have been accidental.

Krysztof continued. "Twenty families attacked in their homes in the United Kingdom alone. Almost half of those families are now either dead or in the custody of the authorities. And you can be certain that this is only the beginning. How long will we sit by, cowering like kicked dogs while our children are slaughtered in their beds? How long must we tolerate these unprovoked attacks? Even here we are hunted. Even now, the Russians launch raids, searching for us. And we hide, afraid and leaderless. Well, I say, we hide no more!"

As a roar of approval erupted from the assembled werewolves, Steffan strode forward. "You are not the alpha of this pack, Krysztof. Or had you forgotten that? Nor you, Lukas. Mikhail is still our leader, and what you are suggesting is insanity. All out war would not have worked in Bosnia and it will not work now. We are too few, and teeth and claws are little use against armour and silver bullets. Or have you forgotten that as well?"

Krysztof snarled and stepped up to him, glaring down into Steffan's eyes. "I. Forget. Nothing. But Mikhail is gone. Captured or killed while trying to save his cunt-sister. The one who brought this down on us in the first place. And if we wait any longer, there won't be enough of us left to take our revenge. I say that the time has come to remind these humans what it is to fear the darkness. To remind them how it feels to be prey. The time has come to take the fight to them. To strike back, and make them remember why they quake in terror at the sound of a wolf in the night. And to do that, we need a new alpha. A strong alpha."

Steffan opened his mouth to argue the insanity of Krysztof's suggestion, but his voice was lost in the cacophony that echoed from the assembled pack members. There was nothing he could do. Not now. With a heart heavy with grief and fear, he pushed his way through the baying crowds towards his waiting vehicle.

25th December 2008. Underhill Military Base. 04:05

Rose rubbed the ligature marks on her wrist. The electrical cable she'd been tied up with had left a sore, red indentation in the skin, but fortunately hadn't been quite tight enough to cut off the circulation. It was tight enough to bloody well hurt, though, and she'd had a hell of a nasty case of pins-and-needles when troops from the base had kicked down the door to her flat and released her a little while ago. None of them had been particularly forthcoming about what had happened that evening. She got the impression that the raids against suspected werewolves up and down the country may not have quite gone to plan, and of course, her own nocturnal visitors had paid a visit to the base once they'd left her gagged and bound in her living room. Beyond that, none of the soldiers would elaborate on what exactly had occurred, only that Colonel Richards had requested her presence and had become concerned when she didn't answer her telephone or pager. Part of her was glad things had gone awry that evening, otherwise she might have been stuck in her flat until someone realised she hadn't reported for duty later that day.

She stepped out of the elevator on sublevel four and turned left towards the medical facility. Even though she'd been told the Colonel was with Steven Wilkinson, she would have been able to find him by following his voice. The Colonel clearly wasn't happy with their guest. While she couldn't make out the specifics of the one-sided conversation just yet, the tone and volume of Colonel Richards' voice told her everything she needed to know. In all the time she'd known him, she struggled to remember him ever raising his voice. That certainly wasn't the case now.

She paused outside the door to Wilkinson's room, which was held open by a Corporal she didn't recognise, and stepped inside. She'd been ordered to come straight down here. No sense in pissing her CO off anymore than she had to by making him wait.

Steven Wilkinson sat on his bed, with Phil Fletcher by his side. The Colonel stood over him, while two armed guards held position by the door. Colonel Richards didn't even look up as she entered and continued his tirade.

"I don't fucking care if things are *complex*, Mr Wilkinson. You categorically told me that John Simpson would not be a problem until the next full moon and that clearly was not the case this evening. And, incidentally, *what the fucking hell was that thing?*"

Steven took a deep breath and closed his eyes before he answered. "What that was, was a werewolf. I told you there was more than one kind. I've told you that over and over again. The quadrupeds and the big, nasty, two-legged bastards."

"Yes, and you told me the bipeds were only a problem on the night of a full moon, and that they were mindless beasts. That certainly didn't seem to be the case this evening."

"What the fuck do you want from me? I told you what I knew. The bipeds I've encountered, John Simpson included, were mindless monsters that only came out to play under a full moon. The four-legged fuckers were always the smart ones. It's not like there's a bloody spotter's guide to these things. In my experience, and from what I got from Carl's journal, that is how it was. Am I surprised that's not always the case? No, I'm not. I stopped being surprised by anything those things do a long time ago. Am I an absolute authority on werewolves? Not even close. What I am is the best you've got."

Colonel Richards' mouth curled into a sneer. "Well, apparently that's not nearly good enough." He seemed to register Rose's presence for the first time and half turned to her. "Doctor Fisher, I'm glad to see that you survived your ordeal intact. Would you mind waiting outside in the corridor for a moment? I'll be with you shortly."

Rose didn't need telling twice. She saluted her Commanding Officer then slipped out of the door, letting it close behind her. After a few more minutes, the door opened and Colonel Richards joined her, along with the two armed guards and Phil Fletcher. The Colonel locked the door behind them then waited until Phil and the soldiers had moved away before turning his attention to Rose.

"I want you to know that I don't blame you for what happened here tonight. Given the circumstances, anyone would have done the same. I'm just glad that you're still alive. We'll have to do a full debriefing in due course, but for now, are you able to work?"

She nodded. "Yes, I'm fine, Sir. What happened here? No one has really brought me up to speed yet."

The Colonel's shoulders sagged. "The facility has been compromised and we're currently making arrangements to relocate to Lindholme. We'll start moving personnel over in a few hours. While the situation here was regrettable, unfortunately that's not our biggest problem."

"The strike teams? Are you saying that the operation didn't...?"

"I'm saying that the operation was an absolute bloody catastrophe. We sent out twenty teams of five last night. One hundred men. Of those one hundred, more than half were killed in action, with another thirty grievously wounded. The United Kingdom's armed forces hasn't suffered a loss like that since the fucking Falklands. Not in a single day. The press will have a damned field day with this, and the Minister wants answers. We did manage to contain almost thirty lycanthropes, but another forty five are unaccounted for, running around the countryside doing God knows what."

Rose's mind reeled. She grappled with the numbers and

the potential consequences. "The wounded men...?"

"Are being taken to Lindholme. The camp there has basic medical facilities, and the prison next door has a reasonably well equipped infirmary that we're going to use. I'd like you to get out there today."

She nodded. "Of course. Can you tell the medics to take blood and tissue samples from each of the men at hourly intervals. Spinal fluid as well, if they can. If nothing else, it should give us a better picture of how quickly the infection spreads through the host body."

"Doctor Channing has already instructed them to that effect, and he's going to accelerate his research, so please relay your findings directly to him. He's confident that we can begin human trials within the week."

This brought Rose up short. "A week? Sir, with respect, that's insane. We have no idea what this is going to do to the test subjects. It could kill them, or worse."

"I've cleared this with the Minister, Doctor Fisher. What tonight has proven is that we are horrendously outmatched when dealing with these creatures. We sent a hundred of our best men into a meat-grinder, and I saw first-hand what they are capable of. We simply cannot allow that to happen again, especially now that we have dozens of the damn things running around out there. We need to be able to meet them on an equal footing."

She sighed. "Understood, Sir. If there's nothing else, I should really begin making my travel arrangements."

A grim smile played across Colonel Richards' lips.

"There is one more thing you should know." He motioned towards an open doorway.

Rose looked into the room, then back to her CO. "Oh good. That's very good indeed. I'll be needing that in Lindholme as well, if it's at all possible."

The Colonel closed the door and engaged the lock, the smile still on his face. "Yes, I rather thought you might feel that way."

Chapter 8

25th December 2008. Trecorras Cottage, Llangarron, Herefordshire. 07:45

The soft buzz from the satellite phone brought Daniel awake in an instant. He sat up on the bed and silenced the device before it woke Michael and Marie, then checked the message. The display showed a phone number with a Moscow area code that he didn't recognise. It certainly wasn't one of the many that Steffan had used in the past. The communication channels with the pack had been severely restricted over the past few weeks, but this new development bothered him. Why send a text message of a telephone number when they could have simply called him?

He slipped off the bed, picked up his boots and pistol, and crept out of his room. He'd not undressed after last night's escapades, simply lying on top of the bed covers in his army issue fatigues. Things had been, and continued to be, dangerous and unpredictable. If a situation developed, the last thing he wanted to be doing was scrambling around for his clothes.

Rhythmic snoring came from Michael's room, while Marie's breathing was shallow and regular. Good. Both of them needed to rest, and he didn't want either of them around when he called the number he'd been sent. Taking care to move as quietly as he could, he made his way downstairs, put on his boots and opened the back door.

The icy air burned his cheeks as he stepped outside. The

sky had cleared overnight, and the temperatures plummeted under the clear skies. The clouds to the east burned crimson against an indigo background, and animal tracks criss-crossed the frost-covered lawn of the cottage. The first chorus of morning birdsong began in the small wooded area to the south, and the air smelled fresh and clean. It was especially welcome after the lingering blood-stench in the cottage. He'd have to burn Michael's combat gear when he finished making his call. The smell was proving to be a distraction, and his wolf had whined and growled at the back of his mind all night as a result.

Daniel walked to the end of the driveway and hopped over the decaying wooden fence that separated it from the farm track, relishing the sounds of the world coming back to life around him. He arched his back, taking some small satisfaction at the cracking of his spine, then rolled his neck to release the knots in it. His muscles still ached from the previous night's exertions, although the cold air was blowing away the last few cobwebs of fatigue better than a cup of Marie's vile coffee. He took a deep breath and let it out slowly, enjoying the tranquillity for a moment. Then he fished the encrypted satellite phone out of his pocket, forced his doubts away and dialled the number he'd been sent.

The phone rang twice before it was picked up. Daniel suppressed a groan as Lukas' voice crackled through the handset. "Comrade Braun, what took you so long?"

Daniel rubbed his forehead with his left hand. "I was sleeping, Lukas. What do you want?"

"I take it then, that you have not seen the morning

news?"

"No, Lukas. As I told you, I was sleeping."

"Yes, I imagine you had something of a late night, given that your description is all over the media. Apparently you are wanted for questioning along with Marie Williams. Strange, but I could have sworn that you were under orders to eliminate her. Was that not the case?"

Daniel's head spun. He should have realised that word of last night's exploits would get back to Lukas. The old bastard never missed a trick. "Other matters took precedence, Lukas. I made the decision that it was more important to secure the release of our alpha than to follow an ill-considered order to the letter."

This time it was Lukas' turn to go quiet, a fact that Daniel took no small amount of satisfaction in. After a few seconds' silence, his voice returned. "And you were successful? In freeing Mikhail?"

"Yes, we were. Michael is out of their clutches and plans to return to Moscow as soon as possible."

"Daniel, there are things you are not aware of. Matters escalated last night. The British launched a number of raids on werewolf families living in the United Kingdom, presumably based on information sent to them by Connie Hamilton before her demise. Twenty families were attacked during the night. Almost half of them were captured or killed. The council decided that we needed to act, quickly and decisively. And act we did. As of two hours ago, Mikhail is no longer the alpha of this pack. That honour now belongs to Krysztof. His first order was to declare Mikhail a traitor and order his immediate execution. You will dispose of our former alpha and his sister, and you will do so immediately."

Daniel massaged his temples. He'd been expecting this to happen, although he'd hoped they would have had more time. "I'm sorry, Lukas, but I'm going to need more than your say-so before I execute anyone. Where is Steffan? I want to discuss the matter with him before I do anything."

"Steffan has been detained until his loyalties can be determined. You will take your orders from Krysztof or myself only, unless of course you decide to turn away from the pack and take your chances with our former alpha. What is it to be, Comrade Braun? Are you with us or not?"

He leaned against a frost-encrusted fencepost and sighed. Michael had been a good alpha over the years and treated his pack mates with respect, for the most part. He couldn't, however, ignore the grave errors that he'd made recently. He'd broken pack law to protect his sister, and his mishandling of Connie had been the main contributing factor in the current debacle. Krysztof was a brash idiot, but Lukas was cunning and smart. Perhaps he'd be able to control Krysztof's more extreme tendencies. If he went against them now, he'd be an outcast, hunted by both the humans and his own people. His chances of survival in that scenario were remote. He gripped the telephone tight enough to make the plastic case groan and his knuckles whiten. "Alright. I'm with you. I'll do as you ask."

The smug satisfaction in Lukas' voice made Daniel sick to his stomach. "Excellent. I'm glad you have decided to stay loyal to your pack. Once you've disposed of their corpses, you are to rendezvous with the survivors of last night's unprovoked attack. We need someone with current field experience to co-ordinate them."

"Co-ordinate? You mean getting them out of the country? Lukas, it will be almost impossible. They are all known to the authorities. If we had to smuggle one or two out, we might be able to do something. But twenty or more families? It's impossible."

Lukas laughed, a harsh humourless bark that set Daniel's teeth on edge. "Comrade, you misunderstand. We do not need you to get them out of the country. We need you to prepare them. Krysztof has decreed that we cannot allow such acts of aggression to go unpunished. You will take the surviving pack members in the United Kingdom and you will use them to strike at the humans. It is time they learned to fear us again."

"That's insane. There are children there. Old people. Most of them have never been anywhere near a field team."

Lukas' voice turned hard. "You have your orders, Comrade Braun. I suggest that you carry them out. We'll be in touch again, after you meet up with the others. Oh, and just in case you were considering letting the traitors slip away from you, I'd like you to send me a photograph of their severed heads before you depart. If I do not get this evidence, then I shall have to assume that your loyalties lie elsewhere."

Daniel began to reply, but realised that the line had gone dead. "Fuck!"

He felt like hurling the phone into the nearest field, or smashing it underfoot, but resisted the urge. There was nothing to be done. His loyalties were to the pack and he had his orders. He retrieved his pistol from his jacket and began to retrace his steps along the frozen track to the cottage, where Michael and Marie lay sleeping.

25th December 2008. Lindholme Detention Centre, Doncaster. 08:15

The first thing Sophie noticed was the nausea. She floated in darkness, aware of nothing but a terrible sickness. It lurked on the fringes of her mind like some vast, unseen monster, gnawing on the edges of her consciousness. *I need to get up and go to the toilet. Mum'll go mad if I'm sick in bed.*

A stab of grief surged through her chest, but her mind was heavy, and she couldn't quite understand why she'd felt that. Something had happened. Something bad. But she was unable to remember what.

She became aware of the pain. A steady throbbing in her chest. An itching, burning ache that pulsed throughout her entire body, setting her nerve endings tingling. She tried to call out for her mother, but couldn't quite get her body to do as it was told. Determined, she swam up through the thick, cloying, narcotic blanket that enveloped her until the darkness began to recede and turn red. Voices were speaking somewhere. She could just make them out, but they were muffled. Indistinct. As if she was listening to a radio in another room. Her eyes flickered open and several blurred faces appeared.

"Mum?"

"Sophie, oh my baby," said her mother, who gathered her up into her arms and held her tight. "My darling. Oh thank God. I thought I'd lost you."

The sudden movement was more than Sophie's delicate condition could handle. Her head swam, and her stomach went into violent spasms, sending a jet of vomit down her mother's back. She wiped her mouth with her pyjama sleeve. "Mum, I'm sorry. I didn't mean to..."

Her mother clucked at her. "Don't be foolish. You've not done that to me since you were a baby, but it's hardly the first time it's happened." The bear hug tightened. "I won't ever let you go again."

"Mum... you're hurting me."

The pressure vanished and her mother withdrew, instead placing her hands on Sophie's shoulders. "I'm sorry, baby. I'm so, so sorry."

Sophie's eyes were beginning to focus properly now. Uncle Dmitri and Aunt Kasha stood at her bedside, next to her mother. That was strange. She was sure they'd gone on holiday. Maybe they'd come back? Her mind struggled to make the connections, the pieces of the puzzle refusing to fall into place. Then she noticed the bed. It was hard, with a steel frame and scratchy grey blankets. The air was cold, and the walls were brick, painted a horrible green colour like they used at school. This wasn't her room! She sat up in bed and looked around. "Mum, where are we? Where's Dad and Adam?"

Her mother threw her arms around her once more and

her voice was thick with barely suppressed tears. "Oh, Sophie. Some men came to the house last night and they... they shot your father. He's dead."

Sophie pulled away from her mother. This had to be some sort of terrible joke. Her dad couldn't be dead. He was big, and strong. He'd have protected them from the bad men. She looked to her Aunt Kasha, but she was weeping into Uncle Dmitri's shoulder, and tears flowed freely down her uncle's cheeks. She jumped to her feet on the far side of the bed and backed away from her family. "No! It's not true. You're just saying that. Take it back!"

"Sophie..."

"No! You're lying. Where's my dad?" she yelled, then ran towards the double doors at the far end of the room and threw them open. The view beyond the doors stopped her dead in her tracks.

Twenty-foot-high steel fences, topped with coils of razor wire, stretched out as far as the eye could see, with tall towers every fifty feet. Rows of single storey buildings, identical to the one she'd just come from, sat in the middle of a large expanse of concrete, and beyond the fence she could see armed soldiers patrolling with savage-looking dogs. Two CCTV cameras whirred and angled themselves towards her as she stepped outside. Her mother came up behind her and put her arms on her shoulders. "Come back inside, Sophie. Please. It's not safe out there."

Sophie turned to her mother, unable to get the words out past the tightening in her throat at first. "Mum... are we in prison?"

Her mother didn't answer, just stroked her hair and guided her back into the building.

She looked up into her mother's tear-filled eyes. "But why? We didn't do anything wrong."

"I know, darling. They didn't come for us because of anything that we've done. They came for us because of what we are. Do you understand?"

"Because we're werewolves? Like they said on the news?"

"That's right, sweetheart. Some people are scared of what they don't understand. They hate anything that's different to themselves. We need to be strong, and we need to help each other. Can you be a big girl and help me?"

Sophie sniffed and wiped her nose on her pyjama sleeve. "Yes. I can be a big girl. I'll take care of you. The others will come for us soon. Michael and the rest of the pack will come and kill all of these bad men and then we'll be able to go home again."

She looked up into her mother's face, hoping to see her agreement, but she turned her head away and wiped her eyes. "I hope so, baby. I really do."

25th December 2008. Trecorras Cottage, Llangarron, Herefordshire. 08:15

Marie rolled over in bed and reached out for the warmth of John's body, but found only empty space where he should have been. She momentarily wondered where he'd gone before the memories of the previous night flooded back and the sudden wave of grief threatened to engulf her. She could smell his lingering odour on his pillow, which still bore the indentation of his head. His clothes were folded neatly on the chair in the corner of the room. It was as if he were still here instead of lying on a mortuary slab in that military base. As if he would come through the bedroom door at any moment with a cup of coffee, kiss her on the forehead and retreat before she could tell him to fuck off and leave her in peace. What she'd give for another chance to have him make her breakfast. To apologise for being such a bitch. To throw her arms around him, hold him close and tell him that she'd always loved him. The crushing loss was like a weight on her chest, making it hard to draw breath or find the will to do so. She felt as if she'd been hollowed out and all of her thoughts and emotions replaced with a terrible, cavernous emptiness that nothing would ever fill.

The first glimmering light of dawn shone through the cracks in the curtains, and she became increasingly aware of her aching bladder and dry mouth. She tried to ignore the sensations, wanting nothing more than to stay in the warm bed and pretend that John still lay there beside her, or that he was downstairs. To hold onto the fantasy for just a little longer. It was no use. The more she tried to ignore it, the more insistent the ache became. She put a tentative foot out from under the duvet, wincing at the frigid air against her toes, then forced herself to get up and scurry to the en-suite bathroom to relieve herself. After that, she resolved to spend the rest of the day in bed. Michael and Daniel could go fuck themselves.

Marie grimaced as her bare backside made contact with

the ice cold toilet seat, then sighed with relief as the pressure dissipated. Her senses instinctively reached out to take in the sounds of the house, a fact that surprised her a little. She'd almost gotten used to the muted, crippled, human awareness that she'd been stuck with for the past six weeks. Now, it was as if someone had turned the dial up to 11. She could hear not only Michael's rhythmic snoring along the hallway, but could also make out the steady beat of his heart through the solid stone walls. She stretched out further, listening to the sound of a mouse scrabbling about in the attic. The sound of the back door to the cottage opening and being very carefully closed. The unmistakable click of a pistol being cocked. The smell of sweat against metal and gun oil, with an undertone of fear.

Oh shit!

She knew it was Daniel holding the weapon. His scent was unmistakable. The lingering after-tones of that terrible aftershave he wore wove through the other aromas like a tapestry. She tried to extend her senses further, to identify some external threat that would justify him entering the house with a cocked and loaded firearm, or explain the sour tang of fear in his odour, but the only sounds and scents from outside were those of the world coming back to life.

That only left one explanation. He was coming for her and Michael.

She tried to remember where her own pistol was, then realised it was still downstairs in the hallway where she'd left it last night. Her eyes darted around the bathroom, looking for something she could use as a weapon, but there was nothing more threatening to hand than a toilet brush. She shook her head, disgusted at herself. Had she forgotten so quickly? She didn't need a weapon to deal with Daniel. She was a weapon.

She eased herself from the toilet and silently crouched on the freezing linoleum floor, then closed her eyes and willed the change.

Nothing happened. And she could hear Daniel's first tentative footsteps on the staircase. There wasn't much time.

She plunged into the darkness of her mind, following her instincts, searching for the animal presence that lurked deep within. That familiar, other part of herself that she'd lived with since she was eight years old.

It wasn't there. Not *her* wolf, anyway. What she found was newborn. Little more than a whimpering puppy. Immature. Still gestating until the light of the full moon gave birth to it. It made sense then. The werewolf side of herself *had* been killed by Steven Wilkinson back in High Moor. She had been human, but the teeth and claws of Anya re-infected her during the battle in Scotland. She was a werewolf, but she was a *different* werewolf, and not yet a mature one. Her emotional state last night had brought on the change prematurely, and she'd been left with some residual capabilities, such as the enhanced senses, but she wasn't certain if she'd be able to fully transform, or what the attempt would do to her.

Fuck it. It's not like I have a choice.

She dug deep, dredging up every scrap of pain and anger she could muster. Reliving the sight of bullets

119

tearing into John as he fell to the tarmac and lay still. Drawing on the pain and loss, not only of John, but at her exile from the pack. The terror she'd felt when Connie hunted her in the woods, or when Oskar, Anya and Leonid had come for them at the cottage in Scotland. The fury at Daniel for turning on them after they'd been through so much together. The thought of his traitorous flesh tearing under her fangs, and the taste of his hot blood as it gushed across her muzzle.

Her skin prickled and itched as thick brown fur burst from her pores. The bones in her back shattered and reformed in an instant. Vertebrae popped and cracked along her spine as it arched, twisted and contorted. Vicious, black talons burst through the ends of her fingertips in a spray of blood. Sharp bone shards split her gums while her skull warped and her jaws elongated.

She could sense Daniel outside the bathroom door. Of course he would dispose of her first. As a trained, experienced field operative, she was far more dangerous than Michael. He hesitated, hand barely grazing the door knob, his sweat reacting with metal. A surge of fear flashing through him, releasing pheromones into the air. He must have sensed that something was wrong. Marie didn't intend to give him time to react. She bunched her muscles and launched herself at the wooden door, shattering it into a cloud of ragged splinters that carved grooves in her flesh, only to heal again in an instant.

Daniel tried to bring his pistol up, but she caught his arm in her mouth and bit down, feeling satisfaction as the flesh parted and bones crunched. The gun went off, blowing a hole in the ceiling, raining plaster dust down on them like snowflakes. Marie ignored it. Her senses were aflame with a glorious bloodlust. She snarled, released her grip on Daniel's arm, and darted her head forward, her fangs seeking the exposed throat of her enemy.

"Marie! Stop!"

Michael's voice rang out, and she paused, delaying the killing blow. Just. Her fangs rested upon Daniel's throat, drawing pin-pricks of sweet blood. She could feel his heart hammering beneath her, the nervous gulp of his Adam's apple against her tongue. It would be oh-so-easy to end this treacherous German bastard and feast on him. And she wanted to. She wanted to more than anything in this world.

"Marie. Let him go. Now."

She angled her head towards her brother, bringing a small yelp of pain from her prey. Marie snarled in frustration then slackened her hold on her enemy, allowing his head to fall back against the carpet. She remained on top of him, however. Pinning him to the floor. She gave her talons the tiniest flex, allowing them to dig through his clothing and pierce his flesh. Just a little. Enough to make the prey cry out.

"Marie. I mean it. Get off him. Let me handle this."

She gave her brother a look of utter contempt, but removed herself from Daniel's shaking body and backed away. Just far enough to allow him to breathe. If he tried anything. If he tried to transform, or if the hand holding the pistol so much as twitched, she'd tear the bastard's head off and damn what Michael said.

Michael made his way along the corridor and removed the pistol from Daniel's hand. "So. It happened, then? Lukas and Krysztof took over the pack and ordered my death?"

Daniel spat blood onto the carpet. "Yes. I wasn't happy about it, Michael, but my loyalties are to the pack. Not to any individual. You know that."

Michael pointed the pistol at the German's head. "I know, and believe me, I'm not taking any of this personally. The question is, I suppose, what do we do with you now? If we let you go, will you leave us be? Or will you come after us again?"

Daniel shook his head. "You may as well kill me. Lukas was very specific in his orders. If I don't send back photographic evidence of your death, they'll consider me a rogue and send enforcers after me."

Michael rubbed his chin, then smiled. "Not necessarily a problem. Have you never heard of Photoshop? However, you still didn't answer the question. If I let you live, am I going to regret it?"

"That all depends, Michael, on what you intend to do with your freedom. Will you and Marie disappear? Or will you simply show up again in a few weeks? If so, then all you are doing is delaying my death sentence."

"I'm sorry, but I need to get back to Moscow and prevent Krysztof and Lukas doing something stupid. No matter what they say, or what Krysztof decrees, I still have support within the pack."

Daniel raised an eyebrow. "So you would throw the pack

into civil war? While we are being hunted by the entire human race? Michael, what on earth gives you the right? This mess is as much yours and Marie's fault as it was Connie's. Can you honestly say that you are still fit to lead?"

Michael slumped against the wall and lowered the pistol. "Honestly, I don't know anymore," he raised his head and fixed Daniel's gaze, "but let me ask you this. What are your orders once you've disposed of our corpses?"

"The humans escalated things last night and attacked every pack family living in the United Kingdom. More than half of them are dead or captured. My orders are to meet up with the survivors and co-ordinate the retaliation."

"Retaliation? Are they fucking insane? That will just escalate things further. Daniel, please, don't do it. Put them off until I can get back to Moscow and try to talk some sense into them."

"I can't. The best I can do is buy you some time. A few days at most. But I won't try and stop you from escaping. Just consider what you'd be walking into, and what the consequences of a civil war will be."

Michael nodded. "Fair enough, but I have to do something, Daniel. I can't just walk away from this. There's too much at stake here." He turned to Marie. "Come on, little sis. Put your fangs away and get your shit together. We've got to be in Folkestone by nightfall."

Marie let out a small whine. Folkestone could only mean one thing. They were going to attempt a tunnel-run.

Chapter 9

25th December 2008. Underhill Military Base, Sub-Level Two. 11:37

Phil flattened himself against the wall as a squad of soldiers hurried past him with a trolley piled high with cardboard boxes. He clutched the bottle in his hands tighter, bringing it close into his chest to protect it. He doubted anyone would oblige him with a visit to the nearest off-licence given the frantic activity taking place around him, even if any of the local shops were open on Christmas day. Crickhowell, the closest town, was hardly a bustling metropolis, and even Abergavenny was still small by most standards. That he'd persuaded one of the soldiers to pick up a bottle for him the day before was surprising. Now, after everything that had happened, there was no chance at all of replacing it if it was knocked from his grasp onto the hard, concrete floor.

He made his way as quickly as he could through the maze of corridors towards Paul's room, passing offices that were being hastily packed into plastic crates by solemn-looking troops. This place was being emptied in a hurry, although after last night's werewolf incursion, he couldn't really say he was surprised. There had been remarkably few casualties in the base. Three men dead, one of those shot by his own squad mates – a miniscule body count when you considered that four werewolves had been loose in the place. But each of the dead men had been known and liked by the other soldiers stationed here, and even a single death would have weighed heavily on those that survived. Of course, he'd heard rumours that those three weren't the only casualties of last night. No one seemed willing to talk about it, but he got the impression that the operation against the werewolves had not quite gone to plan. He just hoped that Paul had come out of last night's events with more than just his body intact.

He knocked twice on Paul's door, then opened it, not quite knowing what to expect. Finding Paul Patterson reclined on his bed, watching cartoons on the small portable TV had not been one of the options that immediately sprang to mind.

Paul raised a hand in greeting. "Alright, Phil. Merry Christmas!"

Phil closed the door behind him and pulled out a metal framed chair. "Erm... Merry Christmas, mate. You seem... better."

"The Doc's got me on a shitload of happy pills. Apparently, I'm fucking depressed. Not that it takes a bloody medical degree to work that out. Still, the little beauties seem to be doing the trick. And they're making these cartoons a load better. Sam used to watch this crap all the time and it bored the piss out of me. Now, it's fucking hilarious. I wish I'd been on these things years ago."

"Well, go easy on them. I managed to scrounge up a bottle of wine for us, but I'm not sure if it's such a good idea if you're on medication."

"Bollocks. I'd love to, but I'd better not. I'm off my tits as it is. Nice thought, though, Phil. I appreciate it."

Phil pulled the chair a little closer. "How are you doing, mate? Seriously? I heard that things didn't go so well last night."

The other man laughed. "Oh, it went fucking brilliantly. The dumb bloody squaddies charged in there like it was some embassy siege and got their arses handed to them. The cleanup crew are probably still scraping bits of the daft bastards out of the carpet. I told them. I fucking warned them, but they thought they knew better."

"Jesus... how many...?"

"Three from our squad. Me and that Sergeant were the only ones that got out, and she was lucky. Her Kevlar was the only thing that stopped her guts from decorating the kitchen wall. Still, we got the bastards. Three werewolves bagged and motherfucking tagged. I tell you, Phil, when I blew one of those cocksucker's brains out, I can't remember feeling happier. Shit, I probably didn't even need the pills today. Natural fucking high. But I thought, bollocks to it. It's Christmas."

Phil shook his head. "Three? Jesus Christ!"

"Pff. That's nothing, mate. Some of those other squads... the poor bastards without the benefit of my experience... total wipes. Every last one of them turned into chew toys. Maybe next time the dip-shits will actually listen."

Phil took a long, hard look at his friend. "Paul, you don't seem all that bothered. Come on, man, it might be just the drugs talking, but people died. People that you knew. Didn't Private Raines have a wife and a kid? The lieutenant too? Try and show some respect, for Christ's sake."

Paul's mouth curled into a sneer. "Respect? They were a bunch of gung-ho fuckwits, Phil. They charged in and they got killed. Boo-fucking-hoo. Maybe the ones that survived will learn their lesson and next time we'll get to do those bastard monsters over properly. Now, if you're done giving me shit, would you mind fucking off? You're making me miss my cartoons and you're spoiling my good mood."

Phil got to his feet, picked up the unopened bottle of wine and walked to the door. He pulled it open and turned back to Paul, but the other man was already engrossed in the television once more. He was about to say something when Paul looked up. "Phil?"

He forced a smile. There was still enough of his friend left to know when he'd crossed a line. "Yes, mate."

"Close that fucking door behind you. You're letting all the heat out of the room."

Disappointment washed over him, but he tried not to let it show. Not that Paul would have noticed in his current state. He wasn't sure whether it was a side-effect of the drugs they'd given him, the psychological hangover from combat or something more fundamental, but he hardly recognised his friend anymore. In every respect that mattered, the Paul Patterson he'd known had died with his family. He shook his head, stepped out of the room and let the door click closed behind him.

With Paul effectively shutting him out, he realised that he didn't have many friends left in the base. He wanted to talk to Sharon desperately. Just a quick telephone conversation so that he could hear her voice. Unfortunately the Colonel had ordered a complete communications blackout in the wake of last night's attack. She'd be around her sister's house, watching the kids open their presents and helping prepare the Christmas dinner. The thought brought a small smile to his face, even though his heart ached with loneliness. At least she was safe and surrounded by her family, and with any luck, the Colonel would turn him loose before much longer. If last night's debacle had proven anything, it was that his limited knowledge of werewolves was next to useless. The surviving members of the assault teams now had as much exposure to the things as he had. He just had to count the days until they let him go back to his wife and try to put this nightmare behind him.

Still cradling the bottle, he made his way back through the maze of corridors until he reached the elevator and hit the call button. After a few seconds, the door pinged open and four soldiers hurried past him, pushing a trolley. They didn't give him a second look. Everyone was much too busy to pay any attention to a middle aged copper wandering about, apparently. Good. If that was the case, then no one was likely to object to him paying a visit to Steven. At this point, all he wanted was to spend some time in the presence of another human being, even if that wasn't strictly true in Steven's case. The old man was still the only friend he had left in this place.

He stepped into the elevator, hit the button for Sub-level Four, and made his way through the bustling corridors to Steven's room. He could tell something was wrong as soon as he turned the corner. The door to Steven's room hung open, and everything had been removed. The monitoring equipment, the commode, the bed, and

Steven himself were missing. The floor was wet and the room stank of disinfectant. He felt a pang of concern for his friend. He'd seemed fine earlier, but he was an old man who'd sustained some grievous injuries. He grabbed the arm of a passing medic. "Excuse me, but what happened to Steven Wilkinson? Is he alright?"

The medic frowned in irritation. "All lycanthrope subjects have been moved to secure accommodation in Lindholme, now, if you'll excuse me, I really must get on."

"Wait a minute... all lycanthropes?"

"Yes, we shipped them both out first thing this morning, on the Colonel's orders."

Phil sighed as the man pulled his arm free and hurried off towards the medical centre. He looked down at the bottle of wine, then unscrewed the cap and raised the bottle to the security camera that swung towards him. "Merry fucking Christmas," he said, took a long swig straight from the bottle and began the journey back to his room. It looked like he was getting pissed by himself for Christmas this year.

25th December 2008. Lindholme Detention Centre, Doncaster. 14:11

The pain was like the worst hangover he'd ever experienced, multiplied a hundred-fold. A red, pulsating coal of agony in the darkness that threatened to split his head open and turn his stomach inside out. He would have cried out, but for the distinct feeling that the slightest movement would make things worse. He was vaguely aware of other people in the room with him. They'd been talking for a few minutes now, but he'd been unable to focus on what they were saying. Every time he tried to gather his thoughts, another wave of pain crashed over him. Cool hands grasped his arm. The brief prick of pain against his elbow, followed by a cold acid-burn that spread through his veins. Miraculously, the throbbing in his head began to subside and, after a couple of minutes, dissipated altogether.

"John? Can you hear me?"

He vaguely recognised the voice. Female, with a soft Welsh lilt to the words, offset by a harshness to the tone.

"It's not working. Give him another shot." A man's voice this time. English. Well spoken.

The woman tightened her grip on his arm again and tapped against the vein. He decided that he'd rather not experience the peculiar sensation of that injection again if he could help it, so cracked open his sleep-encrusted eyes, wincing at the harsh phosphorescent glare from the overhead strip-light, and said, "Okay, I'm awake." It was at this point he realised that he was strapped down and unable to move.

His vision began to clear. The woman and the man standing over him seemed familiar, but his mind was still sluggish and it took him a couple of seconds before he made the connection. Then he remembered where he'd seen them before. "Oh bollocks."

The man gave a grim smile. "I see your memory is returning. Good. That means there's probably no lasting brain damage. Still, as we've not been formally introduced yet, I'm Colonel Richards, and this is Doctor Rose Fisher, who of course, you've already met. I'm very glad to make your acquaintance at last, Mr Simpson."

John tried to move his head, to get a better look at his surroundings, but the nylon straps across his forehead made movement impossible. "Where am I? What happened? Why aren't I dead?"

"Ah, yes. I imagine that it must be a little confusing. You see, we've had varying levels of success containing your kind with silver. Some of you don't seem to be affected at all by it, while it's quite lethal to others. And, as you can imagine, global silver prices have sky-rocketed over the last few weeks. We needed a more practical and cost effective solution to containing individuals like yourself, so we've simply hollowed out our standard munitions and embedded each round with a small, but rather potent dose of an experimental neurotoxin. You regrettably received a rather large amount of it last night, and I was worried that we may have overdone things a tad."

"So where am I? Still at that base?"

"Oh no, Mr Simpson. That location had clearly been compromised, so we've had to make other arrangements for you and your fellow lycanthropes. Don't worry, though, I can assure you that this facility is quite secure."

Rose Fisher leaned over him with what his father would have called 'a face like a smacked arse' and shone a pen light into his eyes. "Pupil response seems normal. Heart rate and respiration are a little below what I'd expect, but still within acceptable levels. I've taken all the samples I need, Sir. If you don't need anything else, I'd rather not be around this *thing* any more than I have to be."

"Of course, Doctor Fisher. Consider yourself excused. Please let me know what your findings are."

Rose turned and walked away without another word, pulling open what sounded like a heavy steel door and slamming it behind her. John attempted a half-hearted smile. "I don't think she likes me."

"Well, considering that you terrorised her in her own home, Mr Simpson, I'm hardly surprised. But seeing as you brought the matter up, I don't suppose you feel like telling me where your friends scurried off to after they abandoned you?"

"You suppose right. Anyway, anything I know will be well out of date by now. They'll have changed their plans the second you caught me. My friends aren't stupid. They're probably already out of the country."

Colonel Richards stroked his chin. "Hmm, I see. Perhaps... perhaps not. It hardly matters. They won't get far. All the airports have been closed, as have the ports. I must confess, though, I still don't understand why you all went to so much trouble for one man."

John couldn't help but laugh. "You really have no clue who you had, do you?"

The Colonel's face darkened at John's taunt, "No, I'm afraid that we don't. Would you care to enlighten me?"

John summoned his most cheerful smile. "Go fuck

yourself."

"I see. Still, I didn't expect much co-operation from you. Not yet, at least." The Colonel reached over and undid the nylon band that secured John's head, allowing him to see the room for the first time. It was small – perhaps twenty feet square, with brick walls painted a garish green colour and a white-tiled floor. A single steel door was the only exit from the room, and a glass cabinet filled with medical equipment covered one wall. Other than that, the table he was strapped to and a CCTV camera in the far corner, the room was empty.

"Welcome to Lindholme detention facility, Mr Simpson. After your time in Durham prison, I expect you'll feel right at home in no time. There are, however, a few subtle differences between these establishments that I think you should be aware of before I undo the rest of these straps and process you into the general population."

John felt a surge of panic. "What? You can't put me in with other prisoners. Are you fucking insane? If a fight started, I could infect them."

"Don't worry, Mr Simpson, the rest of our guests are already much like yourself. Hence the additional rules. The first one, and the most important, is that we will absolutely not tolerate any transformations taking place in this facility. We have a number of armed drones circling the prison, equipped with some rather sensitive infra-red cameras. If we detect any significant change in an inmate's body temperature, then the response will be swift and decisive."

"Drones? Like they use in Afghanistan?"

"Yes, exactly like the ones in Afghanistan. Right down to the Hellfire missiles. I take it I don't need to elaborate further?"

John's heart sank. Werewolves could heal from a lot of things, but as far as he knew, anti-tank missiles weren't one of them. "Understood, although you realise that sooner or later your 'inmates' aren't going to have any choice in the matter? Eventually, we'll all *have* to turn, or it'll happen on its own."

Colonel Richards' lips curled up into a sneer, "Then I suggest you all try really hard to control yourselves."

"You're not listening to me. If we leave it too long, we can't bloody well control it. We have to change once a month."

"That, Mr Simpson, really isn't my problem."

John shook his head in disgust and turned away. "It will be."

The Colonel's hand shot out and grabbed John by the chin, forcing his head back around to look him in the eye. "You need to understand something, Simpson. Durham Prison was a holiday camp compared to this facility. None of you are human, ergo, you have no human rights. You will do as you are instructed by the staff, immediately and without complaint, or the consequences will be severe. You will not eat, sleep or shit without being told to by the wardens first. You will submit to medical examination when required to do so, and any hint of insurrection or insubordination will result in the most extreme response imaginable. Am I making myself clear?"

John's lip curled up into a snarl, and he felt his wolf begin to push its way up through the narcotic fog that clouded his mind. With some effort, and not a little regret, he pushed it down again. "As crystal, Colonel."

The man's smile returned. "Excellent. I'm glad that we understand each other. He turned to the CCTV camera and nodded. A few seconds later, the door opened and a squad of armed soldiers filed into the room, their weapons raised. "Gentlemen, would you please escort Mr Simpson to his new accommodations?"

Two men stepped forward, while the others pulled their weapons into their shoulders and pointed them at John. The straps were quickly undone, and he was dragged to his feet before being ushered at gunpoint out of the room and down a long corridor that ended with a pair of reinforced metal doors. One of the soldiers punched a code into a console on the wall, and the doors clicked open. Then, rough hands shoved him out into the weak, grey daylight.

Rows of single storey brick buildings sat on a large expanse of concrete. A small crowd had gathered outside of the buildings. A group of perhaps thirty men, women and children, all wearing identical prison issue jumpsuits looked at him with a mixture of terror and revulsion. His hearing didn't need to be enhanced to make out the word being whispered between his fellow inmates.

"Moonstruck."

This was not going to be fun.

25th December 2008. Rushtock Trading Estate, Droitwich. 16:04

Daniel parked the stolen car at the entrance to the trading estate and checked for any signs of life. The heavy steel gate lay open, and he could make out the distinct smell of fresh blood emanating from the security office to his right. He'd hoped the place would have been abandoned on Christmas day, but that had apparently not been the case. He cursed under his breath and got out of the car, wincing at the pain from his crushed right arm. Marie's fangs had fractured his radius and ulna, making even the smallest movement agonising. He'd splinted it as well as he could, given the circumstances, but the limb would be next to useless until the next full moon. The joys of being bitten by another werewolf.

The door to the security office lay ajar, and he pushed it open with his foot, grimacing at the wave of blood-stench that washed over him. The guard had been torn apart, no doubt falling victim to the rage of the first families to arrive on site. Throat ripped open down to the bone, left arm severed, abdomen little more than a gaping hole revealing the blue-black bulge of intestines. Blood covered almost every inch of the office. Arterial spray decorated the walls and dripped down the security glass. He shook his head. This was sloppy. Dangerous. If a passing motorist, or worse, a police officer stopped at the window... He picked his way through the gore-soaked remains and extracted the man's mobile telephone, then opened a desk drawer and rifled through the contents until he found what he was looking for. A work roster for the next week, and contact telephone numbers for the security staff. As he'd feared, the next guard was due to relieve this one in around two hours. That didn't give them a lot of time. Working as quickly as he could, he grabbed a handful of tissues from a box in the drawer, wet them with water from the kettle and rinsed the blood off the window. He tried to sluice the most visible stains from the wall using the rest of the water, but only succeeded in making the mess worse.

He didn't have time for this. He opened the dead guard's telephone and cycled through the contacts until he came across the name of the next man on the roster, then sent a text message that simply said.

MISSUS IS BEING A NIGHTMARE. CAN'T BE ARSED WITH THE FAMILY ATM. WANT ME TO COVER YOUR SHIFT?

A few seconds later, a reply came back.

THX, M8. UR A STAR. OWE U A BEER. HAPPY XMAS. SIMON.

Then, he checked the call logs, noticing that by far the most used number was to someone called Joan. To this number he texted.

SIMON'S CALLED IN SICK. HAVE TO DO HIS BASTARD SHIFT. CALL YOU LATER. X

He sighed. It wasn't the greatest plan, but hopefully it would buy them a few more hours, at least until someone became suspicious or the unfortunate guard's wife called Simon to complain about his sickness. He checked the road, straining his hearing for the sounds of approaching vehicles, then dragged the corpse from the office and bundled it into the boot of his stolen car, a job that was made considerably more difficult by his fractured arm. After what seemed like forever, and was certainly much longer than he was comfortable with, the boot slammed shut. Daniel took a minute to catch his breath and bring the agonising pain in his right arm under some level of control, then got back into the car and drove through the heavy steel gate towards the rendezvous point.

It didn't take him long to find the place. An assortment of vehicles, ranging from dilapidated camper vans to sleek, modern saloon cars were parked at the front of a seemingly abandoned factory unit. Most of the windows were broken, and the walls were pock-marked with brightly coloured splashes of paint. This was why he'd chosen the place. The empty industrial units had been repurposed by a company offering a "Wolf Man Combat Experience" to paying customers who wanted to spend their evenings firing paintballs at men in rubber werewolf masks. Today, however, it would house something altogether more dangerous. Also, as well as being relatively isolated, it was about as central a location as he could find in the United Kingdom. It would serve its purpose, but the messy, mindless slaughter of the guard meant they'd need to move on before the alarm was raised. He parked alongside an old BMW with a broken driver's window, got out of the car and pushed open the rotted wooden door.

The building stank of mildew and decay. Plasterboard partition walls crumbled under the damp conditions, and water dripped through gaping holes in the ceiling. Debris was scattered across the floor, along with overturned, rusting filing cabinets and swollen chipboard desks, their laminated surfaces long since having surrendered to the elements. He moved further inside the structure, through dangling fabric strips and a makeshift series of barricades that formed part of the experience, until he stepped out into an open area filled with heavy canvas bags and saw the survivors for the first time.

It was worse than he'd expected. Of the forty or so werewolves before him, almost a quarter of them were children under the age of sixteen. Another ten were elderly – not a single one of them under the age of sixty. Only twenty mature adults were present, and most of them wore nervous, frightened expressions. It was hardly an army. Still, they were all werewolves, and that was a start at least. He strode into the centre of the room, deliberately saying nothing until he was certain that he had everyone's attention. "Good afternoon. My name is Daniel Braun, and if you want to live, from this point onwards you will all do exactly as I say."

A cacophony of noise erupted from the assembled werewolves; questions, demands and complaints – each demand different and each voice filled with fear and outrage. He raised his good arm to quiet the throng. "Quiet, all of you. We will have plenty of time for questions later, but for now we shall need to keep this brief. The mess in the security office will not go undiscovered for long and we'll need to be far away from here when it is."

A young woman, her arms wrapped around a boy who couldn't have been more than ten years old, raised her hand. "Are you going to get us away from here? Out of the country and back to Moscow?"

He shook his head. "No, not yet. All of you have lost loved ones today, and our new alpha has decided that we should not let the humans' actions go unpunished. As of this moment, you are all soldiers of the pack."

The complaints were louder this time, the wall of noise emanating from the group made his ears hurt. Again, he raised his hand for silence. "Once we are in a safe place, I will do my best to answer your questions. For now, I need you to accept what I am saying, gather your belongings and follow me to a safe house a little over an hour away from here."

One of the younger men got to his feet, a vicious gleam in his eye. Daniel saw the bloodstains around his mouth and knew that he'd been the one to slay the guard. "About fucking time. We can't let the humans get away with this outrage. What's the target? London?"

Daniel smiled and shook his head. "No, London is an obvious target and a poor one. Security will be high in the capital, and after the IRA campaign of the 1980's and the 7/7 bombings, people almost expect London to be attacked. Certainly the security services will."

The young man looked confused. "If not London, then

where? Birmingham? Manchester?"

"No. To drive terror into the hearts of the British people, we need them to feel that we can strike anywhere. Not just the cities. So, on New Year's Eve, when most of them are out revelling and drinking themselves insensible, we will converge on the town of High Moor and we will kill or infect every single living soul within it."

Chapter 10

26th December 2008. Castle Hill, Folkestone. 00:50

Marie got out of the car and stared across the motorway at her destination. The tunnel's entrance was obscured behind rows of chain-link fences, each topped with rolls of razor wire and adorned with warning signs. Floodlights blazed down on the entire area, casting stark shadows across the concrete buildings, while CCTV cameras seemed to cover every square inch of the approach to the tunnel. She stuck her head back into the car, where Michael still sat. "Have I mentioned that this is a fucking stupid idea?"

Her brother grinned, which only served to irritate her more. "Not in the last ten minutes."

"Then I'll say it again, in the hope that it might sink into your thick bloody skull. This is a stupid idea. In the history of stupid bloody ideas, it's right up there with the Star Wars Prequels." She reached in and rapped the side of Michael's head with her knuckles. "Any of this getting in there?"

The grin vanished from Michael's face, replaced with an annoyed expression that she was only too familiar with. "Look, I know that the tunnel is going to be dangerous, but if we have to do it, then Christmas Day is going to be as quiet as it gets."

She shook her head in exasperation. "It's not just the bloody tunnel, Michael, although I can't say I'm thrilled to be running through twenty five miles of pitch blackness avoiding oncoming trains and high voltage

142

lines," she nodded towards the chain-link fence, "assuming we even make it past all that security without being spotted. It's the rest of it as well. Why the fuck are we going back to Moscow when there's a death warrant on both of our heads? Let's just get the hell out, while we still can."

Michael's frown deepened. "You know that I can't do that, Marie."

Marie's hands moved to her hips and she glared at her brother. "Why? What the hell do you think you'll accomplish, even if we aren't executed on sight?"

Michael waited for her to get back into the car and close the door behind her. "You heard what Daniel said. Krysztof and Lukas are planning an attack. There's only one way that will end. We have to try and stop them. Talk some sense into them."

It was all she could do to stop herself from laughing in Michael's face. "Talk sense into them? Have you heard yourself? You couldn't talk sense into either of those two when you were in charge. What makes you think it'll be any different now?" She paused, uncertain as to whether she should carry on. "And anyway, I'm not sure you're being completely honest about your reasons for going back."

Michael's voice acquired a sharp edge. "What the fuck is that supposed to mean?"

"You know exactly what it's supposed to mean. Admit it. You don't like not being the big boss dog anymore and you want the top spot back again."

He shook his head. "No, I don't. I mean... yes, I'm pissed off that Lukas and Krysztof made a play for the alpha position when I was away, but I'm not surprised. And what Daniel said has been playing on my mind. I fucked things up, Marie. Pretty much everything that's happened was down to bad decisions that I made. I don't deserve to be alpha anymore, but I'm not ready to give up on the pack just yet. Apart from you, they're the only family I have."

Marie let out a long sigh. "Well, you don't have the monopoly on making bad decisions, and I have to take my share of the blame. If I'd done things differently... then maybe..."

Michael took her hand in his. "What's done is done. There's no point in agonising over it. We just have to make the best of a shit situation. Maybe try to make things better. That's why we have to go back."

She rolled her eyes. "Alright, we'll go back. Lukas will probably have us killed the second we set foot in Moscow, but balls to it. It's not like I have anything better to do, and there's nothing here for me anymore."

Her brother's smile returned. "Good. Now, what do you think our next move should be? How are we going to get into that tunnel?"

"Well, we're not going to manage much from here. There's too much security around that control room. Come on. We need to get around to the other side of the facility."

Marie got out of the car, and a moment later, Michael joined her. She threw the keys onto the driver's seat and closed the door. They wouldn't be needing the vehicle anymore, and if they took it any closer, there was a chance that the ANPR cameras on the approach roads would flag it as stolen. The last part of the journey would have to be done on foot. She looked at her brother. "Michael, if we make it through the tunnel, there's something else you need to know. Once we get to the other side, things are going to be difficult. We won't be able to change back until we get to Moscow. Stealing cars... clothes... these things leave a trace for people who know what to look for. We'll have to do the whole thing as wolves."

"I know, Marie. We went over this before, and I know it's not going to be easy. It's a hell of a distance to cover."

She shook her head. "No, you're not getting it. What's the longest you've been in your wolf form for? A day? Two?"

Michael's face darkened. "You know that it was two days. After Bosnia."

"Well, then, you know that after a while you start forgetting that you're anything other than a wolf. This is going to take us five days at least. And a hell of a lot of that time is going to be spent running, with very little rest. If you start to feel like you're losing yourself then let me know straight away. If we push ourselves too hard, we could spend the rest of our lives pissing against trees in a forest somewhere. Okay?"

Michael nodded. "Okay. If I start losing the plot, I'll let you know. Just make sure that you do the same."

"Believe me, you'll be the first to know. Come on then,

let's get this over with."

They walked across the car park and out onto the road. The pavement ended a little way further down. On any other day, they would have no chance of making it across the motorway without detection, but at this early hour on Boxing Day, the road was silent. There was still, however, a risk that a passing police patrol car, goods vehicle or taxi would spot them. And detection was absolutely not an option. She hated this. There were too many variables outside of her control and she was only too aware that her mind wasn't fully focused on the challenge before her. No matter how hard she tried to concentrate on the task at hand, John's death nagged at her, gnawing on the fringes of her consciousness and pushing itself into the forefront of her mind whenever her attention wandered. She couldn't afford to be like this. If she was distracted or not paying attention to her surroundings, the chances of her and Michael making it through this alive would reduce to almost nothing. Michael, for all his bravado, had never been in the field. He needed her, and her brother was the last person on the face of the planet she gave a damn about. She couldn't afford to let him down. She *wouldn't* let him down.

They reached the end of the pavement and checked for any signs of life, but the roads were deserted. Marie strained her enhanced senses for the sounds of any approaching vehicles, but the world was silent and still. The road travelled for another hundred yards before reaching the roundabout on the motorway slip-road. The far exit passed beneath the motorway to a small junction on the periphery of the Channel Tunnel complex that led to the control room. A small track that bore a *No Entry* sign disappeared into darkness on the site's eastern boundary. That was their destination. Five hundred meters. Just over a minute at a flat out sprint. Of course, they'd be able to cover the distance in less than half that time in wolf form, but that wasn't an option. Not yet. She still needed her hands to operate the bolt cutters nestled inside her coat. She gave her brother what she hoped was an encouraging smile, then began running, feeling the adrenaline flood through her system. There was no time to worry about discovery now. No turning back. The time for planning or thought was behind them. She sprinted past the slip-road, over the slippery grass that covered the roundabout and down the other side. There were cameras in the small tunnel beneath the motorway, but they were automated (she hoped), calibrated to read the number plates of approaching vehicles. Not designed to capture the images of two people on foot. No sense in worrying. They were past them in a matter of seconds. Unless someone had been monitoring the video feed, their passage would have gone unnoticed. Moments later, they burst from beneath the motorway and crossed the junction, coming to a stop behind a tree a little way along the dark track.

Marie had hardly broken a sweat, but Michael was breathing much harder than she would have liked. She only hoped that his werewolf form was fitter than his human one. He grinned at her. "Piece of cake. Don't know what you were worried about."

She forced herself to return the smile. "Yeah. Well, that was fuck all. It gets a bit trickier from here on out."

They hurried along the track before turning right into

the woods and ascending a small hill. Once they reached the crest, Marie crouched down and surveyed the landscape while Michael struggled to catch his breath beside her. The Channel Tunnel complex stretched out before them, a blaze of orange light from the distant terminal with the twisting neon snake of the floodlit access road coiling itself around the dark perimeter. She focused on enhancing her eyesight, and watched the colour drain out of the landscape until the scene before her was set in a stark monochrome. She looked over to Michael and saw that his eyes were also shining phosphorescent disks. "There. Do you see it? Just to the right of the tracks. There's a gap in the fence. We can cut the perimeter fence behind that water tower, then it's just a short run along the road. Once we're past that, it's a straight run into the tunnels."

Michael looked uncertain. "That's still almost a hundred meters of road we'll have to run along. I don't like it. Why not just cut the fence straight opposite the access to the tracks?"

She sighed. Michael was great at the bigger picture stuff, but was bloody useless when it came to the practicalities. "Think about it. Cutting the fence is going to take us longer than anything else. If we do it there, we'll be right under those lights. Then we'll have to change once we've made a hole. This way, we'll be shielded from the control room. Yeah, we'll be exposed when we're on that road, but we're talking three, maybe four seconds instead of a couple of minutes. Trust me. I know what I'm doing."

He put his hand on her shoulder. "I know you do, Marie. You always were the smart one, even when we were

148

kids. I've not thanked you properly for coming to get me and... for what it's worth... I'm sorry about John. I know he meant a lot to you."

She forced a grin and tried to ignore the stab of anguish that shot through her chest. Instead, she took Michael's hand. "I would never have left you. You know that. Now, if you've quite finished being a soppy bastard, can we get our heads back in the game? You ready to do this?"

Michael nodded, although the expression of unease on his face told another story altogether. "Yeah. As ready as I'll ever be."

"Then let's stop pissing about and get it over with."

They descended the hill carefully and made their way back to the small wooded area below. Further along, the track split in two, with the left track leading to a small reservoir on the north-eastern edge of the complex. Marie pushed her way through the undergrowth, ignoring the grasping brambles that snagged her clothing, until she came to a chain-link fence. Removing the bolt cutters from inside her coat, she began to snip away at the fence by one of the concrete support posts. Michael began to get undressed behind her, and she made a very conscious effort not to turn around. Despite everything, she couldn't help but smile. They were about to risk their lives, and run for thousands of miles in their wolf form, but she still refused to see her brother naked if she could help it.

In a matter of moments she'd cut away enough of the fence to allow them to pass. Trying to ignore the sounds of Michael's ongoing transformation, she quickly removed her own clothing, gasping as the frigid air brought her body out in goose-bumps. It wouldn't matter in a minute. She'd be warm in a thick fur coat. Still, this situation brought back some uncomfortable memories of the last time she'd tried to transform out in the open, when she'd been attacked by Connie. That hadn't ended well and a small kernel of fear sprouted in her gut that she would fail to coax her fledgling wolf into a full transformation without a clear external threat. She shook away her doubt. Her beast was immature, but she'd managed to bring about the transformation once, and that meant she could do it again. Taking a deep breath, she closed her eyes, cleared her mind and went searching for her wolf.

It didn't take her long to find it. The beast lay nestled in the darkness, and she could almost visualise it leaping up like an excited puppy, eager for attention, at her call. It wasn't the lifelong partnership that she'd had with her old wolf. In some respects she felt guilty for carrying on when her old companion had been murdered, and for the new bond that was forming between her and the young creature. It wasn't anything as straightforward as having a faithful old dog die and getting a new one to lessen the pain. It was deeper. More fundamental. Her old beast had been a part of her since childhood and had sacrificed itself so that she might live. They'd known each other in ways that nothing else could ever match. They were one and the same, while the relationship with the new wolf was just forming and both sides were uncertain of the other. It would not be until the light of the next full moon that the bond would truly be cemented. Until then, she would need to take things very carefully. She was on new ground here. She shouldn't be able to transform at all yet. It was only her experience that allowed her to bring the young monster out from the dark recesses of her psyche and make it flesh. At the same time, the joy at having that again was almost overwhelming. She'd seriously considered killing herself when her old beast died, and it was only from respect for its sacrifice that she'd carried on. When John had been killed, it had almost broken her. Now, though... now she wasn't alone anymore. The bleak, empty, solitary existence she'd been destined to suffer had a glimmer of hope shining in the darkness, and it all became clear to her. She understood why she'd latched on to John in the way that she had. And she understood why his death had hurt her so badly. She smiled and felt a measure of peace for the first time in months, then crouched down onto all fours and began the transformation from woman to werewolf.

Her body felt energised, as if she'd been injected with a powerful stimulant. Clouds of steam billowed from her naked form and the first tingling of the change had already begun in her fingertips. This was really going to hurt, but she'd missed it. The pain, and the power that came with it.

Her spine popped as the vertebrae realigned themselves. Her pelvis cracked, bones splintering then resetting themselves into a new form. A sharp stab of pain as her coccyx elongated, bursting through her flesh to become a heavy tail. Thick, coarse hair flowed from her pores, covering her body in a luxuriant layer of fur. Vicious talons split through the ends of her fingers and toes, shredding flesh, while her face twisted and contorted into a savage, fang-filled muzzle.

In less than a minute it was over. The pain subsided, and

the world around her came into sharp focus. She could smell the heavy musk of Michael as he stood behind her. Hear the steady thrum of his heartbeat and the rush of blood as it flowed through his veins. A myriad scents assailed her sensitive nostrils, mapping out the world around her in a detailed pattern. The delicious tang of fear from a fox further along the trail as it sensed the predators in its midst. The harsh, acrid stench of diesel and oil from the complex before them. The hint of ozone as rain droplets sizzled against the high voltage lines leading to the tunnel. For the first time in months, she felt whole again. It was all she could do to restrain the exultant howl that ached to burst from her lips. Instead, without so much as a backwards glance at her brother, she slipped through the gap in the fence and moved as silently as a shadow, around the side of the water tower.

The road before them was deserted. The freezing moisture in the air formed bright coronas around the floodlights, and two hundred yards away, a brief flare of illumination by the side of the control room, accompanied by the faint odour of burning tobacco, signalled the start of someone's cigarette break. There was no way that they could know when someone was monitoring the cameras from the flat concrete building. One moment was as good as the next. Taking a second to quell the surge of fear that flared from her stomach, Marie broke into a run, with Michael hot on her heels. The road flashed by in a blur, and within a matter of seconds, they reached the gap in the fence – an access track for maintenance vehicles most likely. She didn't bother to break her stride. She streaked over the frost-laden grass, leaped over a small adjoining wall onto the tracks, and ran towards the gaping tunnel entrance as fast as she could.

Once they passed the threshold to the tunnel, the temptation to slow the pace loomed large in her mind. The initial threat of detection seemed to have been overcome, and a deceptive feeling of safety threatened to settle over her. She knew this was a dangerous mindset to fall into, however, and pushed on. To her knowledge, only four attempts had ever been made to traverse the Channel Tunnel in wolf form. Three of those had ended up with the unfortunate werewolves being decapitated by an oncoming train. While the actual tunnel was wider than she'd expected – perhaps four or five meters in width – there were very few places to escape an oncoming express train. Doors to the service tunnel were positioned every four hundred meters or so, but those would be alarmed and the service tunnel would be wired with CCTV cameras. Using them would alert their enemies as to what they were doing, and were an absolute last resort. Other than those access points, there was nowhere to go. The walls were solid concrete panels, featureless apart from thick bundles of electrical cables that adorned the higher reaches where the tunnel arced into a dark, vaulted ceiling. There was a narrow ledge on her right, but while it would be adequate for passengers to evacuate a broken down train, it would offer no protection against an oncoming locomotive travelling at high speed. Anything on that ledge would simply be sucked under the wheels by the air displacement of the passing train. It would take them around forty minutes to get through to the other side of the tunnel, and if something came the other way during that time – a freight train or maintenance vehicle – both she and Michael would most likely be killed. It was that simple. Keeping the grim thought at the forefront of her mind, she pushed on, increasing her pace and trying very hard not to think about what might be coming the other way.

It became impossible to keep track of time in the pitch black. All she was aware of was the feel of the tracks beneath her paws, the burning ache in her muscles and Michael's increasingly laboured breathing behind her. She'd tried to count seconds, to retain some idea of how long they'd been running for, and how long was left on their journey, but had lost count after what she assumed to be about fifteen minutes. Were they past the halfway point? She thought so. Perhaps. Hell, for all she knew they could be about to emerge from the tunnel onto French soil, but all she saw before her was darkness, impenetrable even to her wolf senses.

Then, something changed.

It started off as a vibration beneath her feet. Barely perceptible. If she'd not been engulfed in what felt like an eternal, unchanging darkness, she might not have noticed it at all. Then she began to make out the noise. A rumbling like distant thunder. A tiny pinprick of light in the distance. A single faint star shining in the endless night.

A train, heading towards them. Getting closer with every passing second.

She tilted her head towards Michael, and saw that he'd seen the approaching threat as well. He let out a soft whine and glanced back the way they'd come. They were almost exactly mid way between the service tunnel access points. They'd have to make it two hundred meters before they came to the next one. Unfortunately the train was travelling at speed, and before they could open the door (setting off the alarms) they would have to change back to human form so that they could operate the handle. Fear spurred them on, and they pushed harder, racing the oncoming locomotive.

The light was brighter now, and the approaching thunder of the train was deafening as they reached the access door. Michael began his transformation immediately. He had always been faster than Marie in the change. She held off instigating her own metamorphosis back to human. The last thing she wanted to do was risk being caught midway between woman and beast when the train arrived.

The floor beneath her feet shook, the vibrations making the stone feel almost liquid, and the roar of metal against metal was agony to her enhanced hearing. Michael had finally become human once more and threw himself at the heavy door, frantically twisting the handle, then tugging at it. He turned to her and the look in his eyes said it all. The door was locked. They were out of time and had nowhere to go. The train would be on them in seconds.

Marie snarled, backed herself up against the far wall, and hurled herself at the heavy metal door, just as the blazing headlight of the oncoming train turned her world into a blinding white sea of noise and pain.

Chapter 11

30th December 2008. Lindholme Detention Centre, Doncaster. 07:50

It hadn't taken long for the prisoners to get into the routine of the prison camp. They woke at 6:30 every morning to the high-pitched shriek of a siren, operating at a frequency just high enough to be uncomfortable but not debilitating. John remembered the ultrasonic alarms at Steven's house in High Moor and was grateful that the loudspeakers their captors used didn't seem to be capable of producing that particular noise, or, at least, hadn't decided to use it yet. Once they were up, they had an hour and a half to wash and dress before breakfast, after which they would be left to their own devices until the next meal. Armed guards delivered their food, and it was up to the prisoners to distribute it among themselves. Despite the precautions the military had in place – the ultrasonic sirens, the circling Reaper drones and the blanket CCTV coverage of the compound – it seemed the troops were less than enthusiastic about spending any time inside the fences if they could help it. Apart from the thrice daily food deliveries, the only time they set foot inside the camp was to escort selected individuals to the medical block for experimentation.

In many respects, the camp regime was less severe than what he'd had to suffer in Durham Prison. There was no work detail and he didn't have to worry about infecting any of his fellow prisoners. Hell, he felt safer than he'd done in weeks. Colonel Richards had been clear about what would happen to the perpetrators of any violent incidents, either against the military personnel or the other inmates. That wasn't to say he was comfortable with the situation. The other prisoners were pack werewolves, and they made sure to keep their distance from him. He had one of the low, single storey accommodation blocks to himself. He ate by himself and he showered by himself. He'd attempted to make conversation with one or two of the other prisoners on the first day, to persuade them that he was not the moonstruck beast they thought he was, but his efforts had led nowhere. After several failed attempts, he made the decision not to bother, and was, for the most part, left alone.

This morning was no different to the last few days. He watched through the grimy window as the soldiers placed several large cauldrons of porridge on a table set in the centre of the courtyard, then retreated to the safety of the gates, weapons raised. A line soon formed, and one of the women, Kasha, began ladling meagre portions into outstretched bowls. The food was rank, made with water instead of milk, and unsweetened. Still, it was warming and kept the hunger at bay until lunchtime, when something equally vile and unappetising would be presented. John usually waited until everyone else had been served before going for his own food, by which time it had gone cold and had a rubbery skin across the surface. It seemed like the best way to avoid a confrontation. This morning, however, his stomach growled in anticipation and he decided that he didn't care. He just wanted something to eat.

He opened the door and stepped out into the courtyard, only too aware of the numerous heads that turned in his direction. He walked toward the line, head down, and wished that he were invisible. He made it almost half way before two men detached themselves from the queue and blocked his approach.

One of them, a dark haired man with three days growth of facial hair, sneered at him. "Where do you think you're going, moonstruck?" The man spat the last word, spraying John's face with foul-smelling saliva.

John forced a smile. "I thought I'd have some breakfast. Unless there was something you wanted?"

He stepped around the two men, only to find his path blocked once more. The other man put his hand on John's chest and shoved him back. "Scum like you don't eat with the rest of us. You get the scraps, like the mongrel dog that you are. So go on, dog, get back in your kennel. Maybe we'll leave you something." He smirked and turned his head to the other man. "Maybe not."

John squared up to him and stepped forward so that they were almost face to face. The stench of his breath was almost enough to put him off his breakfast. Apparently these two hadn't bothered to brush their teeth since their incarceration. He fought past the nausea and grinned. "And how, exactly, are you going to stop me?" He angled his head to the sniper in the nearest tower. "Get physical, and that bloke over there will blow a hole in your empty fucking head. Try to change, and those drones will make sure there's nothing left of you but a smoking crater. Unless you're feeling lucky?"

The two men exchanged nervous glances. John smiled at them. "That's what I thought," he said, and pushed his way between them. The two men followed him to the line, but kept their distance and said nothing else. Still, John felt their eyes on him, along with the eyes of everyone else. He found that he didn't care. There was nothing these pack werewolves could do to him. They might talk and act tough, but as far as he knew, none of them were from field teams or had any sort of combat training. Without their wolves, they were just people, and he'd already faced down so much worse. They were no threat to him, and they knew it. He held his head high, meeting the gazes of the pack werewolves until one by one, they looked away. Satisfied that he'd made his point, he joined the end of the food queue and waited to be served.

After a few minutes, he became aware of someone standing beside him. He looked down to find a young girl with blond hair and a serious expression on her face gazing up at him.

"Are you going to kill us?" she said.

The question took him by surprise and, for a moment, he didn't know how to respond. "No, I'm not. I don't want to hurt anyone."

The girl didn't look convinced. "My mum, and my Auntie Kasha and my Uncle Dmitri say that you're a moonstruck, and you'll change and kill everyone on the next full moon."

John shook his head. "I'm not moonstruck. I was, but I learned how to control it. I can change when I want to, just like the rest of you. You don't have to worry about me. What's your name?"

The girl took a half step away from him, tilting her head sideways as if weighing up the truth of his words. Her posture relaxed, and a small, sad smile replaced her frown. "It's Sophie. Do you promise that you won't hurt us? Any of us?"

He nodded. "Cross my heart. I last changed a few days ago, so I won't have to turn on the full moon. I promise."

Sophie's frown returned. "Good. That means we only have to worry about the others."

It was John's turn to feel confused. "Others? You mean the soldiers?"

She shook her head. "No, silly. I mean all the ones who haven't changed in a while. They want to change, but the bad men won't let them. That means..."

Now he understood. "That means they'll all go moonstruck on the next full moon. They'll change whether they want to or not."

A fair haired woman hurried across the yard and grabbed Sophie by the shoulders, ushering her back to one of the accommodation blocks while hissing what John assumed to be Russian at her. He couldn't understand a word of what she was saying, but her tone and the nervous glances back to John told him everything he needed to know. Sophie voice carried back to him: "but Mum, he says he's not a moonstruck. He *promised*!" But her pleas fell on deaf ears, and she was bundled back inside.

John looked up. He'd made it to the front of the queue. The woman, Kasha, glared at him with a murderous look in her eyes. He raised his bowl and she slopped a portion of grey gloop into it, then spat onto his food for good measure. "Moonstruck scum. You stay away from my niece."

John didn't say a word. He turned and headed back to his own barrack block, his mind attempting to process the new information. The next full moon was just under two weeks away. That meant they were all in very serious trouble.

***

The soldiers arrived at his dormitory a little after lunchtime. He still felt queasy from the vile concoction they'd served - some sort of stew with overcooked vegetables and fragments of a mystery meat floating in a watery gruel. The food had a distinctive, pharmaceutical tang to it, and afterwards he felt more than a little lethargic. The drugging of the meals was nothing new, but they seemed to be trying out a new narcotic blend, and the effects were much more pronounced than usual. Still, when the door burst open and he was ordered out at gunpoint, he complied. Arguing wouldn't achieve anything beyond getting him shot, and he wasn't ready to go out in a blaze of glory just yet. Besides, he really needed to speak to someone in charge about the impending full moon. The Colonel hadn't given a shit last time he'd mentioned the matter, but he hoped he might have better luck with one of the medical staff.

They marched him at gunpoint through the compound to the steel gates, while the other prisoners looked on. The red dots of multiple laser sights danced across his chest as the gates were opened and he was ushered through to the other side, across a tarmac courtyard to where a series of Portacabins had been positioned. This make-shift arrangement of temporary buildings was what the soldiers had laughingly called 'the infirmary'. In reality, it was nothing more than a place where the medical staff took samples from the prisoners. One of the advantages of being a werewolf was that sickness was not something they often had to worry about.

One of the guards motioned for John to enter the building with his SA-80, and he obliged, seating himself on one of the hard, plastic chairs within. The soldier then put shackles on his wrists and ankles, securing them to the walls with heavy steel chains. John didn't have the heart to tell them that if he changed, his werewolf form would be able to tear the flimsy walls down as if they were made of cardboard. There was no sense in antagonising his captors. Not yet, anyway. Not when he had a point to make.

The inside of the cabin was sparely decorated. The floor was covered in green carpet tiles and a portable gas heater sat beside an old wooden desk that had seen better days. Several more plastic chairs, all different colours and styles, were scattered against one of the walls. Other than that, the building was empty. He'd seen some of the other prisoners taken to the main prison building, which he guessed had more extensive medical facilities, but so far he'd not had the pleasure of that trip, for which he was glad. Of the half-dozen prisoners that had been taken over there, none had returned. He really didn't like to dwell on what might have happened to them.

The door opened, letting in a blast of frigid air, and Rose

Fisher strode inside. She gave John a look of undisguised contempt, shook off her coat and sat down at the desk.

John shifted on the seat, his discomfort having very little to do with the unyielding plastic. "Doctor Fisher... Rose... I just want to say that I'm sorry for... You know..."

Rose looked up at him and arched an eyebrow. "I know? I'm afraid that I don't. What exactly is it that you're sorry for? For breaking into my flat? Terrorising me and making me fear for my life? Ruining my Christmas? Or for all of the men you killed on that base?"

He looked up at the angry woman, fixing her gaze with his. "For all of it. Apart from the killing. I didn't kill anyone on that base. There was no other way for us to get Michael back. I wish that there had been. I wish that none of this shit had happened, but we are where we are. I just wanted you to know that I was sorry for what we did to you."

Rose removed a butterfly needle and two plastic bottles from the desk drawer and put on a pair of blue disposable gloves. "And that makes it all fine, does it? You're sorry. Well, your apology is noted." She nodded to one of the waiting soldiers, who grabbed John's arm and pulled up the sleeve of his prison issue shirt to expose the vein at the crook of his elbow.

Rose walked across the room and removed the needle from its sterile wrapping, then stabbed it into his arm with more force than was necessary. John winced at the sharp pain. "Doctor Fisher. There's something else that I need to talk to you about. Something important."

Rose left the needle in his arm and secured it with a piece of tape, then attached a bottle to the protruding piece of plastic, all without meeting John's gaze. "Oh? Really?"

"Yes. Listen, it's going to be full moon in a couple of weeks and some of the others haven't changed since the last one. If they aren't allowed to transform before then, we'll all have a problem."

That seemed to get her attention. She looked at him as she retrieved a new plastic bottle from the tray. "And why is that, Mr Simpson?"

John felt his stomach lurch. He hated the thought of telling these people anything about werewolves that they hadn't already found out, but he really didn't see he had a choice. "Every werewolf needs to transform once a month. If they don't, then the wolf side of their nature gets restless and fights against the confinement. On the night of a full moon, the wolf is too strong for them to contain and it forces the change. But if they fight against it, they'll end up caught in a halfway state. What the pack call a Moonstruck. They won't have any control of themselves. They'll lash out and kill anything they see. It'll be a slaughter."

She removed the full blood bottle and replaced it with the new one. "And why should I believe anything that comes out of your mouth?"

"Because the other wolves won't tell you anything. For Christ's sake, there are kids in there. Families. And because of the bloody Reaper drones, they won't even be able to change to defend themselves. It's completely unnecessary. You want to study a transformation? Give

164

everyone a safe place to do it, under controlled conditions, and you'll get all the data you need. If you don't, every single person in that compound will die in two weeks time."

Rose looked at him, scrutinising him as if he were something under a microscope, then appeared to come to a decision. She let out a sigh and nodded. "I can't promise anything, but I'll speak to the Colonel about it. I'm afraid that's the best I can do."

John nodded and gave her a weak half-smile. "Thank you, Rose. You have no idea how much of a relief it is to hear that you'll try."

She sealed the second bottle in a bag, then glared at him. "I'm warning you now. If this is some trick, then I'll vivisect you like a bloody lab rat."

John nodded. "I promise you, Rose. No tricks. You have my word."

"It remains to be seen exactly what that's worth." She looked up to one of the soldiers. "Take Mr Simpson back to the compound, and tell Colonel Richards that I'd like to have a word with him."

30th December 2008. Underhill Military Base, Sub-Level Two. 21:37

Phil leaned back on the hard, metal-framed bed and tried to calm his nerves. The complex was almost deserted now. Most of the essential personnel and equipment had been removed over the past week, ever since the decision had been made to relocate the operation to Lindholme. The frantic activity around the place had gradually eased, then come to an apparent halt. Now, instead of booted feet echoing around the corridors, the only sound was the constant thrum of the antique heating system. Every once in a while he would hear distant voices, or the slamming of a door, but for the most part he was alone. Seemingly forgotten. And that suited him just fine.

He'd not spoken to Paul since Christmas day. When he'd encountered his former colleague in the mess hall, they had avoided each other, with not so much as a nod of recognition passing between them. Paul had been moved above ground, into one of the barrack blocks attached to the training camp. Colonel Richards hadn't been in touch, and after a few attempts to contact him, Phil had stopped trying. He suspected the military simply didn't know what to do with him. He had no tactical value anymore. The survivors of the Christmas Eve raids had much more current and relevant information relating to the werewolves than he did. He didn't know enough to be considered useful, but knew too much to be allowed to leave. He was an inconvenience. A liability. And he'd had just about enough of their crap. He didn't care what Colonel Richards said. All he wanted to do now was go home and try to pick up the pieces of his life. Get back to some sort of normality. Back to Sharon.

A door slammed somewhere further along the corridor. He lay still, trying to slow his heart, and listened as the footfalls faded. There was no point in delaying this any longer. It was time to make his move.

He slid his legs off the bed and began to dress; not in his civilian clothes, though. He'd spent the last few days gathering together pieces of army uniform. A pair of shoes left in a locker. A discarded shirt from one of the empty offices. A pair of trousers taken from one of the sleeping quarters. A jumper from the laundrette. None of the items fit especially well, and the makeshift uniform wouldn't hold up to any kind of scrutiny. He just hoped it would be enough to get him past the guards and out of the building. Beyond that, he didn't have much in the way of a plan, but he didn't really need one. He'd damn well walk back to Durham if he had to. The important thing was getting off this base and out from under the thumb of his military captors. He'd work the rest out later.

He tightened the webbing belt around the trousers, only too aware of the fact that he couldn't quite fasten the top button, and pulled the olive-green jumper down to hide the visible band of his underwear. Taking a deep breath, he picked up a stolen kitbag containing his civilian clothes and stepped out into the corridor, closing the door of his room behind him.

He felt exposed in the empty hallways, as if his every movement was under scrutiny. The thought was ridiculous, of course. No one seemed to have paid a blind bit of notice to him for days, and he doubted they'd notice he was missing until he was long gone. Still, he knew only too well that the biggest risk of failure lay in how he acted in the next ten minutes. He needed to behave as if he belonged here. March through the place with a sense of purpose without obviously rushing. Any furtive or nervous movements would be enough to attract attention, and the moment someone took a second look at him and noticed that the arms of his jumper were too short, or that the legs of the trousers were a little too long, the game would be up. Forcing himself to take steady, measured steps, he made his way through the labyrinthine passageways, past the elevator to the stairwell.

Once he made it through the door he stopped and listened for a moment. There were voices on the level above him. Two people, as far as he could make out. He waited for almost a minute, and when it became apparent that they weren't moving any time soon, he decided to take a chance. He began to ascend the concrete stairs toward where the two men stood, deep in conversation about football. He recognised one of the men, a private who worked in the mess hall. Keeping his head down, he continued forward, but just as he reached them, he felt the trousers begin to slip from around his waist. Panic washed over him, his heart lurching in his chest, and he grabbed at the webbing belt with his left hand. Having his pants fall to the floor was probably the last thing he needed to happen right now. Neither of the soldiers seemed to notice, however, and as soon as he started up the next flight of stairs, he pulled the belt so tight he thought he was going to cut off the circulation to his legs.

Phil paused at the door leading to the ground level. From memory, there was a guard stationed on a desk near the entrance to the underground complex, but with any luck the soldier would be more concerned with checking the ID's of those entering the building than those leaving it. Once he made it through the double doors, it was only a few hundred yards to the main road. From there he was only about a mile east of Crickhowell, or around three miles west of Abergavenny and its train station. He just had one last obstacle to negotiate and he was free. He paused once more, making certain that his rebellious trousers were firmly in place and that his ill-fitting uniform looked at least half presentable, then pushed open the doors and stepped out into the corridor.

Phil almost cried with relief. The desk was deserted. He didn't know whether the guard had taken a break or if they had simply decided not to bother manning it anymore. It didn't matter. He was almost there. Almost free.

The urge to break into a flat run was almost overwhelming. Adrenaline coursed through his body and his limbs tingled in anticipation. He forced himself to maintain the act, however, and marched steadily along the corridor, his heart leaping with every click of his shoes on the concrete, and pushed open the double doors.

The cold, fresh air bit into his skin and hurt his lungs as he sucked it in. He didn't think he'd ever tasted anything sweeter. The orange sodium lights of the A40 twinkled through the trees, no more than two hundred yards away along a dark, deserted road. The real world. So close that he could almost reach out and touch it.

"Phil? What the fuck do you think you're doing?"

Phil's heart sank and a wave of nausea bubbled up from his stomach. He felt his shoulders sag and he turned around to face Paul Patterson. His former colleague had an assault rifle cradled in his arms, and a cigarette hung from the corner of his mouth.

"Paul... mate, listen, they don't need me anymore. They're just going to let me sit and rot down there. Please. I just want to go home."

Paul took a long drag from his cigarette, then flicked it away, the glowing end tracing an arc through the darkness until it landed with a faint hiss on the wet tarmac. "Can't let you do that, Phil. The Colonel wants you to stay put. It's for your own good. Now, why don't we go back inside and forget this happened, yeah?"

Phil shook his head. "No. Fuck that. I'm not going back down there. I've had enough of this shit. I don't want anything to do with it. I just want to see Sharon and you're not going to stop me. Now get out of my fucking way."

Paul took a step forward, shaking his head. "Phil, you're not the boss anymore. And if the Colonel wants you to stay here, then you're going to fucking well stay here. You really don't want to push me, mate. I'm going easy on you, but I'm starting to lose my happy thoughts."

Phil's lip curled up into a snarl. "What're you gonna do about it, Paul? Shoot me in cold blood?"

Paul brought the butt of his SA-80 up into Phil's stomach, driving the air out of his lungs. Phil collapsed to ground, unable to breathe, while Paul crouched down on his haunches. "No, mate. I'm not going to shoot you. But you have to realise that this is for your own good, and Sharon's. You'll just put her and everyone else at risk if you set foot off this base. She's still at her sister's place in High Moor, yeah? Well, believe me, mate, that's the safest place she can be right now."

Chapter 12

31ˢᵗ December 2008. Coronation Estate, High Moor. 18:48

Helen Baxter frowned in exasperation. Her older sister could be a stubborn cow when she put her mind to it. "Are you sure that you won't come with us? We can drop little Matthew off at the church hall and paint the town red, like the old days."

Sharon leaned back in the chair and folded her arms. "No, honestly. I won't be much fun and I wouldn't want to cramp you and Chelfyn's style. I'll go to the crèche with the kids and make sure Matthew gets home safe afterwards."

Helen wasn't going to be put off so easily. "Look, Sharon, I know the last few weeks have been hard, but I'm sure that Phil's okay. You sitting around moping isn't going to bring him home any faster."

The cheerful façade Sharon had worn fell away, and her face creased with concern. "I know, but honestly, it's starting to wear me down. They won't even let me talk to him anymore. National security or some shit. The last time they let him phone me was Christmas Eve. I just can't help but think the worst. That maybe something's happened and they aren't telling me."

Helen crouched down so that she was level with her sister and put her hands on her shoulders. "I know. I get it, and first thing on Monday morning we're going to get onto the solicitors and start getting some answers out of the bastards. But there's fuck all that you or I can do about it in the meantime, so please, get your glad-rags on, come with us to the restaurant and then, who knows... maybe we'll head over to the *Sandpiper*. The DJ this year is meant to be over from Ukraine or something. Been a while since we've been to a proper rave."

Sharon arched her eyebrow. "Some numpty playing hard-house in the *Sandpiper* isn't exactly what I'd call a rave." She winked at her sister. "Not like the old days, anyway. You remember that party on the moors back in ninety two?"

Helen's cheeks turned scarlet and she punched her sister on the arm. "How could I forget, that was the night..."

The door to the sitting room burst open, and Mandy, Helen's fifteen year old daughter, swept into the room like a tornado. Helen hastily put her finger to her lips to prevent Sharon from continuing the conversation. The last thing she wanted to do was put ideas into her rebellious daughter's head.

"Mam, I can't find my stockings. Where did you put them?"

Helen rolled her eyes. "Have you tried the airing cupboard? And if you think that you're going anywhere dressed like that, young lady, then you've got another thing coming."

Mandy puffed up like an angry cockerel at that remark. "What's that supposed to mean? Dressed like what?"

"That skirt might as well be a bloody belt. And if that top showed any more cleavage it would be see through.

Where do you think you're going that needs you to dress up like a tart?"

Mandy's hands went to her hips in an unconscious imitation of her mother's posture. "I'm just going round Anna's house, with Amy and Kat."

"Oh, really. And what are you going to be doing round there?"

"Nothing. Just going to watch some films and listen to some music."

"And you need to dress like that to go round Anna's house, do you?"

Mandy's voice acquired an indignant, whiny edge. "Mam, it's New Year's Eve. We just thought it'd be fun to dress up a bit, you know?"

"Dressing up is fine. You just aren't wearing those clothes. Go upstairs and put something respectable on, or I'll come up there and pick something out for you."

Mandy opened her mouth to protest, but then appeared to think better of it, and instead turned and stomped from the room. Helen waited until her daughter was out of earshot before she burst out laughing. "Oh, God, was I ever like that?"

"You were worse than that. A lot worse. You know what, though? You sounded exactly like Mum just then."

"Oh piss off. You'll be telling me I'm getting bingo wings next."

Sharon smirked. "Well, I didn't want to bring it up..."

Helen's mouth dropped open in semi-mock outrage. "Fuck off, you cheeky cow. I don't even like bingo," she gave Sharon a sly smirk, "anyway, I'd rather have the bingo wings than the turkey neck you're getting."

Sharon's eyes widened. "Turkey neck? I do not have a bloody turkey neck."

"Must be from back in the day. You know... all that 'gobble gobble'. They say you are what you eat."

Sharon was about to respond when Chelfyn, Helen's husband, wandered into the room with his shirt half buttoned. "Do you know where my socks are, Love? Can't seem to find them anywhere."

Helen pointed to the door. "Have you tried the airing cupboard? Or the sock drawer?"

Chelfyn nodded. "Ah, no. Thanks, love," then turned around and started up the stairs. A few seconds later, a muted "Found them," came from the corridor.

"Well," said Helen, "At least I know where our Mandy gets it from."

"Are you sure you won't come with us? It'll be like the old days. Just you and me... well... and that useless bugger, but no change there. Come on. Angela and Tonia are running the New Year crèche and they'll take care of Matthew. Come out with us. Save me from spending a night on the piss alone with my husband."

Sharon shook her head, but the smile on her face remained, and for the first time in weeks, seemed to be genuine. "No. Really. I'll help Tonia and Angela with the kids. You go and enjoy yourself. Sink a few G&T's for me, eh?"

Helen conceded defeat. Decades of experience had taught her that once Sharon's mind was made up about something, that was that. "Okay, but if you change your mind, I'll have my phone on me. Just give me a ring to find out where we are, okay?"

Sharon nodded. "Okay. If I change my mind I'll call. Don't hold your breath, though."

"Oh, don't worry. I know what a stubborn cow you can be when you set your mind to something. The offer's open, though."

The door swung open, and Ian, Helen's oldest son, entered the room with a confused expression on his face. "Mam, have you..."

Helen and Sharon both pointed to the door and said, "Airing cupboard," in unison, and broke into uncontrollable gales of laughter as a confused looking Ian turned around and left in search of his clothes.

Helen hugged Sharon tight. "I love you, you know, you miserable old cow."

Sharon kissed her sister on the forehead. "I know. Now you'd better go and get sorted out, otherwise it'll be gone midnight by the time you plaster your face."

Helen smiled and walked towards the door. "Fuck you, you old trollop."

Sharon grinned back at her. "Fuck you and the horse you rode in on."

31st December 2008. Weardale Industrial Estate, High Moor. 19:15

Daniel got out of the car and sighed. The town of High Moor stretched out below him; an orange neon organism with the white glow of car headlights pulsing through its arteries. Thousands of unsuspecting people were getting ready to celebrate the start of the New Year. Soon, the bars, restaurants and houses of High Moor would begin to fill up. Families and friends coming together to put the horrors of the last few months behind them, and to look forward in hope to what the next year would bring. Hoping and praying that those terrible events of October and November would be the end of their ordeal. Not realising that the worst was yet to come.

He looked across the car park of the deserted industrial estate to where the others waited in their vehicles. Waited for him to give the signal to commence the slaughter of the innocents in the town. Forty werewolves. Men, women and children with nothing but the anger in their hearts and the savagery of their wolves to guide them. He had to try to stop this; talk some sense into Krysztof and Lukas. His heart sank, and he knew the attempt was doomed to failure before he made the call. Even so, he needed to try.

He reached into his pocket and retrieved the satellite phone, then punched in the number. After a few seconds, the connection was made and Krysztof's voice crackled through the speaker. "Comrade Braun. Is everything ready?"

"Everyone is in place, Krysztof, but I wanted to ask you. Beg you one more time. Stop this insanity. Please. This

176

assault will be the end of us. There will be no going back after this."

"Bah, you are going soft, Daniel. You spent too much time with Gregorz. There was no going back once the humans learned of our existence. What would you have us do? Cower in basements like beaten dogs, waiting for them to hunt us down? No. They must learn that there are consequences when they seek us out. For every one of us they capture or kill, we will slaughter or turn a hundred of them. A thousand. Let us see how they handle thousands of moonstruck rampaging through their cities on the next full moon. I think, perhaps, they will be too busy with that to worry about us."

"There is growing support for us within the humans, Krysztof. Some of the media outlets are questioning their tactics. Not all of the humans agree with the actions of their governments. If we do this tonight, that support will vanish. We will prove ourselves to be the monsters they fear us to be."

"What do I care for their support? Their sympathy? They believe us to be monsters, and they are right. They feared our kind for centuries. It is time they learned to fear us again. Now, tell me of the plan."

Daniel's shoulders sagged. He'd known he'd get nowhere with Krysztof. Lukas he could have perhaps reasoned with. Not the big Armenian though. Once his mind was set, there was not a force on this earth that would make him change it. "I have teams assigned to the power substation, the telephone exchange and the mobile telephone towers. We will take out the police station first, and then, on the stroke of midnight, we'll black the town out and begin the assault."

"Good. Good. Now, don't let me keep you from your task, Comrade Braun. We will speak again tomorrow, after your work is done."

The line went dead. He looked at the phone with a mixture of revulsion and fear, but for the second time in as many weeks, resisted the urge to smash the device into fragments. He put the phone back into his pocket, then looked up at the two young werewolves that had got out of their car during his conversation with his Alpha. Matty Cash and Melissa Grove had lost their entire families on Christmas Eve, and had been among the first to volunteer for assignment. They were eager, bloodthirsty, but relatively young and inexperienced. Neither of them older than twenty one or twenty two. Unfortunately, they were also the best he had to work with.

"Well?" said Matty. "Are we on?"

Daniel fought against the wave of nausea that threatened to overwhelm him. He knew the others had been listening in on the conversation. There was no way to hide something like that from beings with enhanced senses such as they possessed. Which meant that if he tried to lie to them, they would tear him apart where he stood, then rampage through the town below without restraint. At least with him in charge of things, some of the humans in High Moor might survive the night, even if it was in an altered state of being. He had his orders and there was no turning back now.

"Yes. We are on. You and Melissa know what to do."

The two young wolves grinned at him, then rushed back to their car and drove away. The plan was in motion now. Nothing could stop it.

Daniel crossed himself. "May God have mercy upon me for what I have done, and for what I am about to do." Then he turned towards the other waiting vehicles and went to give the wolves their orders.

31st December 2008. High Moor Police Station. 20:35

Constable Stephen Bacon got out of his squad car and keyed in the access code for the police station rear door. The magnetic lock clicked open, and he nodded a greeting to Bruce Blanchard, one of the private security staff who administered the station's custody suite, while Constable Pete Gibbons got out of the car's passenger side and stood beside him.

Bruce smiled. "Evening, lads. Looks like the night's festivities are kicking off nice and early this year. What've you got for me?"

Stephen looked back over to the police car, and the two shapes on the back seat. "Two of them. One male, one female. Early twenties. Caught them kicking the shit out of some poor bastard on the high street. The woman bit a chunk right out of the kid's arm. Gave me a couple of nasty scratches as well while Pete and I were getting the cuffs on them. The pair of them have been quiet as lambs since we restrained them though. Not a peep out of either on the journey here."

Bruce stroked his chin. "You think we're going to need

some more bodies to get them inside?"

Stephen thought about this for a second, then nodded his assent. "Yeah. No sense in making this harder than it needs to be. Better get Paul off his fat arse to give us a hand in case they decide to get frisky."

"I heard that, you cheeky tosser," said Paul Mannering's disembodied voice from an adjacent room. After some shuffling and muttered curse words, the large bearded man appeared, fastening his belt as he walked. "I wasn't sat on my arse. I was having a shit."

Stephen winked at Pete and Bruce. "There'd better not be splatter marks on the seat again."

Paul flashed two fingers at the police officers, then tilted his head towards the squad car. "So, what's the story with the two love birds?"

"Assault, GBH and resisting arrest. Usual crap for New Year. This pair started the festivities earlier than most, but they'll have plenty of company by midnight, I'm sure."

Bruce sighed. "No doubt. I fucking hate New Year's Eve. Gives all the piss-heads and idiots licence to run riot. We'll probably be packing them in like sardines before the end of the night." He started towards the parked car. "Come on then. Might as well get these two out of the way before it all kicks off."

Pete joined Bruce by the driver's side door, while Stephen and Paul walked around to the opposite side. Stephen tapped on the glass. "Come on then, you two. Got a nice cosy cell for you to ring the New Year in from.

Still, could be worse. You could be spending it in A&E like that poor bastard you gave a kicking to."

Paul cracked his knuckles. "It's still not too late. Any shit from either of you and you might accidentally fall down some stairs, if you catch my meaning."

When neither of the car's occupants responded, Paul and Bruce opened the doors and hauled the man and woman out, with Pete and Stephen placing a firm grip on their arms as soon as they were clear of the vehicle. The four men hurried the two prisoners inside the station, and Stephen breathed a sigh of relief as the magnetic door closed behind them. Usually, if a prisoner was going to try something, it was in those critical moments between getting them out of the car and entering the station. These two, however, had offered no resistance of any kind. If anything, they'd almost jogged into the custody suite. Perhaps they were beginning to realise how much trouble they were in and were co-operating. That would make things easier on the custody officers, but wouldn't do a damn thing to reduce the charges. His arm still throbbed from where the woman's fingernails had torn through his skin. He was going to have to get a bloody tetanus shot, and for that, he was damn well going to make sure the pair of them were charged with assaulting a police officer, along with anything else he could make stick.

Bruce walked ahead of them and sat down behind his desk once more. He removed two plastic trays from behind him and nodded to the man. "Empty your pockets and put the contents in here. Then take your belt off and the laces out of your shoes and put them in here as well."

The man smiled at the custody officer and lifted his arms to show the handcuffs, then shrugged. Bruce let out an audible sigh of frustration. "Officer Bacon, would you mind taking the cuffs off these two?"

Stephen took out the key to the handcuffs and was about to unlock them when something in the man's demeanour made him pause. There was a tension about both prisoners. An eagerness that made him uneasy. When someone was arrested and brought into the station, they usually acted in one of two ways. Meek and apologetic, often in tears as the reality of their situation sank in, or loud, aggressive and threatening. The man and woman fell into neither category. It felt like they were waiting. Anticipating something. Like they were exactly where they wanted to be. And he didn't like that one little bit. He caught Pete's eye and a silent understanding passed between the two officers. Pete took a step backwards and removed his baton from its holster, while Paul retrieved a canister of pepper spray from his own uniform. If the prisoners felt like trying something, they'd regret it pretty damned quickly. Satisfied that all of the necessary precautions had been taken, he then unlocked the handcuffs on the man and woman in turn.

Bruce tapped on the side of the plastic tray with a pen. "Now, if it's not too much trouble. Pockets, belt and laces."

A grin played across the man's face. "Of course, officers. Happy to oblige." He removed the belt from his jeans, letting them fall to the floor, then stepped out of his trainers and pulled his t-shirt over his head. The woman followed suit, undressing in a matter of seconds. Neither wore any underwear beneath their outer garments.

Bruce put up his hands. "Woah, steady on now. If we wanted you to strip we'd have told you to. Put your bloody clothes back on."

The woman stepped forward, an innocent smile on her lips. "Oh, but clothes are so restrictive, don't you think? Don't you prefer me this way?"

Stephen felt an icy finger of fear run up his spine. This wasn't right. It wasn't right at all. He glanced at Pete and saw his own suspicions mirrored on the other officer's face. There was only one reason he could think of why their suspects wanted to remove their clothes. He grasped the man's right wrist and snapped his handcuffs around while Pete stepped forward and grabbed for the suspects other arm. If he was right, then he needed to restrain these prisoners while he still could.

The man lashed out with his left arm, flinging Pete away from him as if he were a small child. He turned around, and Stephen saw that his eyes had turned a feral yellow and rivulets of blood were running down the man's chin. He smiled at Stephen with a mouth full of bone razors. "I don't think we'll be needing the handcuffs. Tell me, Officer Bacon, will you squeal for me? Squeal like a little stuck pig?"

Chapter 13

31st December 2008. St Paul's Church Hall, High Moor. 21:02

Screams echoed around the church hall. High pitched. Piercing. The sound of over two dozen children running riot. Sharon massaged her temples and wished she'd had the presence of mind to bring some painkillers with her. Or earplugs. Or a bottle of vodka. The New Year's Eve crèche had been established a few years ago to give some of the town's parents the chance to go out and see the New Year in without having to worry about finding a babysitter. Two local women, Tonia Brown and Angela Crawford, ran it every year, and as far as Sharon was concerned, both were either saints or completely insane. Possibly both. Tonia was currently playing a game of musical statues with some of the children, a tactic to burn off some of their excess energy, while Angela read stories to the younger ones. The rest of the little darlings were tearing around the place, howling like banshees.

 One of the rooms adjacent to the main hall had been filled with camp beds and sleeping bags, to allow the children somewhere to take a nap, but the chances of it being used were slim to none, especially with the amount of treats available to them. Sharon's job was to look after the tuck shop – which was, in reality, a collapsible table piled high with cakes, cookies, sweets and sugary drinks that the children could buy. She'd questioned the wisdom of this approach, and Tonia, a cheerful red-haired woman, had just smiled and explained that it was their little bit of fun. They could hand back tired and contented children at the end of the night, sure, but it was much funnier to return bouncing balls of frantic energy, pumped up with caffeine and sugar, to their often slightly worse for wear parents. As a result, she'd forbidden her young nephew any of the items on display, which had not gone down well at all. Matthew was refusing to talk to her, and when she'd offered him some fruit, he'd regarded her with an incredulous mixture of disgust and pity.

The mass of screaming children reached the end of the hall, then changed direction in the same synchronous way a flock of starlings might, stampeding straight towards her. Sharon thought for a moment that they might just crash into the table and send its contents spilling across the floor, but they all skidded to a stop just in time and began clamouring for the sugary treats, each yelling their requests and holding their money out in front of them.

Sharon felt her headache go up a notch, and she began to regret not taking Helen up on her offer. A curry followed by a hot, sweaty pub and deafening dance music seemed like a nice, peaceful way to spend the evening by comparison. She fought to keep the irritation out of her voice. "One at a time. Form a line or nobody will get anything."

The children shuffled and jostled into something approaching a line. A pudgy blonde-haired girl had managed to push her way to the front of the queue and held out a pound coin. "I want some cake and a can of coke and one of those biscuits and..."

"You can have a can of drink and either some cake or a

cookie for a pound, sweetie. Everything is 50p each."

The girl's brow furrowed and her face began to redden. "My mummy says I can have anything I want."

This statement didn't really come as much of a surprise to Sharon. The child had an arrogance about her, and from the rolls of fat that were beginning to jowl under her chin, she was clearly not someone who was told 'No' very often, if at all. She suddenly found herself quite glad that she and Phil hadn't started a family. There was nothing like spending time around other people's offspring to put you off having any of your own. She forced her sweetest smile onto her face and leaned forward so that she was level with the girl. "For a pound, you can have two things from the table, and really, any more than that and you'll end up feeling sick anyway. Those slices of cake are quite big."

The girl rolled her eyes, shoved her hand back into her pocket and produced a slightly sticky five pound note. "There. I want two slices of cake, and a can of coke, *and* a cookie. And make sure you give me the right money back. Mummy says that people like *you* will steal anything that's not nailed down."

Sharon's eyes widened, and her temper began to bubble up through the cracks in her forced demeanour. "I beg your pardon? What did you just say to me?"

The child narrowed her eyes and put her hands on her hips. "You heard me."

That was it. There was no way she was going to put up with being spoken to like that by anyone, especially not some fat, spoiled little brat. "Well, you're not getting anything with an attitude like that, young lady. Go on, get out of the queue. I'm not serving you."

The child's face turned a darker shade of red. "You can't talk to me like that. My mummy says..."

"Well, your mummy isn't here, and to be honest, it won't do you any harm to stay away from cakes for a while. Now stop holding the line up. I have cakes and sweets to give to good little girls and boys. The ones who have some manners."

The child let out a high-pitched wail of frustration; a piercing shriek that seemed to start off at a frequency only dogs could hear, and then dropped down to a level that made Sharon's fillings vibrate. The girl folded her legs up underneath her body, seeming to levitate for a moment, before her not inconsiderable bulk crashed down onto the wooden floor of the church hall. Sharon was a little surprised that the girl didn't go straight through into the basement. As it was, the contents of the table leaped into the air a couple of centimetres.

Tonia, obviously quite experienced at this sort of thing, appeared behind the screaming girl and, catching Sharon's gaze, rolled her eyes and made a face behind the child's back, then kneeled down and put her hand on her shoulder. "Now, Bella, what's all this noise about?"

Bella grunted at Tonia, her breath catching in her throat. A bubble of mucus had formed on her left nostril and was inflating and deflating in time to her sobs. "She... she... she won't let me have any sweets."

"Well, I'm sure that if Mrs Fletcher won't let you have any sweets, then you must have done something?"

The mucus bubble burst and, with that small, moist explosion, Bella's voice returned. "I didn't do anything. She's just a horrible, nasty, mean old bag and she won't let me have any cake. She said I was too fat!"

It was all Sharon could do not to laugh as Tonia puffed her cheeks out and crossed her eyes. She bit her lip before forcing her words out, trying to maintain a serious tone. "I wouldn't serve you, Bella, because you were rude to me."

Tonia's mouth fell open in mock surprise, and when she spoke, her voice was thick with sarcasm. "You weren't rude, were you, Bella? Oh dear, what *will* your mother say when I tell her? I think she'll be very disappointed in you."

Bella mumbled something.

"Sorry?" said Tonia, leaning forward with her hand cupped to her ear. "Were you trying to say something?"

"Mm sorry," muttered Bella.

Tonia winked at Sharon, "Don't say sorry to me. You need to apologise to Mrs Fletcher for being rude."

Bella looked up at Sharon with pure hatred gleaming in her piggy eyes and spoke with a voice that dripped venom. "I'm sorry, Mrs Fletcher. Can I have my sweets now?"

Sharon gave the child a smile that would have been better suited on a shark. "Of course, Bella. You can have a can of drink and one slice of cake. After all, we want to leave something for the other children, don't we?"

Tonia's cheeks were puffed out again, and she mimed shovelling cake into her mouth with two fists behind Bella's back. Sharon couldn't help it this time, and a snort of laughter escaped her lips. Fortunately Bella didn't seem to notice. She handed Sharon her money, made a show of counting the change and stalked away with her paper plate and can of drink towards the back of the hall.

"Tonia, I can't believe you just did that!"

The red-haired woman turned her eyes up and put on an innocent, almost angelic expression. "Why, Sharon, I have no idea what you are talking about." She winked at her. "Give me a shout if any other little darlings start playing up."

Tonia began rounding up the other children, deciding that now was as good a time as any for a snack break, and for the next ten minutes, Sharon busily distributed the remaining cakes, cookies and sweets to the eager children until only a few pieces were left over. Mindful that Bella was watching the rapidly emptying table with interest, Sharon noticed three young children – a girl of around 11 years old plus two younger boys – sitting by themselves. They'd not come to the table for food, and she suspected that their parents had packed them off to the crèche without any money for treats, most likely so that they could spend it down the *Sandpiper* or whichever dive they'd elected to spend the evening in. She put the last three cookies on a paper plate and walked over to the children.

"Here you are. I noticed that you didn't come up with everyone else. I saved you some cookies, if you want them."

The two boys looked uncertain and their gaze flicked to the girl. She smiled at Sharon. "No, thank you. We're fine."

Sharon bent down. "Listen, if it's about money, it doesn't matter. These can be a treat from me."

The girl stepped forward and gently but firmly pushed the plate away. "I said, no. Thank you. We're going to eat later and we don't want to spoil our appetite."

Sharon took a step backwards, suddenly uncomfortable in the children's presence and wanting nothing more than to be as far away from them as she could get. A ridiculous notion of course, but as she made her way back to the table, she was surprised to find her legs felt weak and her arms were trembling. She tried to shake the feeling off, but something gnawed at her. Perhaps it was the way the girl's eyes had seemed almost yellow in the harsh light of the church hall. Or perhaps it was the way all three of them had turned in unison to look at Bella when they talked about eating later.

31st December 2008. Sandpiper Public House, High Moor. 21:07

Mandy wrinkled her nose and tried her best to ignore the stench as she removed her clothes from her bag. Her mother could be *such* a bitch. If she'd just let her wear what she wanted, then she wouldn't have to resort to drastic measures like this. Getting changed in some stinking public lavatory was not the best way to start the evening. God knows what sort of mess her hair would be in. There weren't even any mirrors in here, so she would have to check with her small make-up compact.

Anna hammered on the door. "Get a move on, Mandy. It stinks in here. I think somebody had a piss on the floor and it's making me feel sick."

Mandy straightened her top, then shoved the hideous floral number her mother had picked into the carrier bag. "Just a second. I'm nearly done."

"You said that ten minutes ago. Come on, or we won't be able to get a seat."

Anna's older sister, Julie, after a considerable amount of pleading and a bribe of twenty pounds, had bought four extra tickets for the New Year's Eve party in the *Sandpiper*. Apparently there was going to be a famous Ukrainian DJ playing and people were already saying it was going to be the best party High Moor had ever seen. Of course, the *Sandpiper*'s owner had to do something. Business had not exactly been booming over the last two months. Not since the disastrous Halloween party. Apparently a severed head crashing through the window and landing on the dance floor was the sort of thing that stuck in people's minds and drove custom away. It also meant that the bouncers and bar staff probably weren't going to be too vigilant in checking the age of their clientele. The girls all had fake ID, of course, but Mandy was confident they wouldn't need it. They all definitely looked eighteen. Apart from Kat. Kat had gone *way* overboard with her makeup and she looked like the Joker from the last Batman movie. Anna and Amy had offered to sort it out for her, but she'd gotten pissy about it. Said it was "her look". This was fine as far as Mandy was concerned. It would give her something to laugh about later on when Kat's war paint started to run down her cheeks.

Anna hammered on the door again. "Have you gone to sleep in there? Come on. You're wasting my bloody drinking time."

"Just. A. Fucking. Minute," said Mandy, not bothered that the irritation she felt dripped from her words like acid. It wasn't like she was taking her time on purpose. She sprayed lacquer onto her hair and ran a brush through it until it was sleek and straight. She did her best to check herself out with the tiny circular mirror held at arm's length. Sod it. That would have to do. Anyway, a darkened room and flashing disco lights hid a multitude of sins. She'd still look a million times better than some of the old slappers she'd noticed stumbling into the pub earlier.

She pulled open the door and flashed her best smile at Anna. "Ta da! What do you think?"

Anna regarded her for a moment, her expression still one of mild annoyance. "You look lush, chick. Now come on before the stink of this place starts settling on us. Never going to pull with hair smelling of piss, are we?"

Mandy followed Anna out of the toilets to where Kat and Amy were waiting on a low brick wall. Amy passed a joint to Kat, who eyed it suspiciously for a moment then took a deep drag. A couple of seconds later, she bent double in a coughing fit that an eighty year old asbestosis victim would be proud of and held out the slightly moist, lipstick reddened joint to her friend.

Amy rolled her eyes. "You are such a lightweight. And you've dribbled all over the end of it!" She nodded at Mandy and Anna. "Got there in the end, did you? About fucking time. We've been freezing our tits off out here, and I think it's going to start snowing soon."

Mandy couldn't argue with her friend's reasoning. The temperature had dropped significantly over the last hour, and the leaden clouds overhead seemed almost close enough to touch. Her breath plumed in the frigid air, and goose-bumps had sprung up across her bare arms. "Yeah, let's get inside."

The four girls hurried through the streets as fast as their high heels would permit. The bars were already beginning to fill up, and the only vehicles on the road now seemed to be taxis or the occasional bus. Gangs of young men stood outside *The Wheatsheaf*, smoking and bellowing football chants at the top of their voices, while further along the high street it looked like a fight had broken out between a group of men. Strangely, though, there was no sign of any police. Even on a normal Saturday night, there would be at least two riot wagons parked on the high street. Tonight there was no police presence at all. That meant things were likely to get even more rowdy than usual.

The girls hurried along the shopping precinct, past graffiti-splashed shutters pulled down over shops that had been empty for years, to the small passage that led to the open air car park and the *Sandpiper* public house. The deep bass thud of dance music echoed around the concrete walls and the girls exchanged excited glances. They had been looking forward to tonight for months. Their first proper New Year's Eve party. Mandy couldn't wait.

The pub was a pulsating island of light and sound amidst the darkness of the car park. Groups of young men and women stood around by the entrance, smoking cigarettes and trying not to show how cold they were, while a line of people stretched from the doorway all the way to the edge of the building. Anna stared at the queue and gave Mandy a look that would curdle milk. "It's bloody well packed. We'll never get somewhere to sit now. If you hadn't taken so long, pissing about in the bogs..."

Mandy shrugged, but in truth was starting to lose patience with her friend's constant complaining. "Look, there's nothing we can do about it now. It's not my fault my mam made me wear that minging outfit." She looked down at the carrier bag. "Save me a spot in the line. Going to go stash this somewhere for now."

Anna, Amy and Kat linked arms and joined the back of the line, while Mandy hurried across the dark car park, looking for somewhere to hide the carrier bag containing her sensible clothes until later. Fat snowflakes drifted down from the sky, and she shivered. It really was getting cold, and despite the abuse she'd get from her friends, she really would like nothing better than a big warm winter coat right now. But this was North East England, and such things just weren't done. Not if you wanted to retain any kind of street credibility.

She made her way to the edge of the dark expanse of tarmac, to the rear of one of the few remaining shops, and shoved the carrier bag beneath a large green recycling bin. It should be safe there until they left the bar. Mandy was about to return to her friends when a voice from directly behind her made her jump in shock.

"Excuse me, love. Got a light?"

The man was old. Maybe even thirty, although good looking enough considering he was almost old enough to be her dad. Blond hair. Nice smile. But there was something about the way his smile got nowhere near his eyes that made Mandy nervous. "No, sorry, mate. Don't smoke."

The man shrugged. "Never mind. Really should pack them in anyway. Maybe it's a sign, eh? Give 'em up for New Year." He held out his hand. "I'm Joseph, Joseph Austin, but you can call me Joe if you like."

Mandy arched an eyebrow. "I'm late. My friends'll be looking for me," she said, walking quickly back towards the corona of light.

Joseph didn't seem to be discouraged by this and began walking beside her. "Why do you want to go into that shit-hole anyway? We could hang out. Go somewhere, maybe?"

Mandy hurried her pace. "Or you could just piss off, granddad."

The bar was closer now. She could hear the voices of the people in the line, talking and laughing, from around the corner. To her relief, Joseph was no longer at her side. She risked a glance over her shoulder to see him standing in the middle of the car park, a lascivious grin spread across his face. He waved. "Maybe I'll see you later, then."

The shudder that ran through Mandy had very little to do with the cold, and she breathed a sigh of relief when she turned the corner and rejoined Anna, Amy and Kat. They'd almost made it to the front of the queue. Anna still had a face like a smacked arse and Kat's pale skin had taken on a decidedly green tinge.

Only Amy seemed to notice that Mandy was upset. She put her hand on Mandy's shoulder. "You alright?"

Mandy gave her a half smile. "Yeah, just some perv in the car park. Told him to fuck off. I'll feel better once I get a couple of drinks in me."

They reached the front of the queue and handed their tickets to the doorman, who hardly gave them a second glance. The girls hurried past him before he changed his mind, pushing open the door into a wall of heat and noise. That was more like it. Mandy felt her black mood dissipate, and even Anna was smiling. Kat still looked like she was going to blow chunks all over the carpet, though.

She put her arms around Amy and Anna. "Right then, ladies. Looks like the first round is on me."

31st December 2008. Sandpiper Public House, High Moor. 23:50

Helen linked arms with her husband, using him as support on the slippery pavement. The snow had started falling as they'd arrived at the restaurant and had become heavier in the last few hours, a thick white blanket covering the entire town. This, however, had not stopped the revellers. A large group had gathered in the market square in readiness for the stroke of midnight, and people were already spilling out of the bars. Predictably, snowball fights had broken out between some groups of young men on the periphery of the market square – snowball fights that rapidly escalated into real ones. What surprised her was that there was no police presence to break things up. It had been a while since she'd gone out in town, but a town like High Moor was a rowdy place at the best of times, and some of the scuffles seemed to be getting quite serious. Yet, there wasn't so much as a single squad car in the town centre. She shook her head. The buggers were probably hiding back at their nice, warm station.

She grinned at Chelfyn. "Shall we go for a quick drink in the *Sandpiper*? See the New Year in properly?"

He raised an eyebrow. "What? A crowded pub and some DJ playing techno loud enough to rattle your fillings?" He grinned. "Fuck yeah!"

They hurried through the streets, trying to ignore the biting cold that managed to penetrate their thick coats. Then, something caught Helen's eye. "Love, look at that. In the snow. Is that... is that blood?"

Chelfyn stopped and looked over to the dark stain in the snow, then shook his head. "No, there's too much of it. Someone probably chucked up their snakebite and black. Come on, let's get to the pub before they call time."

They left the main shopping precinct and headed to the small covered passage that led to the car park and the *Sandpiper*. Helen was grateful for the momentary respite from the slush-covered pavement and picked up her pace as they followed the thudding bass beat towards their destination. A homeless man sat slumped on a blanket halfway along the passageway and Helen threw a handful of change down for him. The man didn't seem to notice as the coins hit the front of his blanket, nor offer any form of acknowledgement for the small act of kindness. Helen decided that he was probably hammered on some cheap booze, but was grateful that he'd at least found some scant shelter before the snow had started falling. He'd have frozen to death if he'd stayed out in the near blizzard conditions gripping the town.

She tightly hung on to her husband's arm as they stepped back onto the frozen tarmac, feeling a hint of vague regret at the last gin and tonic she'd knocked back. The last thing she needed was to fall flat on her arse in the icy conditions. She'd have struggled to stay upright on a night like this if she was stone cold sober.

The music was deafening, even outside. The windows of the pub pulsed in time to the bass beats, and crowds of people stood around at the front of the place wearing clothes more appropriate for a warm July evening, huddled in small groups with gooseflesh standing proud on their arms. The doorman barely looked at them as they hurried inside, despite it being a ticket only event.

The blast of hot air, pounding music and screamed conversation was a stark contrast to the frigid conditions outside. Helen removed her coat and tried not to think about the fact that she was probably twenty years older than most of the other patrons. Chelfyn took her by the hand and led her to the main bar, expertly weaving his way through the gyrating mass of people spilling off the dance floor. He made it almost half way, then stopped and looked at the DJ, narrowing his eyes. Then he burst out laughing. He bent over to say something to her, but she couldn't make out a word of it. The track ended abruptly, just as he bellowed into her ear.

"Famous Ukrainian DJ my arse! That's Gary fucking Pennock! He was in our year at school!"

Helen peered through the clouds of dry ice to the man standing behind the decks, remembering a boy in their year with masses of dark curly hair. There was certainly a resemblance. She was about to respond to her husband when she spotted someone else she recognised. Anna Pursey. Mandy's friend. Standing next to one of the bass speakers, talking to a group of young men. And the two girls next to her were definitely Amy Sherwood and Kat Yares. Which meant that, in all likelihood, Mandy was here somewhere as well. The haze of alcohol and happy thoughts vanished in a heartbeat, replaced with a mother's righteous rage. She strode across the dance floor to where the girls stood, oblivious to the people she knocked out of her way in the process. She reached them and just stood there, hands on her hips and eyes blazing in fury. Anna looked up and met her eyes just as the music started again. Helen couldn't hear the words that came out of her mouth, but she didn't need to. "Oh fuck" was not a difficult sentence to lip read.

Anna's eyes flicked nervously to her right, and Helen followed her gaze to her fifteen year old daughter, weaving her way across the dance floor with four bottles of WKD in her hands. And wearing the slutty outfit she'd been ordered to remove earlier. That, as far as Helen was concerned, was the last straw. She set an intercept course and stormed across the dance floor. Mandy spotted her at the last moment and her eyes widened with mute horror. The bottles fell from her hands, exploding into four fountains of blue liquid and glass shards. She turned to run, but it was too late. Helen's hand whipped out and closed around her daughter's wrist in a vice-like grip.

Mandy tried to pull away, her face a mask of mixed emotions. Helen tightened her hold until her knuckles went white and pulled her daughter away from her friends, towards the hallway, where the music faded to a dull roar.

"Where are your clothes? The ones you left the house in?"

Mandy's eyes darted around as if looking for some escape route, then resignation set in and she looked down at the floor and mumbled a response.

"Look at me when you talk to me, young lady. Where is that nice dress your Grandmother bought you?"

"Outside. In a bag. I stashed it under a wheelie bin."

"Right. We are going to go out there to get it, right now. Then you are coming back in here, getting changed out of those rags, and we are going straight home."

"But Mam…"

"But nothing. I don't want to hear another word out of you. You're in enough trouble as it is."

Mandy glanced up to where Chelfyn stood with Ian, her older son. Ian caught her gaze then looked away as her eyes burned into him. Oh yes, he was not going to escape her wrath either. He'd clearly known all about this and had decided to stay silent. Big mistake.

Helen strode outside, past the groups of drunken young men and women. "Where are they? Where did you leave them?"

Mandy's voice hitched in barely restrained sobs. "Out the back of Poundland."

"You'd better pray that nothing has happened to that dress. I don't know what we'll tell your Gran if it's been stolen."

Helen and Mandy tottered through the driving snow around the side of the pub. The snow seemed to glow under the distant street lights, providing at least a degree of illumination as they slipped and slid across the car park. After what seemed like forever, they finally arrived at the rear of the shop. Helen said nothing and stood back with her hands on her hips while Mandy began pushing the snow aside. Moments later she retrieved a rather soggy looking carrier bag from beneath the green plastic bin.

"There," Mandy said with a touch of defiance in her voice. "Got it. Safe and sound."

Her tone managed to annoy Helen even more. "Well, that doesn't mean you are in any less trouble. You're fifteen years old. You're lucky you didn't get arrested, or worse. Now, get back in those toilets and change out of those clothes. You look like a bloody slapper."

"But Mam, this dress is soaking. I'll freeze!"

"Well, you should have thought about that before..."

Helen's tirade was cut off by a polite cough from behind them. She turned around to find a young man, probably in his late twenties or early thirties, standing a little too close to them for comfort. "Excuse me, ladies. Don't suppose I could trouble either of you for a light?"

"No, I'm sorry. Neither of us smoke. Now, if you don't mind, I'm having a conversation with my daughter."

The man smiled with a grin that sent a shiver down Helen's spine. She was suddenly very aware of how far they were away from the pub. "Mother and daughter, eh? Now you mention it, I can see the resemblance. Thought you might have been sisters at first."

Mandy stood close to her, her hands gripping her arm. "He's some perv that was hassling me earlier on."

The man's smile widened and he took a step back with a mock flourish, bowing as he did so. When he stood back up, the smile was gone, and a knife glinted in his hand. He shrugged. "You know what they say. Old enough to bleed, old enough to breed. Now, I've got a van parked just over there. Why don't you two lovely ladies come with me? You scream, or try to run, and I'll slice up those pretty faces. Starting with your gobshite of a daughter."

Helen's limbs went numb as her body dumped adrenaline into her veins. There was no way that either of them would be able to outrun the man. Not wearing heels. And the bass thud of the music from the pub would drown out any cries for help. She looked around frantically for anyone that might be able to help, but there was no one visible through the driving snow.

The clock on the town hall began to chime. Each peal ringing in the New Year. She could hear the muted cries of people counting them down from the market square and from the pub, which was only just visible through the white blanket. At this moment in time she would have given anything to be with them. Warm, happy and safe with Chelfyn and Ian.

The clock chimed nine... ten... eleven... twelve.

And then all of the lights in High Moor went out.

Chapter 14

31ˢᵗ December 2008. St Paul's Church Hall, High Moor. 23:59

Sharon glanced at the clock, praying that the night would end soon. What had started off as a distraction from worrying about Phil had, as the night progressed, become an exercise in endurance. Even the children that had been well behaved and polite earlier in the evening had become belligerent, grizzling balls of mucus, tears and temper as the sugar rush subsided and fatigue kicked in. Tonia and Angela's demeanour seemed to be slipping as well, with a few genuine looks of irritation breaking through the smiles.

The children had been gathered together in a circle, holding hands as they waited for the clock to strike twelve. Then, after the obligatory singing session, all that remained would be the uncomfortable wait for the parents to arrive and take their offspring away. Sharon really hoped that Helen had some booze back at the house. All she wanted to do now was put her feet up and do some real damage to a bottle of Chardonnay.

All eyes were on the clock at the rear of the church hall as the seconds ticked away. A few nervous giggles escaped from the children. Bella's face was still creased into a scowl over the tuck shop incident and she refused to hold the hands of the two little girls to either side of her, something that neither of the other children seemed to be bothered about.

Angela caught her eye, raised her eyebrows and gave

her an encouraging smile. The message was clear. One last push. We're almost done. She forced her most cheerful smile onto her face as the clock ticked closer to midnight.

Tonia's voice held a tiny, almost imperceptible strained edge as she spoke. "Alright, Children. It's almost time. Ten. Nine."

The children joined in with a weary monotone, all of them presumably as ready to go home as the adults. "Eight. Seven. Six. Five. Four. Three. Two. One."

The lights went out, plunging the church hall into pitch blackness. Even the comforting orange glow of the streetlights outside was gone. Children squealed in alarm and Sharon heard Tonia curse under her breath from across the hall.

"Okay, everyone, it's just a power cut," Angela shouted above the screaming children. "Stay where you are and behave. I'll go and get the torch from the kitchen."

Quite predictably, the children neither stayed where they were, nor behaved. The little blonde girl to her left released her hold on Sharon's hand, although when Matthew tried to do the same she tightened her grip on his wrist.

Squeals and laughter echoed through the darkness, despite Tonia's exasperated pleas.

"Woooooooooo!"

"Johnny poo'd his pants! Johnny stinks!"

"Get off, you booger!"

"Miiiiisss! Someone just hit me!"

The removal of sight seemed to sharpen Sharon's other senses. There was a faint, musky odour to the church hall that had not been there before, and beneath the squeals of misbehaving children she could make out another sound. A snapping, tearing noise, as if someone were cutting through an old hessian sack with a fistful of sharpened twigs.

The children heard it too. The jubilant cries of mischief lapsed into an uneasy silence as the strange sounds continued at the rear of the church hall. Sharon tried to visualise what could even make a noise like that, or what could possibly be happening in the darkness. She tightened her hold on Matthew and tried to open her eyes wider in the hope that she would see something – anything.

The noise stopped and, for a moment, there was silence. Then something let out a savage animal growl.

1st January 2009. Sandpiper Public House, High Moor. 00:01

The town was plunged into darkness and silence. Mandy didn't stop to think, adrenaline and alcohol coursed through her body and she just reacted, lashing out with her foot to where their would-be assailant had been standing. She was rewarded with a satisfying crunch of shoe against something soft and a cry of pain. She grabbed her mother's wrist. "Come on, Mum. Run!"

Her mother didn't need to be told twice, and they both

kicked off their shoes and ran towards the relative safety of the pub. The music had stopped, but that had not apparently dampened the spirits of the *Sandpiper*'s patrons. A rowdy chorus of Auld Lang Syne, interspersed with cries and cheering, echoed across the empty car park.

Mandy lost her footing, tripping over a buried kerb that sent her sprawling. Pieces of gravel shredded the palms of her hands and knees, but she barely felt it.

Her mother reached out her hand. "Come on, love, we've got to get inside before..."

Helen didn't get a chance to finish her sentence as the man who'd called himself Joseph Austin crashed into them. Mandy tried to scramble to her feet – to get away from their attacker – when her stomach exploded in agony and the breath was forced from her body. She collapsed back into the snow, desperately trying to suck air back into her lungs.

"You fucking little bitch! How do you like that? Did you really think you were going to get away with kicking me in the bollocks?"

She heard the whoosh of air as what she assumed was a booted foot connected with her left side, sending another bomb-burst of pain through her. Her mother let out a scream of rage and hurled herself at the man, but he seemed to have anticipated the attack. His fist lashed out and connected with the side of her mother's head with a loud crack that seemed to resonate around the car park. Her mother collapsed face down in the snow and did not get back up.

The man wiped his hand across his face then kicked Mandy again. "You two are going to pay for that. I swear to God, I'm going to make you wish you were dead."

Mandy found her voice and screamed for help, praying that someone from the pub would come to their rescue, but her cries were lost in the cacophony emanating from the building. She crawled to where her mother lay and wrapped her arms around her. "Please. Leave us alone. We won't tell anyone. Just don't hurt us."

"It's too late for that, you little cunt. I'm going to fuck your bitch mother, then I'm going to cut her while you watch. I'm going to..."

The man's voice faltered and he took a step back, away from them both. Mandy couldn't make out the expression on his face, but she didn't need to. It was clear from his body language that Joseph Austin had just seen something that had terrified him. Something that was just behind her. She had to see. Mandy forced down the wave of terror that threatened to drown her and slowly turned her head.

Two glowing green eyes shone out from the darkness, and a deep, guttural snarl echoed around the empty car park. Mandy got the impression of immense mass and power from the shape. Given recent events in the town, it really didn't take long for her mind to realise what it was she was looking at. A werewolf. Less than ten feet from her.

She let out a small whimper of terror, draping herself over her mother's prone body as the creature bunched its muscles and pounced.

Mandy squeezed her eyes tight closed, waiting for the terrible pain of the werewolf's fangs rending her flesh. She felt the air displaced by the monster's passing, but the expected agony did not materialise. The thing had leaped straight over her and her mother and was stalking towards Joseph Austin, who backed away from the creature, waving his knife out in front of him.

"Stay back. Get away. I'm fucking warning you!"

That, apparently, was all the prompting the werewolf needed. With a roar, it hurled itself at the man, knocking him to the ground. Talons tore through fabric and flesh as if they were as insubstantial as gossamer. Jaws crunched through bones, and within a matter of seconds, the man's screams had turned into little more than wet gurgles, while the snow beneath him blackened and steamed.

Mandy was in no doubt they would be next. She shook her mother, desperately now. "Mum, wake up. You've got to..."

Her hands were sticky and the air was filled with a thick, coppery stench. She looked down at her mother and saw that her eyes were wide open, an expression of surprise on her face. Black ichor dribbled from an inch long hole in her temple. Austin hadn't just punched her mother. He'd plunged his blade into her skull. Her mother was dead.

A terrible keening sound filled Mandy's ears and it took her a second to realise that the source of the noise was her. Her mam was dead and it was all her fault. If she'd worn what she was supposed to, they would never have had to come out here, and Joseph Austin would never have murdered her. The loss was a raw, aching chasm opening up inside of her. Her mother would never call her down for breakfast again, or hold her tight, ruffling her hair and kissing her on the forehead in the way she did when she was in a good mood. She was dead. Dead. The world contained nothing but grief. Pain. Loss.

Then Mandy remembered the werewolf.

Part of her wanted to just lie there and wait to feel the beast's teeth and claws tear her apart. She deserved to die. Everything was her fault. But then she remembered her Father. Ian. Anna, Kat and Amy. Matthew and Auntie Sharon. There were werewolves loose in High Moor and she needed to be with her family. Warn them. Keep them safe. Save them to atone for failing her Mother.

She kissed her mother once on the forehead, mirroring what her mum had done to her so many times, not caring that she could taste blood in her mouth. Then, she carefully laid the body in the snow and backed away from the feasting werewolf, towards *The Sandpiper*.

1st January 2009. St Paul's Church Hall, High Moor. 00:03

Sharon's stomach tightened into a hard knot of raw terror and her legs seemed unable to support her weight. The utter darkness was more than disorienting; it was all-encompassing – more like a presence than a mere absence of light. If not for the sensation of her feet against the wooden floor and the sudden awareness of gravity bearing down upon her, she might have struggled to know which way was up. As it was, in the wake of the massive adrenaline surge, she struggled to clear her mind long enough to orient herself. And in this situation, to hesitate would almost certainly result in her death and the death of her nephew. She was under no illusions about what shared the darkness with them.

The children began to scream as they realised that they were trapped in absolute blackness with monsters. Monsters that could see in the dark. Monsters with razor sharp fangs and claws that could slice through flesh with ease. Monsters that had not yet moved from the far end of the church hall. Sharon knew why with a sickening certainty. They were savouring the terror of their captives. Choosing their targets. When the end came, it would come swiftly, and she knew then who the first three to die would be. Tonia, Angela and herself. Kill the adults and the children would be easy prey. As if to confirm her suspicions, the growls dropped an octave. She pulled Matthew behind her, putting herself between the creatures and her nephew for all the good it would do.

The snarling became a roar of sheer bloodlust, and the glowing eyes streaked across the dark expanse of the church hall. The terrified screams of the children increased in pitch and volume. Racking sobs mingled with howls of anguish. Bella's voice rang out, louder than the others. "No, get away! I'm going to tell my mammy! NOOOOO! IT HURTS! MAMMMYYYY!!!"

Wet ripping noises, like someone peeling an over-ripe orange, mingled with the agonised screaming. Some of the children ran from their attackers, colliding with each other in the darkness, while others curled up, sobbing quietly as they waited for death or salvation. Part of

Sharon was glad of the darkness. She really didn't want to see the source of some of those sounds. However, the mute terror of not knowing when the creatures would turn their attention towards her and Matthew was so much worse.

Something brushed against her leg – a brief sensation of coarse fur on skin and a residual sticky wetness on her flesh. She yelped and leaped away. Her foot slipped on something soft and wet, and she fell to the floor, her ankle twisting sharply beneath her as she landed. Sharon ground her teeth at the searing pain, but refused to cry out. Hoping – praying that the beast would pass her by. Choose a different victim.

Hot rank breath on her face. The barest hint of a snarl held in check. The screams from the children faded into the background; the only thing she was aware of was the sound of her own heart pounding in her chest and the sense of something powerful mere inches away from her. She could visualise the mouth curling back into a snarl and hoped that it would be over quickly. Then a beam of light cut through the darkness as Angela arrived from the kitchen with the torches.

Time slowed, and in that dilated, drawn out, terrible second, among the deep, dancing shadows, Sharon saw a werewolf for the first time. Oddly enough, it wasn't as big as she'd expected it to be. More like a large dog – an Alsatian or a Husky – than the dreadful things she'd seen on the internet. The creature's muzzle was soaked in blood and its snout was indeed wrinkled into a snarl, revealing fangs that no mere dog could ever possess. Another of the creatures had its snout buried in Bella's stomach, its head thrashing from side to side as the girl screamed in unimaginable agony. Bella's size had protected her to an extent. The monster had needed to chew through layers of fat before it got to her vital organs, but that had just prolonged her suffering. The other creature was stalking two young boys in the corner of the church hall, seeming to relish the fear emanating from its intended prey, while two more children lay face down in spreading pools of blood. The rest of them were either curled up in foetal positions, crying, or had their backs flat against the far wall.

Sharon saw all of this in a fraction of a second, the scene burned onto her retinas. Then time reasserted itself and all hell broke loose.

Tonia let out an inhuman screech and hurled herself across the church hall at the beast stalking the two boys. Somehow she'd managed to pick up a heavy wooden chair and she swung it at the unsuspecting werewolf with all her might. The force of the impact shattered the wood into jagged, foot-long shards. Tonia didn't hesitate and drove one of them into the creature's back with so much force it burst out of the werewolf's stomach.

The monster howled in pain and surprise and began to snap at the makeshift stake that remained just out of reach. Tonia took a step back, apparently surprised at the success of her attack. That was when the other two creatures turned their attention to her. The beast before Sharon leaped over her and barrelled into Tonia's side; its jaws clamped down on her arm, severing the appendage in a single bite. The other creature tore itself away from Bella, trailing a streamer of the girl's intestines behind it, and slashed the woman's Achilles tendon with its talons. Tonia's leg buckled under her and she fell to the floor, vanishing in an instant beneath the enraged monsters.

Sharon couldn't move. The horror she was witnessing was too much and, for a moment, her mind seemed to shut down. Tonia was still screaming beneath the onslaught of claws and fangs from the two werewolves, while the injured one whined and snapped at the makeshift stake that impaled it. It would only be a matter of seconds before she shared her friend's fate, she knew.

It was Angela that snapped her out of her resigned fugue state. "Everyone. The cellar. Get into the cellar. Now."

The torchlight seemed to be a beacon of hope, illuminating Angela and an open door that ran beneath the stage to the storage room below. Sharon pulled herself to her feet, ignoring the white bomb-burst of pain erupting from her injured ankle. Matthew was by her side, trying to help her, and while he lacked the strength to be much use, his presence banished the last of her hopelessness, replacing it with a righteous anger and a determination to get her nephew through this ordeal. She didn't dare look back until she reached the doorway and had ushered Matthew safely inside.

Tonia's corpse was spread over an eight foot patch of gore, hardly recognisable anymore. One of the werewolves continued to feast on the bloody fragments, while the other had turned its attention to its stricken companion and had fastened its jaws around the wooden stake. In a matter of seconds the object would be removed, and Sharon had heard stories of how quickly these things healed.

Most of the children were now in the relative safety of the cellar, but the two boys that were being stalked prior to Tonia's assault were still frozen in place in the corner of the room, their faces blank masks of terror. Sharon started to move towards them when Angela put her hand on her shoulder and shook her head. "No. Get downstairs. I'll get them."

The look on Angela's face said it all. She knew the chance of getting to the children was slim, but she had to try. She was responsible for these children, and to abandon those two boys would have made Tonia's sacrifice mean nothing. Sharon nodded her understanding and Angela ran across the slippery, blood-drenched floor to where the children cowered, gathering one up under each arm. She'd made it almost halfway across the room when first one child, and then the other were torn from her grasp.

She turned and screamed out in fury, advancing on the werewolves that were tearing the young boys apart, all reason long gone. Then the third werewolf, apparently already healed from its wounds, hit her square in the chest and began to tear into her body while she beat at it.

Sharon couldn't watch anymore. She pulled the heavy steel door closed, fastened the bolt and descended the stairs to the crowd of weeping children.

Matthew hugged her fiercely then stepped back and held her at arm's length, regarding her with a strange expression on his face. "Auntie Sharon?"

215

She somehow managed a smile. "Yes, Matthew?"

He pointed to her leg. "Does that mean you're going to turn into a monster as well?"

She looked down and saw four deep, parallel gashes across her calf. The marks of a werewolf's claws.

Chapter 15

1st January 2009. Sandpiper Public House, High Moor. 00:06

Mandy stumbled out of the car park towards the front of the pub. A few people stood close to the building, backs pressed against the wall in an attempt to avoid the worst of the falling snow while they smoked their cigarettes. Of the two bouncers that had guarded the door earlier, only one was present. A bald man in a heavy black jacket who leaned against the door frame talking to a couple of girls that were in Mandy's year at school. She pushed her way past the girls to stand in front of the doorman.

She'd been trying to frame a coherent thought, but as soon as she opened her mouth, the words rushed from her in a torrent. "You've got to help me! There was a man in the car park and he killed my mum and then a werewolf killed him you have to call the police and get everyone inside then lock the door before... oh, God... before it comes and kills everyone!"

The doorman's face creased into a frown and his eyes narrowed. "Steady on love. Just calm down and get your breath back. What have you taken? Coke? Pills?"

Mandy shook her head. "I've not taken anything. You have to listen to me or everyone is going to die. Do you understand? There's a massive fucking werewolf in the car park!"

The bouncer appeared a little taken aback but quickly regained his composure. "Look, I don't know if you're trying to wind me up..."

He never finished his sentence. A howl echoed around the building, the sound reflected from the unyielding concrete of the shopping centre until it seemed to surround them. It was answered by another, and another, and another from all around the town. A joyful lament that combined in a primal chorus, drowning out the sounds of drunken revelry from within the pub. The colour drained from the bouncer's face and the smokers near the doorway looked up, eyes wide with terror.

The doorman seemed convinced by this. "Inside. Get inside, all of you. Now!"

Mandy needed no further encouragement and ducked beneath the man's arm into the dark, cavernous interior of the *Sandpiper*. She felt her way along the cheap wallpaper, her eyes registering only vague outlines of doorways or the tacky wildlife pictures that adorned the walls. Then the front doorway slammed shut with the finality of a closing tomb, and what little ambient light there was disappeared, plunging her into absolute pitch darkness.

She knew she should have felt safer once the door was closed and the bolts in place, but she didn't. The darkness was all-encompassing and the urge to curl up on the floor was almost overwhelming. *Maybe they won't come. If I hide here, or lock myself in the toilets, then maybe I'll be safe. The police will come soon. Or the army. I should just hide until they get here.*

The thoughts were seductive whispers in the back of her consciousness, born from terror and desperation. Her limbs felt numb, heavy. As if the nerves had died and she was hauling around lumps of dead meat instead of arms and legs. She knew that what she needed to do, above everything else, was get back to her dad and Ian. She didn't know what she'd say to them, but being with family would at least provide her with a temporary refuge - an illusion of safety. And if the werewolves came, then at least she'd die with people that loved her. She willed her leaden legs into motion once more and felt her way along the wall, guided by the raucous laughter in the main bar area, until her hands found the heavy wooden door.

A wave of heat and noise washed over her. People laughing, singing and drinking as if everything was normal. As if every single one of them was not in mortal danger. Mandy wanted to scream at them - make them understand - but instead she pushed her way into the room. One of the staff had the presence of mind to light some candles and position them along the bar. It meant that, along with the weak glow from the emergency exit lights, there was at least some illumination. The flickering light and dancing shadows were a stark contrast to the utter blackness she'd emerged from and, more importantly, it meant she had a chance of finding her family. She threaded her way through the room, desperately scanning the faces of the people she brushed past, hoping to find someone familiar, yet dreading the moment that she'd have to explain things to her dad.

A hand fell on her shoulder, and she let out an involuntary shriek of alarm. She span around to find Anna regarding her with a look halfway between amusement and concern.

"Where the hell did you piss off to? You missed the

countdown? Is your mum still here? She looked really fucking mad."

Mandy's throat constricted and she struggled to force the words out. "My mum... Mum... she's dead... she..."

Anna gave her a playful punch on the shoulder. "Piss off, Mandy. That's not a nice thing to say, even as a joke."

Mandy held up her blood-soaked hands. "Does this look like I'm joking? Listen, Anna. Get Kat and Amy then find me. I've got to find Dad and Ian. The fucking town's full of werewolves, and they're killing people."

Anna's face fell and she took a step back from her friend. "Mandy... I... Is this for real?"

Mandy grasped Anna's shoulders, leaving bloody prints on the white fabric. "Anna. I mean it. We haven't got much time. I need to find my dad."

Anna nodded her assent. "Okay. He was over by the DJ earlier. Maybe he's still over that way. I'll get the others and meet you there."

She watched Anna disappear into the crowd before pushing her way through the forest of bodies towards the DJ booth, doing her best to avoid the flailing arms and elbows of the revellers. Mandy was not a tall girl, and she struggled to fight off the crushing claustrophobia she felt as the sea of people closed around her. The crowd seemed to surge away from where she wanted to be, carrying her back towards the bar. She was never going to make it to the DJ booth in time to warn her dad. An idea flashed across her mind.

Something Ian had told her about how he got through

the crowds at festivals and concerts. She put her hand against her mouth and began making tortured retching noises.

"Oh my God, I'm going to be sick... I'm going to be..."

The crowd parted before her as if she were Moses standing before the Red Sea. Where there had been nothing but a seething, impenetrable mass of humanity a moment before, there was now a clear path forming as people frantically pushed themselves away from the obviously distressed girl. Within seconds she had cleared the dancefloor and stood before the DJ booth. Unfortunately there was no sign of either her father or Ian. A pungent cloud of marijuana smoke hung in the air above the console. Mandy peered around the corner to find her father and Ian passing a joint between them and the Ukrainian DJ.

Her dad coughed when he noticed her there. "Oh, Mandy... I didn't see you there... I was just... erm... I mean... this is Gary... your mum and I went to school with him and we were just... erm... your mother's not there, is she?"

Mandy threw her arms around her father and let the tears come in great, choking sobs. She felt her father's strong arms around her. Holding her. Keeping her safe the way he had done when she was younger. It was an illusion of safety, but one she grasped and clung to for dear life. No one would be able to hurt her now she was with her daddy. He'd hold her and protect her from everything and everyone that meant to do her harm. Only that wasn't true. It wasn't true at all. It was her turn to try and keep him safe. Save all of them. She

221

pushed herself away and wiped her tear-streaked face on the sleeve of her top.

Her father looked confused. "Steady on, Mand. What's the matter? Did your mum go overboard about you being here?"

Mandy shook her head and forced the words out through a throat that felt too small. "No... Dad... you... you need to listen to me. There was a man outside. He... attacked us. Mum's... I mean... Mum is gone. He killed her with a knife."

Her father's face fell as he processed what he'd just been told. He got to his feet and began to move out from behind the DJ booth. Mandy grabbed his arm with both hands.

"Dad, where are you going?"

"I need to get your mother. If she's been hurt... she's going to need help."

Mandy tightened her grip, and her voice rose to a yell. "Dad – you're not listening to me. That man stabbed her and then a werewolf tore him to pieces. You could hear them howling outside. The bouncer locked all the doors before any got in."

He looked uncertain. "But... your mum. I need to..."

Mandy threw her arms around her father again, letting the tears flow. "Dad, she's gone. And if any of those things get in here, we'll be next."

***

Anna pushed her way through the crowds, back to where Amy and Kat had been. Amy had pulled some bloke who, while a bit weird, had seemed cute enough. She'd just wished that Amy would stop calling him tastyface. You'd think she'd never snogged anyone before. Kat had not really recovered from her whitey earlier in the evening, and the drinks hadn't helped. She'd been sick at least twice and, as predicted, her makeup had slithered off her face until she looked like a demented clown. She didn't know what to think of Mandy's story. Her friend had been a pain in the arse all night, but she wasn't one to make something like that up for a joke, and the bloody handprints on her top lent credence to her story. If she discovered later that this really was some kind of wind up, she'd beat the shit out of Mandy – for ruining her top if nothing else. In the meantime, she decided it was better to be safe than sorry. Besides, once the power had gone out, the bar had stopped serving drinks, so there really wasn't much point in staying here. At least at home she wouldn't have to contend with random blokes grabbing her arse in the darkness. The whole night had been a bit shit really, and Anna was ready to pull the plug on it. New Year's Eve had been something of a letdown, all things considered.

She pushed her way past two pissheads and was not in the least surprised to find Amy locked in a passionate embrace with the bloke. Anna struggled to remember his name – Matty? Was that it? Beyond his thick Glaswegian accent, she struggled to remember much about him at all. She tapped him on the shoulder and tried to prise the two of them apart.

"Amy, put him down. I need to talk to you. Mandy's gone

off the deep end. She reckons towns full of werewolves."

Amy didn't seem too inclined to listen to her, and the sucking, slurping noises coming from the pair of them was making her feel sick. She felt a surge of annoyance and shoved her hands between them, using all of her strength to separate Amy and Matty.

Her hands were wet. Warm and sticky. She didn't want to think about how much drool would have been needed to get their clothes that soggy. She turned Amy around and felt her heart lurch in her chest. She tried to scream, but the sound caught in her throat. Where Amy's pretty face had been, there was only a bloodstained skull. The bone had deep gouges carved into it and Amy's beautiful blue eyes stared out of the gore at nothing. Her friend's body stood on its own for a second, then fell to the floor in a crumpled heap. Anna couldn't help herself. She turned to Matty and was met by a visage from the depths of hell. The boy's eyes were flat, reflective disks in the flickering candlelight. His face was distorted – the bone had stretched out into a snout filled with row upon row of razor sharp fangs. A mass of bloody flesh and muscle dangled from between those terrible jaws. They crunched once, then swallowed. Matty brought up a clawed hand and wiped his mouth. "Aye, she wasnae wrong. She did have a tasty face."

Anna's voice returned and she let out a scream of abject horror. A scream that turned into a wet gurgle as Matty's talons flashed out and slashed her throat open down to the bone.

***

Kat felt a warm splash across her face and wrinkled her nose. When the power had gone out she'd been relieved. The flashing lights and pulsating music had done nothing to stop her head from spinning or to alleviate the persistent, bubbling nausea that had plagued her all night. She never should have taken Amy's spliff. Her mouth felt gritty, her teeth coated with the acrid remnants of her evening meal and regurgitated alcohol. But, for the first time in hours, she was beginning to feel more like herself again. She'd try to persuade Mandy and Anna to take her home soon. The thought of her soft, clean bed brought a smile to her face. Then the warm spray continued and a terrible thought occurred to her. What if someone was taking a piss in the dark corner where she lay and simply hadn't noticed her? Her eyes snapped open and she immediately wished they'd stayed closed.

Anna slumped to her knees before her, her eyes wide and her mouth opening and closing like a goldfish out of water. Her hands were clasped to her throat and jets of thick, dark liquid sprayed out from between her fingers. Then Anna fell backwards into a pool of what could only be blood, beside Amy's faceless corpse. The spurts of liquid became smaller and smaller, until they finally stopped altogether. Kat's hand flew to her mouth as her stomach lurched. *No,* she thought. *I can't. God, Anna – Amy – I'm so sorry.* Kat had thought that her previous bouts of illness had emptied her stomach. She was amazed to discover she'd been very wrong about that. A jet of alcohol and partly digested food erupted from her mouth, spraying the mutilated corpses of her friends

225

with what looked like a thick, foul smelling vegetable broth. Kat fell to her knees, only vaguely registering the warm liquid oozing through her tights, and let out a strangled sob of misery. Then something approaching awareness leaked through the alcoholic haze clouding her mind. She looked up and saw something out of her worst nightmares.

The boy that Amy had been getting off with was convulsing beside her. At first she thought he might have fallen prey to whatever had killed her friends. Then she noticed he wasn't wearing any clothes, and that his body cracked and shifted as spasms racked him. She could hear the bones snapping and reforming. Even as drunk as she was, Kat knew exactly what was taking place before her. Panic threatened to overwhelm her, and for a second, she froze, caught between her fight or flight response. Unsurprisingly, flight won that particular battle incredibly quickly, and Kat scrambled to her feet, pushing her way through the crowds towards the heavy wooden doors that led to the exit.

Kat could hear the cries of alarm from behind her as other people realised what was happening. Fear surged through the crowd, transmitting from person to person like a virus. The sounds of animal rage were clearly audible behind her now and the patrons of the *Sandpiper* charged towards the exit as one, pushing Kat forward like a surfer riding a wave. She slammed face first into the wooden doors at the far side of the dancefloor, tasting the metallic tang of blood in her mouth. There was no escaping the forward momentum of the panicked crowd, and she knew if she slipped she'd be trampled underfoot by two hundred and fifty people desperately trying to escape the monster in their midst. The exit was before them – the door closed. And something else. A pair of green eyes shone out from the blackness by the door and a guttural feral snarl echoed out. There was another creature guarding the exit to ensure no one escaped. Kat tried to push her way back through the surging mass of humanity – she cried out, pleading for them to turn around. Her cries were joined by those beside her who had seen the monster at the end of the corridor, but it was no good. They were forced forward towards the huge, snarling werewolf. Kat didn't even see the attack. She just felt a sharp pain across her abdomen, followed by a horrible sensation of unravelling as her innards spilled from her stomach cavity onto the ground. The air stank of blood and shit. Worse; those behind began catching their feet in her guts, tripping over them, hastening the *emptying* of her.

Don't do that! I need those! She thought absently, the shock momentarily numbing her mind, the pain not yet properly registering. Then the strength left her legs and she was dragged down by her intestines to the forest of pounding feet behind her. Bodies slipped against her. A man stumbled, and as he put his hand out to arrest his fall, it vanished into the wet cavity of Kat's stomach. She was beyond pain. Her breath wouldn't come, and although she felt the urge to vomit again, she had no stomach. She opened her mouth to cry out for mercy – for someone to notice and save her from the terrible fate. Then a heavy, steel toe capped boot came down on her head, forcing the bone of her nose deep into her brain, and Kat, mercifully, knew no more.

***

The *Sandpiper* erupted in chaos. People ran screaming from the horror stalking across the dancefloor towards them. The creature seemed to be in no rush, circling the outskirts of the panicked crowd in the same way a sheepdog would direct its flock. Anyone who came too close was mauled – legs torn out from underneath them with the beast's savage claws and quickly shredded into bloody ribbons before the werewolf resumed its herding.

Mandy crouched behind the DJ booth with her father, Ian and the famous Ukrainian DJ (whose real name was apparently Gary). Her father's face was drawn and grey while Gary took a very long drag on the last remains of his joint and suppressed a cough before stubbing the roach out on the carpet. Ian's eyes darted from left to right, the nervous tension visible in his every action. He leaned closer and whispered, "We've got to get out of here. That thing's going to slaughter everyone."

Mandy shook her head. "There are more of them outside. I heard them howling."

Her father rubbed her arm. "No, Ian's right. Even if there are more outside, they'll be going for the people in the market square. At least we'll stand a chance. If we stay here, we're dead."

Gary looked up with red-rimmed eyes. "Chelfyn, mate, I'm right there with you, but the fire escape is on the other side of the dancefloor and the front door's a bit congested right now. How the fuck are we going to get past that thing? All the exits are blocked."

Mandy risked a glance over the top of the console,

immediately regretting it. The werewolf had its jaws clamped around a young man's throat and was shaking its head from side to side like a dog worrying a rag. The man's screams were little more than a strangled gurgle, drowned out by the cries of terror from the other people in the pub. She dropped her head back down before the monster saw her, an idea forming. "If we can't get through the exits, why don't we make our own? Mate, how heavy is that record box?"

Gary looked confused as he glanced at the aluminium flight case. "I don't know? Heavy. It's full of vinyl. 20 kilos maybe. Why?"

Ian looked at his younger sister, grinned and kissed her on the forehead. "Plenty heavy enough to go through one of those windows, then? Dad, grab the other side of it. Gary, try and block that doorway up with some chairs or something. Anything to slow it down. It'll be after us the second the glass goes."

Mandy helped Gary create a makeshift barricade with a trestle table propped up with a couple of wooden chairs. As barriers went, it was terrible. But it was the best they could manage under the circumstances. Ian and her father exchanged worried glances, then both bent to pick up the record box. A shadow fell over them, blotting out the candlelight. Mandy looked up and screamed as the werewolf crouched on top of the DJ booth and snarled. One huge taloned paw scraped against the record decks, while the other flexed against one of the mixers in anticipation. Mandy sensed the creature bunching its muscles for the attack. The monstrous beast growled, and hot, rank saliva sprayed Mandy's face. She could see the bloodstained enamel daggers that would end her life; feel the rancid breath on her face. She wanted to close her eyes and look away, but couldn't. Somehow the thought of waiting in darkness for those teeth to tear her flesh apart was worse than seeing it happen.

A whoosh of air above Mandy's head. A screamed war cry that sounded something like "Fucking have some ya bastard!" A yelp of pain and shock as Gary smashed a bottle of Newcastle Brown ale into the werewolf's slavering maw like a club, shattering the monster's fangs into fragments of bloody bone.

Ian looked at his father. "Now!" he yelled, and both men got to their feet, swinging the aluminium flight case at the large plate glass window. The record box crashed through the glass, large sheets exploding into vicious splinters that rained down across Mandy and her family.

A terrified scream rang out and suddenly Gary wasn't standing next to Mandy anymore. She only caught a glimpse of his trainers as he was dragged over the top of the DJ console. Mandy reached out instinctively, trying to grab the man. Save him from the fate that he'd saved her from, but she was too late by far.

Her father grabbed her by the shoulders. "Mandy, listen to me. If we get separated, then get to the church. Get to your Auntie Sharon and Matthew. She'll keep you safe."

Mandy nodded. Ian kicked the last of the glass shards out of the window frame and hoisted his sister up. She looked back into the bar and saw that Gary's assault had galvanised the patrons of The *Sandpiper* into action. Many of them lay dead or dying on the dancefloor, but many more were taking the attack to their assailants.

Men leapt on top of the snarling creature with nothing but chair legs, pool cues and broken bottles for weapons. The werewolf was a brutal killing machine, but it was badly outnumbered, and the townsfolk of High Moor had a certain reputation within the area. The town was not considered to be a rough shithole for nothing. Astonishingly, fuelled by terror, rage and alcohol, they seemed to be winning. One man speared a broken pool cue through the back of the thrashing monster. Another man wrapped his arms around the beast's neck and was trying to saw its head off with a broken bottle, despite some grievous injuries.

Something collided with Mandy, sending her flying back into the pub. Something huge, heavy and covered in thick, foul smelling fur. Another werewolf, presumably stalking the outside of the pub to prevent anyone escaping, had hurled itself at her and now stood on her chest, vicious claws penetrating her clothes, pinning her to the floor. It snarled at her and brought its fangs to her face. The beast's lips curled back, spraying her with blood-flecked foam. Mandy closed her eyes. Then suddenly, the weight was gone. She opened her eyes and saw her father and Ian wrestling with the huge, enraged werewolf on the dancefloor. Others moved to help, brandishing makeshift weapons. She cried out, "No! Dad! Ian!"

Her father looked at her and yelled, "Go!" Then the creature's jaws closed around his head and crunched down, turning his skull into a jellied mass of blood, bone and brains.

The monstrous beast vanished beneath a sea of drunken, enraged northerners, lashing out with anything they could get their hands on, and failing that, using their fists and feet. Mandy couldn't see Ian anymore, and knew she couldn't wait to find out if he was still alive or not. She'd lost both of her parents in the space of half an hour. She needed to get away, get to Auntie Sharon and Matthew. Ignoring the pain from her wounds, Mandy vaulted onto the window frame, then leaped out into the night.

She groaned as her bare feet plunged into the snow. Shards of glass from the broken window stabbed into her, but the cold soon numbed the pain. She knew that she couldn't stay here. Pain and fear surged inside her, but she blocked them out, concentrating on the present. The church was normally less than a ten minute walk from here – a journey to the top of the high street, then up the hill for half a mile until the narrow terraced houses opened out to the green expanse around the old stone church and the hall behind it. From the screams emanating from the high street and market square, however, she knew that wasn't an option. Instead, keeping low to the ground she hurried across the road into the housing estate beyond.

Despite the lack of lighting, the snow made the ground glow with enough ambient light to allow her to make out some details of her surroundings. The door of each house lay open, the locks shattered and the wooden frames splintered. Whatever had happened in High Moor that evening had clearly not been confined to the pub and the town centre. The werewolves had gone from door to door, slaughtering people as they slept or celebrated the New Year. Occasionally she would come across dark patches in the snow where some unfortunate had met their end, but mostly the streets were pristine, white and empty. Her ears strained for any sign of life as she scurried from garden to garden. A telltale crunch of snow that would indicate a survivor or a lycanthrope stalking her, but the town was silent save for the occasional distant scream. The monsters had done their work and moved on, spreading out from the town centre to the outlying houses like ripples in a pond.

It took her almost half an hour to make her way through side streets and gardens to the church hall. Like everywhere else, the door swung open on the frigid breeze and the interior was dark, cavernous and silent. She stepped inside, expecting to be attacked at any moment. The floor was wet and sticky, with soft things squelching between her frozen toes. The werewolves had obviously been here as well and did not appear to have spared anyone. The last shred of hope that Mandy had been clinging to evaporated. Her Auntie Sharon. Her little brother. Dead. Slaughtered like her mum, her dad and Ian. She fell to her knees and began to sob, the wall inside her crumbling and the emotions flooding out. She was alone. Everyone she knew and loved had been killed. Torn apart for no reason she could understand. At that moment, Mandy longed to join them. Wanted death more than anything else in the world. She didn't even react when she sensed something behind her. A presence in the darkness. She closed her eyes and waited for the end. Instead she felt the light touch of a hand on her shoulder.

"Mandy, love. It's Sharon. Come with me. I'll keep you safe."

Mandy let herself be led towards the basement door, her

mind numb. She only knew one thing. She wasn't safe. She would never be safe again. The puncture wounds from the werewolf's claws on her shoulder guaranteed that.

Chapter 16

1st January 2009. Lindholme Detention Centre, Doncaster. 06:50

John crouched before the small electric fire and tried to warm himself. The siren had sounded at 6:30 as usual – apparently Colonel Richards didn't believe in allowing his guests a lie in on New Year's Day – and he'd showered and dressed without enthusiasm. The water had only been lukewarm, and the temperature in the barrack building hovered just above freezing. He glanced from the threadbare curtains at the floodlit compound and sighed when he saw it was covered in snow. He hated snow at the best of times, and the flimsy gym shoes provided by the military wouldn't do much to keep his feet warm and dry as he waited in the line for breakfast. He considered skipping the meal, but the growling in his stomach persuaded him otherwise. As rank as it was, and despite the fact it was laden with narcotics, he knew he needed to keep his strength up. The rations they were given were not quite small enough to make them starve, but they were definitely enough to keep the prisoners weak. He'd already had to tighten his belt two notches in the short time he'd been here. If he went without too many meals, he wouldn't have the strength to leave his bunk, let alone defend himself if some of his pack friends decided to challenge him again. No sooner had the thought flashed across his mind than the door to his hut opened. He snapped his head round to find Kasha, her husband Dmitri, Sonja – Sophia's mother, and two large, heavily muscled men entering and closing the door behind them.

John got to his feet, eyes searching desperately for something he could use as a weapon, knowing it was no use. The beds were bolted to the floor. He supposed he could hit one of them with the electric fire, but in reality, the only weapons he had were his fists, feet and, if it really came to it, claws and teeth. There was no way he would go down without a fight, even if it meant a Hellfire missile obliterating the hut and everyone else in it.

Kasha stepped forward, her hands raised. "We did not come here to fight you, Simpson. Relax."

John's muscles remained tensed. "Really? Then what are you doing here? You've all made it perfectly clear that you want me dead. Forgive me if I'm struggling to believe you've all come for a friendly chat."

Sonja joined the other woman, while the three men remained by the door. "I wanted to thank you. For what you did. For persuading them to let us change. Some of the others are angry, but they are complying, and even those among us who are unhappy with changing in a cell at least know it's the only way we'll survive the full moon. You saved us. You saved my daughter." She paused and looked back to Dmitri, who gave a small nod. "We wanted you to know that there won't be any more trouble for you. Not from us. Not anymore."

John unclenched his fists, but remained tense. "Really? It's that simple. We're all best friends now? Sorry if I have trouble accepting that."

Sonja walked across the room, took John's hand in hers and kissed it. "Believe it. As a mother you have my gratitude. Dmitri and Kasha have spoken to the others.

236

But you must be honest with us. Sophie says that you are not a moonstruck. Is this true? Because if you are, then your efforts to save us will be for nothing. In a few weeks, you'll change and kill every one of us. We need to know. We need to be certain that you are not a threat."

John looked into Sonja's eyes and saw no trace of a lie in them. "I used to be. Marie taught me to control the change. When I do turn I'm... well, I'm not like the rest of you. I think my body got so used to being in that form that it's what I become now. But I can think. I'm rational. I'm just... different."

The woman nodded. "You may be different, but you have more in common with us than with those animals," she spat on the floor, "that cage us. That take us away and experiment on us. It's time we all accepted that."

The tension left John's shoulders and he nodded. While he was not about to take this change of heart from his fellow prisoners at face value, all he could really do was play along, hope for the best and watch for any sign of betrayal. In the short term, at least it might make his life a little easier. At least until one of his new friends cut his throat while he slept. "Okay. I'll believe you. Not saying I completely trust you, but I'm willing to put the past few days behind us." He looked at Sonja and held out his hand. "Fresh start?"

Sonja clasped John's hand in hers and shook it. "Yes. Fresh start."

The other pack members joined her, each shaking John's hand in turn. Then Dmitri put his huge hand on John's shoulder. "They say you were with Mikhail. When you were captured. Is that true?"

"Yeah. We broke into the base where they were keeping him. Marie, Daniel and I. They got me, but I think the others got away. I hope so, anyway."

Dmitri smiled and clapped John on the back. "That is good. Very good. We can only pray that they managed to prevent Krysztof doing something stupid."

The loudspeakers crackled into life. "All prisoners must remain in their quarters until further notice. Any deviation from this order will be met with lethal force. I repeat. All prisoners must stay in their quarters until instructed otherwise."

Kasha, Sonja and Dmitri exchanged worried glances. John moved to the window and pulled the curtain aside. It was still dark outside, but the floodlights illuminated the compound, casting a glare from the unblemished snow. The main gates were open and rows of armed soldiers took up position inside with their weapons raised. Behind them, John could make out a line of heavy lorries, each fitted with a crane and carrying a Portacabin. The trucks made their way to the exercise area and began unloading the temporary buildings while more soldiers made their way into the compound and took up position.

Sonja stood beside him. "What is happening?"

John turned back to the pack werewolves and shook his head. "Nothing good. I think we're going to have some new arrivals."

1st January 2009. Underhill Military Base, Sub-Level Two. 15:40

Phil wriggled on the hard mattress, struggling to get comfortable. Ever since his failed escape attempt he'd been confined to his room on Colonel Richards' orders. He was escorted to and from the mess by armed guards, and he'd been reduced to using a bucket in the corner of what he now considered to be his cell as a toilet. That meant, given the reaction the mess food was having on his stomach, that the atmosphere in the small, claustrophobic room was rarely pleasant. He thumbed through the paperback he'd been given without much enthusiasm. A bloody horror novel – and about fucking werewolves at that. As if he wanted to have anything to do with werewolves again. Clearly his military captors had a warped sense of humour. He glanced at his watch and sighed. Another two hours before he was taken for whatever slop was served up as his evening meal, then back into solitary confinement until morning. He dreaded to think what Sharon must be thinking. He'd not spoken to her since Christmas Eve. She must be going out of her mind.

The sound of a key turning in the lock made him sit up, and he put the book down on the bed. A break from the tedium of his daily routine was welcome, but he also knew that if someone was bothering to visit him, it probably wasn't good news. Of course, the Colonel might have decided to let him go, but he wasn't holding out much hope.

The door opened and Paul Patterson, dressed in full combat gear, stepped into the room and locked the door behind him. His face was pale and his expression pained. Phil's hands gripped the side of the bed. "What's this? Come to put me out of my misery? Colonel Richards sent you to tie up loose ends?"

Paul leaned the weapon against the door. He didn't say anything at first, as if he couldn't find the words. "Phil... I..."

"What? What's happened?"

Paul pulled out the red plastic chair and sat down. Phil couldn't help but notice his former colleague's hands had a distinct tremble to them, and a sheen of sweat glistened on his forehead. Paul paused, taking a deep breath as if to steel himself, then began speaking.

"Phil. There's been an attack. Christ, more than an attack - a fucking slaughter. God knows how they did it, but..."

Phil felt his heart drop through his stomach. He didn't want to hear the rest of what Paul had to say. He already knew.

"It was High Moor, Phil. I was on the QRF team that went in, but by the time we got there it was all over. They cut the town off, took out the power and mobile phone masts, and then went door to door. Fuck... I've never seen anything like it. It was... monstrous."

Phil got to his feet and grabbed the younger man by his webbing. "What about Sharon? Are you telling me my fucking wife's dead, Paul? Are you telling me that the military and the government just let a pack of werewolves wipe out an entire bloody town and kill my wife?"

Paul shook his head. "No, Sharon's alive. I found her myself. She was in the basement of a church hall with a bunch of kids. Saved them by all accounts."

The strength drained out of Phil and he collapsed back on the bed, tears of relief streaming down his cheeks. "Oh thank God. Thank fucking Christ. When you said... Jesus."

Paul sat down beside his former boss and put his hand on his shoulder. "Phil, it's not all good news. She got scratched in the attack. Most of the survivors were scratched or bitten. She's infected, Phil. Sharon's a werewolf."

He turned his head to Paul, lips curling into a snarl. "Where is she, Paul. Where have they taken my wife?"

Paul sagged. "Lindholme. They've taken all the survivors to the internment camp at Lindholme."

Phil got to his feet. "Then get off your arse. You're taking me to that camp so I can have a chat with Colonel bloody Richards."

1st January 2009. Lindholme Detention Centre, Doncaster. 17:35

Sharon stared out of the bus window at the snow-covered landscape, trying to make sense of what had happened, and what was going to happen. Matthew had finally fallen asleep, fatigue and grief getting the better of the boy. He sat between her and Mandy, his head resting against her arm. Mandy hadn't said a word for hours and just stared ahead. Any attempt at conversation had resulted in grunted responses. She couldn't imagine what the girl had gone through. From what little Mandy had said, it had been appalling. Worse even than what she and Matthew had survived in the church hall.

Sharon had broken down in tears when the army had found them that morning. The relief had almost been too much to bear. That one of the people through the door had been Phil's colleague, Paul Patterson, had reduced her to a weeping mess. Paul had escorted her and the children from the basement towards an army truck. She'd done her best to ignore the carnage in the church hall. Most of the corpses were unrecognisable, but the glance she'd taken had burned itself into her consciousness. So much blood – made worse when she recognised pieces. A sweater worn by one of the children. What remained of Tonia and Angela, their mouths open in silent screams. The wide eyed look of anguish and terror on what remained of little Bella. She hadn't allowed herself to feel at the time, making herself strong for the sake of the children. Telling them not to look and to keep their eyes on the floor instead. A few wretched sobs and sniffles from her charges had told her that some of those children had ignored her, and had seen things that would haunt them for the rest of their lives.

The town itself had been just as bad. Every door hanging open with claw marks carved into the wood and the frames splintered. Windows shattered, some with ruined corpses impaled on the glass. The snow had long since stopped falling, but it seemed that almost everywhere she looked there were red stains on the pristine white blanket covering the town.

The soldiers had taken everyone to the town hall, where

medics had dressed injuries and handed out blankets along with hot cups of sweet tea. The air was filled with the sounds of orders being shouted and the almost constant hum of helicopters landing and departing from the market square. There were so few people there. The town of High Moor had thousands of residents. Thousands. Yet, by her reckoning, there were fewer than two hundred people gathered in the building, and most of them bore terrible injuries. A man beside her had a blood-soaked field dressing over what was left of his face. Others were even worse. At least three people had died from their wounds before an officer informed them they were going to be moved to a temporary refugee facility near Doncaster, and those who were able to walk had been shepherded onto four buses. Four buses holding all that was left of the town of High Moor. It seemed impossible. The sort of tragedy you saw on the news but never imagined it could happen here, in such an ordinary little town. A place that should have been a safe environment for families to raise their children but instead became a slaughterhouse.

She glanced around at the others on the bus. No one was speaking, although a few women wept softly. Most of the other passengers were silent, with haunted expressions that she was sure mirrored her own. The only hope she held out was that Phil would be waiting for her at the other end of the journey. All she wanted right now was to feel her husband's arms around her, holding her close and telling her everything was going to be all right. That they would be able to prevent the wounds she'd received from turning her into a savage monster like the things that had killed so many last night. She couldn't bear the thought of becoming *that*.

243

After everything that had happened in the last few months – from what happened to Olivia, Paul's family and now Helen, Chelfyn and Ian – it seemed that almost everyone she knew and loved had fallen prey to the teeth and claws of something that, up until November, had only existed in horror movies. She'd kill herself first.

Sharon shook her head, trying to banish the dark thoughts. She couldn't think like that. She needed to be strong for Mandy and Matthew. She was the only family they had left and couldn't afford to lose hope. Hope was the only thing that any of them could cling to anymore.

The convoy of buses and military vehicles turned off the motorway onto a long straight road surrounded by flat, featureless fields that stretched off as far as Sharon could see. It felt strange for there not to be any hills on the horizon. She'd spent most of her life in County Durham, and the openness of the countryside here made her feel somehow lost and exposed. As if the flat expanse of farmland went on forever. There was almost no other traffic on the roads, and the small villages they passed through seemed deserted. Cars were parked in driveways with a covering of snow across their roof and bonnets. Only the warm glow from behind closed curtains gave any indication of life. She imagined the families warm and safe behind those windows and wished that she was one of them. There with the people she loved instead of being driven to a refugee camp in the middle of nowhere.

The buses slowed and Sharon spotted a sign on the carriageway. HM Prison Lindholme. A small coal of fear ignited in her stomach and she felt her shoulders tighten, although she tried not to let it show. Mandy didn't seem to notice and continued staring into the middle distance, although Sharon couldn't fail to see the tears dampening her niece's cheeks. She reached across and put her hand on the girl's arm, making her flinch. "Mandy, love. It's going to be alright. I'm here for you both and I'm not going anywhere."

Mandy turned her head and gazed at her with hollow, empty eyes, then turned her head back to the front of the bus without uttering a word. Sharon felt her heart break a little more, wishing she could do or say something to help her niece, but knowing that there was nothing she could do but be there for her when the walls inside her finally crumbled and the pain and grief came flooding out.

Their bus arrived at a huge set of steel gates topped with razor wire. The gates swung open and Sharon's heart sank further. The compound was filled with armed soldiers, with sniper towers every two hundred meters along the perimeter. A series of low brick buildings sat near the entrance, with rows of Portacabins and concrete barrack blocks behind them. A soldier with a pair of glowsticks directed the buses to the right, away from the entrance, where they parked side by side. Armed troops flanked the vehicles, weapons raised. Then the doors hissed open and they were instructed by the driver to step out.

The cold bit into Sharon's face as she filed out with the rest of the passengers. Matthew had grumbled and called for his mother as he'd woken, but now stood next to Sharon, gripping onto her injured leg so tightly that it was all she could do not to cry out in pain. Her twisted ankle no longer seemed to be bothering her, but she didn't want to think too hard about what that meant. The blanket she'd been given at the town hall did little to keep the chill wind from bringing her arms out in goosebumps. More soldiers arrived, flanking the survivors of High Moor, while others arranged themselves in outward facing ranks, crouching down and pointing their weapons at the concrete barrack blocks. A man dressed in an immaculately pressed army uniform, accompanied by a young, dark haired woman, marched to the front of the crowd.

"Good evening. My name is Colonel Richards, and this is Doctor Rose Fisher. I apologise for the surroundings, but given the short notice, I'm afraid we will have to improvise as best we can. You will each be shown to your accommodation shortly, and then Doctor Fisher and her staff will assess each person's injuries. In the meantime, I would ask that you remain in your assigned accommodations. There are other residents in this facility who I would not recommend mixing with. I should also regretfully point out that, as of now, you are all in quarantine, and any attempts to escape from this facility will result in swift and decisive action. Any questions you may have will be answered in due course. In the meantime, I suggest you all make yourselves as comfortable as possible."

As the Colonel turned and walked away, and the soldiers began ushering them towards the Portacabins, Sharon felt that small ember of hope she'd frantically clung on to fade and die.

Chapter 17

2ⁿᵈ January 2009. Lindholme Detention Centre, Doncaster. 10:45

Rose adjusted the stack of folders in her arm and rapped twice on the door to Colonel Richards' office. The military had taken over a wing of the prison, as well as the administration centre, much to the displeasure of the warden. The regular prisoners had been shipped out to other facilities and the only people she saw now were wearing olive green army uniforms. The military could be a slow, ponderous machine at times, but when the shit hit the fan, they could operate with surprising speed. Not that this was much comfort to her. She was still reeling from the events of the day before. Everyone was. An atmosphere of fear had gripped the country. The tabloids were busy spreading panic, but in all honesty, they didn't need to. That the worst terrorist incident on record had happened in an insignificant little town like High Moor meant no one felt safe. Everyone was potentially in danger, not just those in the big cities like London or Manchester. The werewolves could not have picked a better target. The fact that the monsters responsible for the assault had then vanished without a trace did nothing to calm the public. Already, the papers were screaming for blood – for some reaction to the atrocity. She shuddered to think what that response might be. But for now, she had a bigger problem to deal with. She rapped again, feeling impatience bubble up within her. This time, the Colonel's voice responded with an abrupt "Enter." She pushed open the door, holding the folders under one arm and saluted her commanding

247

officer.

The Colonel was reading something on the antique PC in front of him and didn't look up as he waved her towards a wooden chair with faded, frayed fabric arms. "Please take a seat, Doctor Fisher. I'll be with you in a moment."

Rose sat down and placed her folders on the desk. The office had belonged to one of the middle managers, and Colonel Richards hadn't even bothered to remove the former occupant's personal effects. Books on accounting theory sat on dusty shelves, along with several photographs of a severe looking man, a mousy woman and two red-faced, overweight children. Stacks of paperwork were piled in a corner. Only the desk had been cleared; a new plastic in-tray placed on one corner, already overflowing with documents stamped *Top Secret*. A lingering smell of tobacco smoke seemed to ooze from the furniture and the walls. Clearly the former occupant had believed that the smoking ban in public buildings only applied to other people.

The Colonel looked up from the computer screen and sighed. "Are those the casualty reports on the High Moor refugees?"

She nodded. "Yes. Almost all of them have injuries. Most are clearly the work of lycanthropes. Others... well, my findings are inconclusive. Even those with obvious bite or claw marks are claiming they cut themselves on broken glass while escaping. I can't say I blame them, really. But some of the others might be telling the truth. I suggest we remove those without injuries and the borderline cases to another part of the facility for observation."

"Out of the question. You've seen how things are here. They are in the most secure location as it stands. We can't take the risk of moving them. If even one of them is infected and turns, the damage they could inflict doesn't bear thinking about."

Rose leaned forward in her chair. "Some of them are children, Colonel. There are a number of them that I've examined from head to toe and there's not a scratch on them. Surely you can't mean to keep them locked up with the others?"

Colonel Richards' face was an immobile mask, his eyes cold and emotionless. "My orders stand, Doctor. We absolutely cannot risk any of them getting out of here, or running rampant through this facility. We simply don't know enough about how this contagion spreads."

"We know it spreads through scratches and bites. That's it. If there's an incident, those children will be slaughtered. We have to move them somewhere else."

"Doctor Channing tells me he's isolated a viral component, but is unclear as to exactly how it's transmitted, or whether there is a chance it could mutate and become airborne or transmissible through contact. Just think about the ramifications of that for a moment, Doctor. My orders stand."

Rose's stomach did somersaults at the thought, but she fought to retain her composure. "If that was going to happen, don't you think it would have happened before now? These things have been around for hundreds, if not thousands of years. Everything we've seen - everything we've been told - backs that up. The condition is transmitted by a bite or scratch from the infected."

The Colonel fixed Rose's gaze and she felt herself wilt a little beneath it. "I have very strict orders on the matter, Doctor. I am passing those orders to you and I expect them to be obeyed. To the letter. Am I making myself clear?"

Rose felt the fight drain out of her. "Yes, Sir. I understand. But what happens on the full moon, Sir? Everything we've been told says that those infected refugees will turn on the eleventh. And they won't be like the pack ones. They'll be like John Simpson, if I understand matters correctly."

That got a response from the Colonel. His marble facade cracked for a fraction of a second to reveal something of the emotions beneath. She was sure she saw fear in her superior's eyes, but it vanished as soon as it appeared, and the walls came down once more. "As I understand it, there's nothing we can do about that. They will change on the next full moon, and won't be able to initiate the change in a controlled manner. When that happens, we will simply have to be prepared to handle matters."

"What do you mean? Handle matters?"

"That, Doctor Fisher, is none of your concern. Circumstances within our chain of command are in flux. I take it that you are aware of the fact a vote of no confidence has been passed against our current government? I fully expect that the leader of the opposition will be sworn into power as an emergency measure in the next few days. He has already been in direct communication with me regarding this, and has outlined a number of measures to deal with things on the eleventh. One thing is certain, however. We shall not allow any of the infected to leave the compound. For any reason. Any medical examinations you feel necessary will be conducted within the confines of the detention facility. Now, if there's nothing else, I'm sure you have things you need to attend to."

Rose got to her feet, feeling sick to her stomach. She was only too aware of what those measures were likely to involve. There was a reason all of the infected were being kept in a relatively confined area. It made extermination that much simpler. She got to the door, then paused and turned around to face her commanding officer. "One more thing, Sir. Where's Steven Wilkinson? I've not seen him since he was transferred here. As his Doctor, I..."

"Mr Wilkinson has been transferred to Doctor Channing's care. He is no longer your concern, Doctor Fisher. Now, if you please, I have other pressing matters to attend to. As do you."

Rose saluted Colonel Richards and let herself out of the room. Her emotions were in turmoil. All of those people. All of those families - after everything they'd been through - had less than two weeks left to live. And Steven Wilkinson... She didn't want to think about what might happen to him in Doctor Channing's care. The man was as much a monster as the things he experimented on. She wiped a single tear from the corner of her eye and did her best to push her emotions down. Something terrible was going to happen, and there wasn't a damn thing she could do about it.

2nd January 2009. Lindholme Detention Centre, Doncaster. 11:17

Matthew Baxter was bored. The last two days had been horrible – the worst he'd ever experienced in his short life. When he thought about his mum and dad, and how he'd never see them again, his throat constricted and he couldn't hold back the tears. But because he saw that Auntie Sharon and Mandy were upset, he did his best not to let his mind travel along that path. The last thing he wanted to do was upset them even more. He was the man of the family now, and he needed to start acting like a big boy if he was going to take care of them. Despite the pain, things had seemed exciting at first, once the danger was over and the monsters had gone away. All of the soldiers, with their guns and helicopters and tanks, had been, quite frankly, awesome, although he'd secretly been disappointed that he'd not had a ride in one of their helicopters or even the big green trucks with canvas sides. Even so, if he didn't think about the other things, this was very cool – like being in a movie. He wanted to tell some of his friends about it and found himself looking forward to telling the story in school. Then he remembered that his friends were mostly dead, along with their parents and his teachers, and again the tears came. The day after, he'd found himself able to focus on the flurry of activity around him, keeping his thoughts on the present and trying to identify the different vehicles or weapons the soldiers used. He'd found enough that was interesting to distract him from the large, empty pain in his chest. Even when they'd been put on the buses and brought here, it had been new – scary, but sort of exciting at the same time. Now though, the novelty had worn off and he was bored. Which made it so much more difficult to keep the sadness at bay. Mandy didn't want to talk to anyone, and the other children on the buses were mostly the same; either that or their mums seemed to have them locked in a permanent death-hug and refused to let them out of their sight, even for a second. There was no TV, no video games, and no comics. Not even any books. As far as Matthew was concerned, this was just cruel and unnecessary punishment.

He looked up from his lumpy, uncomfortable camp bed as two soldiers entered their cabin. They walked all the way down to where he was, and a surge of excitement and guilty terror ran through him. Why did he feel as if he'd done something wrong when he'd just been sitting here, minding his own business? The feeling intensified as the soldiers got closer, replaced in an instant with a strange mixture of relief and disappointment as they stopped by his Auntie Sharon and asked her to come with them. Part of him wanted to go with her, to break up the long hours doing nothing but staring at the walls and listening to people weeping. At least now he had a narrow window of opportunity to relieve his boredom and explore the compound. Maybe even find some more children to play with.

He glanced across to Mandy's bunk, but his older sister lay with her back to him, knees pulled tight against her chest. No one else seemed to be paying any attention, so he slipped from his bed, put on his shoes and jacket, then walked purposefully towards the door that his Auntie Sharon had vanished through a few minutes before. His heart began pounding in his chest as he approached the door and his hands were slick with cold sweat. The temptation to turn around and see if anyone was watching became overwhelming, but he ignored it. He'd learned from Mandy over the years that you could get away with almost anything if you acted as if you were supposed to be doing it. One guilty glance over his shoulder could alert some goody-two-shoes grown up, who'd make him go back to his bed and tell on him to Auntie Sharon. His hand closed around the cold metal of the handle – his heart lurched in his chest and, for a moment, he felt lightheaded – then the cold bite of the January wind stung his cheeks and he was outside, the door clicking closed behind him.

Now that he was out, he felt exposed. Auntie Sharon might come back at any moment, and he really didn't want to get caught right away. There were soldiers outside the gate, and stationed in the towers along the fence, but they didn't bother him. They were the good guys, after all. Just there to make sure that no more monsters could hurt them. His eyes darted around the compound, taking in his surroundings and seeking out anything that seemed interesting. The building he'd just escaped from was modern looking, like a bigger version of the sort of thing you'd see on a construction site. It sat in the middle of a whole lot of identical ones, and he assumed that this was where the other people from the buses had been put. That would be no fun. They'd probably be full of the same crying adults as the one he'd just left. It looked like they'd been put on some sort of exercise yard, like they had at school but a lot bigger. Across the way, there were rows of older, wooden buildings, with a large, official looking brick and concrete structure behind them.

He could make out movement in the older buildings. There were definitely people inside. There was a chance that they would just be other people from the town, but there wasn't much else to do so he decided to take a look. He shoved his hands deep into his pockets and shrunk down inside his jacket to keep the bitter wind off his cheeks, then began marching across the open ground towards the low wooden structures.

The feeling of exposure – of dozens of watchful eyes marking his progress – intensified as he left the shelter of the temporary buildings. He felt an urge to run, but knew that would just draw attention so he forced himself to maintain a steady, even pace. He was almost three quarters of the way across the compound when he noticed a red dot dance briefly in the snow before vanishing. He smiled. His friend Billy had a little laser pointer that he tormented his pet cat with. Or he had, until the cat had brought down the curtains in the living room and knocked a vase over onto the laminate floor. Then Billy's mum had taken it off him. He wondered if maybe Billy was in one of the wooden buildings, and was signalling to him. Someone was. There wasn't any other explanation he could think of for the red laser light. Grinning, he made his way towards the nearest building and pressed himself against the wall. The windows were too high for him to see through. He tried jumping, stretching his neck, but he was still too small. There were definitely sounds from within, though. There were people in the building. He could hear them talking in low whispers and could make out the shuffling of feet. He decided to try something else, and, gripping the window ledge with cold, numb hands, he scrambled against the wall, feet flailing as they searched for something to give

255

him leverage.

The red dot was back. It appeared on the wall beside him, then disappeared again. He creased his brow and turned his head, only to find his world turned red. Just like it had when Billy shone the pointer in his face. That had made him see spots for almost a week and had made his eyes hurt. Instinctively he put his arm over his eyes, just as a pair of strong hands grabbed him and whisked him off his feet.

"Hey, get off! I didn't mean anything. I'm sorry! Don't tell my Auntie Sharon!"

Matthew looked around him. He'd been carried inside the wooden building so quickly, he'd hardly noticed the transition from outdoors to in. An array of faces looked at him with a mixture of surprise and suspicion. The arms released their hold on him and he turned to see a woman, her dirty face wearing an expression that was somewhere between concern and anger - a look he'd seen on his own mother's face on many occasions. He felt the memories try to push their way into his consciousness, but he forced them down. No way did he want to start blubbing in front of these strangers.

The woman gripped his shoulders, and spoke with a thick accent. "My God, boy, are you trying to get yourself killed? Another second and they'd have shot you."

Matthew furrowed his brow. "Shoot me? Who was going to shoot me?"

The woman bent down until she was level with him. "The soldiers. Who else do you think?"

Matthew laughed, the first genuine one since New Year's Eve. "The soldiers are the good guys. They're here to protect us from the monsters. You're just being silly."

The woman turned to look at some of the other people. Matthew couldn't see her expression, but he saw some of those gathered around – another woman around the same age, a man the same age as his dad and an old man with one leg – nod as if in agreement. The woman turned back to him. "What is your name, little one? Why are you here, in this place?"

He beamed and held out his hand. "My name is Matthew Baxter. Pleased to meet you. I don't know why I'm here. They brought us all here after the monsters came. The ones that were left, anyway."

"What monsters? What happened to you, Matthew?"

"They came in the middle of the night. The werewolves. They killed nearly everyone. They..." his voice cracked and tears began streaming down his cheeks, "they killed my mum and dad and Ian..."

He couldn't carry on – giving voice to his pain had suddenly made it all far too real. The woman gathered him in her arms and held him tight until, eventually, the tears stopped. Matthew wiped his nose with his sleeve. His throat felt tight and the empty hole within him had grown into an aching chasm. The others in the room were muttering to each other, and the atmosphere had definitely taken a dark turn that he didn't understand. The expressions on the other people's faces were strained and drawn with worry. The woman brushed the hair back from his eyes. "Why did they bring you here?

257

Did the werewolves hurt you?"

He shook his head. "They didn't hurt me. They did hurt almost everyone else, though. My Auntie Sharon got clawed on the leg, and Mandy on the shoulder. A lot of people were worse though. My Auntie Sharon got me into the cellar before they could eat me."

"Well, it's alright now," the woman said, although there was a strange wavering in her thick accent. "Sophie? This is Matthew. You go play with him while we work out how to get him back to his Auntie Sharon."

A pretty blonde girl, maybe a year or two older than him, pushed her way through the crowd and held out her hand. Matthew felt his cheeks flush. She really was very pretty. He took her hand and she led him back through the sea of adult legs, towards the back of the building. "I'm Sophie, "she smiled at him. "Don't suppose you brought a Nintendo or anything with you?"

He shook his head. "No. I didn't get to bring anything. I've been soooo bored!"

Sophie grinned. "Don't worry, I scrounged a deck of cards from one of the guards. Do you know how to play Fish?"

Matthew returned the smile and nodded. Suddenly his new surroundings didn't seem so bad after all.

2nd January 2009. Lindholme Detention Centre, Doncaster. 11:20

Sharon felt nauseous with fear. Two days ago she

couldn't have imagined that she would ever be in the position of being led at gunpoint to some unknown destination, but here she was, flanked by two armed guards, being marched towards the gates they'd been driven through last night. She turned to the man on her left and said, "Can you tell me what this is about?" but the man just motioned forward with the barrel of his gun and returned her gaze with a look that made her heart lurch. There really was no question in her mind as to what would happen if she gave them any trouble. They would gun her down without a second's hesitation. Then there would be no one to look after Matthew and Mandy. She tried to calm herself and will life into her numb legs. One step after another. Trying to ignore the dancing red beads of laser sights on the snow ahead of her, the sudden ache of her bladder and the urge to lie down on the cold, wet ground and weep.

The journey across the compound seemed to take an eternity. Beyond the gates, the place was a hive of activity. Squads of armed men marched in ranks around the perimeter while others unloaded crates from the olive green Bedford trucks. A helicopter gunship roared overhead, so low that she could feel the downdraft from its rotors. It felt like she was in a war zone. To all intents and purposes, she supposed she was. The werewolves had declared war on the British people and she was at the epicentre of the response, or at least it seemed that way. For all she knew, there could be dozens of places just like this all around the country. She shuddered, the chill of the bitter January morning only partly responsible.

They led her to the main prison complex and ushered

her through a series of heavy steel doors, the unlocking of each accompanied by a loud buzzer and the clank of metal. They walked down long, featureless corridors, past empty offices, until they arrived at what could only be described as a cell. The man she'd spoken to opened the door and motioned for her to go inside. Whatever they'd brought her here for was inside that room. Fighting down a fresh wave of adrenaline, she accepted her fate and stepped inside.

The room was small with no windows; a flickering fluorescent light encased in a reinforced steel cage the only source of illumination. Two armed men stood in the corners of the room, their rifles raised. She registered all of this, but none of it mattered. The only thing in the room that did was the man sitting behind an ancient laminated table in the centre of the room. Phil.

She rushed forward to embrace him, weeks of suppressed emotions surging to the surface. Not knowing whether he was still alive. Wanting nothing more than to be in his arms and have him tell her that everything would be all right. The world slowed down. Phil began to get to his feet, his face concerned but also showing delight and relief. Her heart sang and tears streamed down her face. Then the two soldiers pulled their rifles into their shoulders, aimed them at her and screamed, "Don't move!"

Sharon froze, the joy vanishing in an instant. "I... I don't understand."

The soldier motioned to a plastic chair on the other side of the table from Phil. "If you attempt any form of physical contact, we have orders to open fire. Now sit down. You have five minutes."

Phil turned to the man. "Hey, this is my fucking wife. There's no need for any of this."

"Sir, Colonel Richards' orders were explicit. I suggest you make the most of the four and a half minutes you have left."

Phil muttered a curse under his breath and sat back down. Sharon did the same, doing her best to stop the tears from coming. Phil went to put his hands across the table, an instinctive reaction, then realised what he was doing and pulled them away once more. Sharon's heart broke. In some ways this was even crueller than her confinement. To be so close to the man she loved, but unable to reach out and hold him. If she'd had any doubts as to her status before, they evaporated. She was a prisoner – worse actually – the military looked at her not as a victim or survivor. To their mind she was already a monster, and they would gun her down given the slightest excuse.

"Phil..." she managed through her constricted throat, only too aware of how cracked and strained her voice sounded, "I'm so happy to see you. For so long I thought... I thought you might have been hurt. When they... when they stopped letting us talk I worried that something had happened to you."

Phil's expression was a mixture of impotent rage and concern. "I tried to get away, Love. They didn't need me anymore. I don't think they knew what to do with me, but after everything that happened they just locked me up. It wasn't until... well... you know, that I could convince Colonel Richards to let me see you. God, I wish

I'd brought you to me at the base. I thought you would be safer with Helen. I thought..." Glistening beads of moisture formed at the edges of Phil's eyes. He took a moment to regain his composure before continuing. "How are the kids? Paul told me that Matthew and Mandy were with you. Are they holding up?"

She shook her head. "Mandy hasn't said a word since it happened. Matthew seems alright, but he misses his mam and dad. Bless him, he's putting a brave face on but you can see it in his eyes. Phil... What's going to happen to us? Mandy and I... well, I'm sure they told you that we've been scratched. Matthew though... he's alright. They didn't touch him. He shouldn't be in there with everyone else. It's not safe for him there. Can you speak to the Colonel? Maybe he could stay with you instead. In case..."

Phil nodded. "I'll see what I can do. About everything. It's not right, what they're doing to you. You're all victims in this and they're treating you like..." His face reddened, and Sharon could see that he was doing his best to keep his temper under control. Her heart ached for him. She could see he was in as much pain as she was, but they were separated by the table and the soldier's watchful gaze. Those couple of feet might as well have been a hundred miles.

The soldier who hadn't spoken stepped forward. "Okay, that's it for now. Mr Fletcher, if you would please remain seated. Mrs Fletcher, can you slowly stand up with your hands above your head and face the door."

Sharon did as she was told and very carefully stood with her hands raised. She risked a backwards glance as one of the soldiers moved to the cell door. "I love you, Phil."

Phil managed a smile. "I love you too, pet. I'll see you again soon."

She let herself be led away, tears flowing freely down her cheeks. She couldn't shake the feeling that she'd never see her husband again. They marched her in silence through the cold, featureless corridors, out into the snow and back to the prefabricated buildings. Sharon felt exhausted, her nerves raw and shredded from the experience. All she wanted to do was collapse on her bed and cry, but she knew she couldn't. Not in front of Mandy and Matthew. They'd been through more than enough and she needed to maintain the façade for their sake. She reached the end of her bed and looked up and down the building. Mandy was still staring at the far wall, but there was no sign of Matthew. Panic began to blossom in her stomach. She tried to remain calm, walking slowly up and down the narrow walkway between beds, checking every group to see whether her nephew was among them, and under the metal bunk beds to see if he was hiding from her as a joke. It didn't take long before she came to the inescapable conclusion that Matthew was not here anymore. The cold knot of fear began to turn into something else. Anger. There were fifty people in this building. *Fifty*. And they were all so absorbed in their own personal tragedies that they had, apparently, not thought to watch out for anyone else but themselves. One person in particular should have been taking care of Matthew in her absence. One person whose inattention was no longer even remotely acceptable. She strode over to Mandy's bunk and kicked it. When she spoke, there was no hint of anything but anger in her voice. "Mandy, where the hell is your little brother?"

Mandy seemed dazed, but her eyes focused on her aunt for the first time in two days and there seemed to be some awareness creeping back. "I... I don't know. I thought he was with you?"

"For Christ's sake, Mandy, I know you've been through a lot, but so has everyone else here. If I'm escorted out of the building by armed bloody guards then I expect you to step up and make sure that your brother's alright."

Mandy sat up and looked around the building. "Have you checked everywhere? Did you ask anyone if they've seen him?"

Sharon's cheeks flushed at this. "Of course I've checked everywhere," she snapped, but then walked towards the group closest to the door with Mandy following behind her. She was angry, embarrassed at being called out by her niece for not doing the most obvious thing and actually asking someone if they'd seen him, but most of all, she was worried about what might have happened to Matthew. The soldiers were not there for the protection of the survivors. She knew that now. And she doubted if any of them would think twice at shooting a child. Especially one they considered no longer human.

She stood before the closest bed to the door, where a woman with haunted, empty eyes sat cradling a little girl. "Excuse me, but I can't find my nephew. He's seven years old, with dark brown hair."

The woman moved her head and looked right through Sharon, her mouth hanging slack. After a moment she seemed to wake up a little and said, "Sorry, what?"

"My nephew. He was here before they took me away, but now I can't find him. Have you seen him? Did any soldiers come after I left?"

The other woman seemed confused, as if she had just awoken from a dream. "No... I'm sorry... I wasn't paying attention... where did you say he went?"

Sharon turned away from the woman and projected her voice so that it cut through the silence of the hut. "My nephew, Matthew has gone missing. Did anyone see where he went? He was here twenty minutes ago."

Silence.

She couldn't believe it. In a room full of fifty people, not one of them had paid the slightest attention to what happened to Matthew. "Anyone? Are you saying a seven year old boy just vanished into thin fucking air?"

A small voice spoke from the bed beside her. "He went out to play. I wanted to go as well, but Mummy wouldn't let me."

"He went out to play? On his own? When?"

The little girl, still held fast in her mother's arms, smiled. "Right after the men came for you. He opened the door and went outside." She glared at her mother. "When I asked if I could go with him, Mummy just hugged me so hard I couldn't breathe."

Sharon turned, opened the door and stepped outside. Immediately she saw three red points of light appear on her chest, but she didn't care. "Matthew? Matthew, where are you?"

Mandy appeared beside her. "There – in the snow," she said, pointing to a trail of small footprints leading across the empty yard towards one of the low, wooden buildings.

They set off across the yard, Sharon setting a steady, determined pace, trying to push the knowledge that they were both a finger-twitch away from death out of her mind. The distance to the wooden building seemed vast, the white glare of the snow distorting her sense of perspective. As they arrived at the hut, the door burst open and a woman ushered them inside. "Get inside, quickly, both of you, before they open fire."

The relief as the door closed behind them was palpable, and Sharon realised that her heart was racing. She felt quite nauseous, but also enormously relieved. She looked up to the woman. "I'm looking for my nephew. A little boy called Matthew."

The woman smiled. "It's fine. He's here and he's safe."

"Oh, thank God. If anything had happened to..."

The words dried up in Sharon's throat and she recoiled in absolute horror. The crowd parted and she saw Matthew, but standing beside him, with his hand on her nephew's shoulder, was her worst nightmare. John Simpson. Murderer. Serial killer. Werewolf. Monster.

He raised his hands. "Look, Sharon, the things you've read about me in the papers might not be completely accurate. I'm not going to hurt you, or your nephew. But we need to talk. Everyone's life depends on it."

Chapter 18

3rd January 2009. Romashkovsky Forest, Moscow. 22:17

The she-wolf sniffed the air and moved cautiously through the snow, taking care to remain downwind of her prey. The elk, a huge black-haired bull, remained unaware of the predator stalking it, content to forage for green shoots beneath the snow. The wolf knew instinctively that the elk was a threat. Despite shedding its antlers, the beast outweighed her by a significant factor, and the sharpened hooves would inflict terrible damage if they connected. The darker furred creatures tended to be the more aggressive, and the she-wolf had never seen an animal with fur so close to black. It stood out against the white backdrop as if it were a shadow brought to life. She would have selected easier prey if there were any to be found, but the smaller game – the rabbits, foxes and squirrels – had all either hibernated or retreated in fear to their burrows when they sensed the hunter moving through the forest. Even now she could smell their fear as they cowered in the darkness, and hear the frantic flutter of their hearts. The elk was the only potential meal she had encountered for days, and a terrible hunger gnawed at her stomach. The cold had sapped her strength, and she could feel herself becoming weaker by the day. Soon she would not be able to take on such a formidable opponent. If she was not already too weak to do so. There was no choice in the matter. She needed to eat. That was the only thing of any consequence.

She dropped to her belly and began wriggling closer to

the feeding animal. She'd learned through painful experience that there was no safe side to assault these creatures from. Their vicious hooves were capable of striking out in any direction. Her only chance was stealth. To slay the animal before it realised the danger it was in, and before it had a chance to retaliate.

She covered more than half of the distance, then froze, flattening herself into the snow as the elk raised its head, its ears twitching as it tried to locate any potential threats. If it ran, there was a slim chance she could catch it before it was able to reach full speed. The elk were fast, agile prey, but were slow to start and took several strides before they reached their top speed. If the animal turned and charged, however, then it was fully capable of inflicting terrible damage to her. It might not kill her, but the chance of the meal would be lost, and the next hunt would be so much more difficult.

The elk looked around the forest, uncertainty and fear in its eyes. It sniffed the air and let out a snort, then returned to its foraging. The she-wolf waited until she was certain the beast had relaxed, then resumed her approach. Slowly. Cautiously. Freezing at the slightest hint of detection. She was almost close enough now. Just a little further and the elk would be in range. She tensed her muscles, feeling what strength she had left flow through her. Judging the distance to the target. Preparing for her assault. Trying to ignore the growling of her stomach.

The elk raised its head and snorted, then turned around and let out a monstrous roar that sent a shiver of fear along the she-wolf's spine. The massive animal lowered its head and pawed at the snow-covered ground, ploughing deep trenches in the frozen earth. The wolf snarled in response, its muscles coiled. It knew that the situation had become extremely dangerous. She might have been able to subdue the animal with the element of surprise, but now, faced with a full frontal attack, her options had become limited. One mistake would send her beneath those sharp hooves with almost a ton of pressure bearing down on each. Their eyes locked – predator and prey – assessing one another. Staring each other down. Waiting for the slightest hint of weakness before they attacked. Fear fluttered in the wolf's stomach again. The elk was massive. A bull in its prime. Difficult to take down with a pack. Almost impossible for a single wolf to defeat. Yet she was keenly aware of the hunger and the cold sapping her strength. Retreat was not an option. She readied herself to attack. Then the elk charged.

The wolf feigned to the left, then changed direction and bounded to the right, trying to confuse the elk. This, however, was no young calf. The scars along its hide bore testament to the many battles this animal had endured. It recognised the ploy for what it was, and a hoof crashed into the wolf's flank with sufficient force to send her careening into one of the towering, spindly pine trees. She scrambled to her feet, tasting blood in her mouth. One of her ribs had been broken and she whined as the bone slid back through her flesh and reset itself. The elk was not prepared to give its enemy any respite, however, and changed direction with alarming speed before charging headlong at the predator once more, hoping to catch the wolf before it had recovered sufficiently to mount a proper defence. The she-wolf lunged to the left, desperate to avoid being caught under the trampling hooves of the enraged animal. Despite this, a hoof scraped across her leg, tearing a strip of fur and flesh free. The elk however, was unable to halt its momentum in time and collided with the pine tree that, only seconds before, had arrested the she-wolf's flight. The trunk of the tree gave a loud crack, and a flurry of snow from its skeletal branches rained down on the stunned animal.

The wolf seized the opportunity, knowing that she could not hesitate for even a second. She ignored the burning pain and hurled herself at the elk. The massive animal saw the danger, and managed to lash out with its hoof once more, but too slowly to prevent the wolf's fangs sinking into its throat. The impact of the hoof shattered bones and again, hurled the wolf away into a bramble thicket. The damage, however, was done. Hot blood streamed from the wound, staining the snow crimson. The elk staggered back and tried to roar at its attacker, but all that came out was a bubbling wheeze. The she-wolf took a moment to recover, whining in agony as the shattered bones began to reform. The elk tried to attack again, but its movements were slowing and its legs were unsteady. The she-wolf evaded the renewed assault with ease, despite her injuries, snapping at the elk's exposed flanks, making the animal expend the last of its energy. The dance continued for a few minutes more before the elk finally collapsed in a rapidly cooling pool of its own blood, eyes rolling in panic. When the wolf's jaws clamped around its throat this time, the beast was no longer able to resist and the end came quickly in a final bright red arterial spray.

The wolf stepped back from the corpse and howled in

triumph, the sound echoing through the empty woods. After a few seconds, a response rang out, and before much longer, her companion limped into the clearing. She couldn't remember how he had lost his leg. There was a vague recollection of sound and noise that she couldn't articulate or reference. It seemed that he'd always walked on only three legs as they were drawn towards the rising sun. The urge to press east had been insistent, and she couldn't fathom the reason why she allowed her injured companion to slow her down and share the food when it would have been much easier to simply tear his throat out and feed on his corpse to keep herself going. Every time she considered it, an unfamiliar pang of disgust surged up from within, and the thought was discounted almost as soon as it formed. They were connected, the crippled male and she. She just had no idea as to how or why.

The male approached the fresh kill cautiously, head lowered and tail between his legs. A sign of deference. He sniffed the rapidly cooling carcass of the elk, but would not dare start feeding. The she-wolf acknowledged his submission and sank her fangs into the back of the elk, chewing through bone and muscle until she found her prize. She ripped her head back, tearing the creature's heart from its torso, relishing the taste of the blood on her tongue as the organ burst between her teeth.

Now the male joined her, hungrily stripping muscle from the creature's flanks. The two monstrous wolves tore into the carcass, rending the flesh, savouring the sweet meat of the organs. They feasted for over an hour, until both of them had eaten their fill. Ordinarily a kill of this size would feed the wolves for days, perhaps even longer. However the female felt the insistent tug eastwards once more as she lay beside the male. She was aware of other predators nearby. A bear circling them cautiously at the edge of her senses. A pack of smaller wolves lurking in the tree line. Carrion eaters, scavenging the fruits of her labour. An urge to protect her kill rose up, but it was overshadowed by the need to keep moving. She understood that the end of her journey was close, and felt a sense of urgency, as if time were somehow a factor. She got to her feet and nudged the male with her snout, then loped off into the forest at a casual pace, leaving the elk's carcass to the scavengers.

The two wolves ran through the night, past ancient stone ruins and rusted iron railings. On occasion, the she-wolf picked up the scent of fresh death in the air, and when the two of them happened across an old stone mausoleum, the air crackled with an atmosphere of malevolence that raised both wolves' hackles and forced them to back track to find another path around the place.

The horizon was invisible through the impenetrable rows of pine trees, but a change in the depth of the shadows told her the sky was beginning to lighten, and she knew they would need to rest before much longer. Already her nose detected the acrid stench of the human city, and the low bass rumble of the metal things that moved along the black rivers at terrifying speeds – faster than even she could run. She knew to avoid the humans at all costs, although she didn't fully understand why. They were weak, slow. Prey. Yet they had taken great care to avoid them, only moving through villages and towns when necessary, and then, only in the darkest parts of the night when the humans nestled in their homes, unaware of the creatures stalking the night beyond. The answers to these questions seemed to dance on the edge of her consciousness, along with the reason for their journey, but the concepts and sounds were alien to her, feeling more like the noises the humans made than her own thought patterns. These thoughts frightened her, although she would not allow this to show. She didn't understand what they meant, but she was left with a series of feelings and urges. Travel east as quickly as possible. Protect the male. Find the others.

She paused, and the hackles rose on her neck. The bitter arctic wind had, for a moment, changed direction as it whistled through the forest. And with that change of direction, she caught a scent. Just the tiniest fragment, but enough to confirm the nagging suspicion she'd had since she'd killed the elk. They were being followed. Stalked. By wolves just like them. The beasts were using the same tactics that she used when hunting. Staying downwind, keeping their distance and waiting for their moment to strike. The alarm calls of birds from behind them had been the most obvious giveaway, and now the hint of scent confirmed it. The change in the wind had been too brief for her to properly assess those hunting her. There was a tang of familiarity to it, but she couldn't tell how many of them there were, or how close they'd managed to get. The male hadn't noticed, fortunately. She'd managed to crush the stab of fear before it could affect her own scent and alert those stalking her. The male was unlikely to be able to perform that feat, especially given his injury. He was no good in a hunt, would be a liability in a confrontation, and he was

273

all too aware of the fact. The stench of fear would billow from him like a cloud.

The options were limited. She could probably run and outdistance their pursuers, but the male would have no chance. Similarly, in a direct confrontation, they would be at a disadvantage if there was more than one stalking them. And she was certain that there was more than one of them. That meant the only viable option was to change the odds in their favour. She growled at the male, letting him know that he should continue on without her, and to increase his speed as much as he could. The male didn't understand the reasons why, but he complied, picking up his pace and trotting off into the forest. She waited until he was out of sight, then veered sharply off to the left, darting through the trees at right angles to the male as fast as she was able. If nothing else, this should split the pack of wolves that followed them. As long as the male was not alerted to the presence of the pursuers, his more relaxed pace would, she hoped, mean that the others would not have the urgency in intercepting him. Of course, they could all attack the injured male now that she had left his side, but she hoped that her more energetic run would draw them to her, to prevent her escape so they could finish the male off at their leisure. A calculated risk, but not one she saw any way around.

She vaulted a log, sending a shower of snow into the air behind her, then turned to the left again and raced through the forest towards where she'd sensed the other wolves. It was a dangerous gambit. Until she drew level with them, they would know exactly where she was by her scent on the wind. She hoped they would simply think she was fleeing and pursue her, not realising that she was about to go on the offensive. There it was, the scent again. Five of them. Two continued after the male while three broke away and began running towards where they'd last caught her scent. She turned towards them, angling herself to remain downwind, moving through the forest as silently as a shadow. As she'd hoped, the three wolves began spreading out in a wide semi circle, hoping to catch her within it, not realising that she was already outside of their sphere of influence. They would, she knew, widen their search radius and attempt to get downwind once more when they failed to detect her. She hoped that by the time that happened, she would have killed at least one of them.

She began her approach to the closest one, creeping forward at a slow but steady pace. This one's scent seemed very familiar to her, but the corresponding images and thoughts that flashed through her mind were, again, alien. She saw an old human when the beast before her was clearly a wolf like her. She tensed her muscles, curling back her lips to expose her fangs. The old wolf was oblivious to her approach. She would be on him before he even registered her presence. She prepared to pounce, but froze as she heard a growl from directly behind her.

There had been more of them than she realised. Another group following behind the vanguard. She'd circled behind the first but had been completely unaware of the second. She knew the mistake would cost her and the male their lives. There was no way that she could hope to fight so many. The best she would be able to do was ensure that their victory was costly.

The other three creatures joined the five behind her, forming a wide circle around her, cutting off any avenue of escape. She whined, then snarled at the other wolves, baring her teeth in a futile gesture of aggression. Then something strange happened.

The old male that she'd been about to pounce on walked forward and lay down on the ground before her. She backed away a step, not knowing what to expect. Then the old wolf rolled over and exposed its belly in a show of submission. She had not expected that at all, and although the temptation to surge forward and eviscerate the creature was strong, the wolf's actions and the nagging feeling of familiarity stayed her hand. The old wolf got to his feet and backed away a few steps, head low and ears flat. Then its body began to crack and contort. Bones shattering beneath the flesh, rupturing and twisting into new, unfamiliar shapes. The wolf's thick grey hair retreated into its skin, and its vicious fangs pushed their way back into the rapidly shortening snout. The she-wolf took another step back, whimpering. This was not natural. This was not how things were supposed to be. And yet, again, there was a familiarity about the horrific process. As if she'd seen it somewhere before. Perhaps even experienced it.

Within a matter of moments, the old wolf had gone, and in its place stood an elderly naked human. "Bozhe moi! I am getting too old for this. Marie? Do you recognise me? It's Steffan. Please, Marie, try to remember who you are."

The old man's words resonated through her. How could she understand them? Steffan? The name was one of the alien phrases that her mind had conjured when she caught his scent. Marie? The name seemed familiar. Marie? Marie Marie Marie. The she-wolf played the noise over and over in her mind, feeling the shape of it, allowing herself to immerse in the array of images that flashed through her consciousness. Her eyes widened in recognition, and then an agonising pain tore through her. She howled in confusion, then yelped as her talons retracted themselves into her paws, which separated and began to stretch. Her skin burned as thousands of thick hairs pushed their way back into her pores. Her face was the worst. Every nerve ending in her mouth was ablaze with bright blue streaks of agony. Every tooth crying out in torment at once. Her body was aflame with pain, the likes of which she'd never experienced... or had she? Even in the midst of this terrible, never ending torment, she felt a pang of familiarity. As if this were something she'd experienced time and time again.

Then, as suddenly as it had begun, the pain stopped. She shivered and looked down at her naked body. Her naked human body. She whimpered, but it only came out as a groan. The old man stood over her. "Steady, Marie. You've been in your wolf form for too long. It may take a little time for your memories to return. You're safe now. We've come to take you and Mikhail home."

4ᵗʰ January 2009. Krasnaya Presnya, Moscow. 14:25

Michael walked to the window and raised the stump of his right arm, then shook his head and pushed back the curtain with his left hand. The loss of his arm was going to take some getting used to. Even now he struggled to remember everything that had happened, only that the train they encountered would have killed them both if Marie hadn't managed to break through the door to the service tunnel in time. As it was, he had been a fraction of a second too slow, and the speeding goods train had torn his trailing arm off at the elbow. After that, things had become a blur. A sequence of images flowing into one another with no real concept of time or place. They'd escaped from the tunnel via the service tunnels, that much he'd been sure of, but how they'd got out of the compound beyond, or how Marie had managed to keep them on course after their humanity had been subsumed by the animal part of their nature, he had no idea. He only knew that without her, he would certainly have died.

It felt strange to be in a house after so long in his wolf form. Claustrophobic. He cast his eyes across the frozen Moskva River and the snow-covered buildings, wanting little more than to be back in the woods. It had been a simpler existence. Cleaner. Now that he was back in his human form, and his memories had begun to return, the burden of responsibility weighed heavily on him.

Steffan had refused to talk to them about what had occurred in the last few weeks, insisting that they needed time to recover properly and allow their human aspect to become dominant once more. He could see the sense in that, he supposed. The transition back to human had been unlike anything he'd experienced before. Even after Bosnia, when they'd stayed in wolf form for two days, he'd never known such a complete loss of self. If Steffan hadn't found them when he did, they might never have come back from it, spending the rest of their lives stalking deer in the forests.

The bathroom door opened, letting a billowing cloud of steam into the room. Marie strode into the living room wrapped in an enormous white towel, with another smaller one around her head. She gave him a small smile. "I thought I was never going to get the smell of wet dog out of me. I swear, if I'd scrubbed any harder I'd have taken my skin off. And you would not believe some of the places I found twigs."

Michael smiled at her. "Spare me the details, please."

She gave him a lopsided grin, then finished rubbing the towel through her hair, wincing as her fingers caught in the tangles. "What I wouldn't give for a bottle of conditioner right now. And a decent razor. The way my legs look, you'd think I hadn't changed back."

"Well, maybe Steffan will pick something up at the shop. He said he needed to go and pick up supplies."

Marie rolled her eyes. "Knowing the pair of you, he went to pick up a bottle of vodka. Did he say anything while I was in the bathroom?"

"No. Said he wanted to let us get back into a proper human mindset before he discussed anything. I didn't like his tone, though. Something's wrong. More wrong than usual, anyway. Did you see the date? We were wolves for a week and a half. The way things escalated during the last few months, I'm not sure I want to know what's happened."

Marie's expression darkened. "You can bet that if something has gone tits up, Krysztof's big, stupid Armenian fingerprints are all over it. I take it you've realised what's wrong with this place?"

Michael hadn't seen anything amiss, but it was hardly surprising. Marie was trained to notice the small details that would mean the difference between life and death out in the field. His skills were more attuned to the big picture. Still, he didn't like his sister's tone and began scanning the room, looking for anything out of place. It took him a few minutes, but then he noticed the clean area amidst the dust on the sideboard where a television had recently been. He looked for a telephone, and similarly discovered a light area around the socket that would have, until recently, housed an internet micro filter. He frowned. "No TV, no phone, no internet. Steffan really meant it when he said he wanted to talk to us later."

Marie finished drying her hair and flopped down in the chair opposite him. "I don't like it. I get that he doesn't want us picking information up out of context, or tipping anyone off that we're in town, but this is... off." She got to her feet and walked across to the front door, reached out and turned the handle. "Locked. And this door is a lot heavier than it looks. It's been reinforced. Same goes for the frame and hinges. I don't think I'd be able to get through this, even in wolf form."

Michael felt an unfamiliar flutter of fear in his stomach. "Steffan's probably just taking precautions. You know how cautious he can be."

Marie shook her head. "I don't know, Michael. This could just be a secure location, but it's starting to feel like a prison cell with carpets and a sofa. How sure are you that we can trust Steffan?"

"Marie, this is Steffan we're talking about. For God's

sake, he's been like a father to us both. Apart from you, there's no one I trust more."

Marie walked across to the window and examined the frame and glass. Then she began tapping the plaster of the external walls, listening intently as her knuckles rapped against the solid wall. She disappeared into the kitchen, then went through each bedroom before going back into the bathroom. "Michael, this is more than secure. The glass is bulletproof and the whole damn place is hardened. Window frames, walls and doors. The floor and ceiling are solid concrete all the way through. And try to listen for any other noises? Or scents?"

Michael cocked his head and strained his hearing. In a building like this, he should have been able to pick up conversations in adjacent apartments, but there was silence. He brought his wolf a little way further up, which, in theory, should have allowed him to hear every conversation in the building, but all he could hear was the steady thrum of his and Marie's heartbeats and the groan of the antique heating system. He sniffed the air and again, could sense nothing at all beyond the confines of the apartment. This was wrong. This was *all* wrong. He prayed that Steffan had simply brought them here, to this sealed building, to keep them away from the prying eyes and noses of the Moonborn pack factions, but the doubts that had been gnawing at the edge of his nerves leaped fully formed into his mind. He sighed. "You're right. We need to be ready to move."

Marie nodded, and disappeared into the bedroom - emerging a few minutes later wearing a pair of light jogging bottoms, trainers and a loose fitting sweatshirt several sizes too big for her. She shrugged as she

281

noticed his expression. "It's not like we've been left with much in the way of clothing. Better than nothing though. So... what's the plan?"

"There's not a lot we can do until Steffan gets back. I hope we're just being paranoid, but if we're not, then at least he'll have the key to the front door. Honestly, though, if Steffan's turned then we are basically fucked. He's the only ally I thought I could count on. If we don't have him on side then we need to get the hell out of here."

She nodded. "I agree. We're right in the heart of pack territory here, so we're both going to be twitchy and nervous, but if I get even a hint of bullshit from Steffan, we get the fuck out. I'm thinking Australia or a nice, secluded island in the south pacific. Somewhere warm."

He smiled, in spite of himself. "That does sound like a plan. Warm sun, sand and a cold mojito. Better than winter in Moscow. For the record, though, the more I think about it, the more I'm sure we're just jumping to conclusions. Steffan would never betray us."

The lock clicked, and the reinforced door swung open. Steffan stood framed in the doorway, with a pack member holding a submachine gun on either side of him. The old man's face seemed to sag, as if he'd aged decades in the last few hours. A large, hulking figure pushed its way past Steffan and grinned at them. Krysztof gave a mock bow. "Greetings, my friends. You have no idea how very glad I am to see you both."

Marie looked across at her brother and raised an eyebrow. She didn't say a word. She didn't have to. Her meaning was clear. They were both absolutely fucked.

Chapter 19

5th January 2009. Nauchnnyy proyezd, Moscow. 17:25

Michael paced back and forth within the abandoned storeroom that was their prison. There were no windows in the room. The only entrance was a heavy steel door on rusted rails and the only illumination the light that seeped through the gaps around the door frame. Water dripped from the concrete ceiling with the regularity of a metronome, and the room stank of ancient rat piss. Marie had examined their accommodation as soon as they had been incarcerated, and had simply shrugged her shoulders before retreating to a relatively dry corner and closing her eyes. Michael envied his sister's calm demeanour. He had no idea how she was able to relax, given the predicament they found themselves in. The waiting was the worst part. Krysztof intended to kill them both, of that Michael had no doubt. Killing them, however, was not enough. The Armenian's position as alpha was precarious, especially after the slaughter in High Moor and the imprisonment of so many in Lindholme. The Moonborn factions sided with Krysztof, but from what he'd been able to gather from the guards, there was still support for him among the turned. Krysztof intended to make a public spectacle of his death. Stage a trial for them both, then perform the execution himself. It was the only way he could be certain of complete control. Especially after the destruction his actions had brought. They had been too late to stop the assault on High Moor, but even if they had gotten to Moscow in time, there would have been no guarantee of success. Certainly, he could not have reasoned with the man, and he was no match physically for him either. What other options would have been open to him? Assassination? Civil war between the pack factions when they were at their most vulnerable? He'd been a fool to return. To believe he could have made a difference. The latest, and most likely last, in a long line of mistakes that may very well have doomed his species to extinction. He deserved everything that was coming to him and more.

Marie opened one eye and glared at him. "Any chance of you packing that shit in? Or are you trying to tunnel out of here by wearing a hole in the floor?"

He sighed. "I'm sorry. I just keep playing things over in my head. I can't believe that Steffan turned us over to Krysztof."

Marie nodded. "We don't know what happened. Chances are he was being followed, and no matter what precautions he took he would have had our scent on him. Or... the fucker stitched us up." She shrugged again. "None of it makes any difference now. All we can do is wait. Save your strength for whatever comes next."

Michael sagged. "What's the fucking point? We both know what's coming next. We're going to get hauled out of here and executed."

"If you don't stop your whining, you won't make it that far because I'll put you out of your bloody misery right here. For fuck's sake, Michael. You are the one that wanted to come back here. You were the one that wanted to try to put things right. Yeah, maybe we are screwed, but if you start off with an attitude like that then you might as well give up now. We watch. We wait.

We save our strength, and if an opportunity to get ourselves out of this mess presents itself then we jump on it. Or you can give up. Your choice, big brother."

Michael felt shame flush his cheeks. "I'm sorry. I know I'm being a miserable bastard. But I really screwed things up. If I hadn't..."

"What? Saved my life? We are where we are and there's no point dwelling on the past. When life gives you lemons you take the lemons and shove them up its fucking arse sideways." She got to her feet and put her arm on his shoulder. "We'll get through this. We always do." She gave him a lopsided smile. "Trust me."

The bar on the other side of the door clanked, and the door slid open with a torturous squeal of metal against metal. Michael saw his sister's posture change – becoming tense – then immediately relax again when she saw what was on the other side of the door.

Krysztof's massive frame filled the doorway, flanked by two Moonborn cradling sub machine guns and another two in wolf form. If they tried anything, they'd be cut to pieces before they managed a step. Still, Michael imagined his hands around the big Armenian's throat and couldn't suppress a sardonic smile. Krysztof threw two pairs of silver manacles into the cell. "It is time that you both answered for your crimes. Put these on and follow me. I'm sure I don't need to tell you what will happen if you resist."

Michael thought about this for a moment, and from the expression on Marie's face, he knew that her thoughts were walking a similar path. Was it better to go out in a blaze of glory now and deny Krysztof his moment of victory? No. He would face this with as much dignity as he could muster. He had made mistakes, but no one could have imagined what Connie would do. No one could have foreseen this. The issue with Marie was a minor thing by comparison. It was Connie who had doomed them. He bent down and fastened the silver strap around his wrist. The manacles were for show, really. The silver would not affect him in the slightest, and he'd be able to tear the malleable metal into pieces if he brought his wolf up to the surface. Anyway, with his missing hand, all he would need to do to remove the chains was to point his stump down and they would simply fall off. This was all about ceremony. He held his head high and followed the new pack alpha, flanked on either side by the two huge werewolves, while the armed Moonborn brought up the rear. He watched Marie out of the corner of his eye, ready to react if she made a move. His sister seemed uncomfortable, however, and he noticed tiny wisps of smoke coming from her wrists where the silver touched her skin. He was confused for a moment, then realisation struck. Marie was not immune to silver anymore. Her resistance must have died with her old wolf. His mouth suddenly went dry. They were in more trouble than he thought.

He didn't need enhanced senses to guess their destination. The low murmur of conversation and the myriad scents of the assembled pack members were like a beacon. Michael knew this building well. Perhaps too well. The pack had a number of properties they used around the city, but this abandoned industrial unit was easily the biggest and had been used many times recently, even before the current troubles. They were led along the corridor towards one of the warehouses, past walls with flaking paintwork and over sodden carpet tiles towards a set of heavy steel shutters. There was, of course, a faster route to the warehouse that would bring them to a rather ordinary wooden door, but again, Krysztof seemed determined to make an entrance. If the situation had not been so grave, Michael might have admired his flair for the theatrical. As it was, his stomach felt heavy with dread. This would all be over very soon, and try as he might, he could not see any way out of it.

Krysztof reached the shutters and dragged them open with considerably more force than was necessary, causing them to crash into the housing above. The warehouse erupted in shouts of outraged anger. The place was filled to bursting point. Every werewolf in the country – perhaps even every pack member in Europe – was present. Krysztof wanted his audience. He wanted them all to see what happened to those that broke pack law.

Lukas stood to the left of a raised platform, with Steffan by his side. His old friend cast his eyes down as they approached and wouldn't meet his gaze. Clearly the old man felt at least some guilt for his part in this. Michael would have loved to know whether he'd given them up of his own free will or if he'd not been left with a choice. From the look on Steffan's face, he suspected the latter, but it made very little difference now. The outcome would be the same.

He and Marie were pushed at gunpoint to stand in the centre of the platform. He looked across to his sister, hoping to see a reassuring look. Marie was nothing less than resourceful, and if anyone had a plan to get them

287

out of this, it was her. He saw moisture glisten on her cheeks and the hollow, hopeless expression in her eyes, and realised that their time had indeed run out. There was nothing she could do here. Their fates were already sealed.

Krysztof strode to the centre of the platform and raised his arms. The place erupted in a solid wall of noise that, even with his wolf suppressed, made Michael's ears hurt. The two Moonborn in wolf form must have been in considerable pain, a thought that didn't cheer him up as much as he would have liked. Krysztof motioned for quiet, and the roar of discordant voices faded, although there was still a considerable amount of murmured conversation going on. "Brothers and Sisters. Please. I bring this court to order." The last voices ebbed away until the vast room was silent. Then, Krysztof continued. "We are in one of the darkest times of our history. The humans not only know of our existence, but have declared open war upon us. There is one person, and one person alone, responsible for our plight. Our former alpha, Mikhail Williams. The accursed creature you see before you today.

"The charges against him are as follows. Firstly, that he willingly and openly ignored the decree of the council with regards to the death penalty issued against his sister, Marie Williams, putting her wellbeing over that of those he was supposed to protect." The noise in the room returned with a vengeance. Krysztof did not wait for silence this time, however, and simply bellowed over the cacophony. "Secondly, that he acted against his fellow pack members and assisted in the murder of the field team assigned with tracking down his sister and the moonstruck, John Simpson. And finally, that his mishandling of the situation in England, in particular with regard to Connie Hamilton, resulted in our existence being proved to the humans." He turned to Michael and his lips curled up into a snarl. "Do you deny any of these charges?"

Michael felt his stomach flip and a tidal wave of guilt crash over him. It was all true. When the facts were laid bare before him like that, there was no way that he could deny it. He had done all of those things and more. The reasons didn't matter. The simple fact was he let his anger at the way Connie butchered the police woman cloud his judgement. Connie had known she was going to her death and had lashed out. He had gone against the judgement of the council to save Marie, and he had slain fellow pack members to protect her. He had been the one in charge. The one the others looked to for protection. And he had betrayed them all. He raised his head and looked Krysztof in the eye. "No, I don't deny it. The responsibility is mine, but..."

Krysztof's hand lashed out, so quickly that Michael was barely aware of the movement. His chest erupted in a white blaze of agony as the Armenian's talons shattered his sternum and tore through his flesh. The wall of sound that erupted in the warehouse was muted, as if he was listening to it from underwater. He could hear Marie screaming, but it seemed far away. He couldn't breathe. Couldn't move. Krysztof leaned closer to him, so that the pack leader's fetid breath filled his nostrils. "As pack alpha, I sentence you to death."

Then Krysztof ripped his clawed hand free, with Michael's heart clutched in his talons. The hot coal of agony in his chest flared into a sunburst. He tried to speak. Tried to cry out, to tell Marie that he was sorry, but the darkness around the edges of his vision closed in around him and he couldn't force the words past the bubbles of blood in his mouth. He was dead before his body hit the floor.

***

A solemn silence fell over the warehouse. Even the Moonborn seemed shocked at the sudden brutality of the execution. Michael's corpse slumped forward and lay face down in a spreading pool of blood. He was gone. Her brother was dead and she was all alone in the world. For the next few minutes anyway. She knew she'd join David, Michael and John very soon. The loss consumed her – a savage pain in her chest like a fist of ice clamping around her heart, squeezing every last shred of her out. Her love, her compassion and her humanity. What was left was an arctic inferno of pure cold rage. She sensed her young wolf recoiling from the burning silver, but also feeding on her fury. Gaining strength. The loss of herself in the run across Europe had changed her. Made her more in tune with her animal nature than she had ever been before. And cornered animals did not lie down to die. They fought their way out of the hunter's trap or died in the attempt. Krysztof turned his back to her and held her brother's dripping heart aloft for all to see. Displaying his trophy. Then the hulking Armenian brought the organ to his lips and bit into it in a spray of blood.

That was as much as Marie could take. More. She surged forward, her arms held high, and wrapped the silver chain of her manacles around Krysztof's throat.

Krysztof yelped in surprise and pain as the metal burned his flesh. For all his size, he'd never been on a field team, and had never gone through the silver immunisation process. He was as vulnerable to the metal as she was. And Marie didn't need her wolf to be deadly. Her muscles bunched as she tugged tighter, using her arms in a sawing motion, cutting into the hulking werewolf's throat. Blood trickled through the links in the chain. She relished the coppery stink and the stickiness of it on her hands. The strangled cries from Krysztof as she tried to cut the bastard's head off. Then a sharp pain erupted in the back of her skull, forcing her to relax her grip. Strong arms seized her, dragging her away from her victim. Marie cried out in fury, thrashing against her captors, while Krysztof sagged to one knee, gasping for breath.

The Armenian got to his feet, hands around the raw wound in his throat. His eyes burned with rage, but also delicious fear. She'd wounded him. The scars around his throat would never heal. They would be a constant reminder to him for the rest of his life of how close he had come to dying by her hands. He strode forward and punched her in the face. Marie spat blood back into his.

"Fucking bitch-whore. I'll gut you for that!" he said, smashing his massive fist into her face again.

Marie grinned at him through a mouthful of blood. "You're weak, Krysztof. And you're a fucking idiot. Even after things went public, the situation could have been handled. Instead you started a war. A war we can't win. Michael may have made some terrible mistakes, but what you did means there can never be any going back. You want to find someone to blame? Take a long look in

291

the mirror, you mindless fucking moron. This is your doing as much as Michael's or Connie's."

Krysztof spat a wad of stinking phlegm into her face. "You talk too much, bitch. Past time you joined your brother in hell." He raised his hand and his brow furrowed in concentration as he willed the change. Nothing happened.

Marie grinned at him again. "What's the matter, fuck-nugget? Can't get it up?" She was still grinning as she brought her foot up into Krysztof's testicles with enough force to lift him off the ground.

He staggered away from her, then fell to the ground, clutching his ruined balls and gasping for breath. "Bitch! I'll fucking kill you! I'll feast on your heart. I'll..."

Then the door at the rear of the room exploded.

Marie didn't need to use her enhanced senses to understand what was happening. The Russians had found them. And Krysztof, in his arrogance, had gathered almost the entire pack in one place. A single, well placed bomb would have wiped them out. Fortunately the Russian commanders had yet to face werewolves and had elected to send in teams of Special Forces troops.

Not that this made a vast amount of difference. The deafening roar of gunfire echoed around the warehouse as the soldiers charged into the room. One of the concrete walls blew inwards, knocking her and the Moonborn holding her to the floor. Silver bullets, fired from automatic weapons, tore into the assembled werewolves. There were field operatives here, but the vast majority of those present were not immune to silver, and were cut down in a steady hail of automatic gunfire. Krysztof got to his feet, opened his mouth to speak, and then the top of his head exploded, spraying blood and grey brain matter across Marie's face. Jets of sparkling fire burst from the nozzles of flamethrowers, turning everything they touched into screaming torches. Men, women, children – the fire made no distinction, and as most of the wolves present were not combat trained, there had been, as yet, no response to the slaughter.

She had to do something or it would be a massacre.

More troops streamed through the breach in the wall behind her, firing as they went. The turned Moonborn wolves hurled themselves into the throng, tearing and rending flesh in gouts of bright arterial blood. Body parts sailed through the air, and the highly trained Russian shock troops began to panic. Gunfire stitched the creature's flanks, but clearly these wolves were field operatives and they simply shrugged off the wounds. For now at least. They would fall if they were damaged badly enough. Marie snatched up the submachine gun from one of her stunned captors, then rolled and opened fire. The soldiers wore bullet-proof vests as part of their combat equipment, so Marie sent a hail of bullets across them at groin height. Men fell screaming to the ground, only to have their throats torn out by the turned werewolves in their midst. Soon the entire pack of soldiers lay dead on the floor. Marie yelled at the wolves. "Both of you – to the rear. Protect the civilians." When the two Moonborn looked uncertain – this woman had, after all been a prisoner only minutes before – she stepped forward, snarling. "Did I fucking stutter? Move!

Now!"

With the alpha's headless corpse lying not five feet from them, and Lukas nowhere to be seen, the two werewolves came to a decision and darted across the warehouse to where the other soldiers were firing into the mass of panicked lycanthropes.

Her wolf still recoiled from the silver shackles. It was young and strong, but not strong enough to fight past the poisonous metal. She retrieved a knife from one of the fallen soldiers and used it to break her bonds; the shackles clattered to the floor at her feet. Her wolf surged forward, but she held it at bay. Just below the change threshold. Teeth and claws were not going to win this. A trained killer with heightened senses, strength and reflexes, however... that was a different story entirely. She picked up a blood-soaked AK-47 from one of the corpses and brought it to her shoulder. The main battle was utter chaos. Some of the werewolves had tried to turn, only to find themselves caught mid-transformation by the terrible sparking gouts of flame. Ordinarily, it would take a lot more than a flamethrower to stop a pack wolf, but she instinctively knew that the sparks within the flames meant the fuel contained silver particles. She followed one of the flame-jets back to its source, took aim and fired.

The effect was instantaneous. The 7.62mm rounds pierced the fuel tank and a ball of flame engulfed the soldier and everything around him. Secondary explosions ripped through the warehouse as other flame units ignited. The air was filled with the smoke, the stench of burning flesh and the screams of the dying. The Russian shock troops couldn't see through the smoke, and the intense heat of the fires made their night vision equipment useless.

The surviving werewolves, however, did not suffer from this problem.

The brief respite Marie's actions had won them gave some of the survivors the time to begin their transformations. The throng of bodies twisted and contorted amidst the burning corpses of their friends and family members. Where moments before these people had been frightened civilians, fleeing for their lives from an assault force, they now showed their true nature. An apex predator on its own territory. One by one, the great beasts bounded off into the smoke and flames, seeking an outlet for their sorrow and rage. From the shrieks of terror that emanated from the billowing smoke, it seemed that they had found exactly that.

Dozens of werewolves had been killed. Perhaps hundreds. The dead and dying covered the warehouse. Those too injured to fight staggered away from the carnage, towards the relatively clear space where Marie stood. She had to get them out of here. No matter that the tide of battle had, momentarily, turned their way, she knew they could not survive a sustained assault. It would only take a well placed missile or the arrival of heavy armour to finish the job. She motioned to the running survivors. "This way, quickly. We need to get out of here. Now."

The werewolves did not need to be told twice. They came to her, many bleeding from grievous injuries. Those who were unable to walk were carried by the more able survivors. Those with silver wounds would not be able to change until the next full moon. They needed another way out.

Then she had an idea. Those troops had not walked here. There would be transports outside. Almost certainly guarded, but it at least gave them a fighting chance. If not, then the werewolf species would essentially be wiped from the face of the earth. She whistled, and two turned werewolves came bounding over to her. One still had a Russian soldier's severed arm in its mouth. "We need to clear a passage to the troop transports for the wounded. Both of you, go out there and take care of any guards. We'll follow you in a couple of minutes."

There was no other word for it – the two huge werewolves grinned at her, then loped off through the shattered wall into the night. After a few moments, there was a rattle of gunfire and a series of long, agonised screams. Then the night was silent once more. Leading what remained of the pack, Marie hurried out into the bitter night towards the waiting transports.

6th January 2009. Romashkovsky Forest, Moscow. 03:10

Tendrils of freezing fog swirled under the truck's headlights as they pulled into the forest clearing. Ethereal and wraith-like, it formed indistinct yet vaguely recognisable shapes in its dance, before dissipating back into the impenetrable white blanket shrouding the trees. Marie turned off the engine and got out of the vehicle, wrapping her arms around herself in a vain attempt to fight off the chill of the frigid Russian winter. The convoy halted behind her. Two more trucks and a couple of cars. A little under a hundred werewolves - most of them families - were all that remained of their species. Krysztof's arrogance had come close to wiping them out. It still might. They were a long way from being safe, even now, hidden in the forest to the west of the city. It would not take long for the authorities to track them down and mount another assault, and she doubted they would make the same mistake again. The next time the Russians came for them, it would be in helicopter gunships and armoured personnel carriers. They would not risk losing any more Spetsnaz in a ground assault. The Russians were many things, but they were not idiots. The next attack, when it came, would be decisive.

The others had gotten out of their vehicles and stood behind her, silhouetted against the billowing mist. Steffan stepped forward and put his hand on her shoulder. "Marie. What now? What do we do next?"

She turned slowly and regarded the old man with confusion. "What do you mean? How the hell should I know?" she snapped.

Steffan stepped closer and gripped her arm with surprising strength. "These people are lost, Marie. They are injured - mostly civilians. There are only fifteen left with any field experience, including yourself. They are looking to you for direction. You are now the alpha of the pack."

Marie recoiled in horror. "What? No! Fuck that! I'm no alpha. I'm as much to blame for this mess as anyone. I can't think of anything I want less than to be in charge. Fuck!"

Steffan gave her a small, sad smile. "Don't you see? That is exactly why you are the only person who can do it. You turned an impossible situation to our favour and saved their lives. You can't turn your back on them now. They need you. All of us need you. There is no one else they can turn to."

She staggered back, then looked at the expectant faces. All of them watching her every move. Like fucking children, waiting for their mother to tell them what to do. "Fuck!" she hissed, and kicked the tire of the army truck. She turned back to the survivors and took a deep breath. "Okay. I'll get us out of here. We still have safe houses and weapons caches for the field teams all over Europe. We have to leave Russia. Get somewhere remote." Her mind raced, trying to wrap itself around the problems they faced. She knew they would be hunted anywhere they went and, based on the methods they'd used in Britain, the humans were getting better at detecting them. Nowhere in their world would be safe. Nowhere within their towns or cities would they be able to blend in or disappear for long. The assault on High Moor had guaranteed that. Any newcomers would be treated with suspicion and it would only be a matter of time before the authorities came to investigate.

Then it hit her. There really was only one way out of this situation. The only thing they could possibly do to survive. It was a big step – no, it was a colossal one. Something that they would never be able to come back from. But it was also the only way out she could see. Marie raised her voice once more. "There is a way we can stay safe. But it will mean leaving all of this behind. The lives you knew will be gone forever. Is that something you all think you can live with?"

A woman stepped forward. Around the same age as Marie, blonde and attractive, but Marie couldn't place her name... She looked uncertain, but then raised her head and looked Marie in the eyes. "There's nothing for us here anymore but death. I want to live. Wherever and however that might be. If that's something you can offer, then I'm all for it."

Others joined her, each stating the same thing – slowly at first, but then more and more, until the entire pack cheered their would-be saviour. The woman who would save and damn them.

No, she thought. Not the entire pack. According to Steffan, there were still almost forty pack members held captive by the British military. A sizable number before, but now almost a third of the total werewolf population on the planet. There was no way she could let them rot there. She'd seen what the bastards had done to her brother during his incarceration. There was no chance in hell she would condemn those families to the same fate.

She turned to the old man beside her. "Steffan, I need you to liquidate as many of the packs assets as you can. Michael told me once that you and he had talked about a last resort. A plan that could be put into action if the shit ever really hit the fan."

Steffan's eyes widened. "You can't be serious?"

"Can you see any other way? I'm open to suggestions."

He thought about this for a moment, then shook his head. "No. You are right. There really is no other way.

299

Alright. I'll make the necessary arrangements, but it might take some time."

"You have until the next full moon. If I don't join you two days afterwards, then take these people and get them safe."

A look of confusion crossed Steffan's face. "You're not coming with us now? Why? What on earth are you intending to do."

She gave him a lopsided grin. "I'm going to take what's left of the field teams, and we're going to get the rest of our people back from those bastards in England."

Chapter 20

6th January 2009. Trecorras Cottage, Llangarron, Herefordshire. 11:15

Daniel sighed and threw the novel he'd been reading onto the bed. He couldn't concentrate and really wanted nothing more than to sleep. The only problem was that for the last few days, sleep had eluded him. The pain from his broken arm aside, every time he closed his eyes he saw the faces of those he'd killed and those who, by his actions, had been allowed to die. He'd killed before, of course. Over a decade working on field teams had made him as efficient and ruthless a butcher as it was possible to be. The attack on High Moor though – that had been something different entirely. The people in that town had stood no chance. Well... almost no chance. The patrons of one of the public houses had somehow managed to subdue and kill Matt Cash with nothing more than broken bottles – sawing the young werewolf's head off as he howled and thrashed beneath them. But for the most part, it had been a massacre. Hundreds of people dead. Hundreds more maimed and cursed to become ravening moonstruck monsters in a couple of short weeks. That he'd been following orders did nothing to assuage his crippling guilt. As a German, he appreciated the bitter irony more than most. Hitler's thugs had, after all, just been following orders as they committed genocide. As far as he was concerned, he was now no better than the worst of them. He hated Krysztof for putting him in that position, but even that was a pale shadow compared to the depths of loathing he had for himself. He'd considered ending his life, but it would not be an easy thing to accomplish. His silver immunity meant traditional methods of despatching his kind would be ineffective. And there was also the question of what the pack of young lycanthropes in his care would do if he was not there to lead them. Already they grew restless – Melissa and others had been continually harassing him about what their next target was. They had a taste for blood and vengeance now. In all honesty, they were little better than moonstruck. Worse, actually. A moonstruck was nothing but instinct, pain and rage – an elemental force of nature that destroyed everything in its path. There was no rational thought behind it. No malice or intent. It simply was. The creatures he now commanded were calculating, brutal murderers with a taste for slaughter unsurpassed by anything he'd ever encountered. They were monsters, pure and simple, and they terrified him. As much as he dreaded whatever their next 'assignment' would be, he feared not getting one more. Sooner or later, he knew, they would tire of being told what to do and seek their own entertainment. They would become a roving plague of teeth, claws and death.

He wanted a drink. Wanted nothing more than to escape into oblivion, but this also was impossible. His heightened metabolism aside, there were already rumblings of discontent. To show weakness now would be to invite one of the others to challenge his position and, in his current state of mind, he feared he would not be able to muster enough enthusiasm to mount a proper defence. He almost wanted it. An end to the guilt of what he had done and what he had created. An end to the responsibility. Let the rabid dogs turn on their leader and do as they would. It would not be his concern after they'd finished tearing him apart.

Melissa Grove knocked twice on his door and, without waiting for a response, let herself in. Another display of his weakening authority and dwindling respect. She appeared excited. Agitated almost. She held out the satellite phone to him. Daniel felt a sudden wave of nausea and regarded the object as if it were a venomous snake. *Be careful what you wish for. You might just get it.*

He sat up on the bed. "What is it, Melissa?"

She beamed at him. "A message came through just now. Said you should call straight back."

Daniel sighed, got to his feet and took the device from her. When she didn't leave he raised an eyebrow. "Was there anything else I can help you with?"

The woman's smile slipped a little. "No... It's just... well, we can't wait for our next mission. Everyone's anxious to know what our target is going to be. I thought I'd..."

"I am the sub alpha of this unit, Melissa. This call is for my ears and mine alone. If we have another assignment, I'll relay the information to the rest of you in due course. Now... if you don't mind?"

He could sense the disappointment and anger radiating from her. Melissa was going to be a problem. The young wolves had, sickeningly, kept a tally of their kills in High Moor and Melissa was top of their league table by a significant margin. The loss of her family to the human assault on Christmas Day made her single-minded viciousness understandable to a point, but they all

303

treated this like it was some sort of sick game. She reminded him in many ways of Connie. That thought alone was enough to trace an ice finger of fear down his spine. He wasn't sure what he could do about it, but it was becoming very clear that he would have to do something soon. He waited until the blonde woman turned and stormed from his room before putting on his shoes and jacket. He walked out of his room and down the stairs, past rows of expectant faces, then picked up a set of car keys, left the house and drove along the farm track to the snow-covered village a mile away. He did not want any of his young charges listening in to what was said. Not on this call. He refused to be responsible for another massacre. Krysztof and Lukas could go fuck themselves.

He drove for another ten minutes before pulling the Ford Focus into a lay-by on the A40 and took a few moments to slow his breathing until the adrenaline had subsided. Then he picked up the satellite phone and called the number he'd been given.

The phone rang five times before it was answered. He didn't give the alpha time to respond. "Krysztof, listen to me..."

The voice that cracked through the speaker, however, did not belong to Krysztof. The person he was speaking to was the last person he would have expected. "Daniel, it's Marie."

"What? Marie? But how..."

"Listen to me. It all went to hell over here. Krysztof executed Michael, then the Russians attacked. It's... it's not good, Daniel. There are only about a hundred of us left, and hardly any with field experience. Steffan is making preparations to keep them all safe until I get back from England."

"England? You can't be serious? They've increased security at all the ports and the military are on full alert. It's suicide to come here, Marie. Take the others and save yourselves."

"I can't do that, Daniel. Not when almost a third of us are locked up in that internment camp. I'm going to get them out. And you're going to help me."

Daniel managed a small smile, in spite of himself, and felt the cold fist around his heart relax its grip a little. "What do you need me to do?"

"I need intel. I need you to run reconnaissance on Lindholme until we get there. Defences. Troop movements. The whole lot. We can't risk going in there blind."

"Understood. When will you get here?"

"Soon. I have a few things over here that I need to take care of, then I'll be coming over with whoever I can find that's combat ready." Her voice softened. "Daniel, I know what you had to do, and I know *you*. You can't hold yourself responsible for that. It was all on Krysztof. You were just..."

He gave a bitter laugh. "I know. I was just following orders. My grandfather would be so proud."

"Daniel, I need you on this. I can't do this without you. Get the intelligence and don't take any stupid risks. We can't risk alerting them. If they know we're coming it

305

will get very ugly. Take care of yourself, Daniel. I'll see you soon."

The line went dead. Daniel looked at the satellite phone in his hands, then smiled. Perhaps God did answer the prayers of the damned. This solved all of his problems. He could never undo the terrible things he had done, but perhaps he might be able to earn a little redemption.

6th January 2009. Lindholme Detention Centre, Doncaster. 13:35

John leaned back, taking satisfaction at the popping in his spine. Their captors had seemingly relaxed their restrictions on the High Moor survivors and the pack wolves mixing, although the two groups still regarded one another with fear and suspicion. It was hardly surprising, given the circumstances. The pack wolves looked on the two hundred infected as a potential army of moonstruck that would tear them apart in a little over a week, while the survivors drew little differentiation between those they were incarcerated with and the pack of monsters that had swept through their town on New Year's Eve. If not for Sharon Fletcher's assistance, he doubted if he'd have been able to get them to listen to him at all. As it was, almost three quarters of the survivors had done their best to put their differences aside and work with the pack wolves – Dmitri, Kasha and Sonja – to at least try to learn how to understand and control the changes they were about to go through. Those who refused had been moved into a single structure, the one closest to the main gates, and were left alone. Still, that meant that when the moon rose, there would still be around fifty moonstruck werewolves loose in the compound. That really was not good. John knew better than most what just one moonstruck was capable of. Fifty of them... well, dangerous didn't even come close.

The lack of military interference bothered him as well. There were no more tests. No more visits to the medical centre and, apart from the thrice daily deliveries of drugged food, no soldier set foot inside the compound. John wasn't sure what that meant, but he had a nagging suspicion it was not a positive thing. If the military had no more use for them, chances were their life expectancy was days – perhaps less.

He brought his thoughts back to the present, to the group of people sitting before him. Thirty men, women and children. All infected. All werewolves with no idea of what to expect when the moon rose and the change tore through them. All relying on him to somehow explain the unexplainable. Tell them how to come to terms with the fledgling monster growing inside them. Teach them somehow to control their fear of the thing all of them feared the most. He'd been at this for a little over a week and really didn't feel as if his efforts were getting through to them. It was not like he was an expert. For most of his life he was a prime example of exactly what you should not do. All he had to go on was what Marie had taught him in that cabin. The thought terrified him. All it would take was one person to push too far and initiate the transformation unbidden, and one of the circling Reaper drones would drop a Hellfire missile on the building. Every one of these sessions was akin to playing Russian roulette with high explosives. The thought did little to calm him.

"Okay, I'm going to go over what we did last time. Close your eyes and slow your breathing. Concentrate on it, and on my voice. Breathe in... and out... in... out. Feel the rhythm. Imagine that everything around you is fading away. The only things that exist are my voice and your breathing, and with every breath you take the more relaxed you are getting."

Some of the people in the group were fidgeting. Not really managing to come to terms with the relaxation exercises. John took a mental note of who they were. If things didn't improve, it may end up being necessary to move them to what some of the pack were calling *Moonstruck Mansion*. He wouldn't give up on them, though. Not until the very last minute. Until then, he'd pray that somehow these people would learn to accept their 'other self' and keep pushing in the hope that he'd get through to them.

"Now, I want you to sink deep into yourself. There is another within you. It's young. Little more than a puppy right now. You'll find it by following the heat it emits. Imagine turning your face towards a heater. Feel the warmth on your face, then will yourself to get closer. Not quite close enough to touch, but close enough that you can feel it, and it can feel you. There is nothing to be afraid of. This is part of you. No different to your arm or leg. It can't hurt you and you can't hurt it. Accept it. Feel it. Let any fear you might feel fade away and just be there beside it in the warm and dark. As if you were sitting by a fire with a dog by your feet. Relax, concentrate on your breathing... and just be."

His attention was caught by Sonja waving at him through a window. He quietly got to his feet and let himself out of the building. "What's up, Sonja? I'm in the middle of a session. Can't it wait?"

She shook her head and pointed to the flurry of activity beyond the chain fence. Troops were packing equipment into trucks, and as one was filled, another took its place. "What do you think is going on?"

John felt sick to his stomach. The military were clearing out. Removing themselves from the facility. It was possible they were setting up somewhere else, another internment camp more suited to the population, but somehow he doubted it. What he'd learned of the military during his confinement was that they rarely did things quickly. "I don't know, Sonja. But something tells me whatever's happening isn't good."

7th January 2009. Lindholme Detention Centre, Doncaster. 13:35

Rose strode along the corridors of the prison, keeping her gaze fixed straight ahead. The clipboard she carried was just for show. The soldiers had gotten used to her presence, and none of them gave her a second glance as they went about their business. The removal of the majority of the research equipment and files had all but ended. The Colonel had tried to reassure her that they were moving the sensitive material to a more secure site, but had refused to elaborate further. Rose may have had her share of flaws, but she prided herself on being able to spot bullshit a mile away, and every word that came out of Colonel Richards' mouth had reeked of it. Something was up, but whatever it was, no one was letting on. She'd already made her mind up to do some digging of her own and get to the bottom of this surprise redeployment, but first there was another pressing matter she needed to attend to. She needed to find out what had happened to Steven Wilkinson.

Her enquiries about the old man had been savagely rebuffed by the Colonel, and Doctor Channing was equally evasive about him. She liked Steven. His brusque, flirtatious manner had been charming after a fashion. More to the point, he had been nothing but helpful during his time on the base. Most of the knowledge and countermeasures they'd not got through direct contact had come from the old werewolf hunter. Doctor Channing had a certain reputation among his peers, and she was not about to see Steven mistreated by the vicious son-of-a-bitch. She had been his Doctor, and that still counted for something. She needed to know that he was all right. Besides, it was not like she had much else to keep herself occupied. Her own research had effectively been put on hold after she'd assessed the refugees from High Moor. She desperately wanted to find out what her colleague was up to.

Rose used her key card to gain access to the makeshift medical facility, but instead of continuing to her own offices, she carried on along the corridor, through two more sets of doors to where Doctor Channing had set up shop. There didn't seem to be anyone around, but she didn't want to risk being discovered. She had a flimsy excuse prepared if she was challenged, but knew that it would not stand up to close scrutiny. The last thing she wanted right now was to get another bollocking from the Colonel. She felt that she was on rather thin ice with him as it stood. Any more insubordination from her was likely to see her being put on a charge at the very least.

She paused outside Doctor Channing's laboratory – in reality it had been the prison's medical centre before all of the inmates had been shipped out to other facilities. This was it. The moment of truth. She fought to contain the nervous fluttering in her stomach, then pushed down all the fear and uncertainty and strode through the doors, ready to face the consequences or, if need be, lie through her teeth.

She breathed a sigh of relief when she found that Doctor Channing was not in the room, but regretted it when the stench of the place hit her. The smell of disinfectant did little to disguise the mingled stink of blood and human excrement. The laboratory was disgusting. Surgical implements covered in drying blood covered every surface. Microscope slides were scattered across benches and empty food wrappers rested in pools of gore. Canisters of volatile chemicals were stacked haphazardly on top of one another. Blood-stained curtains were drawn around individual beds, with some of the blood-spatter bearing the unmistakable patterns of arterial spray. This wasn't a laboratory. Any samples in this room would be hopelessly contaminated – worthless. It was like something out of a horror movie. Or a slaughterhouse. Doctor Channing had clearly lost his grip on what little sanity he had left.

She reached for a blood-stained stack of medical charts. The writing was largely indecipherable, even for a doctor's handwriting, but she eventually managed to find Steven's among the dozens of others. Dozens? What the hell was going on here?

That question could wait until she found Steven. She checked the bed number on the chart and carefully made her way across the filthy room, making sure to avoid any obvious patches of blood or other bodily fluids, until she came to the curtain around Steven's bed. Taking a pen from her pocket to avoid touching the soiled plastic sheeting, she pushed them aside, crying out in spite of herself. She thought she'd prepared herself for the worst. In reality, she couldn't have expected this. It was... inhuman.

Steven Wilkinson was strapped naked to a bed. No one had bothered to clean him up, or even attend to his most basic of needs. The mattress was stained with blood, urine and excrement. They'd not even bothered to catheterise him. But that was far from the worst thing. It was not even close. The old man had been opened up from crotch to throat – his entire torso cut open and laid bare. Silver clamps prevented the wounds from healing themselves. His ribs had been sawn open and some of them removed to allow Doctor Channing easier access to his internal organs. He had, in essence, been autopsied while he was still alive – and worse – fully conscious. There were no drips beside his bed. No fluids, morphine, blood or antibiotics were being administered. He rolled his eyes towards Rose and there was, for the briefest of moments, a flicker of recognition among the unmistakable clouds of agony that he was clearly in. A tear rolled down his cheek and he mouthed the words. "Help me..."

Rose backed away, her hand across her mouth. This was

worse than anything she'd ever witnessed. It was beyond barbaric. It was absolutely monstrous and she knew that she had to stop it. Colonel Richards, for all his faults, would never have agreed to this. No one deserved to be condemned to this living hell. She didn't want to look behind the other curtains. She had a pretty good idea of what she would find. Instead she turned and hurried from Doctor Channing's 'laboratory' and made her way back towards Colonel Richards' office, any pretence of composure long forgotten.

The door to the Colonel's office was slightly ajar. She was about to knock, then let herself in, when she heard a voice she recognised. The voice of the country's new interim Prime Minister. A man that had visited the facility at Crickhowell before events had escalated. She paused outside the door and listened into the conversation.

"How are matters progressing with the relocation, Colonel?"

"We've moved out all essential personnel and most of the pertinent research material. We've had to keep a strong enough force in place to avoid suspicion, and of course, Doctors Fisher and Channing are still at the facility. They will be among the unavoidable casualties when the plan goes into effect."

"Good. Very good. We can't take any chances, Colonel. The timing of the strike needs to be precise. The public outcry would be unfortunate if they discovered we were targeting civilians and members of our own armed forces along with the lycanthropes."

"Everything is arranged, Sir. When the moon rises on

the eleventh, we will have a Hercules inbound from Brize Norton and the thermobaric device will be deployed before any of them have a chance to complete their transformation. The complex and anything within it will be utterly destroyed, but in the event that anything manages to escape the blast, the drones will finish them off. We can then explain that we were left with no alternatives."

"Very good, Colonel. What about collateral damage outside of the target area?"

"I'd expect catastrophic damage to anything within a mile of the target, and probably significant structural damage to anything within five. It might be wise to close the motorway and Doncaster airport to be on the safe side."

"Out of the question, Colonel. This cannot appear to have been premeditated. If the press get a sniff of it there will be hell to pay, and I don't need to remind you that there will be a general election in the next few weeks. Rest assured, Colonel Richards, there will be a rather comfortable position for you in the MOD after this operation concludes."

"Thank you, Sir. I won't let you down."

Rose didn't wait any longer. She'd heard enough. She fought back her tears and hurried away from Colonel Richards' office. They were going to sacrifice her – sacrifice everyone not already redeployed from the facility – to wipe the werewolves off the face of the earth. She had to do something, but for the life of her, had no idea what. She was utterly alone here, with no one she could enlist for help. Then a thought occurred to her. There was one person she might be able to turn to. One potential ally. Rose straightened her clothes, wiped the moisture from her eyes, and headed towards the room where Phil Fletcher was being held.

9th January 2009. Newcastle International Airport. 21:55

Marie stepped out of the KLM twin prop aircraft and made her way towards the waiting shuttle bus. The frigid air stung her cheeks and hurt her throat when she inhaled it, but it was still considerably warmer than Moscow had been. Her wolf was forced as far down as she could and it lay quiet in the depths of her subconscious, making her more susceptible to the cold. It may have been warmer than Moscow, but she felt the chill much more keenly than she ordinarily would. The journey had been considerably less fraught than she'd imagined. While there had been increased security at the airport in Moscow, there had not been, as far as she could tell, any special measures put in place. Not yet, anyway. The Russian's experience with werewolves was limited and, for the moment, it didn't look like the British had shared much intelligence on them. Certainly not the countermeasures they'd had from Steven Wilkinson. They'd boarded the Aeroflot flight to Amsterdam without incident and the transfer to the KLM flight had been similarly straightforward. It was only here that they were in any real danger. She remembered the video footage of Dmitri, Kasha and Adam trying to flee from Exeter and suppressed a shudder. Silver bullets would not affect the other field operatives, but the scars on her wrists left her under no illusion that she

315

wouldn't be so lucky if things went wrong.

The flight had been almost empty. Only around a dozen passengers had boarded in Amsterdam in addition to herself and her strike team. Most of them were dazed-looking young men, clearly returning from the Dutch capital. There were not many flights in or out of Newcastle at this time of night and she hoped the police officers present would be more interested in the other passengers and any souvenirs they may have brought back from the coffee shops than in a well-groomed woman wearing a business suit. If not... well, at least if things got bloody there would be limited civilian casualties.

The bus lurched into motion and headed towards the terminal building. Marie made a show of checking her telephone and avoided eye contact with the others. She'd been in dangerous situations before, but this was different. There had never been so much at stake. Fifteen field operatives, plus those with Daniel, against an army who were as prepared for the enemy they faced as they could be. She'd made contingency plans, of course, but even those were as dependent on luck as sound strategy. Steffan had put things in motion at his end, and she'd done her best to cover as many angles as she could, but in the end, she'd simply run out of time. The full moon was less than thirty hours away. Whatever actions she took needed to happen by then.

The bus came to a stop and the passengers filed off, hurrying to get into the warmth of the terminal building. The airport was almost empty now. Most of the shops had closed, or were in the process of closing, and bored staff members looked at their watches, hoping they would not have to deal with any more passengers for one day. She stopped at a coffee shop and ordered an espresso, to the dismay of the girl behind the counter, then followed the rest of the passengers towards baggage collection and passport control. The other wolves had also held back, allowing the returning stag party to get ahead of them. How the customs officials treated those new arrivals should at least give some indication as to how closely they were monitoring things. If they were lucky, the border control staff would be as tired and ready to go home as the people in the shops and cafés.

It only took a few minutes for their luggage to appear on the carousel. Some of the stag party seemed content to wait for the rest of their friends, while others grabbed rucksacks and began making their way towards the exit. When the first few made it through without opposition, she followed, trying to control the racing of her heartbeat and fixing her face in a mask of irritation to hide the nervousness she was sure must be radiating from her.

She need not have worried. The customs official at the desk barely glanced at her passport and she made it out into the empty foyer without incident. She almost felt like crying out in relief. Instead she took her phone out of her pockets and sent a single text message, then made her way out of the airport towards the car park, with the other members of her team following behind her. Once out of the terminal building, she removed the earplugs she'd been wearing. A white minibus waited for them at the entrance, with a young blonde woman in the driver's seat. Marie opened the side door. "Melissa?"

The girl grinned. "Welcome back to the UK. No problems on your flight, I hope?"

Marie climbed into one of the empty seats and fastened her seatbelt. "No, plain sailing. The security measures don't seem to be in place for inbound passengers. Not yet anyway. Is everything ready?"

Melissa nodded. "Everything is set. The others are ready and Daniel... well, he's got a surprise for you. Apparently he ran into an old friend of yours."

Marie's brow furrowed in confusion. "Old friend?"

Chapter 21

Earlier that day...

9ᵗʰ January 2009. Finningley, Doncaster. 17:10

Rose sat in her car and drummed her fingers against the steering wheel. The village of Finningley was quiet. A few cars were parked outside the public house; people unwinding after a long week at work, or stopping off for a meal. She herself had gone there several times when off duty, preferring the food and the company to that served up by the army chefs at the detention facility. She'd found it relaxing to sit and watch the other customers, appreciating the interactions between them. It reminded her that outside of the confines of the prison and the horrors it contained, real people were happily living their lives. Normal lives, with no monsters and no imminent threat of death. That was the pretence she'd used when she'd driven out of Lindholme earlier. She was just sticking to a routine that she'd established and she hoped that no one would consider it in any way out of the ordinary. Not that she was planning to eat at the pub today, despite the protests from her stomach. There was another reason she'd come here. Finningley was right next to Doncaster Airport.

There were not many flights in or out of such a small place at this time of year. Most of them were to skiing resorts in France or to popular destinations like Dublin. Those destinations were not the ones she had in mind, however. She needed to disappear. The shit was going to hit the fan in two days' time, and when that happened, she wanted to be as far away from it as she could be.

Somewhere she could hide out relatively inexpensively until the dust settled. Of course, there was a damned good chance that they would hunt her down, especially when she released what evidence she'd been able to gather to the media. It wasn't much, but if she couldn't prevent the tragedy, she was at least going to make certain the bastards who orchestrated it were held accountable for their actions.

She checked her watch again. There was a flight to Wroclaw in three hours' time. Poland was not the most glamorous destination on the planet, but it was part of the European Union so she hoped she'd be able to pass through customs relatively easily. Once she was there, she'd find a way to cross over into the Czech Republic or Romania. She didn't have a lot of money on her – a couple of thousand pounds that she'd exchanged into euros over the past twenty four hours – but it was a start. The last thing she wanted to do was draw attention to unusual activity on her bank account. She would simply hit Eastern Europe and fade away. They'd be able to track her flight of course, but hopefully, by the time the shit hit the fan, they would be too concerned with other things to come straight after her. She would have a few days, and you could travel pretty far in that time.

She looked out across the village. It was like a picture postcard. The snow was still falling and the icy air formed glowing nimbuses around the streetlights. She was parked on a residential street, where hopefully it would take some time for them to find her car. She'd considered using one of the car parks at the airport, but with the CCTV coverage and the increasing unpaid parking charges, sooner or later someone would work out where she'd gone. Here at least, there was a chance of her vehicle going unnoticed for longer. She did her best to quieten the butterflies in her stomach, then got out of the car and retrieved her suitcase from the boot. There were no personal belongings. Everything she owned was either still in her rented flat in Crickhowell or in her room at Lindholme. She hoped her parents would understand why she'd done this. Grief welled up inside her, but she steeled herself. She needed to be strong and not act in any way that would draw attention. She'd simply go into the pub and call a taxi from the payphone near the toilets to take her the rest of the way.

Rose made her way across the road, cursing as the wet slush oozed through her shoes. It wouldn't matter soon. She'd get to the departure lounge and reward herself with a large gin and tonic to calm her nerves. Not too many, though. She needed to be alert. But one wouldn't hurt. Or two. Three at the absolute most.

The warmth of the pub hit her like a wall as she opened the door. The place was busy. It always was on a Friday. Good. People were not likely to notice a woman sitting in the corner for a few minutes until her taxi arrived. She made her way to the bar and ordered herself a drink, then walked towards the rear of the establishment where the payphone hung on the wall in a small alcove. She paused as she reached it. This was it. The point of no return. As soon as she made this call, she was committed. In all honesty, though, she'd been committed from the time she'd told Phil Fletcher of her plans and given him her key card. She hoped that he'd at least be able to find a way to get Steven clear. She'd given them both a fighting chance. That was really all she could do. At the end of the day, she needed to get the hell away from this place, and the monsters – both human and werewolf – could take care of themselves. She'd seen what a fuel-air bomb could do when she'd been stationed in Iraq and had no intention of being within a thousand miles of Lindholme when it hit.

"Here goes nothing..." she said, and reached for the handset.

A large hand grabbed hers before she could pick it up. She stood, frozen in place, expecting Colonel Richards or one of the base security team to be standing there. She turned to face her captor, but discovered that it was worse than that. So very much worse.

Standing beside her was the large German man who had broken into her flat on Christmas Eve with John Simpson and Marie Williams. The big werewolf bastard whose wrist she'd broken.

He smiled at her and tightened his grip on her arm. "Rose. It's so very nice to see you again. I'd like you to come with me, if you don't mind. We need to have a little chat."

10th January 2009. Moorends Business Park, Doncaster. 01:20

Marie was on edge. She'd been unable to relax on the trip down from Newcastle. That the heaters in the minibus were broken and Melissa had insisted on tuning the radio to some godawful dance station hadn't helped.

Her heartbeat seemed to synchronise with the pulsating bassline of the music, heightening her state of anxiety. At least it had been better than Melissa's relentless chattering for the first hour. The other members of the assault team had taken their seats and promptly fallen asleep, leaving her as the only person for the young werewolf to talk to. And some of the things she'd been saying disturbed Marie quite a lot. Melissa seemed far more concerned with vengeance against the people stationed in Lindholme than rescuing the captives. Well, she would get her wish. Marie had already decided to send the young woman in on the first attack wave. She could not afford to have another bloodthirsty rogue werewolf on her hands. In many respects, she seemed even more unbalanced than Connie had been. It was hard to believe that less than a month ago, Melissa had just been living with her family somewhere in Oxfordshire.

Marie felt a pang of guilt. The repercussions of her actions in High Moor had affected so many people – brought her species to the brink of extinction. She didn't feel fit to lead them. Part of her wished that Krysztof had finished the job and executed her along with Michael. Then, perhaps, she would have been with her brothers and John again instead of existing with the terrible burden of responsibility, not only for her past actions, but for the choices she was about to make. It made her sick to her stomach, but there was no one else to do this. Daniel had seemed a shadow of his former self when she'd spoken to him, and the surviving members of the field teams were little more than soldiers, lacking any sort of vision or imagination. It was all up to her. The only consolation she had was that when all of this was over, she would not have to carry her guilt for long.

The minibus slowed then stopped by the entrance to an industrial estate. Melissa got out and unhooked a chain that ran across the entrance, then returned to the vehicle and drove down the long gravel track, past the dark silhouettes of skeletal trees against the flat white expanse of snow-covered fields. The moon was almost full now – Marie could feel its insistent tug and knew that the others could feel it as well. The newly bitten survivors of High Moor would not know what was happening to them, and tomorrow night they would transform for the first time. The thought made Marie shiver. She didn't know exactly how many people were held in Lindholme, but chances were most of them would go moonstruck when the change hit them. Most of the moonstruck would slaughter each other or, if they were really lucky, turn on the soldiers guarding the base. Even so, she knew that to reach the pack wolves and mount a rescue they would need to get past not only the British Army, but a horde of ravening monsters. It was their biggest challenge, but also their biggest asset. With any luck, the military personnel would be too busy fighting for their lives to pay her pack of raiders much attention. She hoped, anyway. The worst case scenario really didn't bear thinking about.

The minibus pulled up in front of a looming building – an empty warehouse on an abandoned industrial park. It was the best option for staging a mission such as this, with so many people involved, but the slaughter in Moscow was still fresh in her mind and it did little to dampen her anxiety. The sooner this was over and they were all out of the country the better. She stepped out into the frigid night air and followed Melissa through a fire door into the cavernous interior of the industrial unit.

The place was a hive of activity. Daniel had evidently been rather busy over the last few days. It looked as if he'd managed to empty every one of the pack's weapons caches in the country. Everything from 9mm pistols to assault rifles and even a couple of high calibre sniper rifles littered the work benches, while eager conscripts stripped, cleaned and checked them, or catalogued the number of silver rounds available for each. The arsenal was impressive. Marie estimated that there were almost forty individual weapons here. Not enough to take on the might of the British Army head on, but hopefully sufficient for what she had in mind. Besides, it wasn't as if firearms were their only weapons.

She spotted Daniel explaining how to strip an AK-47 to a small group of young werewolves. He looked up as she approached, smiled, then walked forward to embrace her.

"Marie, it's good to see you. I'm so sorry about Michael."

Marie returned the hug and swallowed the lump that had formed in her throat. "Thank you, Daniel." She released him and turned away so he wouldn't see the moisture dampening her eyes. "You seem to have things under control here. What's the situation at Lindholme?"

"Not good. Follow me. It's better if you hear this yourself."

Daniel walked towards a series of prefabricated offices in one corner of the warehouse with Marie following closely behind. He opened the door and extended his arm, leading her inside. Marie wasn't sure what she'd expected to find, but Rose Fisher had certainly not been it. The woman was sitting on a plastic chair, nursing a steaming mug of tea. She looked up when Marie stepped inside and managed a weak smile, then stood and extended her hand. "Daniel said you'd be arriving soon. I wish I could say that it was nice to see you again, Miss Williams, but... you know."

She turned to Daniel. "What the hell is she doing here? If they realise she's been taken it could put the entire operation at risk. What the fuck were you thinking?"

Daniel raised his hands. "I'd been watching the base, as ordered, when I saw her leave. I followed her on a whim, hoping I might be able to get some more concrete information about what's going on in Lindholme. Turns out that Doctor Fisher was getting ready to abscond when I caught up to her. The rest... well, you really need to listen to what she has to say."

She turned back to Rose. "I'm listening?"

Rose took a sip of her tea and sat back down, then looked directly at Marie. "They're going to kill everyone in that base tomorrow night. They've got the essential personnel and research out, with just a skeleton security staff in place to keep things under control. The second the moon rises tomorrow night, they're going to drop a thermobaric device on Lindholme and vaporise everyone and everything within two hundred meters of the place." She gave a bitter laugh. "I was, apparently, not considered to be essential personnel. They were going to kill me along with everyone else. Those troops, the people that survived High Moor and your friend, John. All burned to ashes."

Marie's mouth fell open. "What do you mean, John? John is dead. I saw him gunned down when we broke Michael out."

Rose shook her head. "They hit him with enough tranquiliser to put an elephant out then locked him up with the others. He's alive and well – for now at least. In twenty four hours it won't matter though. They've got two Reaper drones circling the place at high altitude, ready to drop a missile on anyone that even looks like changing before then, and there are still enough soldiers on station to make short work of any uprising. I don't know what your plan is, but whatever you're intending to do, you'll have to do it soon. I've seen fuel-air bombs used in Iraq. There's not a lot left afterwards."

Marie's emotions were in turmoil. She'd suspected the military would have some plan in place, but she never expected something so brutally efficient. And John was still alive. She couldn't believe what she was hearing, and the thought both excited and terrified her. If she failed here, she'd lose him all over again. She'd been detached in many ways, believing that she no longer had any personal stake in proceedings beyond guilt and obligation. Now that had changed. Everything had. She'd hoped to use the chaos of the newly transformed moonstruck to her advantage, but now that option was denied to her. She felt lost, unsure of what the hell she could do to prevent the slaughter.

Daniel seemed to sense her concerns. "Don't worry, Marie. I have a plan. Come on, I'll walk you through it."

10th January 2009. Lindholme Detention Centre, Doncaster. 16:15

Mandy watched the last golden sliver of the setting sun slip beneath the horizon and stifled a sob. That was it. The last time she'd ever see daylight and still be able to pretend she was a human being. Perhaps the last time she'd see the sun, full stop. She wasn't alone in her observation. Almost all of the survivors of High Moor had maintained a similar vigil, either standing at the windows of their accommodation or in small groups outside. Every single one of them wore an expression of hopelessness and fear. In some respects, despite their surroundings and the constant training from the more experienced werewolves they were locked up with, they'd been able to push the impending transformation, and the awful knowledge of what was to come, out of their minds. Last night had been the worst so far though. The moon had almost been full and she'd felt that awful, alien thing within her stir – gnawing at the edge of her consciousness. Testing her. Probing for weaknesses in the defences she'd been putting up. It left her in no doubt whatsoever that when the moon rose tonight there would be nothing she could do to hold it back.

Oh, she'd listened to everything John Simpson and the others had told her. Tried to feel comfortable with the monster that lurked in the depths of her mind. It hadn't worked, though. She'd done her best to appear calm and act as if the lectures and exercises had been effective – the alternative was to be banished to what the others had started calling *Moonstruck Mansion*; to join the ones who were, in all likelihood, going to die awful, violent deaths when the change tore through them. Almost seventy men, women and children, some as young as eight years old, who would transform into ravening beasts in just a few hours' time. People like her. She knew some of them. A few classmates from her school. Mrs Matthews from the end of her street. Even now, it didn't seem real to her. Like some horrible story she'd been told. In other respects it felt as if she teetered on the edge of an abyss. A deep, dark hole that contained terrible things. Hungry, savage things with razor sharp teeth and vicious claws, designed to rip and tear through flesh.

John Simpson and the other pack wolves strode over to the centre of the courtyard, then a few she recognised, Sonja, Kasha, Dmitri and a few others, broke off and headed towards the buildings. After a few seconds, the door to her hut opened and Sonja stood there. "Come on. We need to talk to you. All of you. No exceptions."

Without waiting for a response, the woman turned on her heels and marched to the next wooden hut. Mandy sighed, retrieved her jacket (not that it would make much difference to the freezing January air outside) and filed out with the others. They shuffled into a large group and stood in front of Simpson. She pushed her way through the crowd until she found her Auntie Sharon, who stood on the periphery of the group, holding little Matthew's hand. It took a few more minutes for everyone to assemble. Even those condemned to *Moonstruck Mansion* were present, although they kept their distance from the others, huddling together and casting hurt, angry looks at their friends and neighbours who'd seemingly condemned them.

When everyone was present, Simpson raised his hands. "Alright. I'm not going to sugar coat this. Tonight is the night that we've been preparing for. It's going to be dangerous. Not everyone here will live to see tomorrow morning. But some of us will. Those of you who manage to keep your heads, stay calm, and no matter how scared you are, and no matter how much the change hurts, just find it within yourselves to go with it. You can't fight this. Fighting is the absolute worst thing you can do."

He turned to look at the smaller group. "Those of you in the first cabin, know that you are only there for the safety of everyone else. You've had the same instruction. When the change completes and you find that you are able to think for yourself, get the hell out of there. Go through a window, door or wall. Find the fastest route out of that building and come find the rest of us. We'll be back against the furthest set of huts, as far away from the main gate as we can get. The same goes for the rest of you. You change, get to the rest of us. We have the drones and the soldiers to contend with, and honestly, it's going to be loud, terrifying and dangerous, but if we stand together, we all have a chance. No more than that, but a chance all the same. There is no difference between us. After tonight, those that make it through will understand. The moon will rise at half past three in the morning. Be ready for it. Be safe. And if you see the person next to you get up from the change on two legs instead of four, get the hell away from them. We'll be around for the remainder of the night, and if you want to talk, or have any questions, then ask us. I want *all* of us to get through tonight. We're family now, whether we like it or not. And all we have is each other."

Simpson turned and walked away from the group, with most of the pack wolves following behind him. Sonja and little Sophie held back until the crowd began to disperse, then walked over to where Mandy and her family stood. Auntie Sharon leaned down and hugged Matthew tight. "Sweetie, I need you to go with Sonja and Sophie now."

Matthew held her tight. "I don't wanna. I want to stay here with you and Mandy."

Sharon stroked her nephew's hair. "I know, honey, but it's only for a little while. Until tomorrow morning. They'll keep you safe."

Sophie stepped forward and took Matthew's hand. "Come on. It'll be fun. Like a sleepover. Plus we'll get to stay up *really* late."

Matthew detached himself from his aunt and gave them both a long, solemn stare. "Just for tonight? And you both promise that you'll be alright?"

Mandy did her best to smile, then leaned down and kissed her brother on the forehead. "Of course we are, you little snot. Now go. Do you really want to see everyone in our hut without their clothes on?"

Matthew wrinkled his nose. "Ew! No! That's just gross," and allowed himself to be led away with Sophie and her mother.

Mandy and Sharon stood and watched them walk across the compound until they vanished through the door of the furthest building. Then Sharon turned to Mandy and took her hands. The older woman's eyes were damp with tears, but despite this she managed to force a smile. "Alright, kiddo. Just you and me now. Come on, let's get back inside and go through those exercises again."

Mandy nodded, knowing it to be pointless, but humouring her aunt anyway. The last thing she wanted to do was add to her worries. Sharon seemed to sense her niece's concern. "Mandy, we're going to get through this. I promise. I won't let anything happen to you."

Mandy forced a smile, but knew deep down that everything was not all right. After tonight, things would never be all right again.

11th January 2009. Lindholme Detention Centre, Doncaster. 01:45

Phil checked his watch and swore under his breath. He was cutting things fine. Too bloody fine, he knew. He'd promised Rose that he'd find Steven and get the hell out of there before midnight. But he wasn't going anywhere without Sharon and the kids. There was not a chance in hell. He'd do what he could for Steven, he owed the old man that much, and from what little Rose had told him, there was no way he could leave his friend to such a terrible fate. But his wife, nephew and niece were the only family he had. The only people left on this planet that he gave a flying fuck about. He would get them to safety or die trying, even if the latter option seemed the more likely of the two.

He'd spent the evening pacing the small room he'd been locked up in, trying to recall the layout of the camp. Desperately trying to formulate some sort of plan that would get them all out of there without being gunned down by the soldiers left on duty, or vaporised by the thermobaric explosive that was, in all likelihood, already in the air.

The prison had gone quiet since the turn of midnight, as if the concrete walls themselves were holding their breaths in anticipation. He had an hour and forty five minutes until the moon rose. An hour and forty five minutes until the survivors of High Moor began to twist and transform into the very monsters that had slaughtered their loved ones. A little over one hundred minutes until everyone within a mile of Lindholme perished in searing fire. He hoped that, this close to the event, all eyes would be turned towards the compound. Chances were, once he got Steven, the two of them could slip away undetected without too much trouble. Assuming Steven was in any state to walk. Rose hadn't gone into detail, but he got the impression that whatever was being done to the old werewolf hunter was unpleasant to say the least. He hoped he'd be okay. If nothing else, he was going to need all the help he could get if he stood a chance of breaking into the compound and getting his family out of there in one piece. He had a few ideas, but really that was all they were. Ideas. Nothing resembling a plan. Hell, they were barely concepts, but they were all he had to go on. Phil had never been one for winging it. His career as a police officer had been based on applying methodology and observing the facts – a far cry from what he was intending to do tonight.

He removed Rose's key card from beneath his pillow, used it to unlock the door to his cell, then pushed the door open a fraction of an inch and listened. Nothing. The prison was as silent as a tomb – an analogy that didn't exactly reassure him. He waited for another few moments, straining his ears for the slightest hint of guards walking the corridors, and when he heard nothing more than the groan of the prison's antique heating system, pushed the door open and slipped out into the corridor.

He remembered his failed attempt to escape from Underhill a few short weeks ago, and wondered if he'd suffer the same fate as last time. If it was Paul who intercepted him this time around, he hoped he'd be able to talk some sense into him. Following orders without question was one thing, but suicide was something else entirely. Not that his former friend would mind that either, he supposed. He was a different man these days. Not surprising given the circumstances, and at least his new role as Colonel Richards' go-to psychopath seemed to have pulled him back from the brink somewhat. Given him a purpose, even if it was nothing more than vengeance. Still, Phil hoped his former colleague would survive the night. No matter what had happened between them over the last few weeks, he still considered Paul a friend, and would warn him if he could. If he tried to stop him, however, Phil knew he would kill him without hesitation. When his life was weighed against Sharon's, it barely registered.

Phil reached the metal doors leading to the medical facility, swiped Rose's key card through the magnetic lock and stepped inside before anyone noticed him. This corridor was as empty as the last. A fluorescent tube flickered halfway down the bare concrete walls, and beneath the overpowering stench of pine disinfectant was another smell. The familiar sickly sweet stink of decay. What the hell was going on down here?

He decided the time for caution was long past and hurried through the double doors at the end of the passageway. The smell almost brought him to his knees and he had to put his hand over his mouth to prevent himself from gagging.

The room was more like an abattoir than a medical facility. The stench of rot mingled with the distinctive ammoniac tang of urine and faeces, permeating everything until the air almost felt as if it had a texture. Dried black blood covered every surface. Long drag marks stretched across the floor, only to vanish behind the plastic curtains around each bed. Phil had to check his watch to make certain that the moon had not risen because the supposed laboratory looked as if a slaughter had taken place here, but it was still only a little after two. Whatever monster had been at work here, it was decidedly human in nature. He dreaded to think what such a man might have done to his friend, and hurried to the last bed, not wanting to waste another second in this awful place. He ripped the curtains back and was unable to stifle the cry that burst from him.

Steven Wilkinson's body was laid open before him. The bastard had performed an autopsy on him while he was still alive. Phil could see the weak flutter of the old man's heart. The slight rise and fall of his lungs through the shattered ribcage. Whatever damage Connie Hamilton had done to him was nothing compared to this. In fact, it looked as if the wounded flesh and bone had actually been cut out, then placed in an array of glass jars on the shelf above him. Blood-stained silver clamps held his friend's body open, preventing the terrible wounds from healing. Steven's eyes flickered open, but didn't seem to be able to focus on Phil at all. Hardly surprising, considering the pain he must be in. That he was alive at all was nothing short of a miracle.

"Motherfucker!" Phil hissed through his teeth. He had no idea how the hell he was going to get Steven out of here in this state. If he sat him up, his guts would simply slop out across the bed. Perhaps it would be a mercy to let him die here when the bomb fell. Get the hell out and focus on saving Sharon, Mandy and little Matthew. He turned to leave, but stopped. He couldn't. There was no way he was leaving Steven in this state for another second, let alone another hour and a half. He'd do what he could for him, even if it meant putting him out of his misery.

He winced and fought the rising wave of nausea, then reached forward and began removing the silver clamps that held Steven's torso open. Each jingled like the peal of a bell as they bounced off the filthy tiled floor. When he was almost halfway through his gristly task, Phil noticed that Steven's wounds were healing. They were healing fast. Bones began to regrow to replace those that had been cut away. Flesh and muscle knitted themselves together. The silver had suppressed Steven's healing ability, but once removed, his repair mechanisms kicked into overdrive. He remembered how quickly Connie had recovered after Rick shot her in the face and shuddered. In his confinement, he'd almost forgotten how formidable a werewolf could be. How quickly their bodies could recover from catastrophic damage. And now the wounds that Connie inflicted had been removed, even those areas were reforming. It wouldn't take too long before Steven Wilkinson was back to his old self, as fit as he'd been the night he'd broken into Phil's house and told him what he was facing.

But even the time it would take for the old man to recover was more than Phil had to spare. He couldn't wait for Steven to recover. He needed to get to Sharon – find some way of getting them out of here before they were turned to ash. He leaned forward. "Steven, its Phil. They're going to bomb this place flat in about an hour and a half. Get the hell out of here if you can. Turn right when you get out of the room and just keep going. I've got to get my wife."

A hand grabbed Phil's wrist as he turned to leave. He looked back, and Steven's eyes were open. Despite the agony he must be in, the werewolf hunter managed a half smile, then nodded a thank you. Phil returned the gesture then stepped out from behind the curtain into the laboratory.

To find a small, greasy-haired man in a filthy lab coat pointing a gun at him.

"Mr Fletcher. I'm Doctor Channing. I've been expecting you."

Chapter 22

11th January 2009. Peak District National Park. 03:15

Squadron Leader Ryan Lockwood checked his watch. It was time. He'd been in the air for almost two hours now, essentially doing laps of the National Park at twenty five thousand feet. It made sense. The area was in relatively close proximity to the target and sparsely populated. They could be on station in less than ten minutes when the order came through from Brize Norton. The order that he honestly hoped would not come.

He was conflicted about his mission. He'd been a career pilot for more than twenty years now, had seen action in both Gulf Wars and had flown missions in so many minor conflicts and skirmishes that he struggled to tally them all up. This one was different, though. He understood the rationale behind it. The absolute necessity of containing the werewolf threat and preventing any further outbreaks. He understood that the infected survivors of High Moor were no longer human and were as much of a threat as the creatures that spawned them. Even so, using a weapon as appalling as the one currently nestled in his cargo hold on UK soil, against not only the werewolves but the soldiers stationed at Lindholme, unsettled him. The American made GBU-43/B was the most devastating non-nuclear weapon in existence. One thing was certain. There would be nothing left alive anywhere near Lindholme once he deployed it.

He turned on his radio. "Delta Papa Three Zero this is Ascot Four Six Three One. We are zero five two kilometres from objective, on a heading of zero zero five degrees. Request authorisation to commence operation."

The radio crackled into life. "Roger Ascot Four Six Three One. Proceed to target on a heading of zero three five degrees. Mission is a go, I repeat, mission is a go."

"Acknowledged, control. Proceeding to target area."

He engaged the aircraft's countermeasures almost without thinking, then clicked the intercom to the army munitions experts in the cargo bay. "We are approaching the target. T-minus ten minutes. Cargo ramp will deploy in T-minus five."

He turned to Flight Lieutenant Dave Fowler, his co-pilot, and gave him a grim smile. "Okay, Dave, we're on. Let's get this over with." Then he banked the C-130J Hercules to the North East, towards where the full moon crested the horizon.

11th January 2009. Lindholme Detention Centre, Doncaster. 03:25

Phil looked at the clock above the door and sagged in the chair he was tied to. That was it. Even if he somehow managed to get free of the cable ties securing his limbs and overpower Doctor Channing without getting shot, he didn't even have time to get out of the facility before the bomb hit, let alone reach the distance he'd need to escape being torn apart by the blast. He'd failed Steven, but more importantly, he'd failed Sharon and the kids. After everything he'd gone through over the last few months, it seemed almost ridiculous that his life was about to end in a wave of searing heat that would turn the earth to glass and melt steel like wax. All things considered, he supposed there were worse ways to go. He thought back to his friends. Olivia – slaughtered in the most appalling way imaginable, with her unborn child torn from her stomach by the monster, Connie Hamilton. Rick Grey and Mark Briggs – eviscerated in Steven Wilkinson's home. All of them dying in blood and terror, screaming in agony as their lives ended. In many ways he was getting off easy. At least he, Sharon and the two children wouldn't suffer. At least his family would never have to go through the excruciating transformation from human to monster. Their lives would be snuffed out in an instant. Quick. Painless. Clean. All fear washed out of him as he accepted his fate. Hell, once he stopped to think about it, he almost welcomed it. The nightmare would be over in a few short minutes. He relaxed and turned his head to Doctor Channing, who was busying himself with an array of video cameras, hastily erected on tripods, or balanced on chairs. "I don't know why you're bothering. They're going to bomb this place flat any minute. And it won't be a second too soon, you sick fucker."

The Doctor chuckled. "Nonsense. My work here is far too valuable. Colonel Richards appreciates what I've achieved, even if it's beyond someone like yourself. Perhaps in a few minutes you'll understand."

Doctor Channing walked over to the first of the bays and pulled back the stained curtains. Phil gasped. He recognised the sedated woman on the bed. Sergeant Peyton. The woman who'd been with Paul's unit on Christmas Eve. The only other person to survive. But he was sure she hadn't been injured. What the hell was she doing here? Doctor Channing adjusted the video camera to ensure it was pointing at the bed, then proceeded to repeat the action on the other bays, revealing five more unconscious soldiers with IV drips in their arms.

"You see, Mr Fletcher, I've managed to isolate the viral strain that causes the transformation. Culture it. Even improve it. Increase its virulence while exponentially reducing its rate of infection. Your friend, Mr Wilkinson," he nodded towards the final, as yet unexposed bed, "was convinced that there was some other factor at work. A curse he called it. Superstitious mumbo-jumbo of course. It was simply a matter of extracting the canine DNA strands and replacing them with the subject's own genetic material."

Phil was unable to speak for a moment as the Doctor's words sank in. "You don't mean... all of those soldiers?"

"All willing volunteers from the Christmas Eve missions. They all wanted to be able to meet the lycanthrope threat on even terms. I can hardly say I blame them, given the casualties of those missions. The infected ones had to be euthanized, of course, but I'm confident that these fine people will become a new breed of soldier in..." he checked his watch, "a little over three minutes."

"Are you out of your fucking mind? You've not even restrained them!"

Doctor Channing laughed – a thin, reedy noise that set Phil's teeth on edge. "Oh, they are heavily sedated, Mr Fletcher. And you forget, these are trained, disciplined soldiers. Volunteers. Even if they do manage to overcome the effects of the tranquilisers, after a period of disorientation I'm confident that they will adjust to their new-found state of being rather quickly."

Phil's stomach felt as if someone had just pushed his chair off a rather large cliff. This wasn't even remotely ethical, legal or sane. He now understood why Doctor Channing hadn't been evacuated with the other medical staff. Colonel Richards might be a lot of things but stupid was not one of them. He intended to wipe the Doctor and his abominations off the map along with the werewolves. And not a second too soon. Phil found himself wishing the bomb would hurry up and fall. He did not want to spend his last seconds on earth witnessing whatever Doctor Channing had cooked up down here. He'd seen some terrible things lately, but felt with a sick certainty that all of it would pale into insignificance once these *things* turned into whatever-the-fuck they were.

"Now, just Mr Wilkinson to deal with. I have to admit, I am fascinated as to how the transformation will affect his internal organs. I've watched the change from the outside, of course, but this will be most illuminating, I'm sure."

The Doctor pushed back the blood-stained curtains around Steven's bed, then let out an abrupt, strangled squeal. His body went into spasm and a pool of blood, urine and faecal matter splashed around his feet. Steven stepped forward with his hands gripping an IV stand. He'd forced the front of it through Doctor Channing's mouth with sufficient force to tear his cheeks open and burst from the back of his neck. Steven's mouth was curled into a snarl, and he gave one last hefty shove that almost severed the man's head above his jaw before letting the twitching corpse fall to the floor. He regarded his tormentor for a moment, then spat on the man's ruined body and turned his gaze to Phil. "Alright, Phil. Did I miss much?"

Phil tried his best to avoid looking at the ruined corpse of Doctor Channing and to ignore the sour taste in his mouth. He shuffled around so the cable ties were facing Steven, and craned his neck. "Not that it's going to make a blind bit of difference, considering Colonel Richards is about to bomb the place back to the stone age, but if I'm going to die, I'd rather not do it tied to this bloody chair. Any chance you could give me a hand?"

Steven took a step forward then cried out and fell to his knees. Phil watched in mounting horror as the old man's body began to twist and contort. As one, the eyes of the soldiers on the beds snapped open and they began their own transformations. The moon had risen. There had been no explosion. No cleansing fire to wipe away the monsters. And he was still tied to the chair.

"Bollocks!"

11th January 2009. C-130J Hercules, Doncaster. 03:28

Ryan Lockwood hit the intercom button again. "We are two minutes from the objective. Are you ready to deploy the package?"

The radio crackled static.

"Sergeant? We are almost at the drop zone. Respond. Is the package ready to go?"

Silence.

Dave Fowler removed his headset and undid his harness. "The fucking intercom's probably on the blink again. I'll go back there and make sure everything's okay." He got up from the co-pilot's chair then paused and removed his browning service pistol. He grinned at Ryan. "Better safe than sorry, though."

"Dave. Be careful."

"Careful's my middle name. Don't worry. I'll give them a kick up the arse if they're pissing about. Damn squaddies probably just yanking your chain. You know what the pongos are like when it comes to us flyboys."

Dave eased himself past Ryan, unlocked the reinforced cockpit door and swung it open. Ryan was very aware that his colleague didn't venture any further into the cargo bay.

"Dave? What is it? What's going on?"

"Oh, God. It's... it's like a fucking abattoir in there. They're..."

"Shut the damn door then, you bloody idiot. The ramp's down. I'll pull the nose up and drop the damn bomb that way. We're close enough now. The GPS should take it in. Now get back in your fucking seat."

Dave didn't move. Ryan could see his friend standing motionless in the doorway.

"Dave. Get the damn lead out and shift your arse."

He turned around, but Dave wasn't there anymore. Instead, a large man covered from head to toe in blood and entrails stood framed in the doorway. "Good morning, Squadron Leader," he said in a thick, German accent. "I'm afraid there's been a change of plans."

Ryan reacted with reflexes born from years of combat missions. He grabbed the control yoke and pulled it toward him. The aircraft responded and began to climb at a rate the airframe was, quite frankly, not designed for. The metal groaned and creaked under the strain and Ryan wished he'd been flying something more agile. The Hercules was a great aircraft, but it was as manoeuvrable as a truck sometimes. Then he felt a fist slam into the side of his head with more force than any man should have been capable of. Even through his Kevlar helmet, he barely held onto consciousness. The German grabbed the flight controls and pushed them forward, sending the nose of the aircraft straight down towards the city below them.

The German's face was fixed in a maniacal grin. "My name is Daniel Braun and I'll be your pilot for the rest of the flight. We'll be on the ground in around twelve seconds."

Then the man punched him again with sufficient force that Ryan felt his neck snap. The last thing he saw as his vision faded were the streetlights of Doncaster growing closer and brighter by the second.

11ᵗʰ January 2009. Lindholme Detention Centre, Doncaster. 03:28

John didn't have to see the rising moon to feel its effect. In a few short minutes, the survivors of High Moor would begin their first transformations within the flimsy prefabricated huts. And as soon as that started, the circling Reaper drones would unleash their arsenal of Hellfire missiles on the buildings, obliterating everyone within them. That is, unless they were given other targets to keep them busy. He nodded to the pack werewolves, then sprinted towards the perimeter fence closest to the guard towers. Seven of the pack wolves followed suit towards their designated spots by the fence, covering the distance before the snipers in the towers could react. He saw the dancing lights of laser sights on the ground behind him, but he was on the brink of his transformation and his movement, and the movement of the other werewolves, was too fast to follow.

He reached the perimeter fence and let his wolf out. Even now he felt fear as the familiar agony of the transformation tore through him. He'd only managed to change twice before and remain in control. Those two successes were weighed against decades of failure, where he'd become a mindless, savage monster. At least, if that happened this time and he lost himself in the change, the missiles from the circling drones would put an end to any threat he posed. Even if he held onto himself through the pain, there was a very real chance that would happen anyway. If he was too slow in turning, he would be blown to pieces by the high explosive warhead before he could react.

The change took hold and John fell to his knees. The colour leached out of the landscape and he cried out as his spine contorted and his jaw dislocated to allow the rows of bone daggers to burst from his gums in a spray of blood and foam. His hands stretched and twisted, fingernails splitting in half as vicious talons slid from his fingertips. His bones shattered then reformed in seconds, each crack and splinter a white-hot blaze of unendurable agony. Every second appearing to stretch out into hours of abject misery. He felt his face warp, and a strangled cry escaped his throat – more howl than scream. Then, as quickly it had begun, the change from man to monster was complete.

His senses were alive, picking out the frantic heartbeats of the soldiers in the towers, the panicked cries of the snipers as they tried to locate their targets, the thick stench of fear emanating not only from the soldiers, but from the survivors huddled in the huts, who would endure the same agony themselves in a few short seconds.

John didn't waste any time. He began running around the perimeter of the compound. He couldn't afford to wait. He knew the Hellfire missiles were already inbound and, as they travelled faster than the speed of sound, even with his enhanced senses, he would never hear them coming. But they were. He knew without a shadow of a doubt that the remote pilots of those drones would see the spike in heat signatures by the perimeter fence and react accordingly.

Sure enough, he'd not made it twenty feet when the area he'd been standing moments before erupted in a ball of flame, noise and shrapnel. The blast threw him from his feet, hurling him forward, while red hot shards of metal tore through his flesh, slicing through muscle, rupturing internal organs and shattering bone. His ears rang with the sound of the explosion, and warm, wet fluid trickled down the side of his head. He struggled to get to his feet, trying to force the pain of his injured body from his mind. Trying to ignore the red dots on the ground that were zooming towards him at impossible speed. Willing his wolf to heal him enough to avoid the next missile strike.

Then he felt it. The tug was unmistakable. The full moon had risen.

All hell was about to break loose.

11th January 2009. Scarborough Barracks, Doncaster. 03:28

Colonel Richards' fists clenched so tightly, his knuckles turned white. "Would you mind repeating that, Corporal?"

The young man before him looked uncertain. His eyes flicked between his companions, as if looking for someone to help him or an escape route. "We lost contact with Ascot Four Six Three One a few moments ago, Sir. It's not known if it's a radio problem or something more serious. No word on whether they delivered the package before we lost them on the radar."

"Of course they didn't deliver the bloody package. Or did I miss an earth shattering explosion? What about the Reapers. Are they on station?"

"Yes, Sir. We're getting reports that the drones have already engaged their targets. Four missiles away. No confirmed kills as yet, though."

"Four? You're telling me that the damned drone operators have fired off half their bloody armaments before the moon has even risen? What the hell are they shooting at?"

"Erm... They reported confirmed heat spikes consistent with transformations at eight separate locations by the perimeter fence. The pilots..."

A vein began to pulse in Colonel Richards' head. "Those morons fired Hellfire missiles at targets alongside the perimeter fence? And we've lost contact with the Hercules?" He turned and stormed across the temporary command station to where Paul Patterson stood with the other members of the Quick Reaction Force. "It's all gone to hell down there, Patterson. I want us airborne and on our way to Lindholme in three minutes."

Paul snapped a salute. "Yes, Sir. But... Sir... Us?"

Colonel Richards' mouth curled into a snarl. "Yes, Patterson. Us. I clearly can't trust the cretins around me to do the job properly, so I'll be leading the assault. Now, you have your orders. Get on with them."

11th January 2009. Lindholme Detention Centre, Doncaster. 03:28

Sharon removed the last of her clothes and placed them on the bed. It seemed ridiculous to take the time folding them, considering what was about to happen, but that simple act of normality helped distract her from the terror that threatened to overwhelm her. The air in the hut was freezing and she wrapped her arms around herself in an attempt to keep warm. Not that she'd be cold for long.

The other occupants were mostly sitting on their bunks. A few paced back and forth, wringing their hands. Mandy sat beside her with a blanket draped across her shoulders to stave off the cold and hide her nakedness from the others. Not that anyone was paying attention. Each and every other person was lost in their own thoughts. All of them trying to come to terms with the monster within them, whose presence was becoming more apparent with every passing second. Sharon felt the creature on the edge of her consciousness, growing more powerful as the moonrise approached. She sensed no malice or anger from it, only an excited eagerness, like a dog waiting to be taken out for a walk. She did her best to hold on to the image. That was all it was. A puppy, longing to be let out for the first time. She put her hand on Mandy's shoulder and almost recoiled from the heat emanating from her niece. The wool blanket was soaked through with sweat. "Are you alright, love?"

Mandy looked up at her aunt, and Sharon could see the terror in her expression; her face drawn and her eyes haunted. "I don't want this to happen, Auntie Sharon. I don't want to be like them. I'm scared."

Sharon hugged her. "I know, sweetheart, but there's nothing we can do to change that. We just have to remember what the others told us – not to fight it, not to try and stop it. If we do that, then everything will be okay. I promise."

A tear rolled down Mandy's cheek. "I wish I could believe that, Auntie Sharon."

"You have to trust me, Mandy. You have to…" She didn't finish the sentence. A sharp pain lanced through her torso and sweat burst from her pores. She fell to the floor as another wave of pain hit her, worse than anything she'd ever experienced in her life. It felt as if someone had stuck a blade in her stomach and was twisting it slowly. She felt the bones in her hands break as they began to stretch, healing in an instant, and then shattering once more as they warped into massive paws. The building was filled with screams of agony as the change tore through the others, but Sharon was barely aware of it, lost in her own torment.

Her skin felt as if it were on fire as thick, coarse hair pushed its way through her flesh, and the sensation of internal organs shifting within her was both terrifying and absolutely agonising. Every part of her body was being torn apart and reformed, but she was keenly aware of every last terrible change: Her coccyx splitting through the flesh at the base of her spine as it grew into a tail; her mouth feeling as if she were chewing broken glass; the thick, coppery taste of blood; nerve endings blazing in a white hot fury that it seemed would never end.

Then, as suddenly as it had begun, the transformation stopped. She felt clumsy, uncoordinated, as she pushed herself up on her four legs. Her senses were alive and she struggled to process the massive amount of information flooding through her mind. Individual heartbeats of not only the others in this building, but in the adjacent ones. Thick animal scents she couldn't identify. Her body felt energised. Powerful in ways she could never have imagined. Sharon had never felt so alive in her entire life.

Then she remembered Mandy. She turned to her niece and let out a yelp of terror as the girl beside her stood up on two legs instead of four, then let out a savage roar of pain and rage.

Chapter 23

11th January 2009. Lindholme Detention Centre, Doncaster. 03:30

Phil struggled against his bonds and did his level best to ignore the terrible sounds coming from behind him. His heart raced in his chest as adrenaline flooded his system. He had no idea whether Steven Wilkinson was able to control the transformation. From what he remembered from the hospital reports, the old man had escaped on two legs instead of four, which meant that he was in serious trouble. And that was before he factored in whatever was happening to those soldiers on the beds. One thing was clear. The sedative Doctor Channing had given them was no longer in effect. They could, of course, simply become what the Doctor had intended – enhanced versions of themselves, ready to fight the werewolves on their own terms. Somehow he doubted that. The chances of a lunatic playing with the genetics of the werewolf transformation resulting in anything other than something ungodly were remote to say the least.

The cable ties were not budging. Doctor Channing had done a pretty impressive job of immobilising him. The vinyl straps were not breaking any time soon, and the wet sticky sensation on his wrists told him that his body was going to break before they did. Plus, making yourself bleed in a room full of monsters was probably not the best idea in the world. He couldn't let this happen. There was no sodding way he was going to let himself get torn to pieces tied to this damned wooden chair.

One last desperate thought occurred to him. If he couldn't break the cable ties then perhaps he'd have more luck with the chair. It creaked beneath him as he wriggled, so it was certainly not the sturdiest piece of furniture ever made. And he was not a small man. Whatever was going on behind him was going to end any second, and when that happened, he would be out of time. If he was going to do something, it had to be right now.

He managed to get into a crouching position then threw himself with all his strength to the left, away from where Steven's transformation was coming to its conclusion. The impact jarred him to the bone, but he was rewarded with a loud crack and the splintering of wood. The chair had survived his initial assault, but he'd definitely weakened it. He stood again and threw his entire body weight against it. That did the trick. The chair fell apart beneath him, shattering into long, sharp wooden spikes. Phil rolled over onto his stomach and scrambled to his feet with pieces of the chair still secured to his limbs. Then he saw what Doctor Channing had created and felt what little hope he had left drain out of him.

The creatures that had once been soldiers were horrific. Twisted, misshapen things in shredded military uniforms. The transformation had not gone well. Corded muscles rippled beneath pale, hairless skin. Mouths filled with rows of blade-sharp fangs, sending rivulets of blood trickling across their chins and down their torsos. Fingers tipped with vicious talons. Eyes blazed with pain, hunger and utter malevolence. They weren't werewolves. Whatever Doctor Channing had done had removed a lot of the wolf from whatever they were, but not all of it. Not by a long shot. And every single one of them was looking directly at him.

Then he remembered Steven. He flicked his eyes to his left, dreading what he might find, and while seeing the old hunter on four legs instead of two was a relief, it did little to assuage the absolute numbing terror that left him rooted to the spot. His fight or flight response was conflicted and he was frozen – unable to think of a single course of action that could save his life, or put an end to the monstrosities before him.

Steven let out a guttural roar and launched himself across the room towards where the creatures crouched. Time seemed to slow. The werewolf was fast and incredibly powerful, but the beast that had been Sergeant Jayne Peyton caught him in mid-flight and simply swatted him away. Steven sailed ten feet through the air and crashed into the pile of chemical containers next to Phil, rupturing them and spraying the toxic substances across the laboratory. Smoke curled from Steven's fur, and the stink of the solvents made Phil's head spin. The air was thick with the odour of ethanol, and he realised he was going to lose consciousness very quickly. This was it. Steven was hopelessly outmatched by the things Doctor Channing had created. They would tear them both apart then rampage through the rest of the complex, slaughtering everything they came into contact with. He was going to die. The only choice remaining was how he met his death. He looked at Steven, and in that brief meeting of the eyes, they both understood each other. Man and beast.

"Save my wife, Steven," he said, and pulled his cigarette

lighter from his pocket. As Steven launched himself through the medical centre windows and the creatures surged across the laboratory towards him, Phil struck the flint. He was going to get his cleansing fire after all.

***

John struggled to his feet, despite the pain. His wounds were already healing, but as he moved, he could feel the red hot shards of shrapnel cutting into his flesh and slicing through his ruptured organs. His wolf roared in pain and outrage, wanting to lash out at the enemy that had inflicted so much appalling damage to it, but finding no immediate target for its wrath. It would get its chance, assuming the snipers didn't manage to get him in their sights first.

He realised the snipers were the least of his worries. The air was filled with the furious roars of newly turned moonstruck werewolves and the sporadic crackle of gunfire as the panicked soldiers began opening fire at anything moving within the compound. Four missiles had been fired at transforming wolves by the perimeter fences, including the one that had caught him in the blast. The ploy had worked, however. Each of the high explosive charges had utterly destroyed the fences and, in one case, had brought the wooden sniper post beside it crashing to the ground. They had a way out now, but they needed to act before the Reapers could come around for another pass and before the military personnel could organise themselves.

The pack wolves stayed in formation at the rear of the compound, waiting for those newly turned who had not gone moonstruck to join them. Once they'd gathered as many survivors as they could, the plan was to make a break across the open countryside before reinforcements could arrive. John was very aware that all it would take was for a helicopter gunship or two to turn up for their plan to lie in tatters.

The door to *Moonstruck Mansion* exploded outwards in a hail of wooden splinters, and dark shapes began to pour from the building. John had hoped that the moonstruck would fight among themselves before escaping the building, but it seemed the animal instinct to escape captivity was stronger than even the urge to kill. For now at least. He needed to get as far away from them as possible. He was strong – stronger than most other werewolves. From what Daniel had told him, he'd dispatched two of the pack's most highly trained killers without breaking a sweat at Finchale Abbey. But against this many moonstruck, even he wouldn't stand a chance. Especially not when he was still recovering from his injuries. His body was pushing the shrapnel out, but it was a long, slow and painful process. He needed to buy himself a little time.

The main gates opened and a squad of soldiers swarmed through, firing as they went. Against most opposition, this would have been devastating, and their silver bullets scythed through the charging moonstruck with deadly effect, but they were overwhelmed in seconds, their lives ending in screams of terror and the tearing of flesh. The air was filled with the stench of gunpowder and blood, almost sending his own wolf into a frenzy. More troops emerged from the barracks, filling the air with silver, slowing the monsters down. The moonstruck were forced to filter through the open gates, and being funnelled through such a confined area meant the soldiers could concentrate their fire. The moonstruck people of High Moor were cut down by the dozen, their shattered bodies piled high in the snow. Still, some escaped the initial onslaught and covered the distance to the soldiers. Then the screaming began anew.

John knew their window for action was limited, growing smaller by the second. These few brave, doomed men would not stem the tide of the moonstruck for long, and Colonel Richards, having seen what sort of mess a werewolf could do to trained military personnel, would not have left anything to chance. There would be reinforcements coming. Most likely in something that was impenetrable to teeth and claws. Like a helicopter gunship. Or a tank. Worryingly, though, so far, not one newly transformed werewolf had emerged from the other three huts. He tried to focus his senses on the closest, but there was too much noise and too much blood in the air for him to make out anything specific in the building.

He struggled to his feet and made a decision. He needed to get whoever was left out of those buildings and fast. He knew that not everyone in the other huts would have managed to transform properly. There would be moonstruck in there with them, of that there was no doubt. And, as those who retained their minds struggled with the influx of sensory information, the moonstruck would tear them apart. Ignoring the agony of his ruptured insides and the buzzing of high velocity silver rounds whizzing past him, he raced across the compound to where the first of the wooden shelters stood. He didn't stand on ceremony and threw his entire weight against the door, shattering it into kindling as easily as if it had been made of balsa wood.

He brought himself up short as he surveyed the interior of the building and cursed himself for being so stupid. He was too late. Perhaps twenty eviscerated corpses were spread over the walls, floor and beds – it was hard to tell because their destruction had been so absolute. He took all of this in in a fraction of a second because his attention was drawn to the other occupants of the wooden hut. Moonstruck werewolves. Around thirty of them. Every single one of them regarding him with a look of utter feral rage.

***

Sharon looked up at the towering monster that had been her niece, trying to find some fragment of recognition in those blazing yellow eyes, some hint that Mandy knew who she was, and came to the conclusion that there was nothing of the young girl remaining in the creature before her. Mandy was lost. A small, insignificant voice trapped within the consciousness of the werewolf.

The beast was nightmarish. Sharon had thought the monsters that had slaughtered so many on New Year's Eve in High Moor had been bad, but she understood now that they had been nothing at all compared to what she faced now. It stood almost seven feet tall, with corded muscles moving with liquid ease beneath thick brown fur. Its hands were still roughly human shaped, but were elongated and misshapen, with a vicious curved talon at the end of each finger. Ragged triangular ears protruded from the side of its head, flattened against the fur in aggression, while the long snout that had once been her niece's pretty face wrinkled in a snarl, with black lips pulled back to reveal glinting ivory fangs the length of Sharon's forefinger. A howl rang out from somewhere behind her – a joyous lament filled with anger and loss. Another beast joined the chorus. Then another. And another. Then Mandy threw her head back and let out a long, pained wail that broke Sharon's heart. She knew, at that moment, at least half of the occupants of her hut were like Mandy. Savage, unreasoning monsters that would kill without pity or remorse. To remain here would seal her fate. As the chorus of howling reached its crescendo, Sharon bunched her muscles and launched herself into the air, twisting mid-flight so that her clawed feet connected with Mandy's chest, using the moonstruck as a springboard to propel herself straight towards the window.

The glass exploded in a shower of razor fragments, each seeming to slice through Sharon's flesh in a brief but painful burst of discomfort. She barely noticed them, and the wounds had healed before she landed on the snow-covered ground outside. The air was filled with the smell of blood and smoke, mingling with the sound of gunfire and screaming to form a terrible tapestry of sensation that threatened to overwhelm her. For a moment, she struggled to process it all, wanting nothing more than to find somewhere quiet and dark until she could make sense of it. Then she remembered what the others had told her. Get out of the building. Join up with the others. Rely on the strength of numbers to survive.

She took a few tentative steps away from the hut, her mind struggling to co-ordinate movement on four legs instead of two. Then the wall of the hut seemed to fly apart as Mandy hurled herself at the wooden barrier between them.

Sharon wanted nothing more at that point than to run to the others, but she knew if she did, with Mandy in pursuit, her niece would inflict terrible damage on the pack werewolves. They were no match for her individually, and worse, as a group, they would most likely tear Mandy to pieces. And Matthew was with the others. She could not – would not – lead this monster back to her young nephew and put him in danger. If Mandy hurt him, assuming she survived the night, she would never forgive herself. That only left her with one option. Sharon turned to face the monster that had once been the young girl she'd loved from the moment she was born. She tensed her muscles, curled back her lips into a growl and launched herself into the attack.

***

Paul Patterson checked his weapon for the fourth or fifth time and wiped a bead of sweat from his forehead. He hated flying. Even the few rare commercial flights he'd taken had terrified him to the point of gripping the armrests on take-off and landing. And the experience of being crammed into an RAF Merlin helicopter with thirty fully armed Special Forces soldiers was about as far removed from a comfortable commercial flight as it was possible to get. He was in the lead helicopter, along with Colonel Richards and any troops with first-hand experience of fighting werewolves. The other four aircraft followed behind in a tight formation. Each carrying thirty combat ready soldiers within their steel bellies, plus two men manning the heavy machine guns on either side. One hundred and fifty of the most highly trained men in the British armed forces against God knows how many werewolves. Somehow it didn't feel like nearly enough.

Colonel Richards' mood had not improved since they had become airborne. He screamed orders into his headset and was becoming increasingly agitated. The thermobaric bomb was supposed to have taken care of the problem once and for all, but the C-130 carrying it had crashed into an industrial estate on the southern fringes of Doncaster with no one seeming to have any idea as to how or why. At least the airburst weapon had not actually gone off or a large portion of the city would have been levelled. Paul understood the reasons, politically at least, why they'd had to wait until moonrise before wiping the cursed inhabitants of High Moor out, but as far as he was concerned, it had been a ridiculous decision, motivated more by their new interim Prime Minister's desire to hold on to power than practicality. They should have simply walked through the compound, gunning down every single creature inside it while they were still human. Even if they'd held off with the High Moor survivors, they should have at least taken out the pack werewolves. The whole operation was a massive clusterfuck. A balls-up of the highest magnitude. The men in the choppers were supposed to have been a mop-up squad. A massive show of strength to deal with any stragglers or anything else that somehow survived the explosion. Now it seemed barely adequate at best. Pitifully outmatched at worst.

Colonel Richards' face turned a darker shade of crimson as he bellowed into the radio. "I don't give a damn about that. Where are my fucking Apaches? Well, what's their

ETA? Forty five minutes? Forty five bloody minutes? What the hell were they doing in Wattisham? I know it's in fucking Suffolk! What I don't understand is why my air support is half way across the bloody country. What about the drones? I know there are dozens of targets. Well, aim for the biggest bloody groups of them! Yes! Now!" He shook his head in disgust and turned to the assembled soldiers. "We will be onsite in two minutes. I want a fast deployment, form up in squads and shoot anything that moves. The Merlins will stay on station with the machine gunners providing support and taking out any creatures that breach the perimeter. I need you to go in hard, fast and without any mercy whatsoever. If you hesitate for even a fraction of a second, these things will tear you apart. Are we clear?"

The troops turned to face the Colonel and shouted "Sir, yes, Sir!" as one.

Paul checked his weapon one last time and couldn't help but grin. There would be no prisoners. No capture and retrieval. Not this time. They were finally going to put these monsters down, once and for all. "Fucking payback time," he whispered under his breath. Damn, if he wasn't looking forward to this.

Chapter 24

11th January 2009. Lindholme Detention Centre, Doncaster. 03:34

Steven saw the look on Phil's face and understood what his friend intended to do. His every instinct screamed at him that they could find another way. That there had to be something they'd overlooked. Some way they could escape from the monstrosities advancing towards them. There wasn't. As fast and as powerful as he was, just one of those abominations had swatted him aside as if he were a child. They were faster than him. Immeasurably stronger. And completely insane. Their twisted faces held nothing of the people they had been a few short minutes ago. There was a malevolent intelligence there to be sure, but they were devoid of anything approaching compassion or reason. They terrified Steven more than any werewolf he'd ever faced. Just one of them outmatched him by more than he wanted to think about. And there were six of them. Phil was right. They had to be stopped, and there was no way they were both getting out of here alive.

Phil gave him a look devoid of all hope. "Save my wife, Steven," he said, and removed his zippo lighter from his pocket. The fumes in the air were thick; the light distorted by the flammable chemicals. The creatures surged across the room, recognising the danger they were in. Steven gave his friend one last look, wanting to remember the brave man who had come here to save him, then threw himself at the laboratory window.

The glass exploded around him as he twisted in mid-air

so his body was facing along the corridor. He hit the ground in a full run, his claws sinking into the cheap linoleum, shredding the plastic, hurling him away from the laboratory and the horrors it contained. He registered Phil's screams as the beasts fell upon him. Then, for a fraction of a second, there was a horrible silence as the air in the corridor rushed past him. It was as if the room he'd escaped was taking a breath, inhaling every last scrap of oxygen available to it. Steven knew he'd run out of time. He had no chance of getting clear. He threw himself at the door of a supply cupboard to his left, just as the fireball tore through the building.

The world was filled with noise and searing pain. Steven's fur ignited. He breathed chemical fire into his lungs, burning his mouth and throat. His flesh began to bubble, crack and blister. He could no longer see anything other than a terrible redness, and realised his eyeballs had started to boil in his skull. The pain was terrible. Even after the torture Doctor Channing had inflicted on him, he'd never experienced anything like this. The feeling of being slowly burned alive while his wolf side did its best to heal the massive damage. There were limits even to his regenerative abilities, and right at that moment, Steven Wilkinson wished for death. For the sweet, cool oblivion of the grave instead of the endless burning of his flesh. He was in Hell. Condemned to an eternity of agony as he combusted and regenerated, only for the new flesh to be stripped away in the conflagration.

Steven lay in the burning building and waited for death to claim him. When his eyeballs grew back in a white flash of unmitigated agony, he knew that he was not going to be that lucky. Smoke and heat dried out his eyes, but he was unable to blink to clear them. His eyelids had not grown back yet. He needed to get outside, away from the inferno that had been Lindholme Prison. He forced his ruined body to stand, each second more painful than the last, every movement, no matter how slight, sending a cascade of torture through his seared nerve endings as he drove himself to move through the blazing corridors and the thick, acrid smoke to where his tormented wolf sensed clean, cold air.

He remembered his promise to Phil, and this spurred him on despite the protests of his broken body. His friend had sacrificed himself to destroy Doctor Channing's monsters. He had only asked that Steven save the life of his wife. And Steven had no intention of reneging on that promise. He picked up his pace, dodging burning timbers crashing from the ceiling, and running past the mangled corpses of anyone unfortunate enough to have been in the building at the time of the explosion until he saw a glimmer of starlight through the flames. He redoubled his efforts, almost crying out in relief as the frigid air soothed his burning flesh. He leaped out of the remains of Lindholme Prison into the middle of a war zone.

***

The Merlin helicopter banked sharply to the right, allowing Paul his first proper view of the battleground that Lindholme detention facility had become. It was so much worse than he could ever have imagined. The place was swarming with werewolves. And not just the four-legged variety he'd encountered before. Huge, muscular bipeds scaled the observation towers, despite their occupant's best efforts to defend their positions. He saw a man literally torn in half by one creature as he emptied his magazine into another. The unfortunate soldier's torso fell twenty feet to the bloodstained ground, trailing intestines behind it like the streamers on a kite. The few remaining troops covering the entrance were doing their best, but for every one of the monsters their weapons cut down, another two seemed to take its place. One of the wooden barrack blocks exploded in a fireball, swiftly followed by another, while explosions erupted from within the swarming masses that surged across the exercise area. Those were the last of the drone's armaments, he knew. That meant the troops left on the ground, and those within the helicopters, were the only thing preventing the werewolves from escaping. If they should reach a populated area like Doncaster, the damage they would inflict really did not bear thinking about.

The machine guns on their helicopter opened up, tearing into the werewolves scaling the towers and clambering across the roofs of any buildings still standing. High velocity silver rounds shredded flesh, leaving the broken, naked corpses of men, women and children to lie in dark pools of their own blood. It was a slaughter, but there were so many of them that it felt as if they were trying to stop the ocean with a bucket. Two hundred survivors from High Moor, plus the captured pack werewolves, made a formidable fighting force.

A huge fireball erupted from the main prison building, blowing the doors completely off their hinges and shattering the reinforced windows. The shockwave rocked the helicopters and sent most of the soldiers at ground level sprawling face down into the snow, where they were torn to ribbons by the advancing lycanthropes.

Colonel Richards screamed into his headset, "Get us down there, now!" The pilots obeyed the command and dropped the helicopters in formation outside the ruins of the prison. The Special Forces soldiers disembarked and took up firing positions as the helicopters took to the air once more and their heavy machine guns rained death onto the compound.

Paul pushed away any fear or doubt. This was it. Game time. He cocked his SA-80 and began firing at anything with fur. It was exhilarating. And with every werewolf his rounds took down, he began to count. One... Two... Three...

The troops began to move forward, towards the compound, firing at any targets they could while the other squads provided covering fire. The helicopters circled overhead, the tracer rounds from their machine guns lighting up the air like fireflies. Paul realised then that the tide had turned. If they kept this up there was a good chance they might actually survive the night.

***

Sharon honestly had no idea what she was doing. The wolf side of her nature urged her on, its instincts finely tuned to deliver fast, efficient killing blows. Sharon couldn't allow that to happen. She would never forgive herself if she let it take over and seriously injured her niece, or worse, killed her. Unfortunately, Mandy was not under any such constraints. Vicious talons ripped through the air, narrowly missing Sharon as she weaved, feigned attacks and dodged the ripostes from the enraged Moonstruck. She barrelled into Mandy, sending her crashing to the floor, and clamped her jaws around the girl's neck, applying just enough pressure to cause pain but not enough to do any permanent damage.

Lie still! Stay down! She willed, but instead Mandy's arm lashed out, her claws leaving four savage wounds in her side. The impact sent Sharon sailing across the compound. She could taste blood in her mouth and her ribs burned in agony. The wounds were not healing, but she didn't think Mandy had inflicted any serious damage. Not yet, anyway. She struggled to her feet just in time to see the moonstruck hurl itself towards her. There was nothing she could do to avoid the teeth and claws of the beast that had been her niece. She closed her eyes. *Don't blame yourself, love. It's not your fault.* Then the building she'd escaped from erupted in a massive fireball.

Wooden splinters the size of her forearm filled the air, impaling Mandy like a bug. The moonstruck was carried by the blast over the top of Sharon's head before crashing into the remains of the perimeter fence. It howled in pain and fury, struggling to get to its feet while slashing at the wooden shards protruding from its body.

Sharon scrambled to her feet and began rushing to her fallen niece's side, but then stopped herself. What was she going to do? Help her? Remove the wooden stakes so Mandy would be free to attack her once more? There was no restraining her, or reasoning with her. Wherever Mandy was, she was not in control of the savage monster before her. The creature that had been a fifteen year old girl would stop at nothing. It would kill, and keep killing as long as there was something for it to kill. There was only one thing Sharon could do to prevent her from hurting anyone. One mercy she could grant the girl. There was no other choice.

The moonstruck thrashed on the ground, but only succeeded in driving the splinters further into its flesh. Sharon's heart broke, but she steeled her resolve and allowed her feral instincts to guide her, shutting off as much of her humanity as she could. Letting her wolf do what was necessary. She stalked closer, waiting for a moment to strike. Her muscles tensed, and she drew back her lips to reveal her own lethal fangs.

A burst of automatic weapons fire cut through the air between Mandy and herself, the snow erupting in a series of small explosions. Sharon could smell blood in the air and then saw the hole in Mandy's shoulder. Her niece's body began to spasm, contorting as bones realigned themselves. The moonstruck's muzzle shortened and the terrible bone daggers retreated back into its mouth. Hair pushed its way back into Mandy's pores and the creature screamed in utter misery. It took only a few seconds, and the monster was replaced by a naked girl, bleeding from a ragged wound in her shoulder and from the shards of wood protruding from her body.

Mandy looked up at her, her face a mask of agony. "Auntie Sharon? Help me! It hurts. It…"

She never got the chance to finish the sentence. The front of Mandy's head exploded in a spray of blood, bone and brains. Sharon watched in horror as her niece's head seemed to deflate like a burst balloon. That pretty face, so much like her sister had been at her age, erased. Utterly destroyed. Sharon felt the loss and rage wash over her like a red wave. She howled, and when her lament had ended, there was very little of Sharon Fletcher left. Only the wolf remained.

***

John spent an entire half second looking at the thirty moonstruck before him before deciding on a course of action. Ignoring the blazing pain from his still healing injuries, he threw himself away from the door, dropped to all fours and tried to put as much distance between the werewolves and himself as he could.

The compound had descended into absolute chaos. Two of the buildings to John's left exploded in rapid succession. Another missile tore into a crowd of moonstruck as they funnelled through the main gate, while the final Hellfire missile detonated at the rear of the compound where the pack werewolves had gathered. The air was filled with gunfire and the screams of the dying – both human and werewolf. Bodies covered the ground, bleeding from multiple gunshot wounds or torn to pieces by the onslaught of missiles from the Reaper drones. The military forces were not doing much better. Moonstruck swarmed over them like a plague of locusts, scaling the observation towers and butchering them where they stood. The battle seemed to be evenly matched until five helicopters roared over the compound, spraying death from their heavy machine guns, tearing through pack wolves and moonstruck indiscriminately. John knew at that point they were doomed. A werewolf, no matter how dangerous, could not hope to fight against an airborne threat like this. The helicopters landed between the burning prison and the detention facility, and armed reinforcements raced from their holds before they took to the sky again and continued their slaughter.

John, however, had other problems to consider. He didn't need to look behind him to know that the moonstruck were hot on his heels. If he slowed his pace even a little, they would fall on him and tear him to pieces in seconds. His injuries were healing, but even on his best day he could not face so many.

Face them. No. But perhaps he could aim them.

He leaped to his left, towards the perimeter fence, and charged through the burning hole where one of the missiles had exploded a few minutes earlier. Attacking the soldiers head on was suicide. They were moving forward in squads, covering each other's advance with trained military precision. A direct assault would be met with a hail of silver bullets from automatic weapons that would make short work of both him and the pursuing monsters behind him. But they didn't seem to be covering their flanks at all. He increased his speed, angling himself away from the compound, then back towards the attacking troops. The thought of consciously killing another human being sickened him, but at this point he really didn't have a choice. It was kill or be killed, and if he did nothing, every single werewolf in that compound was going to die.

He got to within about thirty feet of the advancing soldiers right flank before they noticed him. By then it was far too late. Roaring with feral rage, John Simpson led his group of thirty moonstruck straight into the heart of the attacking soldiers, abandoning what remained of his humanity in the process.

The moonstruck hit the soldiers like a wave crashing against a rock. John could smell the panic emanating from the soldiers. Silver bullets whined past his head but he didn't stop to think about the danger to himself. The moonstruck had, for the moment, forgotten all about him and were tearing the soldiers apart. In their terror, any pretence at organisation had disappeared. Weapons were discharged seemingly at random, with as many rounds finding soldiers as werewolves. John didn't stop to think. He gave himself over to his wolf, tearing throats out with his claws, spilling entrails across the blood-stained snow. Losing himself utterly in the slaughter he was committing. And, despite the last shreds of his conscience screaming at the back of his mind, he found that he loved it.

***

Marie watched the battle unfold, tears streaming down her cheeks. A conflict like this had its own particular rhythm – an ebb and flow. Timing was everything in a situation like this. If she acted too soon, before all of the players were in the field, she stood to lose it all. But still, even in her long years on field teams, she had never witnessed anything like this. Even the massacre in Bosnia all those years ago was nothing in comparison to the slaughter taking place at the detention centre. So many lives lost. Her every instinct had urged her to act once she'd been certain that Daniel had managed to prevent the thermobaric bomb hitting the prison, but she'd known there would be reinforcements. It was only now, with the arrival of the helicopter gunships and the deployment of the Special Forces, that she was ready to make her move.

She turned to Melissa, who stood eagerly beside her like a guard dog straining at its chain. "Now. Go."

Melissa grinned and let the transformation begin. The rest of her team, the ones responsible for the butchery in High Moor, followed suit and raced towards the battle below. Marie knew they wouldn't stand a chance with the gunships still circling, raining fire on everything that moved. If they'd sent something like an Apache in, there would have been no chance at all. But the Merlins were primarily transport vehicles. Which meant they were vulnerable to small arms fire.

She hefted one of the sniper rifles and lay prone in the snow. Beside her, Andre, one of the few field trained pack members, picked up the other and trained it on one of the Merlins. She allowed her breathing to fall into a steady, predictable pattern, following the movement of the aircraft until she was able to predict its path. Then she held her breath and squeezed the trigger, taking satisfaction in the shattering of the reinforced glass and the spray of blood and brains from the pilot's head. Andre's weapon barked less than a second after hers, and both helicopters veered sharply off before colliding with the burning prison. She already had the next Merlin in her sights as her first target exploded, and within moments, it too traced a steep downward trajectory before erupting in a fireball. Andre's rifle went off twice more, and the last of the helicopters fell from the sky. She didn't take any time to relish the victory, however. Melissa's team had already reached the perimeter of the compound and were slaughtering soldiers and moonstruck alike with unrelenting savagery. She put down the sniper rifle, picked up an AK-47 and turned to the similarly armed members of her field team. Her trained, silver immune field team.

"Come on, what are you waiting for? It's time to get our people out of there. Let's see how the bastards cope with opposition that shoots back."

As one, the werewolves shouldered their assault rifles and raced towards the battle below, with Marie leading the charge. They were going to pay for what they'd done to her people. They were all going to pay.

***

It was all going to hell. Paul honestly had no idea what could have happened to the helicopters, but one thing was for sure: without air support, the chances of them making it out of here alive had dropped to almost zero. The heavy machine guns had torn the monsters to pieces, but now that all five of the helicopters had been taken out it meant the surviving military personnel were very much on their own. There was no chance of an evacuation. The only way any of them stood a chance was to make sure every last werewolf lay dead. And Paul found he didn't mind one little bit. If he was going to die, he'd take as many of the fucking things with him as he could.

He strode through the compound, rifle shouldered, firing at anything that moved. The air was filled with smoke and the thick coppery stench of blood, mingled with burning aviation fuel. Indistinct shapes flitted in the shadows. A pair of phosphorescent green eyes became visible through the smoke. Paul put a silver bullet right between them, feeling immense satisfaction as they winked out. He called on his training and let it guide his aim. One shot, one kill. He didn't have enough ammunition to adopt a 'spray and pray' approach like the yanks tended to do. By his reckoning, he had around fifty silver bullets left. He was determined to make sure that amounted to fifty dead werewolves. If there were any left after that, he'd face his fate without fear. If nothing else, it would mean seeing his family again.

He stepped over a pile of naked, ruined corpses. The Hellfire missiles had certainly been effective at thinning the werewolf ranks, although he cursed Colonel Richards for his complacency. If he'd had the Apache gunships on station, or deployed more drones, or just lined the fuckers up against the wall before they turned, then none of this would have happened. If he saw the Colonel again, one of those silver bullets would have his name on it. The man was a fool, and his incompetence had cost dozens of lives.

The gunfire behind him was growing more sporadic. That either meant there were fewer targets for the surviving Special Forces to engage, or there were simply fewer of them left alive to shoot. It didn't matter. He'd take the monsters on by himself if need be.

A shape rose up from the swirling smoke, arms outstretched, and a roar of fury emanated from its bloodstained muzzle. Paul put a round through its mouth and continued on his way without breaking his stride, not caring that the werewolf transformed back into a teenage girl. It wasn't a girl anymore. It was a thing, deserving nothing less than to be put down like the ravening animal that it was. He reached one of the few buildings still intact – a brick building toward the rear of the compound where the pack wolves had been housed. There was probably nothing inside, but he was not prepared to take the chance. He opened the door and threw a flash-bang inside, then closed the door again. The cries of alarm from within the building after the concussion grenade exploded told him there were, in fact, targets hiding within. He kicked the door open, rifle pulled tight to his shoulder, and stepped inside.

Two shapes were huddled at the far end of the building. Monsters pretending to be children, but monsters all the same. He sighted his rifle at the first, a small boy, then paused as he recognised his target. It was Matthew – Phil Fletcher's young nephew.

The boy rubbed his eyes and squinted at him. "I know you. You're the man that saved us. My Uncle Phil's friend. Have you come to help us? Are you going to save us from the bad men?"

It's not a boy, it's a monster. It's not a boy, it's a monster.

He took another step into the building. "Yes, Matthew. I've come to save you. Why don't you both come out here where I can see you? This will all be over soon."

The two children got to their feet and shuffled into the centre of the aisle between the beds. The other one was a girl. The creature he'd apprehended on Christmas Eve no less. He almost laughed. It was as if the universe was giving him a chance to wrap up unfinished business.

The girl stopped short and looked at him, then sniffed

the air. "YOU! You're the one that killed my daddy!"

Her eyes flashed green in the darkness and he heard the unmistakable cracking of a transformation beginning. *There we are. The monsters show themselves.* He switched targets, letting the red laser dot alight on the transforming girl, took a breath and felt his finger tighten on the trigger.

Something slammed into his back with sufficient force to send him crashing into the nearest bunk. His rifle barked but he knew he'd missed his target. He flipped himself over and started crawling to his feet when something heavy, with a rank animal stink, pinned his shoulders to the floor. He looked into the dripping jaws of a fully grown werewolf, inches from his face. This was it. There was no way he could react in time to save his life. He relaxed. He would see his family soon. Then something unexpected happened.

The creature began to change, hair receding into pores and vicious fangs pushing themselves back into the stinking maw until he found Steven Wilkinson looking into his eyes. "For Christ's sake, Paul, they're children. Think about what you're doing. If you do this, it will haunt you for the rest of your life." The old man sagged and a haunted expression crossed his face. "Take it from someone who knows."

Paul smiled at the old man. "Steven. So glad to see you showing your true colours at last." Before Steven could react, Paul removed his Browning pistol from its holster and emptied the weapon into him. Steven Wilkinson's eyes widened in shock, then glazed over as the life left him. Paul pushed the corpse away, picked up his assault rifle and turned back to the children. "Now, where were we?"

***

Sharon twisted her head and felt the soldier's neck snap between her jaws. She had given herself utterly to the animal side of her nature, but now, with no immediate threat, she felt a little of herself return. The person she had once been recoiled in horror at the carnage she'd wrought on the murderous military personnel. She had torn the man who'd killed Mandy into screaming, bloody ribbons before turning on the others in his squad. The rage had flowed through her, turning her into an unstoppable force of nature that had killed indiscriminately. Her only thoughts had been of vengeance against those who had murdered her niece. She had no idea how she was going to even begin to explain the death of his sister to Matthew, or even look him in the eyes again after the things she'd done.

Oh, God. Matthew!

The realisation hit her like a hammer. She should have gone straight to him. Protected him and made sure he was safe. Instead she'd let the beast take over and go on a murderous rampage. She had to get back to him. Make sure he was all right. There would be time for explanations and recriminations later. Once she made sure that what was left of her family was safe. She dropped the twitching corpse of the Special Forces soldier at her feet and raced across the battlefield to the barrack building where Matthew and young Sophie were hiding.

She'd made it less than halfway there when she heard

the shots. Thirteen sharp cracks in rapid succession coming from the barrack block. Her heart froze and she let out a roar of absolute fury, somehow finding the strength to urge her leaden limbs onwards. She saw Phil's friend, Paul Patterson, push the corpse of an old man away from him. Pick up a rifle. Bring it to his shoulder and aim it at her nephew. What little rational thought Sharon had regained vanished in an instant. Once again, the wolf was ascendant and she flew through the open doorway in a flurry of teeth and claws.

Paul didn't know what hit him. Sharon smashed into his back and the rifle barked once. Then a red mist descended over her and she was lost in a pure, primal rage, tearing, biting and rending the man she'd known for five years into bloody fragments. When the fury abated, there was nothing recognisable left of Paul Patterson. Pieces of the man were spread across the walls, floor and ceiling. Part of his face still hung from her jaws. Despite herself, her wolf wasn't finished yet and swallowed the juicy morsel in a single gulp. The human half of Sharon wanted to throw up.

Then she felt a bright flare of pain in her side and the world began to spin. Her body began to spasm and contort. She cried out in pain as talons slid back into her fingers, feeling like slivers of bamboo being forced under every finger and toe nail simultaneously. Her fangs pushed themselves into her gums, every nerve on fire as if a mad dentist were drilling at her teeth without anaesthetic. She fell to the floor, suddenly unable to breathe. A small, neat hole beneath her ribs oozed blood. She looked up and saw a man in combat uniform holding a pistol. He was covered from head to toe in blood and his eyes bore a crazed look. She realised that she was looking at Colonel Richards. However there was little of the disciplined military man she'd met left. The Colonel's expression was one of sheer rage and bloodlust, in many ways no different from the monster she'd been only moments before. He pointed the pistol at her head.

"Goodbye, Mrs Fletcher. Give my regards to your husband when you see him in hell."

A blur of brown fur caught her eye, and something slammed into the Colonel, knocking him from his feet. The pistol skittered across the floor of the barracks, out of reach. The Colonel screamed as a small werewolf, no bigger than a large dog, bit and clawed and tore at him. Blood sprayed from dozens of wounds. Sharon knew then who the Colonel's attacker was. "No, Sophie. Don't. Don't kill him. Please," she coughed.

Sophie did as she was told and retreated from the injured man, transforming back into a young girl with almost no apparent effort. She got to her feet and glared at the unconscious, bleeding form of Colonel Richards. "He's a bad man. He's a very very bad man."

"Yes, he is. But it's over now. You saved us."

Sharon struggled to her feet, then turned to Matthew and let out a cry. The boy lay in a spreading pool of blood with a bullet hole in his stomach. He looked up at her. "Auntie Sharon. It hurts."

Despite the pain, Sharon rushed to the child's side. His face was pale and his skin clammy, covered in sweat. "Oh, God, Matthew. Don't move, sweetheart. Everything is going to be alright. I'll get help."

Matthew's hand curled around hers. "No. Don't leave me. I'm scared."

Sharon felt a wave of desperation unlike anything she'd ever experienced before. There was no help. No one she could turn to. She couldn't take him to a hospital, or call an ambulance. Soon more soldiers would arrive and finish the job. The last member of her family was bleeding to death in front of her and there was nothing she could do."

"I can save him," said a small voice beside her.

Sharon looked into Sophie's eyes, at the serious expression the little girl wore that belied her age. "How? How can you save him?"

Sophie took Matthew's hand gently, then brought it up to her mouth and bit down hard. Matthew squealed in pain and Sharon snatched his hand away from her. "What did you do? Oh my God, Sophie – what did you do?"

The girl smiled at her. "I made him like us so he'll get better. You'll see. Everything is going to be alright."

Sharon's strength was gone. The frigid air was soothing, but she knew she was going into shock. She gathered Matthew and Sophie into her arms and closed her eyes as the world faded away into blackness.

Chapter 25

11th January 2009. Lindholme Detention Centre, Doncaster. 04:07

An unnatural silence had descended over the remains of Lindholme. Marie felt sick to her stomach and let her empty assault rifle fall to the ground. She wanted to cry. There were so many dead it was almost beyond her capacity to comprehend. Ruined bodies of men, women and children lay beside the ravaged corpses of the soldiers. The members of her field team were going through the bodies, putting any werewolves too injured to escape, and any wounded military personnel out of their misery. In many respects, that order had been the hardest to give, but she would not leave anyone here to be vivisected and experimented on. It was the kindest option, even for those who had done their best to wipe their race out.

She saw Melissa lying among the dead, the young woman's pretty blue eyes wide open, as if gazing at the stars in wonder, multiple bullet holes punched through her torso and limbs.

The moonstruck that had not been killed by the military had been cornered and dispatched with ruthless efficiency by the members of the field team. Given what she was intending to do, and the damage a single moonstruck could inflict to her plan, there really wasn't any choice. If she'd had the luxury of time then perhaps they could have been helped, in the same way she'd helped John. But time was one thing that none of them had. Not anymore. They had to gather the survivors and get away from here before more troops arrived. The window of opportunity for escape was small and they had no time for sentiment. She would mourn the dead later.

The surviving werewolves were emerging from the shadows, many of them wounded. All of them with lost, haunted expressions on their faces. These people were not monsters, or trained killers like her. They were families that had tried to live with their condition as well as they could, and instead had been thrown into a fight for survival. The only consolation she had was that their shock, suffering and grief would be brief. By the time the moon rose again in a months' time, it would all be over. For all of them including herself.

She caught a familiar scent through the stink of blood, shit and fire, and her eyes widened. She had not dared to hope - had been sure she would come across John's bloody corpse among the dead. She'd convinced herself of this, unable to face having that hope torn away again. She began to move towards the scent and then, out of the smoke, she saw him. He was injured, yes. A moonstruck had left savage claw marks across his face that would never fully heal, and he held his arm where a silver bullet had pierced his bicep, but he was alive. The mask she'd held onto crumbled and she raced to him, gathering him in her arms while the tears rolled down her cheeks.

"Oh, God, Marie! I can't believe it's you! I never thought... I never dared to..."

Marie took his face in her hands and kissed him with all the relief and joy she could find. Even in this terrible place, after everything that had happened and with everything that was about to happen, she took this one small moment and held onto it, pulling him to her, kissing him again and again until Andre put his hand on her shoulder.

"Marie, we've got everyone that can walk ready to go. We need to move before..."

She pulled her face away from John's and looked at Andre. "I know. Get everyone loaded up into the transports. Do one last sweep for survivors. We need to be moving in five minutes."

Andre nodded and moved off, shouting orders to the survivors. John took her hands. "I need to check on someone. There were some children hiding in one of the barrack buildings. I have to make sure they are alright."

She nodded and let John lead her through the carnage. Single gunshots rang out, each one making her wince. After a few minutes, the gunshots stopped and she felt a strange mixture of relief and despair. It was over. Finally.

The door to the barracks swung open in the wind and she didn't need enhanced senses to get an idea of what happened here. The remains of what she presumed to be a man were spread all over the entrance. Another man lay unconscious, bleeding from dozens of wounds. She recognised him. Colonel Richards. The man who'd been responsible for running this terrible place. She picked up a pistol from the floor and aimed it at his head. John put his hand on her arm. "No. Not him. Killing the fucker is too kind. Leave him where he is."

She dropped the weapon and followed John to the rear of the building, to where a woman lay cradling two young children. She could smell the blood from here, but when she checked for a pulse, the woman's was strong. The young girl looked up at her and smiled. "She's going to be okay. Matthew too. Is my mummy here?"

Marie smoothed back her blood-streaked hair and smiled. "Yes, your mummy is fine, Sophie. Your Aunt Kasha and Uncle Dmitri too. Come on, I'll take you to them."

The other child, a boy, opened his eyes and regarded Marie with a serious expression. His clothes were covered in blood, but Marie couldn't see any visible signs of trauma on him, even if the blood didn't smell like the woman's. "Are you going to help us? My Auntie Sharon's hurt."

John bent down and helped the boy to his feet. "Yes, Matthew. We're going to take you both away from here. Now, go with Sophie while Marie and I help your Auntie."

The children got to their feet and, hand in hand, ran from the barrack building while John and Marie lifted Sharon's unconscious body from the ground. As they made their way across the compound to the waiting minibuses, John looked at Marie. "So, what exactly do we do now?"

She smiled at him. "Trust me. I have a plan."

YouTube Video Posted 30th January 2009.

A woman sits in a featureless concrete room with a table before her. Her hands are crossed and, despite her well-groomed appearance, her eyes glow an almost phosphorescent green. Her face is a mask of barely contained rage.

"My name is Marie Williams, and I am the leader of the werewolf organisation that was once known as The Pack. For centuries, we have tried to keep our existence from you. We have hunted down and killed the uncontrollable members of our kind known as Moonstruck, for your safety as well as our own. As you are aware, recent events have changed all of that. You know that we exist and your government, and governments around the world, have done their best to exterminate us.

"We have lived peacefully among you for decades. However, when your military executed a series of raids on civilian families and placed them in a death camp at Lindholme, just outside of Doncaster, we were forced to take action.

"The attack on the town of High Moor was regrettable, and those responsible for that atrocity have been dealt with according to our laws. However, what your government did next was worse."

The screen fades to black and is replaced with a series of images. An old man is shown strapped to a hospital bed. His body has been cut open, his internal organs on display, but he is clearly still conscious and very much alive. He tries to focus on the camera, and the words "help me," are just audible. The screen fades and shows the camp at Lindholme, with people in prison jumpsuits moving around in the snow, lining up to receive food. The screen fades again and the woman returns.

"The British Government, under the direct orders of your interim Prime Minister, placed the survivors of High Moor in the internment camp, along with those taken from their homes on Christmas Eve. They intended to use a thermobaric bomb to wipe them out and, when that failed, sent in the military to finish the job."

The screen fades again, and then shows corpses piled up in the snow, riddled with gunshot wounds. The camera focuses on a small child, no more than ten years old, with bullet holes across his chest. The camera pans back to show more bodies, covering the ground as far as the eye can see. Then the screen fades and the woman returns.

"We were not prepared to let your government commit such a slaughter without a response. As you can see, we were not able to save everyone. But we did save enough. The last few members of our species are now far away from the brutality of your government. We are removing ourselves from your world. We will no longer protect you from the moonstruck, should any emerge, but we will no longer live among you. I would strongly advise that you do not try to seek us out. If you do, our response will be swift and it will be terrible. Leave us be, and we will extend you the same courtesy. Ignore this warning and... well... I will leave that up to your imagination."

The screen fades to black.

3rd February 2009. Underhill Military Base, Sublevel Four. 09:52

Colonel Richards' eyes snapped open and he squinted against the harsh white glow of the fluorescent light. He tried to move, but the attempt sent white hot shards of agony through his body. He tried to speak, to call out, but his mouth was dry and his voice came out as little more than a croak.

A figure appeared, but he couldn't focus his eyes. It was just a shape, holding a clipboard.

"Try not to move, Colonel," said a soft, female voice with a welsh accent. "You'll do yourself an injury."

His mind swam, but he recognised the voice. Awareness and memory returned. Lindholme. He'd been at Lindholme and something had happened... Something...

It all came back to him and his eyes widened.

Rose Fisher leaned over him and smiled. "Ah, I see it's all coming back to you now. Good. I was wondering if your mind had survived the trauma. Now you're back with us, we can begin."

Rose disappeared and he tried to move his head. He was restrained – arms, legs and head strapped down. Rose reappeared and gave him a reassuring smile. "There there, Colonel. Don't try to speak." She picked up a small tape recorder and pressed the record button. "This is Doctor Rose Fisher and the time is 09:55hrs on the third of February 2009. The subject has regained consciousness. We will now begin the experiment."

9th February 2009. Kozara National Park, Bosnia. 09:52

John got out of the Land Rover and looked at the forest below him. There was no sign of civilisation. Nothing but towering pines and mountains extending as far as the eye could see. Marie got out of the driver's side and embraced him, then placed a kiss on his lips.

"So," he said, "this is where it all started. And this is where it ends."

She gave him a small, sad smile. "Yeah, this is it. Home, or at least, it used to be."

"Do you think you'll be safe here?"

"It's ours now. Steffan liquidated all of the pack's assets. Every last penny of it. Michael had already made arrangements, a last resort if you like, and bought it from the Bosnian Government. It's private property now and, to be honest, no one comes here anymore. They haven't in decades. The legends keep the locals away, and there are warnings posted on the outskirts of the place about unexploded ordinance from the war. It's as safe a place for us as there is, all things considered."

John looked back along the trail to where the other vehicles were parked. People were already starting to disembark from the rag-tag procession of trucks, ancient 4x4s and cars. He made out Sharon Fletcher with young Matthew and returned a wave.

"Are you sure that this is the only way? We could hide in plain sight again. I doubt anyone will come looking for us after your warning. Fifty million hits on that video pretty much guarantees that your message got out there."

She hugged him. "There's no other way. Now at least, we are out of their world. There shouldn't be any more moonstruck, and after we've been in the forest for a week or two, we won't even remember that we were human. We'll forget it all, and hopefully the world will forget us. We'll fade back into legend. It's better this way. We tried to live as humans and look what happened. It's time we let the other side of us live the life it was supposed to. It's better for everyone."

John nodded, feeling his heart break. He'd been dreading this moment. He paused, then put his hands on Marie's shoulders. "I can't go with you, Marie."

She pulled away. "What? Don't be a fucking idiot. Why not?"

"Because I'm not like the rest of you. You turn into wolves. Big, monster bastard wolves, but wolves nevertheless. I don't. And I can't give myself over to the animal side of my nature. I'd be a monster. Once a moonstruck, always a moonstruck."

"No! It won't be like that, John. You have to come with us. I can't lose you again. Not after everything."

John leaned forward and kissed her, then pulled away. "In a week you won't even remember me. And I can't take that risk. I have to go."

Marie threw herself into his arms, tears running down her cheeks and her body shuddering as he held him tight. He returned the embrace, relishing the feel of her in his arms. Inhaling the scent of her. Committing every last detail to memory. Then he pulled away.

"Goodbye, Marie. Be safe. I love you and I always will."

John turned and walked back to the Land Rover. Marie stood and watched him open the door, then called out to him. "John, what will you do?"

He smiled. "I'll think of something," he said, and winked at her. Then he got into the vehicle, closed the door and drove away, back down the mountain without a backwards glance.

EPILOGUE

28th September 2015. Kozara National Park, Bosnia. 03:00

Walter Parker wiped the condensation from his glasses, then put them back on. "Are you sure this is the place, Joseph? Fifty thousand dollars is a lot of money by anyone's reckoning."

The full moon, stained blood red by the imminent lunar eclipse, hung in the sky to the east and, as if on cue, the forest began to echo with howls. Just one at first, but then answered by another, and another, until the cold night air was filled with their song.

Joseph seemed nervous. "Yes, you hear? This is the place, Mr Parker. You wanted the werewolves. We get you werewolves. We go now. Happy hunting."

"You are not going anywhere. I have to say, I'm not even sure those permits you gave me were official. They didn't have a stamp on them or anything. You are damn well staying here until I get what I came for."

Joseph exchanged a furtive look with his companion – a small, greasy-looking man that Walter hadn't been introduced to. "Mr Parker, are you sure you want to do this? These wolves... they are not like normal wolves. When you kill them, they change back. You aren't going to be able to keep their heads as trophies. I think perhaps the people coming to your dentist's office would be upset at a human head mounted on a plaque, yes? Come back with us. I will return your money and you go back to America. It... it is not safe here."

Walter leaned forward and bared his perfect teeth at the Bosnian. "I have hunted big game all over the planet. One beast is pretty much like another. I don't need a trophy. I'll just take some shots of it for my Facebook page and then we'll head home. But I didn't come all this way to stop now. Do you understand, Joseph? Am I getting through to you?"

Joseph backed away a step, then spoke to his companion in a flurry of dialogue that Walter didn't understand. His companion, however, seemed agitated. Walter picked up his hunting rifle and chambered a round. "We made a deal, Joseph. And I'm not going anywhere without my prize. And neither are you or your friend."

"What good is fifty thousand American dollars if we are not alive to spend it? We should leave this cursed place and never return. It was a mistake to come here."

"I agree with your friend," said a voice from the darkness.

Walter raised his rifle and pointed it at where the voice had come from. "Who's there? Show yourself, right now."

A tall man stepped out from the shadows. He had four scars running across his face, and was wearing a thick pullover, but seemed to be unarmed. "This is private property. I don't know what your friend, Joseph, told you, but there's no hunting allowed here. I suggest you come with me and let me escort you back to your vehicles."

Walter stepped forward until he was face to face with the stranger. "Look, Buddy, I don't know who you are, but..."

The man smiled. "My name is John. I suppose you could say I'm the game warden here. I take care of things. Make sure the wildlife is protected. Make sure that people don't trespass or hurt themselves. These woods can be... dangerous. Please, let me see you safely back to your car. I'd hate to see anything happen to you."

Walter bristled at this. "I don't care if you're the goddamn President of Bosnia himself. I am an American citizen and I paid good money to be able to hunt here. I'm not letting some limey son of a bitch tell me otherwise."

The man smiled. "Then I suggest you ask Joseph and his friend for a refund. As I said, this is private property and you aren't welcome here."

Walter raised his rifle and pointed it at the man. "And what exactly are you going to do if I say no?"

The man's grin widened and, for a moment, it looked like his eyes flashed green in the moonlight. "I was hoping you'd ask that."

THE END

THANK YOU FOR READING

Thank you for taking the time to read this book. We sincerely hope that you enjoyed the story and appreciate your letting us try to entertain you. We realise that your time is valuable, and without the continuing support of people such as yourself, we would not be able to do what we do.

As a thank you, we would like to offer you a free ebook from our range, in return for you signing up to our mailing list. We will never share your details with anyone and will only contact you to let you know about new releases.

You can sign up on our website

Http://www.horrifictales.co.uk

If you enjoyed this book, then please consider leaving a short review on Amazon, Goodreads or anywhere else that you, as a reader, visit to learn about new books. One of the most important parts about how well a book sells is how many positive reviews it has, so if you can spare a little more of your valuable time to share the experience with others, even if its just a line or two, then we would really appreciate it.

Thanks, and see you next time!

THE HORRIFIC TALES PUBLISHING TEAM

ABOUT THE AUTHOR

Graeme Reynolds has been called many things over the years, most of which are unprintable.

By day, he breaks computers for a living, but when the sun goes down he hunches over a laptop and thinks of new and interesting ways to offend people with delicate sensibilities.

http://www.graemereynolds.com
http://www.facebook.com/HighMoorNovel
@graemereynolds

ALSO FROM HORRIFIC TALES PUBLISHING

Of A Feather by Ken Goldman

Whisper by Michael Bray

Echoes by Michael Bray

Voices by Michael Bray

Lucky's Girl by William Holloway

The Immortal Body by William Holloway

Bottled Abyss by Benjamin Kane Ethridge

Angel Manor by Chantal Noordeloos

Wasteland Gods by Jonathan Woodrow

High Moor by Graeme Reynolds

High Moor 2: Moonstruck by Graeme Reynolds

http://www.horrifictales.co.uk

www.ingramcontent.com/pod-product-compliance
Lightning Source LLC
Chambersburg PA
CBHW021127260626
47169CB00005B/1495